Rough Justice

M. E. Braddon

ROUGH JUSTICE

BY

MAXWELL, M. E. BRADDON

Author of "LADY AUDLEY'S SECRET,"
"LONDON PRIDE," ETC.

CONTENTS

CHAPTER I.

" HOW SHOULD I GREET THEE ?"

" Is it really, really you ?"

" Really, and very really. But what in the name of all that's wonderful can have brought my little Mary to South Africa ? "

They had come suddenly face to face in one of the corridors of the Saxon; face to face amid all the hubbub and confusion of a great steamer homeward bound.

They stood there in the narrow corridor, cabin doors on either side of them, spellbound in the glad surprise of meeting, and unconscious that they were an obstruction to the passage of other eager spirits tramping to and fro, looking for lost packages, all more or less frantic, disputing about cabins and berths, in an atmosphere vibrating with farewells. These two forgot everything in the wonder of meeting, after an interval that to young minds seemed a great gap in life. To age it would have been only a parenthesis.He was tall, dark with sun and weather, but originally of the fair Anglo-Saxon type, as witnessed

Rough Justice.

by large, bold blue eyes and crisp, light-brown hair; age about thirty, powerful frame, and easy movements a man who had lived mostly in the open, and had looked the sun in the face, like the eagles. She whom he called little Mary was at least five feet seven, straight and slim as a reed, not by any means a beauty, but full of charm in her fresh youthfulness, with a smile of bewitching gaiety, and clear, dark-grey eyes ; Irish eyes, this old friend of hers had called them, in the days when she was little Mary.

"You had better ask me what takes me home to England," she said, when he had repeated his question—eager, impatient, with both her hands clasped in his.

The people pushing past them took them for brother and sister, or husband and wife, and thought them in the act of parting, and so were more tolerant than they might have been of this obstruction.

"We are awfully in the way here," said Mary Freeland. " Shall we go outside for a few minutes ? You are not going on shore immediately, I hope ?"

"I am going on shore at Southampton not before!"

" What, are we to be fellow-passengers ? How nice!"

"Isn't it?"

Looking into her fresh, frank young face, it flashed upon him that it would be still nicer if they could be fellow-passengers over the wide seas

" How should I greet Thee 9 "of life a passing fancy only, which any man might have about any woman as young and gay as Mary Freeland.Arnold Wentworth and his newly found friend went out upon the upper deck, and stood watching the people thronging the narrow gangway, swarming down to the quay, perturbed by the importunate ringing of a warning bell, excited to fever-point in the final parting. Some might be only friends, some mere acquaintances ; but all were moved to some touch of tragic feeling while the clustered faces looked down upon them from the bulwarks, amidst waving hands and waving handkerchiefs, above and below. At last the bell ceased its clamour, the gangway was raised, the passengers' friends and followers drifted away, and Arnold and Mary were able to look at each other and talk to each other calmly, standing side by side in a quiet corner, away from the traffic of ship's officers and passengers, the latter mostly on the war-path.Table Bay lay around them, and Cape Town gleamed whitely in the clear afternoon light, sheltered in the vast amphitheatre of rock, curtained and protected by those grey cliffs, and dark with the dense growth of pine forests that fill the valley. In the golden light of an African summer it seemed too fair a scene to leave willingly, to exchange summer for winter, the large picturesqueness of South Africa for the fogs and narrow streets of London, and the commonplace of English rusticity. Arnold looked at those jutting headlands

Rough Justice.

and Titanic peaks with something of regret in his gaze.

" I am getting quite accustomed to you again," said Mary, presently; "but it was a tremendous shock to meet you."

" Why ? "

The monosyllable startled her. She blushed rosy red, and answered confusedly

"Well, you see, you left Mervynhall so suddenly—and one didn't know and people said things "

"Said I had gone to the bad, no doubt."

" So shameful of them just because you chose to leave a humdrum little town where you were not properly appreciated."

" Where I was confoundedly miserable. But it's a true bill, Polly, my dear. There is always a scamp in the family, and I suppose it was my mission to fill the part. I have heen to the dogs, Polly, but I contrived to come alive out of the kennel; and—for the last two years I've been doing well."

" In the diamond fields \'7d "

" No ; I turned up the diamond diggings. I have been among the gold miners at Heidelberg. I tried my luck at Kimberley for a bit, but it was no go. And I drifted back to Cape Town worse off than when I landed there, for the clothes I had come in were worn to rags, and then a chap I knew at the 'Varsity, who had also had canine experience, turned up with a little bit of capital, and traded his cash against my

" How should I greet Thee 9 "

knowledge of the mines and capacity for rough work, and the partnership answered better than such one-sided alliances generally do."

"At Heidelberg?" cried Mary. "And I have been at Johannesburg, only thirty miles away. Did you never go to Johannesburg ? "

" Not very often."

" And did you go to the theatre when you were there ?"

" Is there a theatre at Johannesburg ? "

" Is there a theatre ? Why, there are two," cried Mary, with a mortified air. " How little you care for the drama ! "

" Not much. I've been leading rather too rough a life to care for stage-plays."

" I'm glad you and your friend prospered, at any rate."

" Well, you see, we bought a block in the Nigel Reef a very small block, the large ones are owned by companies and we had only a small capital to work with ; but Fortune was kind, and we did well. My chum had fever more than once, and I helped him to pull through, which he called saving his life. And here I am, homeward bound, on a flying visit to see my dear old mother, who never thought me quite the villain I appeared before the paternal high court of justice. And now for your story, little Mary, What brought you to the Cape ; and, above all, to

Johannesburg ?"

" I came with a company."

** A company ? "

"A theatrical company. I'm an actress, you know."

" Indeed, I know nothing of the kind. You were a kid when we last met ; a solitary orphan kid, but as bright and as happy as if you had been the centre of a jovial family. I should have thought your highly respectable aunt would have made a desperate fight against your turning actress."

" So she would ; but she was too unkind, and I couldn't stand her any longer. You would never believe it"and Mary blushed redder than before " bit aunt wanted me to marry Dr. Betts."

" What! Why, the man must be sixty, and he has worn a wig ever since I can remember him !"

" And it's a wig that one can't help seeing. There's hardly any make-believe about it."

" And you plucked up a spirit and refused Betts ? Did he make his offer in person ?"

" Not at first. He only hinted at marriage said he wanted a nice little wife to cheer him of an evening, after a long day's round among his patients. He told me that a doctor appreciated a cheerful home more than any other professional man, and he asked me one day if I thought any nice young lady would accept him. I told him that he ought to look for some amiable person of his own age, if he wanted to be happy with his wife, since in all the novels I had ever read the young women who married old men always eloped in the second volume, and came back to die

How should I greet Thee

miserably in the third. No sensible man would want to begin a story of that kind, I told him. He laughed, and said that the only merit in a novel was not to resemble life, and that he should not despair of winning some nice girl's heart."

" Presumptuous old idiot! " I thought he was only talking for talking's sake—just to fill the time between the porch and the garden gate, for aunt had sent me to see him to his carriage ; but a week afterwards she told me he had proposed for me, and was willing to take me without a penny, and allow me a hundred a year, paid quarterly, to buy clothes. She told me it was a particularly generous offer—for a girl who was almost plain."

" Plain ! That's an outrageous lie."

" I'm so glad you think so. Of course, I know I'm not pretty ; but people have generally liked me, and one doesn't want to think one's self repulsive."

"You were pretty enough to attract Dr. Betts, at any rate."

"Oh, aunt said it was only his benevolence that made him propose for me. He knew that I was entirely dependent upon her, and it was out of pure kindness of heart he offered to make me Mrs. Betts, and the mistress of his beautiful house."

" What rot! what confounded rot! '

"You know his beautiful house a round table in the middle of his drawing-room, and a walnut suite covered with magenta rep. I think I should

Rough Justice.

go mad if I had to live in the midst of a wahiut suite wouldn't you ? Well, I said no, and no, and no—in spite of all aunt could urge about the house, and the silver teapots, and things, and the use of Dr. Betts's carriages when he didn't want them. I went on saying no, though aunt got more and more cantankerous, and would hardly help me to pudding. I believe she'd have locked me up in an attic and kept me on bread and water if she hadn't been afraid of the Society for the Prevention of Cruelty to Children. I was only seventeen, so I suppose I should have ranked as an infant. And to make a long story short, she worried me so that at last I plucked up a spirit, and did just what you did."

"Eh?"

"I ran away. Don't look shocked. No doubt it was all through your bad example."

"But where did you run to, child ." Good God! Seventeen and friendless ! "

" Not quite. I have no more aunts, and, indeed, if I had six I doubt if I should have tried another. But I happen to have an uncle my father's youngest brother who married an actress while he was at Oxford, and went on the stage, and offended everybody belonging to him. I had seen in the papers that he was acting at Cambridge, so I just took a third-class ticket by the first morning train, and was in time for breakfast with my uncle and his wife at Market Hill, Cambridge. It was a very early train, you see, and a very late breakfast."

" low should I greet Thee f

"Poor little waif! Didn't your uncle look rather blue at such an unexpected appearance ?"

" Not a bit of it! Uncle and his wife were both as kind as ever they could be ; and I told them everything. Uncle Joe said I had my father's eyes, and he would have known me as a Freeland anywhere his stage name is Faversham—and they took a room for me at the top of the house a weeny room with a sloping ceiling, and I walked on that very night."

"Walked on.?"

"On the Cambridge stage as a guest in a ballroom scene. Aunt lent me one of her frocks. I had only to stand and sit about and say nothing. It was to accustom me to the foot-lights. Uncle Joe said I was just the right age, and had a good appearance" blushing at the recollection of having been called a pretty girl for the first time in her life "and that I ought to make an actress. He was manager of a touring company, you see, and was taking round his own melodrama, Holding-up the Mail a tremendous success everywhere. People liked it better than Shakespeare."

" Then my poor little Mary fell on her feet ?"

"Immensely. They were ever so good. Aunt is a leading lady, and a really fine actress, though she has been shamefully ignored by the London managers. I went about touring with them for nearly three years, in England, Scotland, and Ireland ; and fifteen months ago we all came to Africa, and we have been acting at Capetown,

Rough Justice

and Port Elizabeth, and Johannesburg, off and on, ever since. My uncle brought me on board the boat. He had not gone ten minutes when I saw you. I was awfully sorry to leave them."

" But why leave them \'7d Have you another good-natured uncle up your sleeve ?"

" I have not another relation in the world."

"Then why abandon these, and face the world alone ?"

"Because I have been left a fortune. Please don't laugh. You would not call it a fortune. Aunt began by disinheriting me a week after I ran away. She made a will leaving all her property to the Asylum for Idiots, and sent me a copy of it. ' I am leaving all I have to persons of your class,' she wrote ; 'I did not know there were so many of you.' "

" The old lady must have thought herself a wit."

" I wrote and told her she was at liberty to leave her money to the shoe-black brigade ; but whatever she might think, I was not ungrateful for past kindness. I had run away from Dr. Betts, rather than from her. And then from time to time I used to send her a newspaper with a favourable notice, just to let her see that I was alive."

" What an artful young woman ! I had no idea that curly brown head was screwed on so tight."

" Uncle Joe gave me the tip. ' Nothing like a good notice to soften the old lady's heart,' he used to say."

"You didn't send her the unfavourable notices the cutters and slashers ? "

" How should I greet Thee "

" The notices that said I was overweighted' or disappointing ? Of course not. Well, I heard no more of her till she had been dead and buried ever so long poor old dear! Then there came a long letter from Mr. Roffey you remember Roffey, the solicitor i to say that my aunt had made a fresh will shortly before her demise he called it demise; so much less shocking than any other word and had left me all her property, on condition that I left the stage, at once, formally, and for ever, Mr. Roffey and a Mr. Middleham, who was a great friend of aunt's, are my trustees, and hold the property in trust for me, to be forfeited and to go to the Idiot Asylum if ever I act in any theatre, hall, or place of entertainment where money is taken at the doors."

"Capital! And you are still free to exercise your talents in the Theatre Royal Back Drawing-room ?"

"Oh, I have no talent. I was just able to get on while I had uncle and aunt to teach me everything; but, of course, I was dreadfully inexperienced ; and I heard a horrid low comedian tell the stage manager that if I hadn't been the Gorger's niece I shouldn't have been allowed to deliver a message in a properly managed theatre ! "

" The Gorger .? "

" Name for the manager ; old-fashioned, I believe. The low comedian must have been eighty."

"And you are free and independent. And pray, what are you going to do when you get back to England ." "

Rough Justice.

"First, I am going to Mei-vynhall."

" To take possession of your estate naturally,"

"And to see old friends, if they will see me. They may cut me, perhaps, for having run away, and for having tried to be an actress."

" Not they! Prejudice in that line is ancient history. Besides, they are sure to feel kindly towards a nice young lady with a snug little property. Pray, at how much do you estimate your property ?"

"Aunt used to say that she had not quite five hundred a year, besides the Briery, and the orchard, and the three meadows."

" Not quite five hundred a year is a very comfortable income for one young woman. You mustn't be in a hurry to marry. You must be on your guard against fortune-hunters."

Mary's cheeks reddened again, and this time the mounting colour had a look of sudden anger.

"I am not going to marry ever perhaps. What a ridiculous warning ! "

"Well, it's not always unnecessary. Nice girls are so soft-hearted ; any plausible fellow can get round them. And I dare say you have a corner in your heart for some Romeo or Benedick you've left behind you."

" Do you suppose I could care for an angel from heaven if he used grease-paints .'* And now I've been prosing for nearly an hour about my adventures, so please tell me yours, and begin

at the
beginning."

" How should I greet Thee 9 "

There was a brief silence before Arnold replied, and then he began, with a sigh.

"Ah, Mary, my dear, my record isn't quite as clean as yours. My story is a long one, and would hardly bear telling ; and all that is worst in it is dreariest, and would be the hardest to tell. We'll sweep it behind us, Mary send it away to sea with a flourish of my arm as Mr. Podsnap used to wave away any subject he disliked ; and you must be content to know that I have led an honest, hard-working life since I came to Africa, and that I have done pretty well as I told you before and am going home for a holiday before setting to work again."

"You mean to come back, then? You like Africa.?"

" It's about the only place I ever liked the only life that ever suited me the only country in which I have had good luck. Everything has gone well with me for the last two years. Indeed, I did so well at the Rand that I thought I was entitled to a bit of sport and adventure before I left Africa so I bought a big waggon, and went off to Bechuanaland to shoot hartebeest, or anything else that came in my way, and look about me a little. The hot weather drove me out of the desert, but I took things very easily. I got back to Johannesburg with waggon and bullocks in very fair condition. I sold the whole turn-out ever so much better than I expected fell in with a young swell who wanted the things, and wasn't hard about price, as an old colonist would have been."

Rough Justice.

" I hope you didn't cheat him ?" said Mary, laughing.

"You don't suppose I'm a swindler? No, I asked a fair price didn't even leave a margin for bargaining. He liked the look of my cattle, and he gave me what I asked, like a brick. Yes, Mary, I have been lucky, luckiest of all in meeting an old friend like you."

"Take care. Scotch people think a man is in danger when he's too happy. They call it being fey. I hope you're not fey."

" I shall be sea-sick by-and-by, perhaps, and that'll check my exuberant spirits. Are you a good sailor, Mary ? "

"A very good sailor. I love the sea as well as if I were a mermaid. But do you know, Mr. Wentworth, now that I am quite grown-up, and we are going to be fellow-passengers for a long time, and among strangers, you mustn't call me Mary."

" What rot! Do you forget that you were a little girl when I was a full-grown man, and that all my recollections of you include short petticoats and a pinafore ? Not call you Mary .? Ridiculous! "

" Life is often ridiculous ; and you will have to call me Miss Freeland, if you please, Mr. Wentworth," she said, smiling at him with mock dignity.

" And you will have to call mc Wildover Alfred Wildover and not Wentworth, if you please, Miss Freeland ; for that has been my name ever since I went under."

" How should I greet Thee ? "

" You have changed your name ? Oh, how dreadful!"

"Not for my people. It would have been dreadful for them to hear of a Wentworth in the gutter. A Wildover might go to the bad as he pleased, and nobody at Langton Park would care. I wanted to cut myself clear of family associations to stand alone and free and so I invented the name of Wildover ; and I think it's rather a good one. I even changed Arnold to Alfred, so that there might be no clue to my identity if I went under altogether."

The great steamer had been lying motionless all this time, for, after all that clamorous bell-ringing and eager hurry to get rid of visitors, the captain seemed in no haste to weigh anchor, and it was dusk before the Saxon steamed out to sea. Mary Freeland retired to her cabin to unpack her trunk, and Wildover went to his own den, and they met no more that day, Mary not caring to appear at dinner, and spending her evening in a cushioned corner of the ladies' saloon.

He saw her no more that night, but she was on deck next morning, as fresh as a rose, and had made friends with a family of children, whose mother and governess were prostrate in their berths, and she was taking care of them, and they were taking care of her. Arnold, who had always been fond of "kids," as he called them, made friends with these young people in five minutes, and attached himself to Miss Freeland's party, which included a black poodle of preternatural

Rough Justice.

sagacity, who had been brought up in the bosom of the family, and received more care and attention than any of the children.

Of these there were five in all—the eldest a sharp-witted damsel of thirteen, the youngest a boy of seven. They were tolerably well-behaved, having succeeded each other too rapidly for any of them to be spoilt, except the youngest, who was still called Baby, and who divided his mother's affections with Chip, the poodle. The lady placidly ignored the other four, and had only one reply to any appeal from them, which was, "Ask Fraulein to do it for you," or " Really you must go to Fraulein."Arnold and Mary and the children found plenty of amusement on the Saxon; and perhaps in all those chequered years which had followed the crisis of severance from home and respectability the young man had never known so placid and blissful an interval as that voyage from summer to winter. He accepted his happiness in the true lotus-eater's spirit thought of nothing, cared for nothing, but the light and frivolous amusements of the passing hour.It was only when the Saxon had passed Madeira that Arnold began to think of anything more serious than deck quoits, or the newest trick he was teaching Chip.Then, one night in his cabin, being lucky enough, on account of the late season, to have a small mid-ships cabin to himself, the second berth being unclaimed, Arnold, after lying sleepless and full

" How should I oryeet Thee "of thought for three or four weary hours, sat up in his berth, turned on the electric light, and unlocked a little cash-box that stood on the table by his side.

It was full of papers, and paper money, chequebook, bank-book, private ledger ; and underneath these, at the bottom of the box, where hope should have been, Arnold found a letter which for him represented despair.

"There's no good in lying awake brooding over it," he said to himself, as he took the thin letter out of the thin envelope ; " I had better read it quietly once more for the last time, and think the matter out."

Enclosed in the letter there was a slip of printed paper—evidently a cutting from a newspaper.

" Among the fortunate adventurers in the South African goldfields, one of the most striking personalities is Captain Wildover, a sportsman and a gentleman, a fine shot at big game, and as plucky as they make 'em. Wildover and his partner are said to have netted a hundred thousand since they started in a modest way at Nigel's Reef"

This was the enclosure which gave the key-note to the letter.

"To think that you should have forgotten me in your riches—you, who were so good to me in our poverty! Oh, Arnold, I could not have believed that you could be prosperous and leave me to starve, even if you had formed new ties ; if you had forgotten all that we once were to each other. No, my dear, remembering what you were,

Rough Justice.

I cannot believe that you would be so cruel; so I am sure you have tried to find me, and have failed, and have thought me dead, perhaps—or worse than dead, sunk in a sinful life, rich with the wages of sin. No, Arnold, I am not dead, nor fallen to that lower depth where your pity could not help me. I have lived on, waiting for happier days ; waiting for you. When you were leaving me alone with my sad—almost broken—heart, you swore that if you prospered you would come back to me, and begin a new life with me, as man and wife. We had been so friendless and alone in our poverty that there would be nobody to say hard things about our past, if fortune should smile upon the future. I believed you, and took comfort from your promises, between kisses and tears, in that dark hour of parting, when I stood beside you in the crowded steerage, and would have given ten years of my life—half my life—to be going with you, to share hardship and danger only to be with you. You will never know what I have suffered in those four miserable years ; the bitter poverty ; the bitter degradation ; turned out of one poor lodging after another, because of arrears in a rent of a few shillings a week ; worried by the burden of debts that are counted by shillings; hunted from pillar to post; tramping all over London in all weathers, in search of employment; trying my hand at anything and everything. All that you and I have suffered together was light compared with what I have gone through since I have been alone. To be alone! Is not that

" How should I greet Thee ? "

enough ? To be alone and almost starving. And then I seem to have grown so common, to have sunk so near the level of my surroundings. I accept favours from such common people, and am grateful. Who else is there to help me "i The woman of this house is the kindliest landlady I ever had, and I have been lucky in getting a little needlework in the house, and have stayed here longer than anywhere else. She gives me my garret for half-a-crown a week, though she might get more for it from any mechanic. She is patient when I am behindhand with my rent ; and she patronizes me and pities me, and makes me go down to her kitchen sometimes when I come in from one of my pilgrimages a little more tired than usual, and gives me tea and toast, and comforts me with the promise of better luck, and tells my fortune in the tea-leaves at the bottom of my cup. Oh, Arnold, I am so weak and wretched that my heart beats and glows with hope when she tells me there is a fair man far off who bears me a good heart. Do you bear me a good heart ? If this letter reaches you will you answer it, and promise to come to me, and send me a little help from your riches, just enough for me to keep body and soul together till you come   I have another friend in this house, one whose pitying kindness— which I try my hardest to avoid—hurts me more than Mrs. Grogan's favours. I have sunk so low as to accept pity from a woman of worse than doubtful character a woman who paints her face, dyes her hair, and lives in a semi-detached manner

Rough Justice.

under the protection of an elderly stock-broker; a woman who goes to a theatre or a music-hall nearly every night, and whose hansom I hear drive up to the door in the dead, dreary hours through which I so often lie awake, waiting for the grey London light.

I had given her a wide berth till one winter evening, when she saw me dragging myself upstairs, feeling so faint and ill that I thought I should never get to the top of the house. She noticed my wretched state, and she put her arm round me and took me into her room. She was just going to sit down to dinner, and she put me in an easy-chair by the fire, and gave me hot wine and water, and was so tender and sweet to me a woman living a profligate life, Arnold, a creature deliberately immoral—not an accidental sinner like me and yet she was so gentle and so compassionate, and so womanly, that I wept tears of gratitude upon her breast. And after that night I could never hold my head high when I met her on the stairs, nor pretend not to see her. We have been friends in a way; and I have sat by her fire sometimes on bitter days when my garret was fireless, and she has told me bits of her story—of the days when she lived with her father, a rich tradesman in a garrison town, and all the officers were in love with her. She must have been really beautiful in her youth ; but she is only a handsome wreck now. She has no visitors, except the highly respectable city person whom she calls her guardian ; and Mrs. Grogan says that her lodgers'

"How should I greet Theef

conduct out-of-doors is no business of hers. Poor wretch, I suppose she gets a better rent for her rooms from Mrs. Delamere than a spotless lodger would give.

"Come back to me, Arnold. Come back, and be my husband, if you think you are bound by old promises. Consider, dear, I have led an honest life since you left me. I have lived on the edge of death for honour's sake. But if not, come back and be my comrade and friend, as in the old days. I belong to you. I have neither shame nor pride where you are concerned. I have repented of my other sins, but never of loving you. If the love is not dead in your heart, come back to me.

"Lisa." The letter was addressed to
"A. Wildover, Esq.,
At the Gold Fields, Witwatersrand,
Near Johannesburg,
South Africa."
Rough Justice.
CHAPTER II.
A FELLOW-FEELING.

Arnold sat staring straight before him across the narrow space of his windowless cabin. He had read Lisa's letter now for the third time, slowly, thoughtfully, realizing the full force of every word ; seeing the vision of the woman he had loved, her sufferings and deprivations, her sheep-like patience, the meek endurance of a woman whom the world had used ill.

To this woman Fate had been merciless. A profligate father, a passionate, hysterical mother, a miserable childhood, the fatal gift of beauty, and, with that essentially feminine beauty, a sensitive, susceptible nature.

Arnold knew the story of her temptation and her fall—how, within a year of her mother's death, she had exchanged a wretched wandering life with her father for a fool's paradise at the West End of London, under the protection of a Viennese banker, with the inevitable result of ill-usage and desertion. She had kept no humiliating circumstance of that cruel story from the man

A Fellow-feeling.

she loved the man who was really good to her, but who was as poor and almost as helpless as she was.

They had found each other in the hour of despair, and their desolate hearts had gone out to each other in an impulse of pity and love.

How well he remembered that meeting; the sultry evening, late in August, when all the prosperous people had left London, and there was a lull in the traffic of the streets, and the lights were fewer because of closed theatres and music-halls. Oh, the stony-heartedness of London streets at this dead season to the man with empty pockets, for whom no friend cares, no hospitable door opens!He had been roaming aimlessly about London all day—lying on the sunburnt grass in Hyde Park for an hour or two in the hottest part of the afternoon, trying to realize the French proverb that he who sleeps dines. He had not found that siesta a substitute for a beefsteak. He had spent his last copper to give himself a meal at a workman's coffee-house, where the eggs were of doubtful freshness, and the tea had a second-hand flavour, as if it had been made with cast-off tea-leaves.As the evening grew towards dusk he had sauntered to Waterloo Bridge, and sat there with his back against the parapet, in the quiet of the deepening twilight, admiring the long Italian façade of Somerset House, and wondering whether he should drown himself.

Rough Justice.

He had carried the idea of suicide about with him for a long time ; and if it had not been for the compunction natural to every prodigal son who has a fond mother, he might have wound up his difficulties before that dreary August night.To-day, however, there had been something in the atmosphere the dusty dryness, the odour of scorching pavements, and stale provisions, and dirty people, and old clothes, the odour of London poverty which had depressed him below his usual low-water mark. There was nothing for it but to enlist let himself out as a machine to carry a musket—or to kill himself; and he thought the bottom of the river might be better than the barrack yard.He waited for darkness, and such an interval in the traffic on the bridge, and on the water below, as would allow him to get over the parapet unnoticed and drop quietly into the river; and while he waited, sitting on one of the stone benches, a woman, who walked slowly past him, looked at him with a curious attention.There was just daylight enough left for them to see each other's faces. He noticed that hers had a faded beauty, which is always pathetic ; and even in that first look as she passed him he could see that she was not an "unfortunate."

She was very poorly clad, in black, and her pale features were innocent of all embellishment. The earnest manner in which she looked at hini could hardly have been misconstrued by the dullest mind.

A Fellow-feeling.

He watched her as she went to the end of the bridge, and in his utter loneh'ness and blank despair he felt a faint sense of regret at seeing no more of her,

"The poor thing saw my sad case, and was sorry for me," he thought, watching the slim black figure as other figures passed it by at the end of the bridge.

He was startled to see her turn suddenly and walk slowly back. It was as if his thought had summoned her; and he, who called thought-transference "rot," and hypnotism humbug, smiled grimly. Of course, his existence had nothing to do with her movements.She came slowly back, and seated herself at the other end of the bench on which he was sitting ; as if he had willed her to come to him, he thought, in spite of his scepticism.They sat thus in silence for about ten minutes, and then in a shy voice she made some little remark about the weather. The night was so sultry, the air so oppressive!He answered courteously, and they talked for a few minutes of indifferent things, the dreariness of London at this season. He knew somehow that she had a purpose in talking to him, and that the serious side of her mind would show itself presently.

There was an awkward silence, and then she said

" I hope you do not think badly of me "

" Impossible! " he interrupted eagerly.

Rough Justice.

" For having spoken to you a perfect stranger. You were looking so very, very miserable as I passed you, that somehow I could not go home in peace and leave you here. Your face would have haunted me all night. I should have dreamt dreadful dreams about you. This is the bridge from which people used to drown themselves years ago."

" Years ago! Do they never do it now ? "

" I think ndt. There are too many people passing now that the bridge is free."

"Ah, the halfpenny toll made a solitude, I suppose, and any poor wretch who was-sick of his life could find time and opportunity to chuck it away."

Again there was a silence embarrassed upon her part, moody on his. He began to understand her now. She knew he meant suicide. It was shrewd of her to have read his thoughts—she, a casual passer-by. He was touched by her concern for him, and began to study her face as she sat at the other end of the bench, looking straight before her in the faint grey light. It was a delicate, prettily modelled face, and it was a young face, though care had written lines upon it, and hollowed the oval cheek, and given a sad downward droop to the mouth.

" Do you live near here \'7d " she asked presently, "and do you come here of an evening for the fresh air from the river ?"

" I live nowhere just at present. I had very decisive notice to leave my lodgings last night. I was locked out."

A Fellow-feeling.

" Poor man! That is hard. And you have nowhere to go ?"

" Yes, I have somewhere—and I am going there presently, when I have enjoyed the fresh air from the river—and your agreeable society."

The defiance of his tone, the cynical sneer, and touch of brutality confirmed her in that conviction which had flashed into her mind at first sight of his face and attitude.

" Oh, don't, don't give way to despair!" she pleaded. " Think as badly of me as you like—for speaking so freely to a stranger for troubling myself about a stranger's fate."

" Think badly of you ! Not a bit. You belong to some rescue society, I dare say, and this is all in your evening's work."

"It isn't kind of you to sneer at me only because I saw a stranger in trouble and couldn't help caring. I can only beg you if you had that dreadful intention I fancied—to put it away from you. Who can ever tell what the future may bring ? So long as one is young, and in tolerable health, racked by no cruel incurable disease, there is always a chance. You know the vulgar proverb —the longest lane! Good night."

She rose towards the end of her speech. The latter part of it was spoken standing, and with the last words she moved quickly away.

But he sprang up, and darted after her, and caught her by the arm.

" Don't leave me just yet! " he said. " Do you think a despairing wretch is to be saved so easily ?

Rough Justice.

Stop! Your pity has touched me. Forgive me for trying to sneer it down. I didn't want to be made to feel human again, I have been feeling an angry devil a lost spirit. I should have gone with clenched fists to meet the Great Judge if there be one or Anything after the weeds in one's hair, and the river mud in one's mouth."

"You won't think of that wicked act any more ?"

" Not to-night, at any rate. You have humanized me. What a good soul you must be to take such heed of a stranger's trouble! "

" I once sat on this bridge for two hours, meaning what you meant to-night."

" And some kind soul guessed .? "

" No, no ; no one spoke to me, no one guessed. I sat and listened to the clocks striking, and I thought in another quarter of an hour it would be darker, and I waited and waited and I was a coward. I was afraid of the jump, and the plunge, so I went back to my wretched room, and let my landlady bully me, and I got some work the next day. My luck changed, and I clung to this poor life."

" Ah ; it was sympathy that made you understand
my case. Well, you are a Good Samaritan "

" Without even twopence to offer you."

"You have given me more than a million pence. You have interested me in something outside my own miserable used-up existence. Be my friend, dear girl. Tell me all about yourself.

A Fellow-feeling.

Who knows ? This may be the turning in my dismal lane. I have need of you, kind, compassionate creature."

He was holding her ; he put his arm round her waist in the darkness, and tried to draw her to him, but she struggled away from him.

"Do you think I am a bad woman because I was sorry for you ." " she asked indignantly.

*' I think you an angel of compassion and goodness."

"You insult me."

" Is it an insult to want your affection ; to yearn for a kiss from those gentle lips .-' You were sorry for me, and pity is akin to love. I am grateful to you, and gratitude is love."

" Good night," she said again, and hurried away from him, walking very fast towards the Surrey shore.

Quick as her pace was she could not escape him. He overtook her a little way from the bridge, and again he took her arm in his strong grip, not roughly, and walked at her side.

"Come, let there be no nonsense between us," he said impetuously. " An hour ago I was a solitary wretch, with nothing to live for, nothing between me and the bottom of the Thames. Your pity something else, perhaps ; something that I have never seen in any other woman has given me back my interest in life. An hour ago I wanted to die ; and now I want to live, because of you. But if you go out of my life again, if you say we are to be strangers, well I fall back

Rough Justice.

upon my original intention ; and so"after a brief pause" good night."

He released her arm as suddenly as he had seized it, lifted his hat, and walked away from her towards the bridge. This time it was she who followed him.

" For God's sake don't go back," she pleaded. " Be reasonable. What can I do but pity you ? What can I—almost as poor as you are—do to make your life better ? "

" Love me ! " he answered passionately. " Love me. My heart has been one great ache for the loneliness of this hideous town. You are the first woman of all I have met and passed in this stony labyrinth—since my ill luck began tht has gone out of her way to pity me. There were smilers enough, and challenges enough from eye and lip while I was prosperous ; but since I have been threadbare and out at elbows not a glance that meant kindness. You could stop to pity me, gentle Samaritan. Give me something more than idle pity."

"You talk as you would to the women of the streets," she said in a distressed voice.

"No, no, no! On my soul, no! Is there no swift sudden love except the love that is bought ?"

" I am not what the world calls a good woman, but I do not belong to that class."

" I know it. Such a thought never entered into my mind. Do you suppose I am such a dolt as not to comprehend purity when I meet it ? Pity,

A Fellow-feeling,

beneficence, the qualities that make ministering angels!"

"Ah, now your praise sounds like mockery. Indeed, there is nothing for us but to shake hands and say good-bye. You will not be so wicked as to think any more of suicide. You will wait and see what Providence will do for you. And please accept this shilling indeed, indeed, I can spare it—and get a crust of bread and a bed somewhere."

He pushed away the slender hand that was trying to slip the coin into his palm.

" No; I will accept no favour from a woman who whistles me off so lightly. Tell me who you are—where you live—when I may see you again. Tell me, and then I will take half your shilling and get myself a supper, and sit in St. James's Park, and think of you till morning."

She refused, but the pleading voice a deep, strong voice that sounded like passionate music— was irresistible. If he were lonely, was she not lonely too." She yielded so far as to promise to meet him in Birdcage Walk at eight o'clock on the following night. She would not tell him where she lived, or her name, yet awhile.

" You will not cheat me ? " he asked.

** I give you my word of honour, if I am alive to-morrow night I will be there."

" I will trust you."

He changed the shilling at a great gaudy public-house, and gave her one of the two sixpences.

"Do you remember how Lucy Ashton and her

Rough Justice.

lover divided a piece of gold between them as a token of lifelong fidelity ? We divide a loaf of bread."

And so they parted." Shall I ever see her again ?" he wondered, as he walked slowly westward. "Will she keep her promise ?"

Could it be love, this warm interest in a woman whom he had never seen before to-night ? Was it love." Impossible, he told himself; but the strange circumstances of their acquaintance, her compassion, her frankness and courage, were enough to account for his keen interest in her, his longing to see her again, to make her in some wise his own.

" She came to me in the hour of my despair. I am not going to let her go," he said to himself, over and over again in the summer night.

He had a hearty supper of bread and cheese and porter—sixpennyworth in all, at one of the taverns that open in the small hours for the market people. He sat in a corner amidst an odour of cabbages with the dew on them, a faint sweetness of herbs and flowers, and ate and drank, thinking of the pale, worn face, and the friendly hand to which he owed the tardy meal. He thought he had never in his life enjoyed a meal so much.

"That swipes was better than all the fiz I ever drank," he muttered, as he set down the empty pot.

He went into the cool dawn like a giant refreshed, and slept sweetly on a bench in St. James's

A Fellow-feeling:

Park, under the rosy morning sky, lulled by the chirruping of London birds, and the flutter of ruffled leaves. And all next day he looked for work with an energy he had not known of late. He had gone about in a low-spirited, ill-tempered way, as if he had been seeking failure. To-day he went everywhere with a bright countenance, a happy-go-lucky air that was irresistible.

Before the day was done he had succeeded in two directions. The editor of a sporting paper had promised to consider any articles upon 'Varsity athletics or 'Varsity sport which he might send in, and to pay him fairly for his " copy " if it were accepted. And, better still, the acting-manager of a second-rate music-hall engaged him as general assistant in front of the house and " chucker-out," at fifteen shillings a week, with a promise of better pay if his services proved satisfactory.

"You won't have to wear a uniform like those big foreign chaps at the West End," said the manager. "We don't run to that. I suppose you've got a dress suit.""

" I have ; but it's—at the cleaner's. You'll have to advance me a week's pay if you want me to wear it."

" And how do I know I shall ever see that good-looking mug of yours again if I do.-' You look like a gentleman—but that sort is sometimes the worst."

" That's your business. With your wide experience of life you ought to know an honest man when you see one."

Rough Justice.

"Well, there's your money. I must risk it. I like the cut of your jib. You look like a 'Varsity man, and you're built for strength, though you're wofully out of condition."

" I've been worrying myself lately."

"And not eating enough, perhaps. You'd better take another five bob, and put a little beef and beer inside you before Saturday."

He was to begin his new duties on Saturday night. He knew enough of such places of amusement to know that his post would not be a sinecure. He was glad that the Hall was a third-rate place, on the Surrey side of the river, since he was less likely to be recognized by family friends, or the men he had known at Cambridge.

He had not a large circle of acquaintance. His father was a small Suffolk squire, living quietly upon an estate that had belonged to his race for nearly three centuries, proud, as such people are proud, of names and acres, never having been ground in that great cosmopolitan mill which reduces all individualities—short of a Prime Minister, a Duke, an inventor, or a quadruple millionaire—to inconsiderable atoms. The Went-worths of Langton Park lived in the narrowest circle, and the majority of Arnold's acquaintance were the friends he had made for himself at Cambridge. These he thought were very unlikely to cross the Thames in quest of amusement, since any new light that illumined those obscure regions would, so soon as discovered by the managerial eye, be invited to blaze upon West End London.

A Fellow-feeling.

He accepted the engagement, therefore, without compunction ; saw no degradation in being hired to keep order among roughs, to show people to their seats, to help the over-worked waiters even, on occasion, and serve drinks. To a man who has been face to face with starvation and death, no honest employment need seem degrading.

Fifteen shillings a week ! He could get a clean attic on the Surrey side for four shillings, spend a shilling a day on food, and have four shillings a week for shoe-leather and laundress. But twelve shillings out of the pound he had just received would go to the pawnbroker, who had custody of his dress suit, and he would have to maintain himself for a week—or perhaps a fortnight—upon eight shillings—a problem in economics, assuredly. But he had other resources.

There was a cricket match on at the Oval that afternoon, so when he had found the room he wanted in a tidy street near the Lambeth Road, and had washed and furbished himself, with much brushing of threadbare tweed and well-blacked boots, so that he might not sink with shame at encountering an acquaintance, he paid his sixpence and watched the heroic struggle of a weak Sussex against a strong Surrey, and joined in the clamour and excitement of the scene, and forgot that he had eaten nothing but a penny roll since two o'clock in the morning.

Luck favoured him so far that the only acquaintance he saw was in the Surrey team, and unconscious of his existence. He stayed till the close

Rough Justice.

of play, took a meal of tea and cold meat in a coffee-shop at Vauxhall, and then strolled through the summer evening to St. James's Park. " Would she keep her promise ?"

He thought she would—thought that her loneliness was little less than his own, that she had almost as bitter need of sympathy. She would not have so felt for his woes if they had not been like her own. He remembered the opium eater's gentle friend—that story of love in poverty. Was not their situation much the same—friendless and poor in the lap of the stony-hearted stepmother, London, the inj'usta noverca to poverty, the sycophant and the ministering slave to wealth ?

She was sitting on a bench in a little bit of ornamental ground opposite Queen Anne's Gate, waiting meekly, very neat and prim in her threadbare black frock, and black straw hat. Last night she had been gloveless ; to-night she wore gloves that were in themselves a history, so carefully mended, so old and thin.

She blushed at his coming, like a girl at the sight of a first lover. The man who could confound her with the vicious classes must have been indeed a thick-skinned brute.

They sat and talked together, and walked about the park together in the summer darkness, till ten o'clock.

He told her the history of his day.

" You are my Mascotte, perhaps," he said. " I have had better luck to-day have got something to do that will just keep me from starving."

A Fellow-feeling

And then he told her about the engagement at the Comet Music Hall; but instead of being pleased, she was shocked at the idea.

" I know you are a gentleman, and have never mixed with such people," she said. " It seems dreadful you should sink so low."

" Oh, I am something of a Radical. I think nothing low that isn't felonious. I don't suppose I shall quite like giving the waiters a helping hand when the Hall's full, but I shall enjoy the chucking out. It will remind me of my happiest days."

" Why not go back to your friends ?" she asked. "I know you must belong to nice people—somewhere."

" I belong to no one but myself, my dear. Besides you I have but one friend in the world— my mother—and she was too weak to shield me from my father's tyranny. He and I could not live in the same house after I was a man. My manhood rose against domestic despotism. I turned my back upon a home that was a wasp's nest of petty irritations, and everybody belonging to me cried out upon my villainy. No, dear little friend, for me there is no going back. I have to make my own life, and to find happiness where I can."

When the Horse Guards' clock struck ten she stopped in the midst of their talk, and bade him good-night.

He wanted her to stay later, but she said her landlady would be horrified if she was not indoors

Rough Justice.

before eleven, and then he wanted to walk home with her, but she was obdurate, and would not even let him know where she lived.

The next night was Saturday, and his engagement at the Comet was to begin. There could be no evening walk in the park. She promised to meet him in Kennington Park on Sunday afternoon.

" It will be nearer where you live," he said artfully.

He put her into a Brixton omnibus at Charing Cross, and then walked to his Lambeth lodging, and sat down to write a criticism on Surrey cricket. He was not literary by any means, had failed to get his degree, and had brought down the paternal wrath upon himself for that and other failures— failure to live upon his allowance, for instance. But he was no dunce, and could write plain English with a good swing in it; and in writing of cricket, football, or athletics, he was writing about what he knew. The editor praised his "copy," and paid him half a sovereign for it on the nail.

" Do you want to sign the article with y-our own name ?" he asked.

" I have no name."

" Oh, then you'd better take a nom-de-plumey said the editor. "We like names. You seem pretty knowledgable. Suppose we call you ' The Man who Knows ' t"

The paper was a new one, called itself In the Know, and aimed at being as modern and as slangy as sporting papers are made. It was

A Fellow-feeling.

printed on yellow paper, and aspired to become popular as the "yaller 'un."

They met in Kennington Park on more than one afternoon in the sultry August. He took her to see a match at the Oval, and they had tea together at a little Swiss shop in the Kennington Road. They were fast friends, and yet he knew only her Christian name. For him she was only Lisa, and for her he was Arnold. And so this gentle friendship continued for nearly a month, the bond strengthening day by day, though she hardly knew how strong it was growing.

And then, one Sunday night;his only free night—they walked longer and later than usual. She forgot her landlady's hours, and the possibility of being scolded forgot the passage of time, as she walked to and fro in the deep shadow of the trees in the most secluded part of Hyde Park, listening to Arnold's pleading. He was asking for more than her friendship he wanted her love, he wanted her. Why should she withhold herself from him \'7d He knew she loved him. She had saved him from an ignominious death. He belonged to her, and she to him. He pleaded in such plain, strenuous language as a working man might have used to his sweetheart. And she accepted him—lover or husband. There were reasons in her own mind which withheld her from even asking what the tie was to be. She gave herself to him unconditionally, having loved him from the night of their first meeting, having

Rough Justice.

melted at his voice, and trembled at his touch in all the time she had maintained an almost severe reserve. The clocks struck twelve while they were talking.

" What will Mrs. Marmian say to me ? She has such a dreadful temper! "

"She shall have no chance of saying anything to-night. My home is your home now you have promised to trust yourself to me."

They went home together. His landlady was of the easy-going type—sat up late herself, and wasn't shocked at late hours in a lodger, and was not averse to the offer of a glass of whisky.

" I've brought my wife home, Mrs. Barwick," Arnold said coolly. "You didn't know I was married, did you ? She has just come from her friends in the country, and her train was late. Her luggage will be here to-morrow."

Alone m London.

CHAPTER III.

ALONE IN LONDON.

Their new lives began in perfect harmony and happiness. There was no question of marriage. If she had possessed that steadfast strength, that power to resist tender impulses, and that lofty-self-esteem which make high principle in woman, she could have made her own terms with him. But she was by nature submissive and unexacting, and she had been crushed under the grinding wheel of poverty, and had suffered the world's contempt. From the first she was his slave— devoted to him, esteeming herself happy if she could but make his life a little happier.

She was the daughter of an adventurer, and had led the casual, shifty life of the out-at-elbows and the homeless ever since she could remember; and in this chequered existence had learnt many small arts. She could cook a dinner, or trim a hat, was an artist with her needle, and so was able to eke out Arnold's small earnings, and to keep the wolf from the door, even when things were worst ; but there were intervals when bt ' tJie

Know was using a good deal of Arnold's "copy," and then they lived merrily.

They had been living thus for a year, and a child had been born to them ; a child that lived only a week, and whose death had a terrible effect upon the mother. She had a long and dangerous illness, through which Arnold nursed her day and night, giving up his engagement at the Music Hall for that purpose, hoping to maintain her and himself by the use of his pen. As "The Man who Knows" he had become a feature on the yellow paper, and as long as the paper and his popularity lasted he was sure of three pounds a week.

It was in the beginning of her convalescence, and while she was still light-headed at night, that Lisa told her lover the secret of her past.

" I dare say you think me worse than I am, because I never asked you to marry me," she said, brokenly, "not even when our baby was coming. If I had been a good woman I should have wanted to be your wife. But you never asked me what my youth had been, and I felt I had no right to ask you to give me your name, unless I could tell you that I was worthy "

"Dear girl, you are worthy. Tell me nothing. I want to know nothing about the past. I know you. Surely that's enough. It is the woman, and not the history, that counts. You have been true and dear, and have loved me as no one ever loved me before you. Make haste and get well, and I will marry you as soon as you are strong

enough to stand up in a church or a registrar's office."

"You won't say that, when you know all," she sobbed.

And then she told him her pitiful story. The daughter of an unprincipled man—steeped in debt and difficulty; shifting his quarters from city to city; clever enough to live where a duller rascal would have starved; utterly neglectful of wife and daughter; unmoved when the broken-hearted wife succumbed to the misery of her existence, and letting his seventeen-year-old daughter tramp the streets of the wickedest city in Europe, and fetch and carry for him.

Young, pretty, ill-clad, with that low standard of self-respect which is the natural result of a childhood steeped in poverty and debt, the motherless waif was an easy prey for a scoundrel. The first man's voice that had ever spoken tenderly to her was the voice of the seducer.

" I was so unhappy, so tired and ill, when he first spoke to me ; and I thought it was only for pity that he took notice of me. He was old enough to be my father. I had no fear of him. I looked up to him as a superior being—my friend, my benefactor. He promised to find employment for my father ; to make our lives happier. I used to see him every day as I went about our poor little marketing—or went to the pawnbroker's for my father—and one day "

Convulsive sobs stopped the pitiful story. Arnold urged her to tell him no more—the past
was past. She was no less dear to him because of her unhappy girlhood.

" No, no, no ; you must know all—all—and then if you still think I am fit to be your wife "

He tried hard to stop her, but she insisted; and in broken sentences, interrupted by hysterical sobbing, she told him how she had been left in London, and how she had starved and struggled, and kept herself out of the lowest depth to which lost women go down. She had been as near suicide as he had. She had lived on a few pence a day; had put her hand to anything that she could find to do; had lived for a week on a West End dressmaker's pay for one day's work.

"Tell me no more, dear, except the name of the man who wronged you. I should like to know, so that I may have a name to hate him by."

" What does his name matter ? He is a great man in Vienna. Everybody looks up to him there, as I did before I knew what he was. If you were to tell people how he treated me they would not believe you. I hate myself for having listened to him and loved him. I did love him, Arnold ; not as I love you, but with the love of an ignorant girl who had never been praised or tenderly treated. He was kind to me—generous, indulgent while his whim lasted ; and then he left me without an hour's warning. His valet brought me a letter good-bye and a twenty-pound note. His master was starting for Vienna at eight o'clock that evening. And then I knew what it was to be alone in London."

Alone in London.

He was tender with her, and seemed full of pity, yet her story chilled him. He had guessed that there was a history; that some deeper woe than poverty had clouded her girlhood ; that her soul had gone down into deep waters. But this story of a middle-aged lover—a street acquaintance —was wanting in every element of romance. She had been fond of her seducer—fond of the man who praised her, and lavished gifts upon her. She regretted him even now, perhaps ; looked back and sighed for the luxury of Brompton lodgings, a brougham, and fine clothes ; looked back from their shabby second floor in Margaretta Street, Lambeth.She saw no change in him yet; but the slow, day-by-day death of a worn-out love had begun. His love was dying by inches, though he hardly knew it. He thought he was tired of this wretched London life this stony labyrinth, and smoke-darkened sky not of her.Things were going badly with them. She was weak after her illness too weak for an occasional day's dressmaking at the West End, and so one element of earning was gone. He had been precipitate in giving up the music-hall, for he found the In the Know people were becoming bad paymasters. He had to call three or four times at the office for the few pounds owing to him. Life was harder than it had been.The rent of the shabby lodging was in arrear, and the easy-going landlady looked at him gloomily in the shadow of the narrow passage as he went out or came in.

Rough Justice.

" If you find seven shillings a week too much to pay, you'd better manage with one room," she said ; and Arnold agreed that in his present circumstances one room must do.

He had taken the extra room when Lisa and he joined fortunes.

Oh, the misery of that one room, where there was room for nothing! The Pembroke table at which he wrote, screwed into a corner where his elbows were cramped by the walls, while Lisa did some bit of fine laundrywork, or prepared their composite meal, at another table—the squalor of it to a man reared amongst ample spaces and pleasant surroundings, and in the clear air of Suffolk fields and woods! An invincible longing to escape from those four walls seized him. He almost regretted the music-hall, the vulgar songs, and stamping dances, the dust and glare, the riot and noise. At least there were movement and life at the music-hall. Here, there was a deadly quiet. Lisa was dull and depressed for want of change of air after her illness; and she had a nervous monosyllabic cough that tortured him by its measured recurrence. There was a loud Dutch clock on the landing, and he knew almost to a moment how many seconds it ticked off between Lisa's coughs. When he was writing for his paper —trying to be bright and lively, to adorn his record of boat-race or cricket match with the highest top-sparkle of Cockney humour—that recurrent cough, slight as it was, made him grind his teeth in nervous agony. Life would have

Alone in London.

been tolerable if he had had a den, he thought, a mere closet, where he could shut himself in, and not hear every movement of his poor companion, and not smell the sausages or the bloaters that she was frying for the tea-dinner, and not be painfully conscious of every detail of this squalid existence.

They were soon to sink into a deeper misery. He had not thrown up his situation at the Comet three months, when that other and, as he once thought, better source of income dried up altogether. In tlic Know died the mute, inglorious death of newspapers that fail. There were no convulsions of the parting spirit. Nobody knew it was passing. The yellow periodical simply ceased to be. Its slang, its stupendous up-to-dateishness, its yellow paper, had not served to keep life in it for two little years. Nobody had ever been induced to call it "The yaller 'un." It died and made no sign. Arnold only knew of his bereavement when he went to the office in quest of a business manager who had been very difficult of access of late, though the editor had been unusually eager for " copy " from "The Man who Knows."

The office a ground floor in a shabby street between the Strand and Long Acre—was shut, and a bill in one of the windows announced that these eligible premises were to let ; for further particulars apply to Messrs. Barnard and Badger, Auctioneers and Estate Agents, Queen Street.

Arnold did not trouble Barnard and Badger.

Rough Justice.

What good could further particulars do him ? He had seen impending ruin in the conduct of editor and proprietor, in the shuffling avoidance of his claim for payment ; in the pacifying him with an occasional sovereign on account, instead of a cheque in full.

The yellow newspaper was dead, and that meant starvation. There were other papers, of course, which treat of athletics, and of manly sports, such as he loved to share in, to witness, or even to write about ; but all the old-established paying papers had their staff, and would hardly desire contributions from an outsider—an outsider in the worst sense of the word, Arnold thought with a pang of self-contempt.He walked homeward by St. George's Circus, and looked in at the Comet. No, there was no berth for him there. They had found an Aberdeen railway porter of six feet four, and proportionate bulk, whom they had put in a uniform, plastered with gold lace, and who gave the hall an air which Arnold's threadbare dress suit could never impart.No, his services were no longer worth bread and cheese at the Comet.Now came the wretched wearing hand-to-mouth existence, the daily fight for the day's food and shelter. How could love live in such an atmosphere ." It did live, for one of the two. The woman went on loving with that love of woman or dog which is deathless. The man sickened of the struggle, and hated his life so much that

Alone in London.

he began to be afraid of hating his life's companion.

They were good and tender to each other through it all. When she was ill—and she was often ill—he nursed her. On those rare occasions when his strong frame sunk under his burden, and the sickness of exhaustion fell upon him, she nursed him, and fed him, somehow, with the earnings of her day's toil. He never knew that at these times she sometimes did half a day's charing for a shilling to buy his dinner.It was the year that the diamond fever raged fiercest at Kimberley, and men in England who knew nothing of the restrictions or the difficulties of the mining district, thought that wealth was waiting for them out yonder, beside the Orange River. One of the contributors to the defunct sporting paper, the man who had written the turf articles, met Arnold walking the Strand, gaunt and shabby, and took him into an oyster shop, and gave him a lunch.This gentleman had been luckier in backing the winners in the great autumn races than those readers who had believed in his prophecies when he wrote for In the Know. He had won a few hundreds, and had heard of that Tom Tiddler's Ground in South Africa ; and, being of a sanguine disposition, was ready to back his luck there.He looked up to Arnold as a man of better education, and better thews and sinews than himself, and offered to take him to the diamond mines. He was not going to Kimberley, but to Barkly

West, twenty miles off the centre of the River Diggings, where a man with a small capital might have a chance of luck, if he worked hard enough. The River Diggings were the poor man's diggings.

"You shall have twenty per cent, of all we make," he told Arnold. " I'm a social bird, and hate the idea of going alone. And if you haven't got the oof for the passage, why, I'll pay your fare —steerage."

"You're very good, but that isn't enough," Arnold answered, his face flushing and his eye brightening at the thought of escape. " I can't leave a friend to starve. I should want a ten-pound note to leave behind me."

The reprobate was good-natured. He lent or gave Arnold ten pounds over and above his passage money, and this a large sum when measured by their late deprivations Arnold gave to Lisa.

" I am no good to you," he said ; " for the last three months you have been the only breadwinner —except for a casual quid once in a blue moon. You have been keeping me, toiling for me, Lisa. Be sure you will do better alone."

" Better!"

The anguish in the voice, the white despair in sunken cheek and quivering lips, smote him with a sense of shame. Pie knew that she was heartbroken, and that he was glad to get away from her; from the four walls ; the London sky ; the cramped, wretched life. Those were the things he

was so glad to leave. And for her? Well, her existence was linked with them.

All that was generous in his nature was aroused by her sorrow. All that man could say to comfort woman those lips of his spoke to her, as she clung to him, and sobbed upon his breast, in that unspeakable agony of parting.

" Dearest, if I live and prosper, I will come back —come back to marry you and make a lady of you. I swear it. Come, love, be brave. Who knows ? I may do well at the Mines. There are men who began there with the clothes they stood in, as I shall, and who are triple millionaires today. I mean to make my fortune, for your sake, Lisa. I shall come back a rich man, and you shall share my good luck, as you have shared my penury."

"No, Arnold, no you will never come back. You have been too miserable with me."

"Ah, but I have been happy, too. You are the only woman I ever really loved; and if I prosper you shall prosper too."

And so they parted on her side with despairing tears, on his with kisses and promises.

The remembrance of the words he had spoken then smote him now, as he sat in his berth, in the night loneliness, with her letter in his hand.

" If you think you are bound by those promises," she wrote. "If!" He knew that he was bound by them. Honour and conscience declared those

vows binding. He had given his promise unsolicited, since she had been ever unselfish and unexacting. And even in reminding him of what he had promised she absolved him in advance, if he wanted to break his word. She urged him only to go back to her ; to be again her protector and her friend ; to love her as he loved her of old.Alas! that could not be. He might go back, and redeem his promise, and marry her. But the love born of despair, the sudden sympathy between two solitary creatures, desolate in a crowded world, was in Arnold's heart and mind only a memory of something that had once been sweet and dear. He could never think of Lisa Rayner without tenderness ; but he had long ceased to love her.The years in which they had been parted were the long years of eventful manhood. He had lived a new life ; he felt himself a new man. That larger life of an adventurer among many adventurers, of the strong man among strong men, had moulded mind and body, and had put a new mark upon him.He had lived in a world where all was young and fresh, eager, courageous, hopeful. How could he expect happiness if he were to ally himself with that broken life he had left behind, the faded, saddened woman, whose mind was shadowed and dulled by bitterest memories, upon whose face care had drawn such cruel lines ?And, worst of all, as he recalled that faded face another face shone out beside it, so fair, so fresh, so radiant with youth and hope, that the contrast

Alone in London.

between the two was wide as the difference between Hght and shadowOh, happy face, in its frank outlook, its innocent fearlessness—the sign and token of an unsullied life! Sweet face which he had been watching and studying in the idle days over that wintry sea, and which had made December bright as June!

"Sweet Mary, it is not for beauty I love you," he said to himself, musing sadly, with Lisa's letter still in his hand. " I have seen prettier faces—but never a face so radiant with youth and hope. My merry Mary, my joyous light-hearted girl! "

He looked back wonderingly at those old days in Suffolk, when Mary had been, in some way or other, his almost daily companion. His mother had compassionated her loneliness in the maiden aunt's prim household ; and Mary had been given the run of the schoolroom and garden, and had been accepted as Beatrice Wentworth's companion and playfellow.

Beatrice was Arnold's only sister, his junior by five years, and two years older than little Mary.

Mary was still little Mary when Arnold left home, still a child, a tall slip of a thing that had just passed its twelfth birthday, and was boastful of being in its teens.I am in my teens, you know," she used to say reprovingly, when Arnold teased her. "You'll have to leave off pulling my hair."

"Then you'll have to leave off having such a preposterous mop. The temptation is too strong for me," Arnold would reply.

Rough Justice.

He was very fond of little Mary his Molly, his Polly, his flippety witchet. He had all kinds of foolish names with which to tease her, but in talking about her she was always "the kid." He teased her, and played with her tennis, cricket, football; tobogganing in a wheelless barrow down a grassy slope in the garden ; blackberrying and nutting in the woods and on the commons ; skating, billiards, archery. Mary wanted to do everything that anybody else in the world could do. Why not billiards \'7d She was sure she could play if they would let her. " Cut the cloth, should I ?" cried she. " Oh, how nasty of you ! "

Mary tried everything, and if she didn't actually adorn everything she touched, she was at least quicker with brain and hand and foot than most girls of her age. She was the kind of child " who feels her life in every limb" a frank, fearless creature.

"Mary Frceland's high spirits are a little boisterous, but she is thoroughly nice," Mrs. Wentworth said ; " and she is a capital companion for Bee, who is much too fond of sitting over a book. And it is a real kindness to have her here. It must be so wofully dull for her at home ; and her aunt is very pleasant about it, and likes the child to be here."

Happily for the little Mary of those days, her aunt. Miss Farmiloe, was a strong-minded person with ample resources, who was bored by juvenile society, and was grateful to the chief lady of the neighbourhood for taking her niece off her hands during the greater part of the day.

Alone in London.

Punctually every evening, at seven o'clock in summer, or at five in winter, Miss Farmiloe's highly respectable parlour-maid or in bad weather the gardener called at Langton House for Miss Mary; and punctually at ten o'clock every morning, except Sundays, Mary appeared, fresh and beaming, at the schoolroom door, ready to share Beatrice's lessons. Beatrice had taken ever so much more interest in her work since she had had a companion, the governess told Mrs. Wentworth ; and indeed Mary's gay temper gave a zest to the schoolroom drudgery; and all those kings and queens in the Primers and Histories who had been such pale abstractions came to life, and were worth reading about.

Mary had been allowed to grow wild till she was ten years old, in accordance with a theory of Miss Farmiloe's, and she was much behind Beatrice when she began to share her studies ; but she soon reached her companion's level, and it required considerable management upon the governess's part to keep the humble friend from outstripping the young lady of the house.

As a child—a graceful, lively, winning child and only as a child, Arnold had remembered his little friend. Looking back at the past, and seeing that graceful childish figure in the picture of his vanished home, it had never occurred to him that the child was growing into a woman—or, indeed, it had never occurred to him that there was in that human Will-o'-the-wisp the germ of the future woman; or that the passing years must

Rough Justice.

change the character of their friendship should they ever meet again.

They had met, and after the first shock of finding her tall and strong, and womanly in form and aspect, he had treated her as if she were little Mary still with the old frankness and freedom ; teasing her, and laughing at her, as in the old times, and spending most of those idle hours in her society. What was there to do at sea but to talk to a girl one liked .- There were the children, too, who were perfect limpets in their attachment to him and to Mary, and who would not let them be apart. They were both indispensable in every kind of recreation. The other passengers noted the merry group clustered on the hurricane deck, with wind-blown hair and frocks, Mary as childish in her mirth as the children ; and most people took it for granted that Mary and Arnold were engaged lovers, going home to be married.

" I suppose you'll be dreadfully busy about your trousseau directly you land," observed one inquisitive spinster, who had been troubled in mind about Mary's chaperonless condition from the beginning of the voyage; and Mary blushed furiously as she explained that she had no trousseau to buy—only a mourning frock or two.

" I ought to be in mourning for my aunt," she said.

"And Mr. Wildover is not yov fiancif How odd! We all took you for engaged people,"

" How silly of you ! Ir. Wildover is an old, old

Alone in London.

friend, who used to be a kind of playfellow when I was little. He would no more think of being in love with me than he would with you," concluded Mary, casting about for an example of the improbable.

She was angry at the spinster's impertinence, and even more angry with herself for blushing so hotly.

"I hate the ladies' saloon," she told Arnold, afterwards. " It reeks with old maids."

When they were within a few days of arrival at Southampton, Mary was hurt at perceiving a change in Arnold's conduct. He left off playing with her and the children—or only joined in their games occasionally, when they were too persistent to be denied.

" Perhaps he is beginning to be ashamed of me because I have no chaperon," Mary said to herself, after crying a little, as she sat alone in her cabin, trying to read an instructive book out of the ship's library—the biography of some one she had never heard of, written by some one equally unknown. "No chaperon! How I shall always hate that word ! As if any girl with a grain of sense wanted an old woman to take care of her! One can understand an old woman wanting a girl—to help her over the crossings, and to put her cap straight. But a girl wanting an old woman is too absurd."

Mary Freeland's African and theatrical experiences had inclined her to protest against the restraints and restrictions of conventionality.

Rough Justice.

At Southampton Arnold bade her good-bye, after having seen her seated in the boat express that was to take her to Waterloo, whence she was going straight to Liverpool Street, and Suffolk. There would have been no word said of any future meeting if Mary had not spoken it.

"You will be coming to Mervynhall to see Mrs. Wentworth," she said ; " so I dare say we shall meet before long."

" Yes, I dare say," he answered, not very cordially. And then, with a sudden change of manner, which was like a flash of sunshine, " Yes, yes, I must see you again—^just once more before I go back to the Cape."

" You mean to go back, then ?"

" Oh dear, yes. What is there for me to do in England .-* I only came home to see my mother, and to look about me a little bit."

" Oh," said Mary, " I thought you were going to settle down as a respectable member of society."

" No, Mary," he sighed, " I fear that isn't in me

—unless—unless Well, it's no good thinking

about possibilities. I may not go back for half a year or so, perhaps. Good-bye."

The train moved as he pressed the slender hand which lay so willingly in his ; he had only time to lift his hat and answer Mary's smile with a smile—so much less happy than hers—before she was carried out of his sight.

" The kid has grown into the sweetest woman I ever met," he muttered to himself, as he walked

Alone in London.

away, and tried to lose himself for an hour or so in Southampton.

He had refrained from travelling in the train that was taking Mary and most of her fellow-passengers, because he had made up his mind that her company was not good for him. There was a train at three that would get him to London at five.

He had a letter in his pocket that lay upon his heart like lead.

Poor Lisa—poor soul—sad companion of saddest days. He looked back and wondered if he was the man who endured that old life, and tramped the shabby quarters of the town in shabby boots, with tired brain and languid limbs; he, whose step was now so elastic, whose frame seemed strung with steel.

" If she will be kind and release me," he mused. He had drifted from the station into the slums of the town—the busy back streets, crowded with a curiously mixed population, foreign and oriental faces among seafaring natives, a crowd that suggested Ratcliffe Highway.

It was Christmas Eve. The shop windows were heaped with food of all kinds, and gaudy with Christmas emblems; and pork-butchers and grocers were vying with each other in the brilliancy of their display—there a prize pig garlanded with holly and coloured paper, here gin bottles blazing with gilt labels, mountains of plums and currants crowned with rocky ridges of candied peel.

Rough Justice.

"Christmas—the rallying time of love and friendship," mused Arnold, "and except Lisa—• and, perhaps, little Mary—and, I suppose, my mother, I doubt if there's a creature in this country who cares whether I'm alive or dead."

Some One loved Him.

CHAPTER IV.

SOME ONE WHO LOVED HIM.

For people who like their scenery flat the neighbourhood of Mervynhall might rank as beautiful. Even for the stranger, and the scoffer at Suffolk landscapes, the river, flowing deep and narrow and straight as a canal through fertile meadows, past old water-mills, and millers' gabled houses, the pine woods on either side the long level roads, have a certain charm. It is a formal, low-toned beauty, no doubt, the homely charm of broad cornfields, and rich pastures ; but then the cottages are old and picturesque, the cottage gardens are neatly kept, and the streets of the little town are broad and clean. The market-place is quaint and odd, and the parish church rises above those modest streets, and prim, square houses, in all the grandeur of Norman Gothic, almost a cathedral.

Arnold Wentworth—alias Wildover—loved the little town for old sake's sake, albeit he would have eaten his heart out had he been forced to spend his life there, in that respectable isolation from everything else in the world which the

Rough Justice.

inhabitants considered a dignified seclusion. The sight of meadows and river, bridge and church, touched him with a sense of pain on this Christmas afternoon, as he walked to the inn, from the modest terminus of a little branch line from Cambridge. There were no Sunday trains upon this respectable line; but the necessities of the lower classes had urged and secured a train in and a train out on Christmas Day.

The train by which Arnold travelled was due at four, and the dusk of evening was thickening to darkness as he approached the town.It was half a dozen years since he had crossed the bridge, and heard that solemn sound of St. Michael's chimes, as he heard it now, telling the quarter after four from a tower that rose dim in the dusk. There were lighted windows shining in a house whose garden dipped towards the river, on his left, as he crossed the bridge—a house to which he looked instinctively, for it was Mary's house now, and he wondered if she was keeping Christmas there, and with whom. He would have liked to find out for himself; but he had another mission at Mervynhall.There were two highly respectable hotels in the town, both of which seemed somewhat over capacious for the requirements of a place that had once bristled with mail-coaches and post-chaises, but which now depended on a branch line, with three trains a day, and had in somewise lost touch with the outside world, save in the shooting season, when the lords of the soil summoned their kindred

Some One who loved Him,

and friends for big shoots, and when Mervynhall awoke and bestirred itself. Arnold went to neither Antelope nor Crown Hotel, preferring the more secluded accommodation of an old inn outside the town, a straggling old house, with an archway entrance, and no expectation of a staying guest on Christmas Day. He came here to avoid recognition, which would have been likely at cither hotel, in spite of bronzed complexion, bearded chin, and the passage of time.

Could he have a bedroom and private sitting-room \'7d Yes, He was shown into a large panelled room next the archway, and a maid-servant, in her Sunday gown, knelt down to light the fire.

What would he like for dinner, and at what time would he please to dine ?

" Oh, anything you can give me ; but not till eight o'clock. I want a letter taken to Langton Park. Have you any messenger who can be trusted to do exactly what I tell him—a sharp, sensible person ?"

The girl stared at him wonderingly.

" We've got the ostler," she said.

" The ostler ? Christmas Day ? I dare say he's been drunk for the last two hours."

" Oh no, sir. The ostler's my father, and he's a very sober man. He don't often take a drop too much."

" Not often—but Christmas ? This would be the very day, perhaps," hesitated Arnold, with a letter in his hand.

" No, sir; I can answer for father. He's been

busy all the morning with the fly—driving people out visiting. He haven't begun to enjoy hisself yet."

"Ask him to come here, then, please."

The girl went to fetch her , father from the untidy purlieus of the stable, which savoured of pigs, and was more agricultural than it had been in the days when the Bear was a coaching house. The man came slouching in, dressed in a kind of compromise between stable fustian and Sunday broadcloth ; and to him Arnold entrusted a letter which he had written in the waiting-room at Cambridge, having found himself with an hour to waste at that unbeautiful station.

" You know Langton House ?"

"Yes, sir."

" Do you know the servants ?"

" The butler, he know me, sir "—as if there were a vast difference.

"Well, then, you can ask him to let you see Mrs. Wcntworth's maid—Mrs. Green— remember. You are to give this letter to her—to no one else —and you are to wait for an answer."

The ostler's eye twinkled. Waiting for an answer in any decent household meant a mug of beer. It might even run to bread and cheese, or to a glass of spirits, at this festive season. Langton House bore a good reputation for kitchen and cellar.

" If I can't see Mrs. Green, sir ?"

" Bring that letter back."

"Yes, sir."

Some Oiie who loved Him.

Langton House was within half a mile of the Bear. A handsome house with an Italian portico, and the rest of the front as flat as the soil it stood upon ; a house standing a good way from the road, in fifty acres of meadow land, which had been promoted to a park by a little extra planting and the removal of two or three hedges, and behind which stretched the woods and farmlands that made up Mr. Wentworth's estate.

The river ran through the grounds, at the back of the house, and made a picturesque boundary line between the formal gardens and the park-like pasture.

The Wentworths stood well among the smaller gentry of the neighbourhood ; very small fry compared with the Earl of Milbank and the Marquis of Cliftonville, who were large landed proprietors ; but entitled to respect by long possession of the soil, and a name that had never been challenged. The present squire was not an agreeable man. He was haughty and arrogant, a quarrelsome neighbour, a very Draco among magistrates ; but he was looked up to for certain qualities that made his neighbours afraid of him ; and he was said to give the best dinners that were given outside the gates of Lord Milbank or Lord Cliftonville. He could not boast a chef, promoted from a West End Club to noble service ; but he had the best woman cook that sixty pounds a year could buy, and he was the most exacting master she had ever served.

Arnold knew from his youth's experience what

this day would be like at Langton House. There would be no Christmas festivities, no Christmas decorations. The day would be a duller Sunday —duller because an additional Sunday inflicted on the dulness of the week. There would be no relaxation in the duties of cook and kitchen-maid, and no high jinks in the servants' hall ; and Mr. Wentworth would be a little more difficult about his dinner than usual because of that extra dulness, the gap in postal deliveries, the hopeless vacuity of London papers which told only of Christmas entertainments and Christmas excursion trains.

Oh, how well Arnold remembered the dreariness of a home Christmas, which had made him long for Cambridge and its free and easy life, even if not a man in the whole University remained "up." How he had pitied his mother, who had to sit and meekly listen to his father's complainings about agents, servants, finances, everything ; and he had pitied his sister for missing the pleasures that Christmas brings to happier schoolrooms. Beatrice Wentworth would have found Christmas duller without "the kid." Arnold looked back and recalled the bright image of a twelve-year-old tomboy. The streaming hair, the gay young face, the lissom figure, slim ankles, long black legs, racing in the frosty garden, tearing across the wintry park ; the riotous games of hide-and-seek, in which he had been made to assist; the afternoons by the schoolroom fire when he had been coaxed to tell ghost stories ; all the most frightening stories that he had read in all the

Some One who loved Hhn,

Christmas annuals of the year. He mixed plots and characters a little sometimes, and was laughed at for incompetence as a story-teller.

" If you have read the story yourself you oughtn't to make me tell it he," retorted sometimes.

"Oh, but we like to hear how you tell it. You're such fun when you mix the white woman in the Lady's Pictorial with the grey Duchess in the Qtceen," protested Mary, or something to that effect.

Poor Mary! She had drawn down Mr, Went-worth's wrath upon her girlish head more than once, by some noisy outbreak in the corridors or on the staircase, and had narrowly escaped perpetual banishment from Langton House,

And now Arnold thought of his sister as grown up, still unmarried, though two or three years older than Mary Freeland, Who would come wooing to Langton Park, where the selfish exclusiveness of the master frightened away everybody except his own particular allies and contemporaries, who were allowed to shoot his pheasants, and eat his dinners, and praise his wine
∧

Poor Beatrice! he thought of her with infinite pity. Yet she doubtless had been taught to pity him, and to think his lot far worse than hers, feeding upon husks among the swine.

He thought of his mother with still deeper pity. Poor soul! she was so miserable, yet scarcely knew her misery. She was one of those weakly amiable wives who hug their chains; who, from a long submission to marital tyranny, and from the knowledge of their own inability to grapple with domestic difficulties, grow to believe in a husband as a heaven-born administrator, to accept his opinions and judgments as infallible, to revere the law that crushes them.

"Will she come to me—dare all—and come to see the reprobate ?" he wondered.

He had chosen his hour with judgment. His father was as methodical as a machine, and arranged his days with automatic precision. The interval between tea and dinner was the time in which he wrote his letters. The post-bag was taken to him at seven o'clock to be filled and locked by his own hands. At half-past seven he went upstairs to dress. His movements might vary once in a way by two or three minutes, but even that irregularity was rare. Clocks were scarcely needed at Langton House; Mr. Went-worth's habits, regulated by Mr. Wentworth's watch, would have sufficed to mark the passage of time.

From half-past five to half-past seven Mrs. Wentworth was her own mistress, unless she wanted cheques for tradesmen ; in which case she was called up before the household judge, and subjected to an exhaustive interrogation as to the particulars of each account, every item of which Mr. Wentworth ticked with his ovn hand, guiding his own massive gold pencil-case. There never was anything in those accounts for which a housemother need blush ; yet Mrs. Wentworth always

Some One who loved Him.

felt like a malefactor during that cheque-writing ordeal.

To-night there would be no cheque-writing, and those hours of darkness before dinner would be her own. Arnold had urged her to come to him at the Bear, if possible. The ostler would walk with her, and she would find her son on the road waiting for her.

He went out soon after his messenger, and strolled along the broad, level road, of which he knew every feature. The old farmhouse and great thatched barns on his right; the cottages— the tiny village post-office on his left—the Vicarage— the mill. The cross roads, with a modest house or two hidden in shrubberies of laurel and arbutus —the bridge. Beyond the bridge, the pine woods spread wide over one-half the landscape, and gave it all that it had of the picturesque, testifying to the happy inspiration which had prompted a certain Sir Felix Vanbury to plant these sandy flats in the beginning of the century.

Half-way between the inn and his father's gates Arnold saw two figures approaching through the darkness, and quickened his pace almost to a run, very sure that the female figure was his mother.

Yes, it was she. He clasped her in his arms, breathless, agitated, clinging to him, and kissing him tenderly.

"Oh, my dear Arnold, what happiness! My dear, dear boy! So long away—so lost to us— except for a poor little letter now and then. Oh, my dear, dear son ! "

Rough Justice.

" Dear mother, how sweet that you should be glad to see me—reprobate as I am !"

" No, no, dear; don't call yourself that. I'm sure you would never do anything really wicked —although you were so unhappy as not to get on with your father."

" I should have been a good deal unhappier if I had got on with him. Oh, my dear mother, forgive me. I know you don't like to hear a word said against your ty—your husband."

" No, Arnold, for he is a good husband, a good father, a good master. But you see, dear, it was not your fault. People say nowadays that heredity accounts for everything; and you always took after my people. You have the Torrington temper —flaming up at nothing, and over in a minute. And it wasn't to be expected that you could get on well with a man of your father's calm and thouditful character."

" It doesn't matter, mother dear, as long as you can get on with him—quite comfortably."

" Oh, my dear Arnold, my life would be a very happy life, if it were not for losing you ; for, you see, with Philip so well married and living in Yorkshire on his wife's property, and with you quite, quite away, I seem to have no son."

"But you have Beatrice, mother. I hope she is good to you."

" She is the best of daughters. We visit a great deal "

" Why, that's a change from old habits."

"Among the poor people, dear. Your father

doesn't like company at home, and he doesn't hke Beatrice to go out much—gadding, he calls it—for you know how he has always looked down upon our neighbours here. But we go to Lady Cliftonville's garden-party, and to Lady Milbank's two Mondays in August, and those are delightful afternoons."

" Three afternoons in a year ? Poor mother I Poor Beatrice!"

" It is rather dull—for Beatrice. And some of the people your father thinks not good enough would be so nice for poor Bee, if he would only let us know them."

" Poor Bee, indeed! She must be as drowsy as a humble-bee by this time."

" She had a surprise at church this morning that almost upset her. I was afraid she would have cried out in the middle of the psalms when she saw her."

" When she saw her ?"

" Mary Freeland! Mary P'reeland, grown so tall and so nice-looking, dressed in black, in the Roffeys' pew."

" Mary Freeland "i Ah, she. didn't lose any time, then. She only arrived in England yesterday morning."

" How did you know that ?"

"Because I came from Africa in the same steamer with her."

"Mary Freeland in Africa! Arnold, what can you mean ?"

" Don't be frightened, mother dear. We weren't

in Africa together. We met most unexpectedly on the steamer."

"But Mary Freeland! What could she be doing in Africa ?"

" That's her story. She'll tell you her adventures, no doubt, by the schoolroom fire, at tea and toast time."

" If your father will let us know her," Mrs, Wentworth murmured, despondently ; " but perhaps he won't, now she's grown up."

"Oh, stuff! He couldn't be sucli a beast as to boycott little Mary."

" Arnold ! " murmured his mother, reproachfully ; and then in an awe-stricken whisper, " They say she has been on the stage."

" And so she has ; earning her own living, like a plucky girl who wouldn't be badgered into marrying an old fool in a wig for the sake of a home. I admire her pluck, and so ought everybody else. And she was in the charge of an uncle and aunt all through her stage career. There's no room for scandal."

" Still, people are shocked, dear. And every one was tremendously surprised at old Miss Farmiloe having left her so well provided for, after all. But tell me about yourself, Arnold, and your own life in Africa. That is what I want to hear. And time is so short,"

" Oh, but we have plenty of time. You don't dine till eight. You are coming to the Bear with me, and we are going to sit by the fire for an hour or so, and talk to our hearts' content. And then I am going to take you quietly home in time to dress for dinner."

They were within five minutes' walk of the inn when Mrs. Wentworth came to a dead stop.

" I couldn't possibly go to the Bear, Arnold. It would be all over Mervynhall to-morrow—and it would come to your father's ears, and he would be horrified to think that I could go to a public-house —to meet my son—surreptitiously."

" If he had not made his son's home intolerable there would have been no need of surreptitious meetings. But are you really afraid to come and sit by the fire at the old inn \'7d The Bear seemed as quiet as the grave just now—except for a sound of voices from the tap-room across the yard."

" Oh, I know the kind of people who go to the tap-room. Our gardeners and grooms, and the sexton, and the men from the mill—lots of people who know me. I daren't be seen there, Arnold."

"Well, then we can only talk here—walking up and down the road. But you will catch cold."

" No, no; I am quite warm in this sealskin coat."

" Happy thought! I saw lights at the Briery ; Mary must be keeping Christmas there. Shall we go and look her up ?"

"My dear Arnold, that would be worse. She will have the Rofifeys with her! "

" It must be the road, then ; and you mustn't walk here a minute longer than you like."

"I should like to walk with you for hours,

Rough Justice.

dearest. I should not know if I were tired, till afterwards."

They turned back and walked the other way, and Arnold told his mother much about his lucky years at Witwatersrand, but not a word of those years of trouble in London. He had written to her even when things were at their worst ; for he would not have her tortured by the thought that he might be dead. Four times a year—wherever he might be—he wrote briefly, under cover to his mother's faithful maid, Anne Green, to report himself alive and well.

And now her heart throbbed with gladness as he told her of his good fortune, and that his future life might be smooth and prosperous, if he were prudent enough to stick to the money he had made, and Hve upon the interest of his capital.

"I shall have four or five hundred a year," he said, " and if I were to marry a nice girl with three or four hundred of her own, we could live somewhere in the country—and we might keep two or three hunters, and some shooting dogs; for we shouldn't want luxuries or finery, both being used to rough it."

"Both! Do you mean that you are engaged, Arnold."" his mother interrupted excitedly.

His sunburnt face reddened in the darkness.

" No, no, mother, not engaged! " with a deep sigh. " I was talking nonsense, that's all."

"Oh, Arnold, I should love you to marry and settle near us. If you were doing well, and had

Some One who loved Him.

married a nice girl, I'm sure your father would forgive you."

" Would he, do you think ? Forgive me for outrunning my allowance at the 'Varsity by a few hundreds, and never costing him a shilling afterwards," Arnold said scornfully.

" It wasn't the money he felt, dear. It was the disappointment. Oh, Arnold, my dear son, you have made me so proud and so happy to-night— so proud to think you were able to make your fortune without a friend to help you."

" You're wrong- there. I had a friend—a college friend ; one of the friends I won for myself while I was spending those extra hundreds. From a purely commercial point of view that one friend was worth all the money, for it was his capital that started me in Africa."

" How sweet of him ! What a dear fellow he must be! How I should love to know him."

"I doubt that, mother. He's as good as gold, but he swears like a trooper, and—and never goes to church."

" How sad! And I was thinking that he would make such a nice husband for Bee."

"Ah, mother, simple and sanguine as of old. Years have not changed you. I wish I could see your dear face. I think I must light a match and look at you."

" Don't, dearest; you would see how old and careworn I have grown."

" Careworn ! Ah, poor mother! And you pretend your life is happy."

Rough Justice.

"There are always cares for the mistress of a house, Arnold, in the happiest life. English cooks are so stupid—and—and—I have never denied that your father is a little exacting. But how can I remember trifling worries now you have come home, and have done so well for yourself \'7d You will never go back to Africa, will you, dear ? Promise me that! "

"No, no, mother dear, I can't. That would be to promise away my life—to make lifelong fetters with words. I hope to stop in England. If I can be happy here I will stop. And if I can live near you, I will. But if I find I can't be happy in England I shall go back to the mines, and make some more money."

His mother pleaded with him, and he answered her with all affection and gentleness, and told her that he meant to make himself a home within easy reach of her, if his hopes could be realized. He would not tell her what those hopes were, though she urged him to confide in her ; and at the lodge gate they parted, with words of affection on both sides, and Mrs. Wentworth walked slowly along the avenue to the big white house, shedding a few tears as she went.

" It is so sad that he cannot get on with his father," she sighed, "and that we must sit down to our Christmas dinner without him."

Arnold was in no hurry to go back to the Bear and to a solitary meal in the panelled parlour, which smelt of wormeaten wood and rotten rose leaves. He walked past his inn, and on to

Some One ivho loved Him,

Mervynhall, and loitered on the bridge for the space of a pipe of tobacco, looking at the lighted windows of the Briery.

How cheerily the warm lamplight shone across the garden by the river. She was there, his little Mary, in the prim drawing-room he remembered in old Miss Farmiloe's lifetime ; a room whose threshold he had crossed with awe, never knowing what he ought to say to that severe spinster. He pictured Mary playing hostess to some of the Rofifey family, elated with the sense of possession and independence, a young woman with a comfortable income, youth, health, good looks, high spirits, and able to dispose of her life as she pleased.

He would have liked to walk in among them and surprise her ; but he was doubtful how he would be received by the Roffey brood. He had left Mervynhall under a cloud, as a son who had been idle and extravagant at the University, and whom his father had cast off. He would be looked upon as a profligate adventurer, no doubt, by those serious church-going Roffeys; more especially as Roffey was his father's solicitor, and afifected a profound veneration for the sage of Langton Park.

No, it would not do to call upon Miss Freeland at eight o'clock in the evening. He went back to the Bear, dined on tough beef, and felt inexpressibly dreary as he sat by a sullen fire, thinking, not of Mary Freeland, but of another woman whose face haunted him, and would not be

Rough Justice.

banished, although he tried his hardest to shut it out of his thoughts.

"What is the use of regretting things that are inevitable ?" he muttered to himself, as he bent over the smoky fire, and knocked about the coals savagely.

He lighted pipe after pipe, smoked till the room was cloudy with tobacco, sat long after everybody else at the Bear had gone to bed, tired but dreading sleeplessness in the bedroom above, and knowing that he should not be able to sleep.

He came downstairs late next morning, looking haggard and unhappy, and at twelve o'clock he went to the Briery and asked to see Miss Free-land.

Mary came singing out of the parlour, while he was talking to the maid. She flushed and brightened at seeing him, and came to him with outstretched hand.

"I thought you wouldn't leave Mervynhall without calling upon me," she said. " I was just going into the garden to look round ray domain. Will you come with me ?"

"Of course I will come. When last I was in your orchard you were being scolded for having picked an apple ; and now the trees and the orchard are yours."

" Poor old auntie! Wasn't it sweet of her to relent, and not leave her fortune to the other idiots? Everybody is so kind. People made quite a fuss about me after church yesterday— ' So surprised '—' So glad ' to see mc. Mr. and

Some One who loved Him.

Mrs. Roffey are staying with me to make things comfortable and correct for me while I am at the Briery ; and they have lent me a parlour-maid to help our old cook, who has been in charge of everything since my aunt's death. It seems wonderful to be well off, and for people to be so prim and particular about me, after running <vild all the time I was with those dear Favershams."

"And now you are enjoying the privileges of respectability."

" Yes; I find it rather nice to be respectable, and to be warned that I must never ride in a hansom or an omnibus alone. Do you know that I am quite a landed person ? I have nearly twenty acres." Here she began to count upon her fingers. "The flower garden and orchard three and a half, the kitchen garden on the other side of the road one and a quarter, the three paddocks fifteen. But how egotistical I am, preaching about acres. Tell me how you found your dear mother—and wasn't she awfully glad to see you.""

" Yes, she was very glad ; though she could only meet me by stealth, poor soul, and would no more dare tell my father of my presence at Mervynhall than she would tell him she had invited a burglar or a forger to dinner. Somebody says all things work round in time and wind up well; and I dare say sooner or later my father will begin to think that a young man who has exceeded his allowance by three or four hundred pounds, and failed to get a degree, may be not quite a malefactor ; and then I shall be readmitted to the

Rough Justice.

pleasures of home life, and hear my father swear at the cook."

" Arnold, you must not be flippant. It is a very serious thing to quarrel with a father. I, who have no father, feel how shocking it is."

" Yes, I have observed that orphans have an exalted estimate of the paternal relation. But, Mary, Mary—never contrary to me—tell me your plans. What use are you going to make of your wealth ?"

" Every use. First and foremost I shall improve myself."

" Don't. There is a kind of dog-rose perfection which cultivation only spoils."

" Nonsense! I am going to board with the Tresillian-Smiths in South Kensington."

" Depressing neighbourhood ! "

" Mrs. Tresillian-Smith is a sister of Mrs. Rofifey's. Their grandmother was a Tresillian, and Mrs. Rofifey's sister has taken the name and hyphen. Her husband is a medical man who is steadily getting to the top of the tree, and she gives a delightful evening party every week, in the London season."

" As you hear from Mrs. RofTey."

" Then I am going to attend classes at the School of Music."

" Oh, Mary, that is contrary—contrary to common sense. Are there not enough piano-torturers in the world, that you should join the ranks ? You, who always rebelled against five-finger exercises as a sheer cruelty!"

Some One who loved Him.

"That was because I was working on a wrong method, and holding my wrist anyhow. I shall enjoy the work when I'm taught in the right way."

"Foolish, deluded Mary!"

"And then I shall go to the Art School and work at the antique."

" Mary, have you one ha'porth of talent for quoit-players and armless Venuses 1"

"I don't know till I try. And I shall have lessons in Parisian French; and I shall learn a little Italian ; and then—I shall travel."

"What! Have you not travelled enough while you were a strolling player .'* You have scoured England and Ireland, and you have been to Africa. Is not that enough ? "

" It IS nothing. I want to see France, Italy, Germany—Spain, perhaps. I shall live abroad for ever so long."

She looked at him searchingly as she made this last announcement. He looked smilingly back at her; but even while the smile brightened his face she could see that he was looking haggard and ill.

"What have you been doing since you left the steamer." You are looking so tired and worn out."

" Am I.? It is not that I have done much to tire myself; but perhaps my dismal Christmas has made me look seedy."

" You look really ill. Did you come straight to Mervynhall on Christmas Eve ? I didn't see you in our train. Mr. Roffey met me at Waterloo. Wasn't it good of him ?"

Rough Justice.

"Very ; but you are his client. No doubt the goodness will go down in his bill."

"Oh, I think not. He said he had made business in town on purpose to meet me and take care of me. He couldn't bear to think of me driving across to Liverpool Street alone. Funny, wasn't it, considering that I had come from the Cape alone? Were you in our train—the 4.50 from Liverpool Street ?"

"No; I stayed in London till yesterday morning."

"And came by the one slow Christmas Day train. How foolish of you ! "

"I had business in London."

" Oh! And how long are you going to stop at the Bear?"

" Only till this afternoon."

"You are in a great hurry to go away again."

" I might make things unpleasant for my mother if I were seen about here. And, Mary, I may call upon you at South Kensington, may I not ? And perhaps, as a very old friend, I might be permitted to take you for an hour's stroll in the Broad Walk —or to look at the riders in the Row."

"I don't think that would be allowed. Mrs. Roffey says that Mrs. Trcsillian-Smith is very particular. I am to drive in the park with her three or four times a week in Dr. Smith's victoria. I am evidently destined to drive in a doctor's carriage."

" Well, at least you will let me call." "It will all depend on Mrs. Tresillian-Smith.

I mean to be intensely respectable," . said Marj', with tremendous emphasis. " After living the dear happy-go-lucky life with Uncle • and Aunt Faversham, and being allowed to do and say just what I liked, prunes and prisms will be an amusing change. I shall have Mrs. Smith's own maid —who is upper housemaid as well—to walk across to the Museum with me, though it's only five minutes' walk. Mrs. Roffey says nothing would induce her sister to let me go out alone."

" Then I shall waylay you, and bribe the housemaid to say she has seen you safe into the Museum, while you have marched off to Kensington Gardens with me."

Mary shook her glove at him. The morning air was so mild that she had been carrying her glove instead of wearing it on the hardy little weather-beaten hand. She was in the gayest spirits, and Arnold inhaled joy from the atmosphere that surrounded her. For him her "aura" was of a brilliant rose colour, and meant happiness.

They walked round the garden two or three times, talking gaily, talking as conscious lovers talk, vv^hen love is freshest and sweetest because still undeclared. Their talk was lighter than vanity, futile, evanescent; but it was happiness enough for each to be with the other.

" Look," cried Mary, " there's the postman. Let's go in and see what he has brought me."

" I hope he has brought you a London paper," said Arnold, " for I haven't seen one since the day before yesterday."

Rough Justice.

"Poor thing!" laughed Mary. "Isn't it dreadful suffering ? That accounts for you looking so ill."

They went into the hall, and found the servant in the act of sorting and studiously examining the letters.

" Here's the Tiuies, addressed to Roffey. Do you think I may open it ?" asked Arnold.

" I think I may," said Mary, tearing off the wrapper. " There, go and read the news, man, while I look at my Christmas cards from the people who were surprised to see me yesterday. And here's an African letter from the dear aunt, and one from Helena Champernowne—such a jolly girl, who gets shoved on for all the wretched old women, and has to make up ugly half her time."

" Shocking murder in Bloomsbury," read Arnold. " What a godsend for Boxing Day newspapers."

Mary was standing with her back to him at the hall table, opening her letters and spreading out her Christmas cards approvingly.

" All sixpenny ones at the very least," she said. " What it is to have come into property! A murder, did you say ? How nice! I hope it is a lovely poisoning case—among genteel people. I hate vulgar murders."

There was no answer.

" Is it poison ?" she asked casually, while she was reading her aunt's letter.

Again no answer.

She looked round, puzzled at his silence, in spite

of her divided attention. He was leaning against the wall, white as death, and speechless,

"Arnold! what's the matter? Do you know the people ?"

" No, no, no—only it's too horrid. It turned me 6ick."

Rough Justice.

CHAPTER V.

AT NUMBER THIRTEEN, DYNEVOR STREET.

It was nine o'clock on the morning of Christmas Day when Mr. John Faunce, Chief Inspector of the Bow Street Division, looked in at the station to see whether the night that was over had been marked by any incident of sufficient importance to spoil his holiday, and to deprive his good wife of the chief ornament to a family dinner which was to take place at six o'clock that evening in the cosiest of dining-rooms on a certain second floor in Bloomsbury. The Chief Inspector lived in his Division, knew every house door in his Division, and the Chief Inspector's wife, however she may have sighed for the pleasantness of a suburban villa, in the smiling valley of the Thames, or on airy heights at Hampstead or Highgate, had to content herself with the upper part of a substantial old house in the neighbourhood of Russell Square, " Nothing that need spoil my Christmas Day! " said Mr, Faunce, when he had heard all that the Inspector in charge of the station had to tell him.

At Number Thirteen, Dynevor Street.

"For once in a way I shall be able to eat my Christmas dinner with the little woman!"

He was leaving the office, contemplating the possibility of attending morning service with his wife, and dropping into a comfortable nap under her favourite evangelical preacher—whose sermons were of the longest—when he remembered a case of a missing child in the sub-division, in which he was personally interested, on account of his knowledge of the parents, worthy hard-working people who kept a small shop for fruit and vegetables, and with whom Mrs. Faunce had dealt for some years. These poor creatures had been thrown into an agony of apprehension by the disappearance of a son of five years old, who had strayed off unobserved on the previous afternoon, and had not been heard of up to midnight.

"I'll see if they've found Hadley's boy before I go home," Mr. Faunce said to himself as he walked briskly towards the sub-divisional office in Gunter Street.

He found a Sergeant in charge in the absence of the Inspector.

" Boy found ?" he asked, before inquiring the cause of this irregularity.

" Yes, sir ; found in Covent Garden, asleep under an orange box at two o'clock this morning. Father has been in the habit of taking him there, now and then, for a treat; boy marched off and found his way there, played about all evening with blackguard boys, and then fell asleep behind one of the orange stalls ; and nobody set eyes

Rough Justice.

on him till one of the constables happened upon him."

"I'm very glad they've got him, and I hope they've given him a sound thrashing ! "

" I'm afraid they're not up to it, sir. They was a-making a right down fool of him when the constable left 'em, cramming him with cakes and tofify."

" Humph! he'll run away again. They always do, if it isn't flogged out of them. Where's the Inspector \'7d"

" He's gone round to Dynevor Street, sir."

"What's up there?"

"Murder, sir. A young woman—shot through the head—number thirteen, Dynevor Street— lodging-house."

" Is it a respectable house ? "

" A doubtful party on the second floor, but no bad goings on inside. I've questioned the neighbours."

" Murderer unknown .'*"

"Not a trace of him, though the second-floor saw him leave the house. It was a most audacious business. The young woman lets herself in with her latch-key at one o'clock this morning—the second-floor hears her go upstairs—hears a man's footsteps following, two minutes afterwards, then hears the report of a pistol, and the second-floor rushes on to the landing and sees a man going downstairs."

" Death instantaneous, of course ?"

" Lord save you, yes, sir," answered the Sergeant, with a look of recalling a dreadful vision.

At Number Thirteen, Dynevor Street.

"Did no one but the second floor lodger hear or see anything ?"

" See ? No one. The landlady heard the shot. She was sleeping on the top floor, you see—room opposite the murdered woman. She sends her slavey shrieking out into the street, in a nightgown and petticoat, and the girl almost tumbles into my arms, screaming murder."

"The murdered woman was a loose character, I suppose ?"

"They say not, sir—honest and respectable— scraping a living somehow—near starving pretty often."

"Do they think she brought the man home with her?"

" Nobody knows, but it seems likely she brought him to the door, anyhow; and she must have left the door open—unless he had a key that would open it."

" Is that all you have been able to find out ?" asked Faunce.

"That's about all, sir. There's nothing but women in the house. The first-floor's husband is a commercial, and he's away; the rest are single women. They're all about mad, poor creatures ; and they all want to talk at once, and tell things that haven't any bearing on the case. But I* expect you'll calm 'em down a bit."

Mr. Faunce nodded, put on his hat and left the office. The morning was dim and dusky— the sun slowly climbing up in a cloudy sky behind the housetops eastward. Dynevor Street looked

Rough Justice.

its worst, perhaps, at this bleak hour, while the winter day was still unvvarmed by household fires, and the monotony of the long, dull street was still unbroken by traffic. The lamps had only just been extinguished by a yawning lamplighter. Here and there a maid-servant with nipped nose hearthstoned a doorstep or beat a dusty mat against the area railings,

Mr, Faunce's keen eye noted the aspect of everything he passed, quickly as he was walking. He knew the character of the street and its population, and he knew the individual differences of every house, as well as he knew the features of his familiar friends.

Shabby-genteel ; affecting respectability; but worse than doubtful at bottom. That was his opinion of Dynevor Street.

There was a little crowd about the door—a cluster of shabby idlers, who had been standing there since daybreak, on the chance of seeing something ghastly ; and there was a policeman on guard in front of the closed street door. He put in a key and opened the door as Faunce approached, and the Chief Inspector went straight up to the third floor, where he expected to find his subordinate, the Inspector in charge of the sub-divisional station.

A tall, elderly woman, in a slovenly gown and a rusty black lace cap—a trap for dust rather than a head-dress—came up the kitchen stairs, and followed Faunce to the top of the house. This was Mrs. Grogan, the landlady; but No. 13 was in the custody of the police to-day, and poor Mrs,

At Number Thirteen, Dynevor Street.

Grogan felt it even less her house than in that dark period when there was a bailiff's man in possession, crouching over a scanty fire in the underground den which she called her sitting-room. She went panting upstairs, and arrived at the top landing breathless ; for, lean as she was, the four flights were too much for her.

The sub-divisional Inspector had the key of the back room, and opened the door for Mr. Faunce.

"You'll find everything as it was when the Sergeant was called in, sir," said the Inspector. " I took care that nothing was touched after I came ; and this good lady told me nothing had been touched."

Nothing—not even that dreadful figure on the ground, lying as it fell, the poor disfigured head half hidden by the shabby black hat; one meagre arm and wan white hand stretched along the discoloured carpet, the other doubled under the body ; the worn-out boots and thin ankles exposed below the edge of a black stuff gown. Nobody—not even a doctor—had touched that sad figure. A doctor's eyes had looked at it, and a doctor's lips had pronounced the fact which was obvious to every eye—"instantaneous death."

The story told by the corpse was brief and conclusive. The story told by the room was of the baldest Faunce's keen eyes scrutinized every object in'that room, and his deft fingers touched and turned over everything movable. The story was of abject poverty, but not of abject vice. The

Rough Justice.

Inspector found no tawdry frippery, no powder-puff and pennyworth of French chalk ; no paper of vermilion ; no tails of false hair ; and, above all, no dirt. The wretched furniture was as clean as a woman's care could make it; a skinny iron bedstead ; a painted chest of drawers with a blurred looking-glass upon it; a basin and jug on a shelf in the corner; on the chest of drawers a crockery candlestick and candle blown out directly it had been lighted, as the state of the wick told Mr. Faunce—a cheap paraffin candle.

He looked in all the drawers. Clothes to speak of there were none—a single change of linen, and a black moreen petticoat that had been mended over and over again till it hung in shreds, were all Mr. Faunce could find in the way of personal property, with the exception of a little black book that had been much read—the New Testament in the German language.

" Honest, virtuous, and pious," thought Faunce, as he turned the leaves of the Testament, and found a violet or a primrose here and there between the pages.

He laid down the little black book on the chest of drawers, where he had found it, and proceeded with his investigation. So far he had not discovered a letter or document of any kind ; but in a corner near the door Mr. Faunce's keen glance lighted on a crumpled brown-paper bag, which he stooped to pick up, and examined as eagerly as if he expected to find the clue to the mystery of the woman's death in a fruiterer's bag. Crimes have

At Number Thirteen^ Dynevor Street.

been brought home to the guilty upon indications as trivial. The bag had held grapes. There were some stalks and a grape or two at the bottom of it. The fruiterer's name was printed on it, "Jakins, Covent Garden." This bag was, from Faunce's point of view, a valuable item in the sum of evidence. He even noted the manner in which it was crumpled, as if it had been crushed in the fevered grasp of a nervous hand. He put the bag in his letter-case, and went on with his investigation.

"There may be something in her pocket," he said.

The two men knelt down, handling the dead form very gently, and Faunce found a pocket in the thin black gown. Nothing in the pocket, except a clean cambric handkerchief, with an embroidered " L " in the corner—very old and thin and worn, but an expensive handkerchief.

" Humph ! " muttered the Inspector ; " not quite so virtuous as I thought, perhaps. A come-downer."

He unhooked the front of the bodice, spattered and stained so dreadfully that even the Chief Inspector's strong nerves, hardened amidst scenes of horror, thrilled as he touched that murdered form.

" She may have carried papers in her bosom," he said. "Women often do."

He was right. Between gown and under-garment he found a little bundle of paper, which he took out and unfolded. It was a bundle of bank-notes

Rough Justice.

carelessly folded across. They were notes on the Standard Bank of South Africa, endorsed with a name and date, and they amounted in all to a hundred and twenty pounds.

• Here was an important discovery, which must needs lead to something. Was the woman murdered by some one who knew of this money, and meant to get it from her.-* One other detail he noted as he knelt beside the lifeless form. The woman had worn a large white silk handkerchief —a man's muffler—tied round her neck. It was very old. The silk was worn and thin, and the edges were ragged, but in one corner Mr. Faunce found a monogram neatly worked in silk that had once been crimson : " A. W." Initials were always interesting to Mr. Faunce. He made a note of these. True, she might have bought the silken rag at a pawnshop ; but initials are always worth recording. Somewhere in the world there was the original owner of this handkerchief; and, wherever he was, it was possible that in the past or in the present might be found some link between him and the dead woman lying here.

The next thing was to learn the history of the crime, as known to the people in the house. The Inspector left the room with his subordinate, locking the door behind him, and addressed himself to Mrs. Grogan, who stood whimpering upon the landing.

- "Have you made out anything, sir?" she asked.

" Not much. I want to hear all you can tell me

At Number Thirteen, Dynevor Street.

about your lodger; and I want to see any one in the house who can tell me anything about the murderer. I'm told that a lodger on the floor below saw him."

"That's Mrs. Delamere, sir. She did get a glimpse of him, there's no doubt—but it was only a glimpse, and she wouldn't rekernise him, if you was to bring him into the house this minute. She's been awfully upset ever since, poor lady, and they've had to give her champagne and chloral to quiet her nerves."

" Never mind her nerves, madam ; I should like to see her. But, first, perhaps you'll be so good as to tell me all you can about the murdered woman and her friends and belongings."

"She had nobody belonging to her that ever I saw, sir," Mrs. Grogan answered; "but, perhaps, you'd step down to my room and talk things over quietly. I've a bit of fire there."

" No, no; there is no one about up here, is there \'7d "

" No, sir. That's my bedroom "—opening a door and shutting it again quickly, but not before Faunce's quick survey had assured him that the room was empty. "That's where I sleep, and the girl. Mrs. Rayner was the only other person on this floor, and Mrs. Delamere has the two rooms below."

"And on the first floor?"

" Mr. and Mrs. Joynson. He's a commercial gentleman in the silk trade, and seldom at home for more than a night or two at a time."

Rough Justice.

*' And on the ground floor ? "

"Mrs. Benning, a widow lady in the dressmaking. She has both parlours, and a workroom at the back. I only hope this dreadful business won't drive them all away. Mrs. Delamere says she can't sleep another night in the house ; but then she saw her. The others didn't. The horror of it ain't brought home to them."

And then Mrs. Grogan allowed the story of Lisa Rayner's death to be elicited from her, clouded with much irrelevant matter about her own affairs and duties—being, as it was, Christmas Eve, and she with more to do than usual—being up till twelve o'clock trussing a turkey for Mrs, Joynson, who expected friends to dinner; her husband's father and mother, and her own niece and niece's husband ; and was to dine at four o'clock, a most awkward hour, wanting everything dished by candle-light, and might as well have made it a rccrular late dinner at once. And she, Mrs. Grogan, had gone up to bed dog-tired ; and she was sound asleep, and the girl, too, when she was waked by the sound of a pistol fired, as it might be close to her ear, and the girl just groaned and turned over and never woke. Them young things would sleep through an earthquake. And she rushed out to the landing, and met Mrs. Delamere coming upstairs ; and they went into Mrs. Rayner's room, and saw her lying there.

And it was an awful sight, which never would she till her dying day be able to forget— nor yet Mrs. Delamere ; and she was afraid that garshly

spekatel would drive away her lodger, the best lodger in her house, though only a second floor; and her with the most feeling heart for another woman ; which there was many lady lodgers would make a slave of their landlady and never say "Thank you," much less offer you a glass of anything warm and comfortable.

And as for the poor creature that had been murdered. Well, all Mrs. Grogan could say of her was " Harmless." A harmless, unoffending creature, whom one couldn't have the heart to turn into the street, though much behind with her rent; but always willing to work at anything, however 'umble—ready to work her fingers to the bone rather than not pay her just debts.

" She's done many a day's chaiyng for me in loo of rent," said Mrs. Grogan, "though anybody could see she was born above it. She hadn't a bit of pride, though she must onest have been very pretty."

" But had she no regular calling ? "

"Well, sir, she was clever with her needle, and off and on Mrs. Benning would employ her for a week or two, and she always gave satisfaction. Those was her best times. But, you see, sir, when you can get 'prentices and improvers that'll work for you for nothing, it ain't likely you'll employ any one as you has to pay, oftener than you can help, and it was only in the busiest times Mrs. Rayner got work downstairs. Other times she managed the best she could, getting odd jobs here and there—always patient, but always melancholy.

And she was a bit eccentric, poor soul, and would wander late of a night—wander and wander, through the quiet squares and streets, as far as Primrose Hill, or even up to Hampstead Heath, and she said it was the only thing as done her good. She got out of herself a bit, she says, when she walked fast under the starlit sky, or could roam about alone on the heath and feel the wind blowing on her face. * I wish I was in Africa—in some wilderness,' she used to say."

" Africa !" Faunce thought of those notes in his charge—notes on the Bank at Johannesburg.

" How long had she been with you.""

"Nearly two years."

"And in all that time you saw no one belonging to her?"

" No one."

"And never heard anything about the people she belonged to, or the kind of life she'd led before she came to this house ?"

"Nothing. She was as close as close. I don't even know where she'd been living last before she came to me. She gave me no reference, but there was a look about her that made me think she was honest and respectable, and in spite of her prowling about at night, I had never reason to think otherwise."

"What time did she go out last night.-'"

" I believe she went out early in the evening; but I didn't see her go. Other lodgers mostly bang the door after them, and shake the house till it makes one nervous to hear 'em ; but she'd go and come like a spirit."

At Nuniher Thirteen^ Dynevor Street.

" Did no one come to see her yesterday ?"

" No one."

" Did she get any letter or telegram ?"

" There was a telegram came for her after dark ▪—the first I ever knew her get, and she was very much upset when she got it. The girl took it upstairs to her, and she said the poor thing was all in a tremble when she opened it."

Mr. Faunce asked to see the girl, who was produced, agitated and grimy, from the kitchen. She could tell him no more than her mistress had done. Mrs. Rayner had snatched the telegram from her hand, and had shook as if she was going to drop. Her hands trembled so that she could hardly tear open the envelope ; but she had said nothing.

"Did the girl know at what hour she left the house \'7d"

" No. She waited upon herself, and nobody troubled about her. She had come down to the kitchen for her loaf and ha'porth of milk before the telegraph boy came, and her tea-things was on the table when the girl took the telegram to her. So it was after tea when she went out."

That was all the girl knew about her.

After this Mr. Faunce asked to be introduced to Mrs. Delamere, and was at once received by that lady, who was anxious to tell him her story, and was less inclined to ramble than Mrs. Grogan. She knew nothing of the telegram, nor did she know when Mrs. Rayner left the house, but she had heard her moving about in her room overhead

Rough Justice.

while she, Mrs. Delamere, was dresshig to go out, between six and seven. She happened to be going to a place of entertainment that evening. She told Mr. Faunce how, lying broad awake a few minutes before one o'clock, she had heard footsteps pass her door and go upstairs. She knew Lisa Rayner's step; and then, not two minutes after, she heard other footsteps following— cautious steps, and not heavy ; but she thought they were a man's footsteps, and wondered how Mrs. Rayner came to bring a man into the house at that hour, knowing her to be a well-conducted young woman. But she had hardly time to wonder before she heard the report of a pistol, and instantly, almost at the same moment, a heavy fall on the floor above. Her bedroom was exactly under Mrs. Rayner's room. She knew something dreadful must have happened ; and she rushed out to the landing in time to see d man going downstairs.

About this man's appearance the Inspector questioned her searchingly. He had seated himself beside her comfortable fire, making himself at home, with a friendly air which was more soothing to Mrs. Delamere's nerves than chloral or brandy. His quick eyes looked round her room in a pleasant way, as if he were admiring the photographs of actors and actresses, and the showy

French lithographs with which she had relieved the dinginess of the sage-green wall-paper. She answered all his questions unreservedly; but she had only seen the man's head and shoulders for an instant, as he ran downstairs. There was no

100

At Number Thirteen, Dynevor Street.

light but the candle she was holding. She heard the street-door shut softly while she stood looking ; and then came Mrs. Grogan's shriek from above, and other doors opened below, and the house was alive with frightened women wanting to know what had happened. She recalled, shuddering, the spectacle on the floor above, and told him how Mrs. Grogan had pulled her out of the room, and had locked the door, taking the key out of the lock.

"They all came tearing up the next minute— Mrs. Benning and her apprentice—a silly, shrieking girl—and Mrs. Joynson from the first floor—but old Grogan was 'cute enough to keep the door locked. ' No one must go in but the police,' she told them. She knew very well that if her other lodgers saw what I saw, she'd have a week's notice from both floors. Nobody would stay in the house to have the horrors as I've had 'em all night."

" But surely, my dear madam, a woman of your superior mind "

" Ah! that's where it is," Mrs Delamere interrupted sharply ; " if I had no imagination I might be able to sleep comfortably in the room under hers, without even seeing her as I saw her last night, and without ever watching the ceiling, expecting to see horrible stains oozing through the whitewash. No, Mr. Faunce, I don't stay an hour in these rooms after I've suited myself elsewhere ; but, of course, that's not an easy thing to do on Christmas Day—no, nor on Boxing Day neither; so I may have to stay till the day after

101

Rough Justice.

to-morrow. Anyhow, I shall pay old Grogan a week's rent. She'll have to fresh paper her rooms, and smarten up the house a bit after the funeral. Goodness knows, the place has wanted it long enough."

The next point was to lead Mrs. Delamere gently on to discourse freely about the dead woman, of whom she affected to have known more than any one else in the house.

" The poor thing was a born lady, however low she might have fallen ; and I don't believe she was ever really low, though no doubt she had had her trials, as we all have when Providence has made us attractive."

" And she had been attractive, you think ?" "That poor disfigured creature upstairs"—with a shuddering sob—"was once a pretty woman. She was the wreck of a pretty woman yesterday when she passed me on the stairs. Oh, if I could forset what she is now!"

Mrs. Delamere clutched a small stoppered bottle from the mantelpiece, dipped a needle into it, and stabbed herself in the wrist half a dozen times in a spasmodic way.

" Don't you think that's rather a bad habit of yours, ma'am?" asked the Inspector, who felt himself on such confidential terms as permitted a friendly remonstrance.

" Oh, I can't help it. I couldn't live if I didn't do it. It's that, or chucking one's self out of a window ; and I suppose chloral's the best of the two."

At Number Thirteen, Dynevor Street.

"An attractive lady like yourself, ma'am, oughtn't to hold life so cheap."

Mrs. Delamere sighed, and shook her head.

" It isn't the pretty women that have the best luck, or that poor thing upstairs would have done better."

"Did she never open her heart to you, and talk freely of her past life ^"

" Never; though I've brought her in here sometimes when I've heard her dragging upstairs, dead-beat, and once in a way she'd accept a trifle of dress from me—a bonnet or such-like. She could do up a bonnet that I should have thrown on the dust-heap, and look the lady in it. She had such clever fingers, and such natty ways,"

" Had she begun life as a milliner's or dressmaker's apprentice, do you think ? "

" Lord knows ; but I believe she had too much education for that. I showed her a letter from a lady friend in Paris, and she read it right off, and wrote the answer for me. French came as easy to her as English. But where she learnt the language, or how she began, I never could find out. I knew nothing except that she was very fond of some one who was far away."

" Did she say where he was ."

" Not she ; indeed, I don't believe she knew. I shall never see him again,' she said once. ' If he is alive, he has forgotten me ; if he is dead, I shall never know where he lies ; and yet our two lives were once so knitted together that I didn't think Fate could part them.' ' Oh, my dear,' says I,

Rough Justice.

' Fate can play us any ngly trick. I've no patience with Fate.'"

Faunce took leave of the lady after this. A respectable, white-headed gentleman, in glossy broadcloth, came upstairs as he opened the door, and said with some asperity

"You really oughtn't to have sent for me to-day, Julia, You ought to know that I have to go to church with the family at eleven."

" I didn't ought to have sent, indeed f Perhaps you would like to find me a raving lunatic when you come here next week ?"

Thus the lady, with hysterical shrillness.

Faunce passed the white-haired gentleman on the landing, and went downstairs, where Mrs. Grogan hovered in the passage waiting for him.

" Have you got a clue to the wretch who killed her ?" she asked eagerly.

" No, ma'am; clues don't grow on trees."

CHAPTER VI.

JOHN FAUNCE'S experiences.

I BEGAN life with a very small stock-in-trade in the way of education. My father was a clerk in an insurance office in a town in the north of England, and I was sent at an early age to a cheap school at Calais, where I stayed five years, during which time I learnt the French language, the coup de savatc, and very little besides. My father died while I was at school, and my mother married a stationer and bookseller in the town where she had lived in all the years of her first marriage. I soon found that there was no home for me with my stepfather, unless I were willing to be a common drudge in his business, and to stand being bullied at that ; so as soon as I was tall enough I entered the force as a raw lad, keen to pick up every scrap of knowledge that came in my way. I was a diligent reader of the daily papers ; and there's a good deal of education to be got out of a respectable newspaper. I was a devourer of novels, and the time that other men gave to out-of-door amusements I enjoyed sitting in a quiet

Rough Justice.

corner, with my nose in a book. Good novels were dear in my young days. I couldn't get "David Copperfield" or "Vanity Fair" for sixpence, or " Ivanhoe" for threepence, as people can now. But if I couldn't buy I could borrow, and books were my only extravagance. I was not a dab at cricket, or football, or any athletic sports ; and so, somehow, my education advanced a good deal faster than that of the fine manly fellows who spent all their holidays batting or bowling on scorched grass, or hustling and kicking one another on a muddy field.In my early days I used to fasten on to any novel that was offered me, good or bad ; but as I advanced in life, and picked up more knowledge, my taste improved; and of late years I have restricted my reading to the works of four masters in the art of fiction—Balzac, Dumas, Scott, and Dickens.The first I read for education. Balzac was a born detective. The second and third serve to quicken my mental circulation when the dulness of the daily papers begins to exercise its deadening influence; the fourth I read for enjoyment pure and simple. The fairyland of Charles Dickens is a paradise whose golden gate I open only when I feel myself brain-weary and heartsick, nauseated by the hideousness of real life. It is only natural, perhaps, that a man of my calling should take a keener interest in stories of crime than in any other form of fiction ; and I am not ashamed to confess a liking for those novels in which some mystery of guilt is woven and unravelled by the romancer. I have read, I believe, all the criminal stories of Gaboriau and Boisgobey. I have hung spell-bound over Bulwer's " Lucretia," over "Armadale," and "The Woman in White," over "Martin Chuzzlewit," "Bleak House," and the unsolved problem of " Edwin Drood ;" and, inspired by this recreative reading, I have been beguiled into writing a detailed account of all those cases in which I have been engaged that have offered any kind of interest to the novel-reader.

But, alas! when I compare the facts of any case, however mysterious, with the complications, coincidences, passions, and counter-passions of love, jealousy, hatred, and revenge which the novelist can elaborate, sitting at ease in his arm-chair, I can but feel the limitations of a writer who recounts actual experiences, and those often of a most sordid kind.

So much for my brief preface, written perhaps rather to excuse myself to myself, than as an apology to future readers, who are not likely to see these lucubrations of mine till I am beyond the reach of criticism. And now for my narrative ; the twenty-ninth in my book of selected experiences, and possibly the last of such records, as I have serious thoughts of retiring from the Criminal Investigation Force. I have dined well, my wife has gone to see the pantomime at Drury Lane with a neighbour. My fire burns cheerily, the house is quiet, and I feel the impulse to authorship strongly upon me.

Rough Justice.

If nature had but gifted me with invention, I am in the humour to begin a modern Monte Christo, or to delve into the dark morass of Louis Phih'ppe's Paris, to pluck out some black pearl of criminals like Balzac's Ferragus ; but, alas ! I can only write of that which I have known and seen. Hard matter of fact is the stuff with which I have to deal.

The Bloomsbury murder offers a more than common interest to the student of crime, firstly, because it is more audacious in execution than the average murder; and secondly, because however close a web I may be able to weave about the murderer, there may at the last remain an element of uncertainty that will prevent a conviction.

The daring openness with which the murder was committed is new in the history of deliberate crime. A man follows a woman upstairs to her room, shoots her through the head, and goes quietly and quickly downstairs again, and is out of the house before any one can stop him.

A cool hand this ; especially when it is remembered that, though the hour was late, the streets were not empty, and that his manner and aspect as he walked away from the scene of his crime could have shown nothing to attract attention, since my closest inquiries failed in discovering any one who had noticed a foot-passenger of hurried or agitated appearance, or in finding a cabman who had taken up a fare between one o'clock and half-past, in Dynevor Street or the immediate neighbourhood. But although I failed in the

endeavour to find any trace of the murderer after the murder, I was so far fortunate as to obtain a very distinct trace of him before the crime was committed. My cautious inquiries among the servants belonging to the adjacent houses—mostly lodging-houses—and the servants mostly of the genus denominated " girl," resulted in the discovery of a maid-of-all-work, at No. 16, three doors from the scene of the murder, who had been waiting at the area gate between twelve and one o'clock, on the watch for a poulterers boy with the Christmas turkey, promised early in the evening, but not delivered till after midnight, owing to the pressure of business on Christmas Eve.

This girl, who is intelligent, and, I think, truthful, related her impressions about a tall, broad-shouldered man, in a "top-coat" and a bowler hat, who walked past the area gate several times in conversation with Lisa Rayner. The girl knew all the lodgers at No. 13 by sight, and she could swear to the woman walking with the tall man as the third-floor back. She had often noticed the third-floor going home late of an evening, and had thought it odd that a prudent young woman should care to walk alone after dark. She had met Mrs. Rayner sometimes in the further squares—Gordon or Tavistock—when she, Phoebe Miller, had been returning from her evening out, and she felt sorry for her, seeing her always alone. Once, on coming home from an evening with an aunt at Walworth, Phoebe had seen the third-floor lodger sitting on one of the stone seats on

Rough Justice.

Waterloo Bridge, "the most desolatest figure as

ever was."

In the course of such inquiries we have to listen to a good deal of irrelevant matter, to swallow a good deal of chaff with our grain ; but I did not consider anything I could hear about the murdered woman's habits irrelevant, or without a certain value.

Phoebe Miller had been all the more interested in the gentleman walking with Mrs. Rayner, because it was the first time she had ever seen her in company; and for a further reason that while Mrs. Rayner was crying quietly behind her veil part of the time, and at one time sobbing violently, the gentleman also appeared agitated. She had heard him say, "for God's sake," more than once in his talk as he passed her ; and once " for God's sake, my dear love," which made her think that he must be an old sweetheart of Mrs. Rayner's.Questioned as to the number of times the two had passed her, she began to waver, as this class of witness always does. She would not pledge herself to any number between three and fifteen. She was sure they had gone by more than three times ; she was sure they had not passed her as many as fifteen times. They walked as far as the first crossing each way, and then came back. I paced the distance when I left her, and found that, taking it at a woman's average pace, the walk each way would occupy five minutes. Say that they passed the girl six times, there was half an hour disposed of, and they were hardly likely to have no walked in that one spot for half an hour. No doubt the girl unconsciously exaggerated the number of times she had seen them go by.Questioned closely as to the scraps of conversation she had caught as they passed her, she could remember only three or four broken sentences. Once Mrs. Rayner had said, "I believed you would keep your promise ;" once the tall man had said, "when we were so miserable together." She had also heard the word "goldmine," and also the word "Africa."This appeared conclusive. The man who gave her the African notes was the man who murdered her.Asked if she would be able to identify this man if he were brought before her, Phoebe gave me a positive affirmative ; yet on my questioning her closely as to his features, she could tell me nothing except that he was dark, and that he had a light-brown beard.

" Was it a long beard ."

"Not long like the man's who sells turkey rhubarb in the Euston Road on Saturday nights."

" What kind of a beard was it ?"

" Short, and square-like, and a very pretty colour—reddish and goldish, but more gold than red."

The man was dark, with a light beard. So far, so good. Of his features she could say nothing; nose might have been aquiline or snub, eyes might have been black or grey. All but the beard v/as a blank, save the dark complexion,

Rough Justice.

which might have been the shadow of the bowler brim. To judge of a complexion in the doubtful light of London gas on a December night would be no easy matter.

Phœbe protested, however, that she would know the gentleman again anywhere.

Experience has taught me what to expect from a witness of this class for the purpose of identification.

Had she seen Mrs. Rayner and the gentleman go into No. 13 ?

No. She had lost sight of them when the boy came with the turkey. She had taken it from him at the gate, informing him that he deserved a hiding for being so late, and she carried it down to the kitchen and shut up the house for the night. Being asked if she could name the time when this happened, she replied glibly that it was a quarter to one by the kitchen clock ; but she confessed that the kitchen clock was generally slow, and never to be depended upon, which had caused complaints from the lodgers upon the subject of unpunctual meals.

Poor Phcebe ! She is a pleasant-spoken girl, full of intelligence, but I foresee in her the worst kind of witness—loquacious, and much too eager.

The notes on the Johannesburg Bank, and the mention of Africa overheard by Phoebe Miller, sufficiently indicated the point upon which my first efforts ought to be concentrated. I had to find the man from Africa. All the probabilities

of the case as at present shown pointed to him as the murderer. He had been with her a very short time before the shot was fired. The unrehability of the clock in Phcebe's kitchen made precision as to minutes impossible ; but a girl living within hearing of more than one church clock would hardly be far out in her idea of time. He had been engaged in a painful conversation with the victim, as her tears demonstrated. There had been words spoken that indicated the breaking of a promise. They were on such terms that the woman would not have been afraid of admitting him into the house ; while the evidence as to her character, from her landlady and her fellow-lodger, would show that she was not the kind of person to admit a stranger.

There remains for after consideration the possibility that a stranger may have got into the house without her knowledge, some one who knew of the money upon her person, and who meant to rob her. But that anybody entering the house for that purpose should have acted as the murderer acted, seems to the last degree unlikely. No alarm was given till the shot had been fired; there was nothing to arrest the criminal in his design. The manner of the murder, and of the man's departure, go to prove that he had but one motive for entering the house, and that was to put Lisa Rayner out of this world.

For some reason or other here was a woman to be suppressed ; and this man took the shortest and boldest way of suppressing her. Was it the

Rough Justice.

man .from Africa? The sum of money which I have no doubt had just passed from his hands to hers a few hours before her death, point to a blackmailer. The fact of her abject poverty during her residence in Dynevor Street is no argument against this supposition, since she told Mrs. Delamere that she had lost .sight of the man she loved, and knew not whether he was dead or living.

The man she loved reappeared on the scene, and sought her out immediately on his arrival. The recent date endorsed upon the notes would show that he received them shortly before he left Africa, since it leaves an interval only long enough for the railway journey from Johannesburg to Cape Town, and the voyage to England. He communicated with her, therefore, immediately upon landing, and he gave her this, for her, large sum of money. Yet her conduct while carrying those notes in her bosom was the conduct of a woman in deep distress. His bounty, therefore, had not satisfied her. There was trouble between them—a promise unfulfilled. Was that trouble sufficient to make him a murderer ? Was it so essential to him to get rid of this woman that he did not stop short of a heinous crime in order to free himself."

The answer to that question depends entirely on the character of the man. There is nothing in which one man differs more from another than in his respect for human life. There are born murderers as well as born poets ; indeed, I incline to believe that the murderer is born, not made.

He is not the victim of circumstances, the creature of environment, that we are disposed to think hin). He comes into the world with ferocious instincts to which bloodshed is almost a necessity; or with a pitiless hardness of heart and mind to which the cold, carefully calculated murder is as easy as a problem to a born geometrician. The murders that have been committed on trivial grounds, for a very small gain, or to escape from a not unconquerable difficulty, go to prove that there are minds which resort to crime at the first temptation, or at the first necessity. The man from Africa I take to belong to this class. The woman had given him the strongest indications that she meant to be troublesome. He had promised her something, most likely marriage, and she meant to make that promise a whip of scorpions for his back. A dull, heavy man, perhaps, brutal, callous, not able to look beyond the narrow circle of his own immediate interests; and thus seeing only one escape from his difficulty. Here was a life that was likely to be a trouble to him as long as he lived. The only remedy was to cut that life short, at once, before the story the woman had to tell had been told where it could most injure him. A weeping, loquacious drab, ready to whimper her tale of wrongs into every ear.

He had been living a wild, adventurous life, perhaps, on the Dark Continent; had lived with a revolver in his pocket, ready to exchange shot for shot, to slay rather than be slain. He had seen sudden death very often in that wild land, no doubt, and the shock of it would hardly touch

Rough Justice.

his hardened nerves. He had his revolver in his pocket while the woman was walking at his side, crying and complaining, upbraiding him for his desertion in the past, urging him to make all good in the future. And while she was sobbing out her reproaches, he was considering how the thing might best be done.

The man from Africa was obviously the first person to be found ; and while I breakfasted at a coffee-house near Dynevor Street I looked up the papers for the arrival of steamers from the Cape. I found the Saxon had arrived at Southampton early on the previous day. On a business day I should have gone straight to the London office of the Company to begin my inquiries, and also to the office of the South African Banking Company in Threadneedle Street, but the day being what it was, I felt that my only chance of doing business was at Southampton, so I made my way to that port by the first train that would take me, which was a slow train, and crowded with holiday people.

At Southampton my business was to get on board the Saxon, or, better still, to find the Head Steward on shore. He was almost certain to be spending his Christmas Day on terra firma, and it would be lucky for me if I found him without much trouble or delay.

The office of the African Steamship Company was closed, so there was nothing to be done there. The ship was lying in the Solent; and if I could get no information on land I should be obliged

to have myself put on board her. The day had turned out badly. A thin, fine rain was falling from a low grey sky. The docks and their neighbourhood were wrapped in gloom, the water was hidden under a grey fog. There was no use in my going on board the deserted steamer till I had tried to find the Head Steward in Southampton, where he was more likely to be spending Christmas Day. If he was an old servant of the Company he was probably to be heard of at some tavern near the docks.

The process of inquiry need not be recorded. It was more tedious than usual on account of the day. It was everybody's dinner-time, or after-dinner time, about the docks. The air was heavy with roast beef and plum-pudding. Turkey and sausages mingled with the odour of strong drinks in bars and bar-parlours. It was night before I discovered the Steward's whereabouts, in a villa on the road to Basset, and it was supper-time when I presented myself in the Steward's snug little dining-room, where he sat in the bosom of his family, embowered in holly, and cooking himself in the heat of a gas chandelier and a roaring fire in honour of the season.

The Head Steward is a man of the world, and accustomed to be intruded on at all hours. He received me very civilly, though the wife and family looked somewhat ruffled at my intrusion. When I had explained myself and the cause of my visit, he insisted on my sitting down to supper, which meal was not unwelcome, as I had been

Rough Justice.

Sustaining life on sandwiches and whisky and soda since I left London. After supper he withdrew with me to the opposite parlour, otherwise drawing-room, where there was more gas and more fire, and where we sat at a circular table covered with devotional books and photograph albums, and where Mr. Palby, Head Steward on the Saxon, answered as many questions as I liked to put to him.

Now, in his capacity as Head Steward it will be remembered that Mr. Palby would not be likely to know anything about second-class or steerage passengers. And what grounds had I for supposing that the man I wanted would be a first-class passenger, making the voyage under the eye of the Head Steward .-'

My reason was that the man who gave a hundred and twenty pounds off-hand to a woman he had wronged was a man who must have been flush of money, and would be, therefore, likely to secure himself as much comfort on a winter passage as money could buy.

These are the facts I was able to elicit from Mr. Palby in a conversation that lasted from ten o'clock till midnight. His family were playing snapdragon in the dining-parlour when we began our talk, and they had all gone upstairs to bed nearly an hour before he let me out into the chill misty night. However prosily the steward rambled in his talk, it was not for me to cut him short. Patience and perseverance, a ready perception, and a quick hearing, are the main requisites in my calling. But, indeed, without egotism or self-praise, I may add that to do well in the Criminal Investigation Force, a man must have all his faculties in good order, and must have the power of sustained attention in a high degree. A man who yawns in the middle of a prosy conversation is not the man to squeeze the gold of fact out of the quartz of twaddle.

There were not many first-class passengers on the Saxon on this last trip. Adult male passengers only six. One of these was a consumptive patient, who had been sent to the Transvaal to be -cured, and who was coming home to die. This poor gentleman hardly left his cabin during the voyage, and was carried on shore at Southampton. Another passenger was an old man, an Afrikander merchant, travelling with daughter and grandchildren. Three others were men with wives and families. The sixth was a bachelor, tall, broad-shouldered, good-looking, with a sunburnt complexion, and a light-brown beard.

Here was Phoebe Miller's description : the dark complexion and the fair beard.

The steward knew very little more about this gentleman than his name—Wildover, Alfred Wildover.

A. W.—the initials worked on the old silk neckerchief which the murdered woman had been wearing!

A young lady, who was travelling alone, was on very friendly terms with Mr. Wildover, and seemed to be an old acquaintance.

Rough Justice.

Asked if there was anything wrong between this young lady and gentleman, the steward assured me that the young lady's conduct was perfectly correct. She had high spirits, and was a bit wild, romping with the children on deck, and Mr. Wildover was often among them, and some sour old ladies on board had talked about it. One of them said that if the young lady was not engaged to Mr. Wildover she ought to be. He gathered from the talk at table one day that Mr. Wildover had been at Kimberley and at the Rand, and that he had made money either in gold or diamonds. He had not heard which it was. There was always a good deal of talk about diamonds or gold at table, and he had left off taking any interest in it. There were names bandied about which he had never troubled himself to remember. The people that were talked about were all millionaires, and they had all gone to Africa without shoes to their feet, if the talkers were to be believed.

I went back to London firmly believing that Wildover was the man who had been seen walking with the murdered woman on Christmas Eve. The steamer had arrived at Southampton early on that day, and Wildover had gone ashore with the other passengers, and his luggage, which was much less than the average quantity, was carried on shore soon after. He had only a cabin trunk and a kit-bag. The Steward knew nothing of his movements after he left the ship, but he concluded

that, like most passengers, he went straight on to Waterloo. I was of the same opinion. He had gone on to Waterloo, and had made his appointment with that unhappy young woman by wire, late in the afternoon. When Mrs. Delamere heard her moving about her room she was dressing herself to go out and meet the man from Africa. That was between six and seven o'clock ; and it was not till six hours afterwards that they had paced the street, engaged in a conversation that was full of trouble, tears, reproaches, recriminations, distress.

I was able through the General Post Office to get a copy of the telegram delivered to Mrs. Rayner on Christmas Eve. It was brief, and without name or initials:—

"Meet me in front of the British Museum at eight o'clock.—Your friend from Africa."

Next came the consideration of motive. The story as I read it was clear enough. Here was a young man who had made his fortune in the Colonies coming home to enjoy life under the best possible conditions—youth, health, and plenty of money. For his companion on board ship he had a girl whom he liked well enough to give his fellow passengers the idea that he and she were engaged lovers. So far all was sunshine for Mr. Wildover. But round his neck hung the millstone of a cast-off mistress—a woman who had suffered poverty and deprivation, and kept herself honest for his sake ; a woman who loved him well enough

Rough Justice.

to be desperate, and who might become his' persecutor if he threw her over and married somebody else.

My experience of Hfe had shown me how heavy these millstones are, and what risks a man will run to get rid of one.

Wildover met Lisa Rayner, therefore, with the idea of a compromise. He told her that he didn't mean to marry her, and he gave her a sum of money, perhaps with the promise to provide for her during the rest of her life.

Now, if this man had intended murder he would hardly have been so besotted as to give his victim a parcel of bank paper, which was calculated to lead to his identification. Notes on a local bank ; notes endorsed with name and date! The indications in a paper-chase could scarcely be plainer.

No! When he gave her that money he thought he was buying her silence. He hoped to pacify her by his liberality—but then came their final interview, and this poor wretch was still harping on the same string,

" I believed you would keep your promise."

Besides tears and reproaches there may have been threats of exposure. A blackmailer would have been bad enough, but a woman whom money wouldn't appease was worse—a millstone of the most dangerous kind.

The man lost his temper—a big, strong, passionate brute—a man who had seen the roughest side of life, civilized and uncivilized—

who had lived in a miner's hut, and herded with Afrikanders and Kaffirs.

A man of that class would be likely to carry a Smith-Wesson in his back pocket—having so shortly landed in England, and not yet abandoned his African habits. And this man lost his temper with the woman who claimed him—urging a claim that was unreasonable, perhaps, from a man's point of view. There may have been some final words on the doorstep—an entreaty on his part— a refusal on hers.

And then he settled his course on the instant; followed her into the house and upstairs; shot her through the head—would, perhaps, have tried to recover the notes, had not the sound of opening doors warned him that he had no time to lose.

The audacity of the crime gives it a certain interest. A bold, resolute, dare-devil brute, evidently, this gentleman from South Africa.

Having made up my mind that the man who gave Lisa Rayner the notes was the man who killed her, my immediate business was to find him, and get him locked up, and in order to do this, and to fill in the links that were wanting in the chain of evidence, I had to trace the South African notes. The easiest way of doing this was to go to the London branch of the Bank, in Threadneedle Street, where I had a satisfactory interview with the Manager, whom I was lucky enough to find at home in his rooms over the Bank, and who undertook to cable to the Johannesburg Manager for all particulars he

Rough Justice.

could obtain about the endorser of the notes, Phih'p Arden, ascertaining if possible to whom and on what day they were paid by the said Arden. That he should have written the date, December 2nd, below his signature was a point in our favour. This inquiry being put in hand, my next business was to track my man from the moment he met his victim, at, say between seven and eight o'clock on Christmas Eve, in front of the British Museum.

To help me in this investigation I had only one piece of evidence—the paper bag from the fruiterer in Covent Garden. Wherever they had spent their evening, whether in a theatre or music-hall, or any less innocent place, they had been in Covent Garden, and had been in Jakins's shop.

It was Boxing Day and Bank Holiday, so I was not surprised to find the Garden a desert, and Jakins's shop closely shut. The class of people who were buying fruit were the class who buy it off barrows in the streets ; so Mr. Jakins could afford to treat himself to a holiday, London was a stony solitude, a wilderness of iron shutters ; but with the murder of Lisa Rayner on my mind I didn't feel up to holiday-making, so I loafed about the neighbourhood of Covent Garden most of Boxing Day, and took my chop at a quiet hotel hard by.

Now, when I loaf there's generally a motive in my loafing, and I was hanging about that neighbourhood on the chance of discovering my gentleman from Africa—or, at any rate, the hotel at

which he had put up when he came to London. As to the man himself, in all probability he was out of London, and meant to get across the sea again as soon as he could. The ports were being taken care of, and he wouldn't find it very easy to leave England. The only difficulty was the chance of half a dozen wrong men being arrested, his description being somewhat vague. He had not come to London intending to commit a murder, and he had behaved as any other traveller would have done. He had gone to an hotel—a young man's hotel, most likely, since, according to the Steward's reckoning, he was about thirty years of age, and, therefore, must have left England a young man. There were three hotels within a short distance of the Garden much affected by

'Varsity and other young men, and at these I looked for traces of Mr. Wildover.

I did not find him by name, but at the quietest of the three houses I found distinct traces of such a man—and, what was more to the point, found that after arriving at the hotel in a hansom, with a cabin trunk and kit bag, this gentleman had engaged a room, and had gone out again almost immediately, not returning till long after midnight, when only the night porter was up to give him his candle and show him the way to his room.

I saw the night porter, who described the gentleman as looking white and worried, not at all like a gentleman who had been enjoying himself at a place of "entertainment.

Rough Justice.

"He asked me to get him a glass of brandy, and was put out when I told him the bar was locked up for the night, and everybody was gone to bed."

Had he noticed the time when he let the gentleman into the house; and did he come in a cab or on foot ?

" On foot. Leastways, I heard no cab stop."

Time, half-past one.

" You were asleep, perhaps ?"

" No!" the porter assured me—he was sitting in the hall reading a newspaper.

So much for Mr. Wildover's return to the hotel on Christmas Eve. The other servants were able to tell me about his departure from the hotel on Christmas morning, after breakfasting in the coffee-room. A cool hand, Mr. Wildover, to sit down to breakfast in a public room, red-handed from a brutal murder.

He left the hotel before noon, in a hansom, carrying his kit bag, and leaving his trunk in his bedroom. I took the liberty of examining this trunk, which was not locked, and which, as I anticipated, contained nothing that could help me in my investigation—only a suit of well-worn tweed and a stock of Colonial underclothing. It was a shabby old wooden trunk, and the initials "A. W." in red paint were nearly rubbed off—but still recognizable. He carried his revolver in his pocket, most likely, unless he had been cautious enough to drop it over one of the bridges before he went back to the hotel.

Time, however, was against the latter supposition, if, as the porter stated, Wildover was in the hotel at half-past one.

I asked the man who had waited upon him a few questions. Had he seemed well and in good spirits ? had he eaten a good breakfast ?

"First-class!" said the waiter. "Ordered a follow of eggs and bacon—said our London rations wouldn't feed a South African, whistled and walked about as cheery as you like, a lookin' at Bradshaw, a smokin' like one o'clock. And to think that he should be wanted, Mr. Faunce! Is it forgery, now ?"

I am pretty well known about town, and the head waiter at Spavins's hotel is an old acquaintance ; but I try to keep him in his place.

"No, James, it ain't forgery, and I never told^ you the gentleman v/as wanted."

"Well, but you come here to look for him, sir. That's tantymint, you know."

James is a terrible fellow for fine words, which he generally mispronounces and often misapplies.

" I have come to look for a gentleman, James," I answered, "but I am far from concluding that this is the man I want."

"Well, sir, any help I can give you "

"Thank you, James. You are always obliging. You saw the gentleman into his hansom— what station ?"

"Liverpool Street."

Antwerp or Flushing, thought I. Antwerp for choice, and then America.

" Did the gentleman say he was coming back ?"

"Yes, sir. 'Keep my room and take care of my trunk,' says he. ' When might you be coming back, sir.?' says I. ' I might be coming back tomorrow,' he makes answer, 'but it ain't hkely. It may be next day—or next week. You can keep my room.'"

" You may keep it till the Day of Judgment, I fancy, James, and the owner won't give you any trouble about it," said I.

" Then you think he is your man ?" cried James, eagerly.

" If he is my man, he's on the sea by this time, or he's caught at Harwich or at Queenborough," said I, " and you'll never see any more of him unless you're asked to look at him at Bow Street. But I'm not by any means sure that he is my man, and all you've got to do is to hold your tongue till you're wanted. He paid his bill, I suppose \'7d"

Yes, he had paid his bill, and had tipped James handsomely, I gathered, which tip did not in the least diminish the waiter's desire to earn an honest penny by getting him arrested for felony.

The likely seaports were being watched, and any man answering Wildover's description would be detained; so I was easy on that point, and expected to find a wire at the office announcing his arrest.

There were no wires. I went home to a late dinner, after telegraphing special instructions to

Harwich and Queenborough. There would be a close watch kept on out-going passengers at both places. If Liverpool Street meant flight, his Christmas journey had not helped Mr. Wildover.

I saw Jakins, the fruiterer, early on Thursday morning. He remembered selling some hothouse grapes—which were scarce and dear at Christmas —to a tall man, in a rough overcoat, and wearing a brown bowler hat. There was a woman with him, youngish, but worn-looking. She looked like a lady, but was very plainly dressed—like a lady who had gone down in the world. Jakins took notice of these two because his shop was empty, and he was just going to shut up when they came in, and partly on account of the man buying grapes at that price. He didn't look the style of customer for hothouse grapes at nine shillings a pound, not in that frieze coat and bowler hat; but he chucked his half-sovereign on the counter, and handed the grapes to the young woman as careless as if they'd been Portugals at one and three.Asked to describe the man, Jakins repeated Phoebe Miller's description: a dark complexion, sunburnt, a light-brown beard ; height over six feet, perhaps as much as six feet two; broad shoulders ; a fine looking man. Anybody would have noticed him; he hadn't the look of a Londoner.Asked if he overheard any conversation between the man and woman while they were in his shop, Jakins replied that they were talking to

each other, " confidential-like," while he was weighing the grapes, but that the only words he had caught were " Covent Garden," and " Concert," and "You was always so fond of music," "which it was him made the remark to her," Jakins said.

After this I had no doubt that they had gone to the theatre hard by, where I knew there had been a promenade concert on Christmas Eve.

Asked if he could say what o'clock it was when these people were in his shop, Jakins was doubtful, couldn't say within half-an-hour, but thought it would be close upon nine, as nine o'clock was his time for putting up the shutters. Then, thought I, they had dined somewhere handy. It would be only natural that this great brute, flush of money, and hoping to wheedle his victim into foregoing all claim upon him, should start by giving her a good dinner.

They were to meet in front of the Museum—on that broad pavement outside the railings—a quiet spot, and within ten minutes' walk of her lodgings. Then came the question. Where would he take her to dine If they walked westward, there was the Horse Shoe, a likely place for Wildover to have known in the past. If they crossed Holborn and went towards Covent Garden, there was no restaurant worth speaking of nearer than the Strand.

I tried the Horse Shoe first, but made nothing by my inquiries. The rooms were too full of diners for any particular party to be noticed. " They'd have had to be Cherokees in paint and feathers for any of us to have remarked 'em," the waiter said.

It really mattered very little where the two had dined, as I had made out their evening pretty well, and I relied upon Jakins to identify the man. Only it is my habit not to leave time unaccounted for, so I was sorry not to be able to trace their movements between eight o'clock, when they were to have met, and nine o'clock, when, or about when, they were at the fruiterer's.After I had left the Horse Shoe I walked along Tottenham Court Road with my face to the North, in a leisurely meditative mood. There was no pressure upon me to superhuman exertion, for I could do very little till I received information from Johannesburg, and in the meantime, if Wildover came within range, I meant to put him in safe keeping. There was evidence enough to justify his arrest.Strolling along, I caught sight of an Italian restaurant on the opposite side of the way, an insignificant little place, which I had often noticed, but never had occasion to enter. Carlo somebody —" Coffee, chocolate, ices," the usual placards, a few cakes in the window. I knew that even at the most insignificant of these places one may get a beefsteak and fried potatoes, and a dish of macaroni with tomatoes, and that the proprietor will send out of doors for any liquor that is ordered. The man from Africa may have chosen just such a place. It lay well within his ken, if he came out of Great Russell Street. I crossed

Rough Justice.

the road, and was soon on good terms with one of the two Swiss waiters.It was early in the afternoon. There was only one customer in the long, narrow shop, a lady of the music-teacher or type-writer species, taking a cup of chocolate and a sponge-cake at one of the marble-topped tables, and spelling over a flabby little French newspaper.Yes, it was here they had dined, in this modest retreat, at a table at the inner end of the room ; a tall, broad-shouldered man of about thirty, good-looking, sunburnt, light-brown beard. Both the waiters were able to describe him. He had ordered the best dinner they could serve at once. He was very hungry and impatient, and he had given them a sovereign to send out for a bottle of champagne ; and he had given the best maftcia Andr6 had received this Christmas.

And they had given him a good dinner.

" Fricandeau de Veau a I'oseille, le plat du jour, oeufs poch^s aux epinards, biftek aux pommes, Gruyre, compote de prunes "—a regular Christmas dinner.

Had Andre observed this lady and gentleman while he waited upon them ?

Naturally! He had observed them much. They were the only customers who had ordered a little careful dinner, or who had sent for champagne. Monsieur was evidently not the first comer. Yes, Andre had observed them. The poor lady had a melancholy air, yet by fits and starts was joyous, and her cheeks flushed and her

eyes shone as she looked at her handsome friend. Once she held out her hand and clasped his across the little table—not without tears. She hardly ate anything, and took only one glass of champagne. She seemed too full of emotion, poor lady, to eat much. The gentleman ate heartily, but he also seemed agitated, and did not appreciate the fricandeau as so excellent a dish deserved. Once Andre surprised Madame in tears. It was when he handed the pattiseries, Monsieur motioned the dish away— brjisqiiemeiit, with an angry gesture. In Andre's opinion they were a married couple, who had agreed to separate, and who faisaient la fete at their last dinner. "Ca avait I'air d'un adieu. J'ai soupgonn6 meme qu'on songeait a se suicider."

They had left the little Italian restaurant towards nine, Andr^ told me.

So now I had their evening laid out like a map ; for I had very little doubt that they had gone straight from the fruiterer's to Covent Garden Theatre. And then, when the concert was over, towards midnight, he had walked home with her. It was a fine evening, exceptionally mild for the season, mild as October. They had walked to Dynevor Street, and perhaps only there, during the walk, in the quiet of after-midnight, had he disclosed his intention of breaking with her altogether—this man whom she had welcomed home with such rapture. Then had come that final conversation while they were walking up and down the street, in which she, poor creature, found

Rough Justice.

how obdurate he was, and during which her distress became uncontrollable. I believe that it was during this last conversation that he gave her the bank-notes. The manner in which I found them, loosely folded, thrust inside the bodice of her gown, indicated that she had put them there carelessly, scarcely knowing what she did. Poverty such as hers would not handle a hundred and twenty pounds so carelessly, except under peculiar conditions.

I asked Andre and his fellow-servant if they would know the man we were talking of among half a dozen other men. Andre protested he would know him among a hundred. Identification in the case of Wildover was therefore easy enough up to a certain point; but what witness could I find to connect the woman who was his companion with that poor soul whose disfigured face the Coroner's jury are to look upon to-morrow." Only Phoebe Miller, who knew Lisa Rayner by sight, and who can swear to having seen her walking up and down Dynevor Street with a man ten minutes before the murder. If Phoebe should falter in her recognition of the man, the whole case against Wildover, as it now stands, must break down. I may succeed in connecting him with the notes I found in her bosom ; but unless I can show him in company with the woman herself, there is no chance of a committal.

The inquest afforded no new evidence of any kind, and passed off very quietly. The public

mind has not yet awakened to the sensational features of this crime ; or it may be that the public mind is temporarily obscured by turkey and sausages. There was no crowd in the Coroner's room—at a tavern near Dynevor Street—and the two reporters I saw there looked half asleep. Yet I have not the sHghtest doubt that in a week's time the Dynevor Street murder will have taken the town by storm, and become the leading topic in all the daily papers.

For cool audacity the man from Africa surpasses anybody who ever came under my notice—always supposing him to be the murderer. I was startled at my breakfast this morning by a telegram from the head waiter at Spavins's Hotel:—

"Wildover returned late last night. Leaving to-day."

I called at Bow Street for one of my best men, and went to the hotel. I was only just in time. There was a four-wheeler at the door, and Mr. Wildover's kit bag was on the roof, while Mr. Wildover himself stood in the doorway, objurgating against the sloth of the Boots for not bringing his trunk.

"That fellow will make me lose my train," he cried, "and if I lose my train I shall lose my steamer, and that means a fortnight's delay."

"You seem in a great hurry to leave England, sir," I said.

He looked at me from head to foot in the coolest way. He is not by any means the rough brute I had pictured him. He is a good-looking

fellow, with a pleasant countenance ; but I have seen a pleasant countenance before to-day with a murderer's brain behind it.

"What business is it of yours if I'm in a hurry to leave your cursed London ?" he said. " Is that luggage coming.?" he shouted, scowling back at the hall.

As he opened the cab-door, Boots brought the trunk, moving at a leisurely pace. He had been held back by my friend the waiter.

"I'm sorry to say that it is very much my business to prevent your starting for Africa," said I, "for I have to take you in custody on suspicion of being concerned in the Dynevor Street murder."

He turned a ghastly white, bold as he may be.

"Oh," he said, as cool as a cucumber, after a few moments' consideration, "then I suppose I'd better go with you."

"Well, you've no alternative. This cab will do for us all. Get on the box, Sergeant, and look after Mr. Wildover's luggage."

When we were seated in the cab I gave him the usual warning, but he hardly seemed to require it. He only spoke twice between the hotel and Bow Street, in the first place to beg me to put him into a clean cell. " I'm used to roughing it," he said, "but I can't stand dirt."

I told him that, as he was arrested upon suspicion, he would be allowed certain indulgences —such as having his meals sent from outside, for instance.

He glared at me like a demon.

" Meals! " he cried. " Do you suppose I shall care about eating and drinking in that d—d degrading position ?"

And that was his second and final remark.

CHAPTER VII.

AT BOW STREET.

Fog and gloom in the Court within, and fog and gloom in the street without, marked the beginning of an adjourned examination before the Bow Street magistrate, in which Arnold Wentworth, otherwise Alfred Wildover, played the leading part.

To that Court and the newspapers, and to the outside world interested in the Dynevor Street murder, he was Wildover still. The name of Wentworth was so far undamaged by the adventures of the black sheep of the family.

He had changed Christian and surname five years ago when the struggle for bread began in London. It was as Alfred Wildover that he took a weekly wage at the South London Music Hall, and it was as Alfred Wildover that he took his passage on the Saxon, and he had given his name as Alfred Wildover after his arrest; so, as his mother had never heard that name, it was hardly likely that she would associate the man under suspicion of a brutal murder with her son,

unless, indeed, Mary Freeland had told her of his alias.

But as the days of his captivity wore on there had been no sign from Mervynhall, and he was, therefore, assured that his mother was spared the knowledge of his degrading position. He had given her no address, had planned no second meeting with her. To see her and talk with her for an hour, and to know that she was well and tolerably happy, had satisfied his filial yearnings in his unsettled state of mind and uncertain future.

And now he looked back at that interview, and was thankful that circumstances had so shaped themselves as to leave all the details of his life in shadow. There could be no obvious link to connect Alfred Wildover with Arnold Wentworth. The fact that the suspected murderer had newly arrived from the Cape could have no significance in days when the intercourse between England and South Africa is a matter of daily occurrence.

Some one had interested himself, or herself, in his fate, and had shown that interest in a very substantial manner. He had been asked if he wanted to engage a solicitor to watch his case, and to defend him; and he had said no. He believed the plain truth would do more for him than any legal sophistry. He wanted no advocate.

But on the day following his first brief appearance before the magistrate, a gentleman was ushered into his cell, who announced himself as

Rough Justice.

Mr. Chilbrick, a solicitor of some standing, but chiefly known in the criminal courts. This unexpected visitor, who was received not too civilly, proceeded to explain that he had been retained to watch the case for Mr. Wildover by a friend who wished him well.

" Be kind enough to tell me my friend's name," said Arnold. " I don't like anonymous benefits. I fear the Greeks and their gifts, if I don't know who the Greeks are."

" Be assured you have no cause for fear in this instance, Mr. Wildover. Your friend is a very good friend, who, hearing that you were undefended and had refused to avail yourself of professional help, called upon me and engaged my services in your behalf. It would be a bad return for that friend's kindness if you were to refuse my assistance."

Arnold moved restlessly in his chair, blushed like a girl, and smiled, with a look half sad, half tender, which Mr. Chilbrick knew meant yielding.

" I have not many friends in England," he said. " I think I can guess the name of this one; and I am not ungrateful for her kindness, God bless her!"

He glanced at the solicitor to see how he took this assertion of his client's sex ; but Mr. Chilbrick's countenance presented a polite mask, which could not have been more impenetrable had it been marble.

Mr. Chilbrick's interview with Arnold, following on this gpnversation, was long, and from the

At Bozv Street.

solicitor's point of view most unsatisfactory. The client was pig-headed in the extreme, and wanted to defend himself, or, at any rate, to be defended only in his own way. The second interview made things no better.

"You don't seem to know that there is a very strong prima facie case against you," said Chil-brick.

"I know that I didn't shoot her. The onus is upon the prosecution to prove me guilty."

"And the onus is upon you to prevent their doing it."

The first appearance of the prisoner in Bow Street had been merely formal, in compliance with the law. Faunce had asked for a remand, as the case was not yet complete. He had an important piece of evidence, which he was not yet ready to produce, and to go into the matter without that evidence would be to waste the time of the Court. So, after a formal setting out of bare facts, the case was adjourned, the prisoner's application for bail being peremptorily refused ; although he was ready to lodge securities for a thousand pounds with the Magistrate.

And now, after seven days and nights of impatience, irritation, and weariness, for the man from Africa, the case was pronounced ripe for hearing, and Alfred Wildover made his second appearance in any court of justice.

That second appearance of his was not calculated to create a favourable impression. He looked haggard, worn out, ill at ease, and irritable.

The cool, frank outlook which had surprised Faunce was gone. A week in durance vile, with the restrictions and discipline to which he had been subjected, had shaken him more than all his hard labour and rough living at Kimberley and the Rand.

Mr. Davenant, a member of the Junior Bar, prosecuted for the Treasury, Mr. Chilbrick, solicitor, defended.

The Sergeant, who had been called immediately after the murder, was the first witness. He described the state of the room when he entered it, and the position of the murdered woman. He was followed by Mr. Faunce, who put in a plan of the room in which the murder was committed, and the landing and staircase, and gave a more detailed account of everything. He described the finding of the German Testament, the fruiterer's bag, and, lastly, the bundle of notes which had been since identified by communication with the Johannesburg Branch of the South African Banking Company, through their London office, as notes which had been given to the Hon. Philip Arden in exchange for his cheque, four days before the sailing of the Saxoji. The notes were endorsed by Mr. Arden more fully than usual, as he had written the date below his signature. Further inquiry at Johannesburg had shown that the notes had been paid to the prisoner for a waggon and team of bullocks, with articles useful in a shooting expedition. The transaction had taken place at the hotel where Mr. Arden was staying, and the

landlord had been a witness of purchase and payment.

The man from Africa heard this latter part of the evidence with a look of angry impatience. The description of the murdered woman's appearance had moved him strongly. If he were the rough brute Faunce believed him, he was not altogether without human feeling. Mr. Chilbrick did not cross-examine the Sergeant or the Detective, nor did he take any objection to the cabled evidence from South Africa.

The Dynevor Street murder had by this time begun, in the language of the music-hall, to " catch on." The reporters were on the alert for sensational evidence and highly coloured detail. Each man after his kind had jotted down a graphic description of the prisoner; while the swift firm strokes of accomplished pencils were doing all that modern art can do to fix the figures of the passing hour. Magistrate, lawyers, witnesses, detectives, and the prisoner in the dock would all be hawked about London by bawling newsboys to-night and to-morrow, to be scattered to the winds the day after.

And now the pencillers became newly alert; for the feminine element was to give a zest to the proceedings. Suddenly, as from the witches' cauldron, there rose in the witness-box an agreeable vision of a sealskin jacket, the smallest and most Parisian thing in bonnets, an alabaster complexion under a spotted veil, and the newest shade of Titianesque hair, while across the foetid atmosphere of a

Metropolitan Police Court floated a delicate odour of Ess. Bouquet.

The witness was a lady who was living in the house at the time of the murder, but who had since removed to St. George's Terrace, Brompton Road. This lady was known as Mrs. Delamere.

" Is that your real name ?" Mr. Davenant asked.

The witness rather reluctantly admitted that Delamere was not her name. It was the name, or possibly the alias, of a gentleman friend who had been acquainted with her father, and who paid her rent, and was, indeed, her guardian ; at least, she had always looked upon him in that light.

The lady was sworn as Anne Wilson, and after the Counsel for the Treasury had elicited a plain statement of fact, she was taken in hand by Mr. Chilbrick.

" It was you who gave the first alarm, I think, after the firing of the pistol.?"

" I don't know. Mrs. Grogan was on the landing before you could say knife."

" But not before the man who fired the shot was able to get off unseen .

"I beg your pardon, I saw him go downstairs."

" Are you able to describe him ?"

"No, I ain't. His back was towards me."

" Was he tall or short, stout or thin >"

"I don't know. I was frightened, and he was running downstairs. There was no light but the candle in my hand."

At Bow Street,

" Then you cannot tell us what he was like in any particular ? His dress, for instance ? Did he look like a gentleman, or a mechanic ?"

"He was in his ordinary clothes."

" Was he wearing an overcoat ?"

" I think so."

" Not a fustian jacket ?"

"No, I am sure of that. If I had time to think about him at all I thought he was a gentleman."

" Did you notice the colour of his coat ?"

"Not particularly. It was dark—that's all I know about it."

" Will you tell us exactly what happened \'7d Were you awakened by the shot ?"

"No—I was lying awake—I am a wretched sleeper, and that was one of my bad nights."

"You had not been in bed very long, perhaps?"

" No. I was rather late home that night. I had been to a place of amusement."

" I will not ask you to name the place of amusement."

This remark and the last question were aimed at the gallery, and a suppressed titter further enlivened the dreariness of the police court.

"Well, you were lying awake. What was the first thing that attracted your attention ?"

" It was footsteps coming upstairs."

" Was that such an unusual occurrence ?"

"No. Mrs. Rayner had a latch-key, and she was often out of a night wandering about—not for any wrong purpose, poor thing—but because

Rough Justice.

she couldn't bear herself indoors. She used to get the horrors sitting alone, she told me."

" Oh, she used to get the horrors sitting alone. I conclude she was living pretty much the same easy kjnd of life as yours ?"

" You have no call to talk about my life. I'm not here to answer impudent questions. As for her life, it was honest enough, and wretched enough ; and it was nearer death than life at the best."

"Well, you heard her come in. Did you notice the time .?"

"Yes, it was five minutes to one."

" How came you to be so precise ?"

"Because I keep a clock on the table by my bed, with a night-light in front of it, and I looked at the clock as I heard her footsteps go up the stairs—and I wondered at her being so late. That's how I come to be so precise."

There was a faint murmur among the audience, as of approval.

" Well, you heard her go upstairs alone ?"

"Yes, and two minutes afterwards I heard a man's footsteps on the stairs, following hers. He trod very softly, but still I could tell it was a man. And I wondered that she should bring anybody into the house at such an hour."

" You thought it was too respectable a house for nocturnal visitors ?"

" I knew it was a respectable house—or I shouldn't have been living in it."

" Perhaps you thought she had found an old

friend of her father's to pay her rent. Well, what next ?"

" I heard the report of a pistol."

" How long after the man's footsteps had passed your door ?"

" Not two minutes. Only long enough for him to have gone up the stairs to the third floor."

"And how long was it before you were on the landing \'7d"

" Hardly a minute. I am very chilly, and I had gone to bed in my dressing-gown, I waited only to put my feet in my slippers and light my candle, before I went to see what had happened. The man was halfway down to the first floor. I just caught sight of him over the banisters. Mrs. Grogan sleeps in the third floor front, and she came out in her nightgown, and was on the landing screaming murder as I went up. Mrs. Rayner's door was open, and me and Mrs. Grogan went into her room together. She was lying on the floor, shot through the head, a dreadful spectacle."

The witness burst into tears, and became slightly hysterical. Some water was brought, and the Magistrate begged her to sit down and rest for a few minutes before continuing her evidence.

When she had recovered from a very natural agitation, and had rearranged her spotted veil over a complexion which had lost somewhat of its alabaster whiteness, the interrogation went on.

" I believe you were very kind to the deceased,

Rough Justice.

and knew more about her than any one else in the house ?"

"Nobody else ever did anything for her. I'd have been kinder if she'd have let me ; but she was very proud. It was very difficult to get her to take bite or sup, though it was plain enough she was half starved."

" Did she tell you anything about her antecedents ?"

" Her family, do you mean ?"

" Yes, her family "—smiling a little at having used a word out of the witness's range. " Her early days—belongings—the circumstances that had brought her to such a pass \'7d"

" No, she was a rare one to hold her tongue. She never told me anything about herself; but I think she must have been brought up a lady. She never talked of herself but once. It was one night that she seemed ready to drop, and I made her take some spirits and water, and it got into her head, and she was half wild-like, and cried and talked about herself; and she told me she had never loved but two men—one who was rich and who led her wrong, and deceived her, and left her to starve ; and one who was nearly as poor as she was, and who was good to her. She loved the rich man when she was little more than a child, and was deceived by the first kind words that had ever been spoken to her. She loved the poor man when she was a woman ; and him she would love till her dying day, though they had parted years ago, and might never meet again."

This closed Mr. Chilbrick's cross-examination.

The servant girl at No. 13, Dynevor Street, was the next witness. She gave her evidence as to the arrival of the telegram for Mrs. Rayner, and a copy of the telegram was produced, and sworn to by a clerk from the Post-office: " Meet me in front of the British Museum to-night at eight.—Your friend from Africa. Received at King Street at 6.40."

Phoebe Miller, the maid-of-all-work at No. 16, was next sworn, and repeated the statement she had made to Faunce, but was weak under cross-examination, and was not certain as to the identity of the prisoner with the man she had seen walking with Lisa Rayner.

The next witness was the waiter from the Italian Restaurant, who had identified the prisoner previously on seeing him in a group of other men, and who described his conduct and that of the woman with him while he waited on them. He described the woman's appearance, and the emotion she had exhibited at one period of the meal.

In the midst of Mr. Davenant's examination of this witness Mr. Chilbrick addressed the Magistrate.

" It would save your time and trouble, sir, if I state that my client has no desire to deny his identity with the person who was seen in Mrs. Rayner's company as late as ten minutes to one on the night of December 24th."

This admission brought the proceedings to an abrupt check. There was no occasion to work

Rough Justice.

any further along the line of Faunae's investigation ; but since his researches of Christmas Day and Bank Holiday the Chief Inspector had become aware of a circumstance which might have a close connection with the crime in Dynevor Street; and he had his witnesses ready.

The first of these witnesses was a cook in the service of a clergyman in Gordon Square, who swore to finding a pistol in the area early in the morning on the 26th of December.

" Did you sweep the area on Christmas Day ?"

" No, the family was dining out, and me and the housemaid was allowed to have a friend each to spend the afternoon, so I left the cleaning up till Boxing Day."

" And on Boxing Day you found this pistol ?"

The pistol was on the table in front of the Magistrate.

"Was it lying where any one might see it from the street ?"

"I don't think any one could have seen it. Missus and the Vicar are great ones for creepers, and the ivy grows all over the end of the area, and the pistol had fallen in a corner, right among the ivy. I mightn't have found it myself, if I hadn't 'It it with my broom. Any one could have put his arm between the railings and slipped the pistol down behind the ivy."

"What did you do with the pistol?"

" I took it upstairs to my room." "Did it not occur to you that it was your duty to inform the police of such a suspicious

At Bow Street,

circumstance, or to tell your master what had happened ?"

" I wanted to show the pistol to a friend of mine first."

"But you finally concluded you ought to tell your master ?"

"When I heard such a lot of talk about the Dynevor Street murder I thought the pistol might be the one as done it."

" Did you know whether the pistol was loaded ?"

" No, but I thought it might be, and I tied it up in a handkerchief and put it on the top shelf of a cupboard, where it couldn't have hurt no one if it had gone off."

"You did very wrong to conceal such a discovery," the Magistrate remarked, in a voice that withered the cook from Gordon Square. "You must be perfectly aware that pistols are not commonly found in the areas of London houses."

The next witness was a gunsmith, who had compared the bullet found in the murdered woman's room with the pistol, all the chambers of which were loaded, except one containing a discharged cartridge-case, when the cook handed it to the constable. Bullet and pistol fitted.

Mr, Chilbrick did not cross-examine either witness, but he begged for a further remand, on the ground that he had been unprepared for this evidence. The Magistrate consented, and the inquiry was adjourned for a week.

The adjourned proceedings opened with the

Rough Justice.

evidence of a witness whose presence there had been procured by Mr, Chilbrick's energetic efforts during the week's respite.

This witness was the assistant of a well-known gun-maker in Holborn.

He identified the revolver produced in court as one which he had sold on the 22nd of the previous November to a young man, who paid for it across the counter, and took it away with him.

Asked if the purchaser was the prisoner, he replied, " Certainly not! Not a bit like him."

" Can you describe the person's appearance ?"

" He was not so tall as the prisoner—a tallish man, but not as tall as the prisoner by three or four inches. He was dressed like a gentleman, but not fashionably, in a rather careless style. He had what one might call a studious look, and was wearing dark-blue spectacles."

"You had no suspicion of any bad motive in his purchase ?"

"Oh dear, no. We should have nothing to do but suspect bad motives if we suspected every purchaser of a revolver. He said something about going to British Columbia, and expecting to fall in with a rough lot there. He was one of your communicative customers, I didn't listen to him, except so far as the business went. He wanted a pistol of the finest quality, small enough for him to carry in his trouser pocket, and I chose that one for him as the best and handiest."

Beyond the fact that the bullet found in Dynevor Street corresponded exactly with this

At Bow Street.

pistol, there was the further evidence of the cartridges, which were of a new make, and identified by the gunsmith as the kind he had supped with the pistol.

Mr. Chilbrick, cross-examining : " Did anything strike you as curious in the spectacles the man wore .■*"

Witness: " They hid more of his eyes and forehead than the common kind of spectacles ; and I imagined that he was a sufferer from some kind of eye-disease."

Mr. Chilbrick: " What time of day was he in your shop ?"

Witness: " I can't name the precise hour, but it was towards evening. The afternoon was foggy, and there had been no one in the shop—except Lord Humberleigh's valet, who ordered some cartridges for Scotland."

Mr. Chilbrick: " You had had a leisurely afternoon, then ?"

Witness: " Yes. I should hardly have remembered the sale of the revolver—it was entered in our books, of course—or the appearance of the man, if it had been one of our busy days. The fog was keeping all our usual customers at home."

Mr. Chilbrick: " Look at the prisoner again. Now, are you quite sure you never saw him before ?"

Witness: " Ouite sure."

After the examination of this witness, the counsel for the Treasury closed the case, and put in a statement written by the accused while under

detention, and handed to the Governor of the prison.

It was the following plain and straightforward recital of the circumstances which had brought the man from Africa into that dock:

"Lisa Rayner was a friend whom I had lost sight of for some years. My first years in Africa were so unlucky, and I was so hopeless of ever prospering there, that I had not had heart enough to write to her. What was the use of writing to say: ' I am starving here—and, perhapSj you are starving in London' ? When the tide turned, and I began to prosper, I wrote, and only waited her reply to send her money; but no letter of mine reached her. She had been driven from pillar to post in the interval. I heard from her just before I left the Gold-fields. Her letter had been waiting for me at Heidelberg for months, while I was amusing myself in Bechuanaland. She wrote to me that she was unhappy and in great poverty; and my first act on reaching London was to appoint a meeting with her. We met at 8 o'clock in Great Russell Street, as the witness Faunce stated. We dined together, and then I took her to Covent Garden, where there was a concert, and where we sat in a back row of the upper circle. It was nearly midnight when the concert was over, and I walked to Dynevor Street with her. We walked slowly, and lingered a little on the way, having a good deal to talk about, and our conversation was not finished when we came to Dynevor Street, so I walked up and down the

street with her—between two turnings—as the girl Miller described. It was during this conversation that I gave her the African notes, which she was reluctant to accept. We parted at the door of No. 13.

"She opened the door with her latch-key some minutes before we parted; and she came down the steps again to speak to me. We stood talking by the area railings during those last few minutes, but whether it would have been possible for any one to go in at that door after she had opened it, unperceived by either of us, is more than I can say. We were both agitated. She was distressed, and I was troubled by her distress. I had given her a promise before I went to the Cape, four years ago—and circumstances had occurred that made it impossible for me to keep that promise. I was very sorry for her, and I wanted to be her friend, and to make her future life as happy as a friend's help could make it."

Mr. Chilbrick briefly reviewed the case against his client, and made a defence which, taken in conjunction with the gunsmith's evidence, and with Wildover's straightforward statement, went a long way towards procuring an immediate discharge. The inquiry was, however, adjourned for a week, to give time for further revelations ; bail was again applied for, and again refused; and Arnold was taken back to Pentonville, angry and almost despairing.

CHAPTER VIII.

A DEATH-BLOW.

No new evidence was forthcoming at the adjourned examination in the Magistrate's Court, and, after some verbal fencing between Mr. Davenant, for the Treasury, and Mr. Chilbrick, for the prisoner, the Magistrate, having briefly reviewed the whole of the circumstances, did not feel justified in remitting the case to a jury. The accused, Alfred Wildover, was discharged; and Arnold Wentworth, like one awaking from a hideous dream, found himself at liberty to leave that place of despair. He thanked Mr. Chilbrick, and begged him to convey an unlucky man's gratitude to his unknown friend, and having shaken hands with the solicitor, and handsomely tipped his custodians, he left that place, as he hoped, for ever.

He was a free man once more, and the world seemed a new world. Even the bleak London streets were enchanting ; swept by a biting March wind, pervaded by the City's dirt, flavoured with sewage, smoke, and an unclean population—yes, even that howling wilderness of brick and stone

seemed paradise to the man who had been enduring an ignominious captivity.

He flung his arms about; he walked with buoyant step; he held his head as loftily as if he had succeeded to a dukedom. He had come into possession of man's best inheritance—liberty; and the sense of freedom was ecstasy.

Mary—little Mary—otherwise the kid ! His first thought after self-congratulation was about Mary Freeland. He was eager to see her, to thank her for her goodness to a friend in distress ; if, as he had little doubt, it was she who had sent the solicitor. It must be she, and none other. Even had his mother discovered his identity with the accused Wildover, it was not within the compass of her mind or means to take so bold a step. What did Mrs, Wentworth know of criminal lawyers.-' Her intellect had been blunted by continual encounters with that awe-inspiring personage, the professed cook, "soups, entrees, ices, etc.," the etc. standing for failures and disappointments.

He had Mary's address in his pocket-book, given to him that December morning at the Briery, when he stood before her, white to the Jips, after reading of the murder in Dynevor Street, and had made some feeble excuse about a touch of African fever, and sudden giddiness, while Mary scrawled Mrs. Smith's address in his pocket-book.

"Be sure you come to see me when I am settled," she had said, as she wrote. " I dare say, Rough Justice.

if you behave very nicely, Mrs. Tresillian-Smith will send you a card for her parties. She may put you on her free list, and then you can come every week, if you like."

He had muttered something about the bliss of such parties, and had left her, after wringing her hand in an agitated way that scared and puzzled her.

" How like a man to make such a fuss about a headache," she thought. "And how could he talk of fever with that ice-cold hand \'7d"

And now he had come through that black cloud of trouble, and was free again ; and that dark past might be as if it had never been. He had shed all his tears for the poor creature whose fate had been so hard (a broken life and a violent and mysterious death) in the solitude and depression of his prison. He would put a slab of marble over Lisa Rayner's grave in Highgate Cemetery, to bear record of her gentle submissive life and unselfish love; and then surely his conscience would allow him to forget her tragic fate, and to remember only the days in which they had loved each other, and been happy together.

A higher kind of happiness was to be his in the future, he hoped—the happiness of union with a pure and guileless woman ; his little Mary, his frank and joyous comrade; the woman out of whose eyes truth and courage looked with bright commanding glance; the conqueror whom his heart acknowledged as mistress and queen.In South Kensington there are long streets o

stuccoed houses on which the sun never shines. These are called Gardens. It may be indeed that on one favoured side of the way and at one propitious hour the sun does look ; but the casual visitor rarely surprises Phoebus in the act. The long stony street, with its pillared porticoes all alike, dwells for the most part in an atmosphere of neutral grey, which is scarcely enlivened by the genteel palms and India-rubber trees in the bay-windows. An Italian grocer's shop, an Indian bazaar, a jutting Moorish sun-blind, striped with vermilion and orange, might afford a relief to the gloom. Anything less vivid is futile.

Hexton Gardens was of this order of architecture, and vainly had Mrs. Tresillian-Smith's artistic fancy struggled against the pervading greyness. The yellowy green of a portiere, between outer lobby and hall, and a beaded bamboo blind before a staircase window, testified to her ineffectual efforts. The gloomy impression of the street which the visitor carried with him into the house was not dispelled by such feeble colouring as came within the range of Mrs, Tresillian-Smith's taste.

Arnold's high spirits yielded to the genius of the place. He was feeling almost unhappy when he pressed the electric bell at No. 19. He felt a gloom akin to despair when he found himself shut in by the black-coated man-servant, in the shadowy back-room which Mrs. Tresillian-Smith called her drawing-room, the two French windows of which were obscured by highly artistic muslin blinds of a sickly yellow and a slaty blue.

Rough Justice.

" Poor Mary! if this is the liveliest room in the house, I pity her," thought Arnold.

He felt as if he were within prison walls again ; but the palms, the silver table, on which the mustard-pots and odd spoons of three generations were paraded, the gorgeous books, inkstands, and candlesticks on other tables, the Indian screen draped out of knowledge, the semi-grand piano muffled in a Japanese curtain, and the general air and manner of the room, testified to its bestness.

Evidently Mrs. Tresillian-Smith's chief reception-room, and a room of which she was proud.

He sat ten minutes in chilling solitude. The fire in the ornamental grate was a miserable fire, and gave neither flame nor heat. He had time in those ten minutes to open and shut every volume on the loaded table. Drawing-room books every one of them : gilded vellum, antique calf, red edges, gold edges: and nothing inside—certainly nothing that he, Arnold, wanted to read.

It was such a long ten minutes; but Mary would come rushing in presently, like living sunlight. Perhaps in strict etiquette he ought to have asked to see the lady of the house first, and her charge afterwards, he thought ; but then the circumstances were exceptional—a man does not come out of prison every day.

The door opened slowly. Not Mary's hand, surely > Yes, it was Mary Freeland; but she came towards him with lagging steps, and a sorrow-stricken countenance, as of one in the

A Death-blow.

house of death. She came about half-way across the room, and then stopped and stood looking at him, with no outstretched hand to welcome him, no smile upon her pale lips, no light in her eyes,

"Mary, are you not glad to see me a free man again, cleared from that atrocious charge ? Have you no good word for me ? I came here hoping to find you half wild with joy ; as I was when I came out of court, a free man."

"I don't think I shall ever know the meaning of the word joy again," she answered, standing before him like a statue.

He put his hands upon her shoulders, as he had done on their first meeting on board the steamer; but this time those strong hands gripped her almost fiercely, and there was anger in the eyes which scrutinized her face.

"My God! Can it be that you believe I murdered that woman ?"

" I believe nothing. I am very miserable."

"You don't know me well enough—you, the child I used to play with—you, who knew my mother, my home, the way I was reared—all this knowledge doesn't help you to know that I am not a murderer ? "

"All that knowledge goes for nothing against the life you led afterwards—the life of deliberate sin. You lived with that woman, and did not marry her, and left her to starve."

" No, no; I gave her more money than I carried away myself when I went to Africa. I wrote to

Rough Justice.

her directly I had money to send her. She had shifted her lodgings, poor soul, and never received my remittance ; but the first money I earned over and above the day's bread and the night's shelter was sent to her."

" Oh, it was base and cruel of you to leave her, base and cruel not to marry her, not to redeem the past, not to atone for the evil you had done— for your sinful life."

"Don't prate about my life," he cried fiercely. "What do you know of a young man's life, flung on the world as I was, without a friend, face to face with famine and suicide \'7d When that dead woman was my friend I had no other. Spare me your schoolgirl sermon, Mary Freelahd, and tell me in plain words, do you believe me a murderer ?"

Tears were her only answer. She flung herself into a chair, clasped her hands before her face, and sobbed broken-heartedly.

" I have your answer," he said. " I knew you were ignorant of life, and the world you live in ; but I thought your womanly instinct would have taught you to read the heart and mind of a man who loved you. Good-bye, little Mary. The woman who can believe me a scoundrel must be a stranger to me. You and I have done with each other."

He went out of the room, and out of the house. She looked up in the midst of her tears, and listened, and when she heard the hall-door shut behind him she slipped from the low chair to the

A Death-blow.

floor, and lay there sobbing and moaning in self-abasement.

Mrs. Tresillian-Smith was making a round of visits in the professional brougham, so Miss Freeland had no fear of interruption. The brazen filigree plate with " Out" was exhibited on the hall-table, and the drawing-room offered the isolation of a tomb.

Poor Mary! Everybody about her had talked of Wildover's guilt as if it were a fact, mathematically demonstrated. She had heard the case discussed again and again ; she had sat, pale and sick with mental pain, while indifferent people went over the evidence, and allowed no loophole for the possibility of innocence.

And then there had been other tortures. It had agonized her to think of his relations with that other woman. She had acted m La Dame aux CaniHias, and had the exalted idea which most innocent women cherish about their fallen sisters. She idealized the guilty love, and told herself that such passions always lasted a lifetime. No man was ever cured of a love like that. And while she had flattered herself that he loved her, Mary Freeland—poor commonplace Mary Freeland— he was bound earth and mind by that chain in the romantic past.

Yet if he still loved that other woman, why murder her \'7d Jealousy, perhaps. He might have discovered that she had been false to him in his absence, and this had been his deadly revenge. Most of Mary's views of life were taken from plays

Rough Justice.

or novels; and revenge was a grand factor in the scheme of existence which she had woven out of drama and romance.

Oh, she feared, she feared that people must have judged him rightly, and that he had done this dreadful thing. How she blessed and thanked Mr. Chilbrick for his successful defence, and the good Magistrate who had dismissed the case against Arnold Wildover! He was free. He had all his life before him in which to repent. She thought that he would turn Roman Catholic and join some severe order of monks. She pictured his future in some Trappist Monastery, never speaking save to remind a silent brother of man's inevitable doom.

Oh, what a sorry end for Arnold, her brave, noble Arnold, the young man whom she had looked up to and admired when she wore a pinafore ! She had carried his image in her heart ever since those childish days ; and the meeting with him on board the steamer had been like the sudden opening of paradise.

Everybody told her that he was guilty. She had sat in her pale silence, with sinking heart, nobody heeding her, while a famous Queen's Counsel expatiated upon the Dynevor Street murder, and shook his head and shrugged his shoulders. Mary Freeland was young enough to believe in the ineffable wisdom of men of fifty, and that a distinguished barrister could not take a wrong view of circumstantial evidence. She had read every word that had been reported of the

A Death-blow.

case; and it seemed to her, in spite of that missing link in the matter of the weapon, that no one could doubt Arnold's guilt.

She did not think of him as a cold-blooded murderer. She tried to mitigate the blackness of that dreadful crime. He had not meant to kill the woman he had loved. Jealousy, revenge, some great convulsion of tragic passion, had maddened him. He had been moved by blind fury, had been for a moment a madman. She made her own theory of the murder, even while she bowed to the superior middle-aged wisdom which denied the possibility of his innocence. If she admitted his guilt, she would at least have him guilty in her own way.

The post upon the evening following Arnold's visit brought Mary Freeland a letter from him. She had not left her room since their meeting, the mere idea of Mrs. Tresillian-Smith's social circle being intolerable. She had pleaded a headache of the most distressing character; and her pallid face and heavy eyelids sustained the plea, together with the fact that she had been looking wretchedly ill ever since she came to Hexton Gardens.

" I really am afraid South Kensington doesn't agree with her," Mrs. Smith said solemnly, as if such a fact hardly came within the range of the possible.

" She wants a tonic," Dr. Smith answered carelessly. " I'll have a look at her before lunch."

Rough Justice.

Mary Freeland allowed her host to prescribe for her, and lay all day in her darkened room persistently miserable. It was the last post which brought her Arnold's letter, a little before ten o'clock. She heard the squeaking of a violin as the housemaid opened the door; and she had been hearing carriages stopping, and bells ringing, and doors opening and shutting, for the last half-hour, inasmuch as this was one of Mrs. Tresillian-Smith's evenings.

She sprang up from her bed directly the housemaid left her, and ran to her writing-table, where there was a candle burning under a rose-coloured shade. Half the elegance of Mrs. Tresillian-Smith's house was expressed in paper candle-shades.

She tore off the envelope with trembling fingers, and her eyes devoured Arnold's letter, which began without any formula of courtesy or affection.

"When I walked into the street yesterday afternoon a free man, acquitted by the Magistrate's dismissal, it never entered my thoughts that any mortal could believe me guilty. How much less, then, could I think that you, Mary, would be my accuser ? You, who know my father and mother, who know from what race I spring, of what stuff I am made ; you to believe me a murderer! It is unthinkable! My mind cannot realize the condition of yours.

" Since I saw you yesterday I have seen the

A Death-blow.

same belief in other faces, I have begun to feel myself a Pariah. My first intention after leaving you was to go straight back to Africa—I even went to the Shipping Agent, and was on the point of engaging my berth on the next outgoing steamer, when I changed my plan in a moment. It would be a craven's part to beat a retreat before an unjust judgment, even though inclination would take me back to the gold-fields and the hard free life that suited me so well. No, I said to myself, I will hold my ground. I will not leave England till I have cleared myself in Mary's eyes.

" That was my resolve yesterday evening, Mary. That is my determination to-day. Henceforth I shall only live to clear myself of this odious suspicion. The sole business of my life will be to prove to you, if not to the rest of the world, that this hand of mine is not the hand of a murderer.

"And that I should murder her, that gentle, unoffending creature, ever ready to expiate her sorrowful past by acts of womanly self-sacrifice. All my business with her that night was to persuade her to one last act of self-abnegation. I was bound to her by every tie of honour and affection ; and I asked her to release me from that sacred obligation in order that I might offer myself to another woman, whose youth and innocence had stolen into my heart unawares.

"And now youth and innocence, for which I was ready to break a loving woman's heart, condemn me unheard. It is the irony of fate, Mary.

Rough Justice.

Her love—guilty as you would deem it—was the rock. Yours is the shifting sand.

"But I mean to prove that I am not the villain you think me.

"A. W."

That was all. There were no tender words; though the letter told her for the first time that he had loved her. Had loved her! His love was dead now, she thought. It had withered at her cruel accusation. She to believe him guilty—she who had known him in his boyhood, she who had spent those happy days with him on board the ship. Could she associate the idea of a horrid crime with the man she had loved and admired and believed in only a few weeks ago ? She hated herself for her conduct of yesterday. There had been time for her to repent of her weak-mindedness, her folly in believing that hateful Queen's Counsel, and all those wretches who were eager to condemn a man of whom they knew nothing.

Of whom they knew nothing. Yes, that was their excuse for harsh judgment. But that she, his playfellow of old, his friend of a few weeks past, she, who knew every line in his face, every tone in his voice, that she could think him a murderer! Well, it only served to prove what a brainless creature she was.

"A woman with brains would never have misjudged him," she told herself.

All her ideas about him had altered since

A Death-blow,

yesterday. She needed only to see him and hear him for her feelings and convictions to change ; not at first, not in a moment, but in those long hours in which she had lain in her darkened room, with aching heart and aching head, that no tonic treatment could cure, recalling his looks and words, living over again that terrible interview which she had meant to be their last.

She had condemned him upon circumstantial evidence, like those foolish drawing-room babblers who had prated about the network of circumstance which enmeshed him.

She had recalled the change in his mood a few days before the vessel came into port—his gloomy manner ; his curious avoidance of her ; his troubled air the morning they parted, the morning of Christmas Eve. She remembered his agitation upon reading the report of the murder; how he had stood before her ghastly and speechless. On such evidence as this, strengthened by the details in the newspapers, and the almost universal opinion of his guilt, Mary Freeland had condemned him. She hated herself now for her willingness to think evil.

"A woman whose love was worth having would have trusted him in spite of the world," she thought. " How he must despise me! What a poor creature he must think me."

She read his contempt for her between the lines of his letter. His allusions to that dead woman— the woman he had loved for years, and who had been to him as a wife—stung Mary Freeland to

Rough Justice.

the quick. She was jealous of his regard for that poor ghost.

" She would have acted like a heroine," thought Mary, "and I have acted like a fool. He can never care for me again. He may want to clear himself from that hideous charge, to make me repent my words ; but not for love of me ; only from a man's natural pride in his own character. He wants to clear himself for his own sake, not for mine,"

There was no address upon Arnold's letter, or Mary would have written to him that night, in her subjugation of spirit. She would have written upon her knees to implore his pardon. She could know no happiness in life till she had made atonement to him.

The next morning she was really ill, and Dr. Tresillian-Smith brought in a brother practitioner later in the day for a consultation. As an inmate of his house, in his wife's charge, almost a ward, he was particularly anxious about her.

" She has looked languid and miserable ever since she has been with us," he told the physician, "though she would never confess to feeling ill. Nothing my wife could do to put her in good spirits was of any use. We were told she was a high-spirited, lively girl; but I really don't believe such a doleful young woman ever came into a house."

" A love affair, no doubt," said the doctor; and having determined that the mind was out of gear, he straightway prescribed for the cure of the body,

A Death-blow.

which, after all, seemed the more important element in the matter,

"The poor child has fretted herself into a low fever," he said. " I should send her to the east coast if I were you, Smith, as soon as you get her up again, and let her ride, or play golf, for a month or two."

Rough Justice.

CHAPTER IX.

MR. FAUNCE'S RECORD.

My good little wife had for a long time been urging me to wind up my association with Bow Street, and retire into private life, and a cottage villa with a garden, at Putney, which neighbourhood she considered a kind of Paradise as compared with Bloomsbury. I own to being fond of Bloomsbury, and to having a liking for a profession which some people might consider disagreeable ; but when Providence has bestowed a good wife upon a man, it is his business to prove himself worthy of the gift. So I had made up my mind to retire for some time past; and I think the Dynevor Street business turned the scale, and precipitated my withdrawal from the Criminal Investigation Department.

I was sorry to part company with the men I knew, and with whom I had worked in friendly association ; but I felt I had had enough of work which took a great deal out of me, and brought me a very moderate recompense. So one fine morning, not long after the break-down of the case against Wildover, I went through the process of securing my pension, and took a lease of Hawthorn Lodge, Putney Hill.

It was a new sensation to be sauntering about Wimbledon Common in the early mornings, a new thing to hear the skylark in the blue above and the cattle lowing in the-meadows. I used to walk for miles and miles through the lanes towards Ewell and Epsom ; for I had never been too good a sleeper, and now that I had nothing to do and very little to think about, I found myself waking with the sun, and it was a relief to get out into the air and see him make his ascent. I had seen the sun rise often enough in the course of my wanderings ; but I had usually seen him at the end of the night—after spending the small hours in London streets, or on the railway, or down the river. It was a new thing to see him at the beginning of my day, fresh from my bed and bath ; and it was a still newer thing to be free from restraint, and to be released from responsibility, no longer to feel that every step in life was a step in the dark—that guilt and innocence, honour and dishonour, life and liberty, were the counters in the game which I was winning or losing—no longer to be incessantly on the alert to check erring comrades, to restrain excess of zeal, and to teach the value of truth to men who were inclined to think they could get along better without it.

My good wife accused me of being restless, and not appreciating the comforts of a retired life, or

being sufficiently grateful to Providence for having given me enough to live upon and pay forty-five pounds a year for Hawthorn Lodge.

" My dear Charlotte Eliza, I dare say I shall get habituated to a life of idleness in time," said I. "But when a man has been working for thirty years, idleness is apt to pall. I confess that I sometimes feel a something wanting; and I'm afraid it's Bow Street."

This inconsiderate admission of mine made the poor little wife cry, and she began to reproach herself for having withdrawn me from a profession I liked ; so I had to assure her I was very happy at Putney, and to take her for a long walk on the Common, where we saw two old gentlemen playing golf.

" There's the garden," said Charlotte Eliza; " I looked forward to your being interested in the garden."

" And so I am, my dear," says I; " but as it only takes me about twenty steps to walk round our lawn and flower-beds, that kind of interest is soon exhausted."

^ "I thought you'd work in the garden, John. People who work in their gardens never seem to have finished, or to be tired."

"Any work I did in the way of gardening would be so destructive that you would implore me to desist before I had been at it two days, Charlotte Eliza," said I; and she sighed, and said no more about the garden.

In sober truth, a life of retirement did not suit

tne. I am not what is called a domestic man. I don't bully the cook or discover cobwebs in the cornice. I have no home occupations, except reading newspapers and novels ; and though I had enjoyed both forms of literature while I was a busy man, fact and fiction lost their zest now that I was an idler.

In this frame of mind I was startled by a visitor whose appearance was as refreshing as a cold douche after a Turkish bath.

I was sitting alone in a little closet of a room at the back of the house, which my wife calls the study, but which I never look at without regretting the spaciousness of our old quarters at

Bloomsbury. It was after our early dinner, and I was smoking the pipe of meditation, having exhausted every scrap of news in four morning papers—down to the markets, although the prices of tallow, and even of mutton and beef by the carcase, could have but the mildest interest for a man whose household consisted of four people, and whose consumption of tallow and butcher's meat was very moderate. I had heard the door-bell, and the opening of the door; but as my wife has a good many visitors, and I have very few, I had scarcely noticed the fact, when the housemaid—she took the superior rank of parlour-maid in the afternoon —opened the door of my den with the grandest air, and announced Mr. Wildover.

There was no card sent in—no preliminary inquiry. The gentleman whom I had last seen in the dock at Bow Street walked calmly into my

room, and the room being only thirteen feet by eleven, was standing in front of me before I had time to think.

I laid down my pipe, and stood up, and I was face to face with the man round whose neck I had tried my best to put a rope.

" I dare say you are surprised to see me here, Mr. Faunce," he said coolly.

"I am really more surprised than I can say, sir," said I.

"You would have seen me sooner but for two circumstances. In the first place, I have been ill; and in the second place, when I was well enough to get about I found it extremely difficult to find you. The people at Bow Street seemed very unwilling to give me your address."

" Oh, you have been hovering about Bow Street, have you ? That seems a curious proceeding for a man in your circumstances. I thought a nice little trip to the Antipodes, or a tour in South America, would have been more in your line."

I had not asked him to sit down, and I was still standing. I had had a good deal of intercourse with murderers during my official career, but now I had retired into private life I meant to have as few dealings as possible with the criminal breed.

And yet I could but own to myself that this man was a remarkable specimen of that class of villain whom nobody would take for a villain. From head to foot I could see upon him no mark of the criminal character. His erect form and easy bearing, the straight and steady look of his

Mr. Faunces Record.

well-opened blue eyes, the firm yet kindly mouth, the broad forehead and finely modelled chin would have made a favourable impression anywhere and upon anybody. If ever there was a criminal who perversely degraded a form and face meant for righteousness, it was this man ; always supposing him to be the murderer I thought him, in spite of that incident of the pistol.

"As I have a good deal to say to you, I hope you will be good enough to sit down and hear me patiently," he said, seating himself in the chair opposite my own, which brought his feet and mine within eighteen inches of each other. "And if, as you were smoking when I came in, you will kindly allow me to light my pipe, we shall feel quite comfortable."

" I don't know your motive for seeking me out, Mr. Wildover," said I, "but I am bound to tell you that I have left the Criminal Investigation Department, and that I take no further interest in crime or criminals."

" Perhaps not," said he ; " but I hope you are interested in a man who has suffered cruelly through your mistake. Come, Faunce, you worked very hard the other day to make me out a murderer, and you succeeded in putting a black mark against my name that has blighted all my hopes of happiness in this life. I want you to work still harder to take that stain off my name and character. It is to be done, and you are the man to do it."

His easy manners and confident tone took me

altogether aback. I had never had to do with such a man. I had seen an innocent man in a hole often enough before to-day; but your innocent man is generally a poor creature, ready to shed tears, and all of a tremble, half out of his wits at the very idea of being suspected. This man was as firm as the Bass Rock. He ordered me to right his character.

I reminded him that I had left the Force.

" So much the better for me," he said ; " you couldn't have worked my business as I want it worked if you were still under the police authorities."

And then he told me that, without being a rich man, he had made a good bit of money in the South African gold-fields, and still owned a share in a mine at the River Diggings, where he could make more money if he cared to go back ; but he had made up his mind not to leave England till he had solved the mystery of Lisa Rayner's death.

"It may have been the most common kind of crime, though it is a mystery to us till we find the murderer. It may have been the work of some loafing scoundrel who saw me give that poor soul the notes, and lurked about and watched us, and contrived to slip into the house behind our backs while we stood talking, believing that he would have time to take the money from her before anybody was roused by the shot."

" He must have been a consummate fool to have thought that possible," said I. "A pistol fired in an inhabited house at one o'clock in the morning,

the fall of a body—enough to rouse any household from attic to cellar."

"Well, the hope of plunder seems to be the only reasonable explanation."

I took a notebook from a desk which was close at my elbow, and referred to Wildover's account of that last conversation in Dynevor Street. I saw that in this statement he said he had given Lisa Rayner the notes during their last turn in the street, and only a few minutes before he bade her good-bye at the door of No. 13.

It was, of course, quite within the range of possibility that some loafer should have seen her take this money, but for that loafer to be provided with a revolver, and to be audacious enough to follow her up to her room and shoot her in a house full of people, hoping to pocket the notes and get clear off after his victim had fallen dead on the garret floor, seemed hardly credible. In my idea of the crime, the murderer must have intended murder only, and must have trusted to rapidity of action for escape. To return to my original notion : here was a life to be suppressed, and all the murderer wanted was to suppress it.

The man fascinated me and won my confidence. There was something uncommonly winning in that handsome face, the frank manner, and the free and easy give-and-take style of a man who had lived and worked under God's open sky, caring nothing for the things which men in cities so much over-estimate—dress, dinner, furniture, society— all the tailor-made stuff that Thomas Carlyle

ridicules. Here was a man not dependent upon his tailor for style or dignity. His rough tweed trousers were kneed and turned up at the ankles; his boots were broad and clumsy ; his frieze overcoat had the marks of long wear; and yet I knew he was a gentleman.

"Well, Mr. Wildover," said I, after turning the business over in my mind, " I thought I had done with criminal investigation for ever ; but I don't mind owning this case interests me, because it is a difficult one, and I don't mind seeing what can be done in it. Not much, perhaps."

"Yes, much—everything—by a man of your experience. The man who dropped the pistol down the area was the man who murdered Lisa Rayner. You have the gunsmith who can tell you what that man was like."

"The man who dropped the pistol may not be the man who bought the pistol. It may have changed hands, you know, Mr. Wildover."

I watched his face closely as I spoke. Much as I was taken by his good looks, and pleasant manner, I was by no means convinced of his innocence. I had seen too much of pleasant-mannered murderers in my time, more particularly in the poisoning branch. There never was a better sort than Bill Palmer till he was found out. It was in Wildover's favour that his was not an arsenic case.

"Yes," said he, "true enough. The pistol may have changed hands. Anyhow, you have to find the man who dropped it down the area."

"I'll do my best, sir. But before I begin I am bound to remind you that you have not been tried and acquitted—and that you might be arrested again to-morrow if any further and stronger evidence came up against you. It might therefore be more to your interest—safer—for you to drop out of this part of the world, and—let sleeping dogs lie."

"I am not afraid of any dogs that you or anybody else can rouse, Mr. Faunce. Don't concern yourself about my safety, but try to clear my name of the foul stain your official skill has put upon it."

I told him my idea of the murder was the putting away of an individual whose existence was a source of trouble and danger to somebody else ; and I asked him to tell me all he knew of Mrs. Rayner's history, omitting no detail that he could remember. He replied with apparent candour, and told me the story of her life before he met her—as she had told it to him—and during the years they spent in poverty together. , There was nothing in this story to suggest a vendetta; no hint of dark secrets or of blackmailing. The Austrian seducer had disappeared from the scene. The father seemed to have made no effort to reclaim his lost daughter, yet the middle-aged seducer and the unprincipled father were the only discoverable personages linked with the woman's story, if she had told Wildover the whole of that story. But there is the likelihood that a woman who has gone wrong—like a man

Rough Justice.

who has got into debt—will always keep back something, and that perhaps the biggest item in the history, or in the list of creditors. I was inclined to believe that in this case all had not been disclosed, and that in the something that had been kept back lay the clue to the mystery.

She had told him the story of her girlhood in outline only. He did not know her father's name, or the name of the Viennese banker under whose protection she had lived at the West End of London. He did not know of any human being whose acquaintance she had made during her season of prosperity, or the address of the house in which she had lived. He had forbidden her to dwell upon that unhappy past. It hurt him too much to hear her talk of her fall.

"You see, I loved her at that time as dearly as if she had been my wedded wife, and her dishonour was my dishonour. She had been a devoted helpmeet to me. I wanted to respect her. I hate, now that she is in her grave, to repeat the confession which she made to me when she was recovering from a dangerous illness."

" No doubt! But if you didn't tell me all you can I shouldn't have the slightest chance of unravelling the mystery," I said. "As it is, I must tell you plainly that I consider the odds against me about a hundred to one; but I am a man of leisure now, and by way of filling in some of the spare hours of my life"—I didn't tell him that I had about ten hours to spare per diem—" I don't

mind trying what my long and varied experience in the C. I. Department may enable me to do."

He thanked me; begged me to consider money no object; wanted to give me his cheque for a hundred pounds there and then ; but I told him that in the present state of things I didn't see my way to spending five shillings on his account; and so we parted, after I had asked him to call upon me that day fortnight, at the same hour. He begged me to make it that day week, but I told him that it was very unlikely I should have anything to tell him after a fortnight's looking about.

I began work with very little hope of success, but I was glad to have something to do and to think about outside my garden at Hawthorn Lodge. I was heartily tired of watching the tulips slowly, and, as it seemed to me, reluctantly, coming out of their green sheaths, and of wondering whether the standard rose trees which had been pruned almost out of existence would really justify the skilled gardener, and break out into branch and bloom before midsummer. Frankly I was delighted to see Dynevor Street again. I told my wife that I had undertaken a private matter, which, if successful, would pay me handsomely ; and I believe Charlotte Eliza was not sorry to see me occupied with business which took me out-of-doors, and left her free to dust the china ornaments, and polish the furniture, without being worried by a husband who didn't know what to do with himself.

Rough Justice.

I saw the gunsmith's assistant, and tried to get" a better description of the man who bought the pistol, but I could extract nothing beyond the impression that he was a studious-looking man, wearing blue spectacles, and his hair longer than the fashion, and that he was several inches shorter than Wildover. The difference in height would alone have been enough to show that the man was not Wildover, but the two men were in all respects unlike each other.

" Should you know the man if you saw him again ? " I asked.

" No. I remember the kind of man—but there was nothing remarkable about him— nothing that would help me to pick him out among a dozen men of the same style. I've seen them coming out of the British Museum of an evening by the score, when I lived in the Hampstead Road and used to walk home by Great Russell Street."

" Do you think the spectacles he wore were intended as a disguise ." "

" Oh dear, no ! His manner was too easy and collected for such an idea to occur to me."

Not much to be made of the gunmaker's assistant. There was only that suggestion of the purchaser's scholarly appearance—the type of man to be seen leaving the Reading-room of the British Museum any evening. I had met them often enough during my long residence in Blooms-bury, and I knew the style.

It is hardly possible for the uninitiated in criminal investigation to conceive the difficulty Mr. Faunce's Record.

of finding any person or any thing in the great ocean of London life, when once the bubble on the surface of the water has broken and vanished. I had started on a wrong scent—if Wildover was to be believed—and I had wasted my time in following a phantom, when there might have been possible opportunities of getting on the right line. I had to begin again with the scent cold ; and I own that I felt nonplussed, and that I only set to work in a dilettante spirit, and with less mental energy than I should have expended upon an acrostic in the World. It was something to do. It kept my mind busy, just as the game of cat's cradle will keep children's hands busy, and it was, I feared, about as futile an occupation.

It is needless to record my investigation step by step. It was several weeks after Wildover's first visit to Hawthorn Lodge when I made my first advance along the line on which I had been working, by the discovery that a person answering to the gun maker's description had been living in Dynevor Street at the date of the murder, and had left so shortly after as to make his removal a suspicious coincidence. I had made a house-to-house investigation of the street, and had in most instances been readily answered ; but there was one house where the people seemed very reluctant to give any information about the persons lodging there in the previous December. The landlord owned at last that he had a reason for this reticence.

" If your business has anything to do with dynamite or Nilerists, I'm not going to be mixed

up in it," he said. " Poor Mrs. Grogan has been all but ruined by that murder last Christmas. She has not been able to let her seconu floor since, or the room where the young woman was murdered, and I know she's half a year behind with her rent; and I don't want my house to be pointed at and boycotted because of some gentleman dynamiter as may have lodged in it—once upon a time."

I assured him that the inquiries I was making had no relation to dynamiters or Nihilists ; and I also gave him to understand that it would be the worse for him if he refused to answer my questions to the very best of his ability. I may add that this was a bit of bluff on my part, as I was assuming my authority of former times, before I retired from the C. I. Department. The effect was instantaneous, for Mr. Durfin's wife, a decent body, who was present at our interview, urged him to comply with my request. The house was a lodging-house, tidily furnished, and as clean as a London house can be ; and it is wonderful what miracles of freshness and cleanliness a hard-working, active woman can achieve, in spite of sea coal and November fogs. Without being directly opposite No. 13, the windows commanded a full view of that house, and a watcher at the window on this side of the way would have been able to identify any one going out or in at Mrs. Grogan's door.

Now for my landlord and landlady's information. Once having relented, they were both eager to tell me all that they could.

Mr, Faunces Record.

They had had a gentleman lodger on their second floor from the 14th of November to the 26th of December, and just such a gentleman as the subject of my inquiry—very studious, very quiet and retiring, spending the greater part of his days out-of-doors—mostly, they believed, in the Reading-room at the British Museum, as he had told them he chose these rooms in order to be near the Museum—and sitting up late at night reading and writing.

He had taken no meal at home, except his roll and coffee in the morning. He had had his own machine for making tea—a Sadover, Mrs. Durfin called it—a Russian machine, "named after the great Russian battle," interjected the landlord.

"There never was a less troublesome lodger. He had his latch-key, and let himself in of a night, as quiet as a ghost. He paid his rent and all extras to the moment. He gave his name as Longman—no Christian name. He received no letters and had no visitors—a most retired gentleman."

Did this lodger wear spectacles ? Yes, always. He was a great sufferer with his eyes—had burnt off his eye-lashes while making a chemical experiment, he told Mrs. Durfin, which admission, with other things—the Russian Sadover, for instance— had made them suspect him of being a dynamiter. He had just the quiet way of a conspirator biding his time—yet quite the gentleman through it all —and must have been at the top of the tree, and one as gave his orders for others to carry out. ♦ 187

They had looked at his kiggage, and they were sure there wasn't an ounce of dynamite in that. A spare suit of clothes and half a dozen shirts was all he brought to the house, and those things were all arranged in the chest of drawers, and everything the pink of neatness. He brought a few books, a writing-case, and a packet of foolscap. He was a great one for scribbling.

Had he left any papers—anything overlooked about his rooms .-•

Nothing except the torn papers in the waste basket ; those had been used for lighting fires directly after he left.

" Did he give you any reference when he came .""

" He gave us a week's rent, and that, with his respectable appearance, was quite satisfactory."

Asked his age, Mr. Durfin guessed it at thirty. Mrs. Durfin gave him five or six years more. He was not bald, but his hair was very thin at the top of his head, straight, dark-brown hair, worn rather long.

Asked to describe him as precisely as they could, Mr. and Mrs. Durfin furnished me with these details.

Height, say five feet nine or ten. Hands and feet small, and particularly well shaped. His boots was a pleasure to black, Mr. Durfin added. Any maker's name in the boots \'7d No. Nose aquiline, small nostrils, chin very square and firm— a chin you would never try to impose upon, even if you was given to imposing, which we Durfins

Mr. Faunces Record.

are not. Complexion pale, nondescript, neither fair nor dark—what Mr. Durfin would call the London complexion.

Any scar, peculiarity of expression, or distinguishing mark about the man ? None,

Did they remember the manner of his leaving their house on the 26th of December > Yes, so far as there was anything to remember. He went out early on Christmas Day, and was absent all day, returning in a hansom before midnight. Mr. Durfin noticed that he was in evening dress when he came home, though he had left the house in his usual dark-grey suit. He went away with his portmanteau in a four-wheeler early on Boxing Day. Mr. Durfin heard him tell the cabman, " Waterloo—loop line," and concluded that he was going out of town from that station. He had told them nothing of his plans, only asking for his account half an hour before he left. He paid a week's rent in lieu of notice.

The second floor had been let to a married couple and baby from Manchester since Mr. Longman left; but these had gone back to the North a fortnight previously, so the rooms were empty, and I was welcome to look at them.

I was sorry to find the rooms had been let—for this fact, taken in conjunction with Mrs, Durfin's cleanly habits, made it very unlikely that so much as a stray inch of paper left by Mr. Longman remained upon the premises. My experience has shown me that people of the criminal class, however careful to remove all compromising material,

Rough Justice.

will almost inevitably leave something in any house they have occupied ; but in rooms turned out and cleaned, and occupied, and turned out and cleaned again after that occupation, I could scarcely hope to find any trace of a departed lodger. I went up to the second floor, however, and used my eyes and my fingers to their utmost power.

My eyes were quick enough to notice an old-fashioned bureau chest of drawers with a sloping lid, which I lifted, displaying that arrangement of small drawers and pigeon-holes which our ancestors loved.

" Did your last lodgers make use of this nice old piece of furniture ^ " I asked.

"Not they, sir," replied Mrs. Durfin, who had accompanied me, being better at stairs than her husband. " I don't believe they wrote half a dozen letters while they were with us. They were always gadding. They came up to see the sights of London, and it was theatres and music-'alls night after night, and supper wanted afterwards ; and it was Crystal Palace and Tussauds or Tower every day. Mr. Longman, he wrote at the desk all the time he was here, and a fine state the mornogany was in with ink when he left it."

" And you cleaned it carefully, I have no doubt."

" I did all that beeswax and turpentine and elber grease could do," she said ; and I hated the woman for her uncompromising cleanliness.

"And you found no papers in any of these

drawers ?" I asked, pulling them all out, one after another, as I talked, and peering into the recesses and secret places of the bureau.

Mrs. Durfin coughed, and paused before replying. One look at her told me that she had found something ; but I went on with my examination of the drawers and pigeon-holes, pretending to be interested in the bureau as a piece of furniture.

Mrs. Durfin coughed again.

"Me and Durfin don't want to be mixed up in no Nilerist cases," she said. " It's difficult enough to make a living in a street that keeps steadfastly going down, without that."

I assured her that I was no Nihilist hunter. I had certainly a motive in seeking information about Mr. Longman; but it had to do with property, and not Nihilism. The good woman's brow lightened at this, and she told me that if she had known I was a respectable family solicitor she would have been more free with me, and on that she produced a very ancient purse from her capacious pocket, and from this purse extracted a small leaf of paper, evidently torn from a notebook, which leaflet she solemnly handed to me.

" That was the only scrap of paper that I found, high or low, after Mr. Longman left," she said ; "and my husband thinks the writing on it is a Nilerist's cypher. Neither me nor him can make out a letter of it."

The cypher was the common, or Pitman, shorthand, and I assured Mrs. Durfin that there was nothing of a treasonable or alarming character in

the document, which I should be glad to keep, if she would allow me,

I slipped a sovereign into her willing hand as I made the request.

" I think you might make it two sovereigns, sir, seeing that it's the only paper as he left, and may lead to valuable information."

" Oh, Mrs. Durfin, what a woman of business you are!" said I, as I gave her the second sovereign, and went off with my find.

It wasn't much, but it was something. I carried it straight to a type-writing office, where there are a lot of clever girls working under a very clever young lady, some of them well up in shorthand. They know me at the office, and are ready and willing to work for me.

" I am coming back for that paper and a typewritten copy of it in half an hour," said I.

"You'd better wait in my room," said the Principal.

"I never wait anywhere, my dear young lady. I can do something better with my time than waiting in a room, if it's only watching the faces in the street."

The copy and the original document were in an envelope ready for me when I went back to the office.

Two pages of widely spaced type-writing— neither beginning nor end—a fragment of an essay or a lecture, I could not tell which—but the indications pointed to oral delivery. Subject, the everlasting working man, his educational opportunities and possibilities of improvement. So much for the one trace the lodger had left behind him. And now what did I think of Mr. Longman as a promising subject for further investigation ? Not much, assuredly. The facts that he had worn spectacles that hid his eyes, and that his description answered fairly enough to the gunmaker's description of his customer, were something, but still not much. Spectacles are so common—even the blue disguising goggle—and all descriptions of figure and appearance are so vague. The circumstance of Longman's departure on Boxing Day was curious ; more especially as that departure was evidently unpremeditated, or the usual notice would have been given. Yet a studious man, with his head in the clouds, might omit such notice, from sheer forgetfulness.

The date of his hiring the lodgings coincided very nearly with the date of the purchase of the pistol. That fact was also curious ; but I have seen too many curious coincidences to attach much importance to them. Altogether the indications pointing to Longman as the murderer were of the most shadowy; but so far I had been able to find nothing better, and I was inclined to follow these feeble lights across the quagmire of the unknown.

The notes of lecture, essay, or book might lead to my identification of the writer, and the man once within my ken it might be possible to make such a retrospective investigation of his life as would reveal a connecting link between him

and the murdered woman. My first business, therefore, was to trace the forty-seven lines of type-writing ; and this was by no means a hopeful business, since it was likely enough that these lines formed part of some unpublished essay or unspoken lecture, and belonged to that vast mass of written thought which never finds a public expression.

CHAPTER X.

CHUMS.

Very bitter was the slow onward progress of the year to Arnold Wentworth alone in London, that stony wilderness which was to his mind lonelier than the great Karroo, more desolate than the lion-trodden sands of Central Africa. He was idle and aimless, waiting for the solution of the mystery that had overshadowed his life, and darkened his dream of the future. Oh, that look of Mary's, that altered face, that agony of unbelief in him! He had left her full of scorn and anger; but afterwards, in the long hours of brooding upon the same miserable theme, he had owned to himself that she was scarcely to be blamed for her want of faith. The web of circumstances encircled him too closely. He hated London, and his purposeless life there, and longed for Johannesburg and the mines ; the fever of the auction mart in the miner's city ; the rough companionship upon the Rand ; the loud talk of mixed nationalities, sitting about under the trees, smoking and drinking in the

starlit evening; the life that was all labour ^nd hope, and the luxury of rest after labour.

And London after this: the burning pavements, the narrow horizons, the dust-laden trees and scorched grass of Metropolitan parks ; the aching sense of loneliness and desertion, of being a Pariah, outside the lives that were going on around him— lives full of action and gladness. He sat in the park for two or three afternoons to enjoy the sunlight and flowers, and he heard people talking at his elbow, a jargon which he understood a little less than the language of Bechuanaland or the Hottentot click. Something he knew of those African tongues from the talk of native workmen in the Compound, but of this modish slang nothing.

He was not rich in the sense that the miner millionaire is rich, but he had made money and invested it in the mine, and he had an income that enabled him to live after his modest fashion, and which would justify marriage with a wife of modest pretensions. He took a fourth-floor flat in a newly built house on the Thames Embankment, between Waterloo and Blackfriars Bridges, He liked the river view and the southern exposure. There was more sunshine here, he thought, than anywhere in the smoky wilderness ; and he liked the river traffic. He felt utterly stranded and alone in that river-side aerie ; but he had no inclination for society of any kind while the shadow of Mary Freeland's unbelief still rested upon him.

One of his first acts after his interview with

Chums.

Mary Freeland had been to sacrifice that fine tawny beard which had given such character to his face. It was with a clean-shaved countenance that he entered upon residence in his new rooms, and the people of the house knew him only under that aspect. Comparing his face in the glass with the rough sketches of the accused that had appeared in the evening papers, he thought that there was little to apprehend from anybody's memory of those rough and ready outline drawings, which, for his good fortune, had not been like enough to be recognized by his family, or any of his English friends. Even should the murderer himself have kept those illustrated pages, he would scarcely identify the smooth shaven face of the living man with those sketchy suggestions of a face in which the beard had been much exaggerated.

The change in his complexion, as the South African bronze gradually faded and left his skin of its original Anglo-Saxon fairness, was almost as marked as the change effected by the razor.

So far his visits to the little villa at Putney had resulted only in disappointment. Faunce had nothing to tell him, and was altogether discouraging,

" I think you must consider the story closed with your dismissal," he said. "The time that was lost while we were following up a false scent is time that can never be recovered. Suppose I were to hear of a man, who, from circumstances of time and place, might be the man we want,

Rough Justice.

how am I to connect that man with the murder? The threads are all dropped or broken. I'm afraid I'm wasting my time, which is not of much consequence, as I have time enough and to spare, and wearing out your patience, which is worse."

"You have found such a man," Arnold exclaimed, all eagerness and fire in a moment.

Mr. Faunce described his investigation of the Durfin lodgings, and produced the type-written copy of the lodger's shorthand notes.

" I have given a duplicate copy to a man I know who is shorthand reporter for one of the morning papers, and who might be able to identify the writer of those notes—always supposing that they form part of an essay or a lecture that has been published and reported," said Mr. Faunce.

" Yes, yes, it ought to be easy to find the writer from such an indication. Longman was an assumed name, no doubt."

"I don't know about that. We have nothing against this man but a coincidence—the mere fact that he left his lodging within thirty-six hours of the murder. We have no more right to think him a murderer than the Durfins had to think him a Nihilist."

" Oh yes, we have. His living in that place— in a secret manner."

*' Why secret ? How secret ?"

"Why, the fact that no mortal ever visited him there would show that he was hidine."

" Not necessarily. He may be a student, of solitary habits."

Chum$.

" There is no man so solitary as to be without acquaintance—to live in a house for six weeks without being visited by any one. And then, the spectacles—the same kind of spectacles which the gunmaker described. A disguise—evidently a disguise."

" All that would go for nothing, Mr. Wildover. If I could put my hand upon this Longman today I have no evidence against him ; and I see no probability of our ever finding any evidence against him, or against any one else. The murder was a clean piece of work. It was easy enough to connect you with the crime. There were the bank-notes—there was the suggestion of motive—conjectural, of course ; but to connect any one else ? Hopeless, I fear."

Arnold went away depressed and disheartened. Should he never be able to prove to that crael girl how shamefully she had misjudged him ." It was of Mary he thought—Mary, who had become all the world to him during that happy voyage from summer to winter—ah! how typical in its climatic changes of the hard fate that he was to find on his native soil!

He was strolling along the Embankment two or three days after his interview with Faunce, when he came face to face with Wilmot Armstrong, his late partner on the Rand, whom he had last seen at Heidelberg.

He would have crossed the road to avoid the man if he could. He did not want to see in another once friendly face the cruel change that

Rough Justice.

he had seen in Mary Freeland. But it was impossible, to escape the meeting. They had almost run against each other.

" Why, this is lucky, old chap!" exclaimed Armstrong. " I have been wanting to see you ever since I landed, but I didn't know where to look for you in this crowded ant-heap."

" 1 wonder you wanted to see me," Arnold answered gloomily. "A man who has been accused of murder is not quite the most eligible acquaintance."

" What, Arnold! Did you suppose I should think any the worse of you for your bad luck last Christmas." You couldn't be such a muff as to think that I could believe you guilty, if the evidence against you had been twice as strong."

Something like a sob choked Arnold's first attempt at a reply ; he turned away from his friend, and stood looking at the river for a minute or so.

"When I came out of prison I found that, though I had been practically acquitted, there were people who still thought me a murderer," he said at last. " It would have been only natural for you to think as badly of me. I suppose you read all about the murder .-• "

"And I suppose I remembered how j-ou and I had slept under the same roof, and lived and worked side by side for two years, and how you nursed me when I was sick, and lectured me when I took too much liquor, and were brother and father to me in one. I suppose that experience would go for something when I saw my

Chtt77tS.

old chum brought before the Beak on suspicion of a cowardly murder. If it had been a plucky, open-hearted murder, between man and man— a scuffle, an oath, a shot—I might have thought my old chum had gone wrong; but the murder of an inoffensive woman ? No, Arnold, I knew that wasn't in your line."

"Thank God," said Arnold, with a deep-drawn breath, " Now I know there is such a thing as friendship in the world."

"Why, you stupid old duffer, what else did you expect ?" asked Armstrong, indignantly,

" Men are better than women, after all," Arnold said to himself, as he walked silently by his friend's side.

This was the first of friendly companionship that Arnold had known since he left the police court. He had talked of Longman's isolation as a suspicious circumstance, but his own solitude in his riverside chambers had been as complete. It was a new sensation to walk the streets in friendly talk with a light-hearted companion. He and Armstrong dined together at the Savoy, and the gaiety and brightness of a popular restaurant afforded a new sensation to the man who had lived alone, brooding over his troubles.

" Did they talk of me—of the newspaper reports —at the Rand \'7d" he asked, later, when he and Armstrong were sitting in the balcony outside his rooms, smoking, in the mild stillness of an evening late in May.

"Why, of course they did, and they said it was

a jolly shame. Come, old fellow, don't let us talk any more of that business. What you have to do is to forget that it ever happened."

"I can never do that, not even if I find the man who killed her," answered Arnold, "Think what a memory it is for a man to carry about with him. She was in tears when I left her. I think I must have been hard and cruel, though I tried to be kind, and meant to make her future life as easy as money could make it. I had been too ready to tell her that I had fallen in love with another woman, and that my happiness depended upon being free from old ties. She seemed heart-broken when we parted ; and then, within a few minutes, she was lying in her wretched garret, brutally murdered. Do you suppose that I can forget that, Wilmot.""

"You must do your best, old chap. And now, what are you going to do with your life ?"

" I don't know."

" Have you made it up with your governor ?"

" No."

"And do none of your people know your assumed name of Wildover ?"

" Luckily for them, they are spared the knowledge of their disgrace."

"And you arc not going back to the Rand ?"

" I think not."

"Then, my dear fellow, all you have to do is to forget that such a man as Wildover ever lived. Henceforth you are Arnold Wentworth."

" That's easily said. I am known in this house

as Wentworth. You can't suppose I would stick to the name of Wildover after it had been dragged through the Police Court and the newspapers. And now that's enough of me and my gloomy-story. Tell me about yourself and your luck since we parted."

This inquiry started Arnold's old friend upon talk that lasted till midnight. He had done well, wonderfully well—had sold his holding in the mine at a large profit, and had come home, hoping to marry a certain distant cousin, who had promised to wait for him when he was down upon his luck.

The assurance of Armstrong's friendship gave Arnold new life and hope. Ever since his interview with Mary Freeland, in the sunless South Kensington drawing-room, he had thought of himself as a creature under a ban, as low in the social scale as a pariah dog; and he had concentrated all his energies upon the task he had set for himself, and which might be indeed an impossible task—hopeless as the rolling of heavy stones up a hill whose summit he was never to reach. But after his meeting with his old companion he began to think better of life, to bear his troubles with a new patience, and even to recover something of that fine, frank outlook which had been clouded over by too much gloomy thought.

One effect of this change was a growing desire to see Mary Freeland again ; and, moved by this desire, he consumed a good many of his idle

hours roaming the streets and squares of South Kensington, or hanging about the entrance to the art school, in the hope of meeting the girl he loved.

He saw her several times, but she was walking with a fellow-pupil, and he watched her unobserved from the opposite side of the road, and noted that she was not looking her best*, and not looking happy. His keen eye could perceive the change even at that distance. The cheeks that had been so plump and peach-like on the homeward voyage were now pinched and hollow ; the eyes had lost their joyous light; and the step, once so quick and free, was slow and languid. Had the air of South Kensington wrought this change, or did remorse for her unkindness to him count for something ? At last he took heart of grace, and having seen her part from her girl-friend, crossed the road, and threw himself in her way.

She was walking home alone, having succeeded in convincing Mrs. Tresillian-Smith that the modern girl did not require to be protected by an upper housemaid in so eminently respectable a neighbourhood as the Cromwell Road.

" The worst that could happen would be for one of those gentlemen tea-touts to introduce himself to me, and beg me to give him an order for some new company's tea," said Mary; " and as for Rebecca, she is far more attractive than I am."

Mrs. Smith was fain to admit that the housemaid in her outdoor apparel was a more conspicuous

figure than the student; so Mary, dressed very quietly in her black frock and straw hat, was allowed to go to and fro unchaperoned, and thus Arnold was able to waylay her and walk by her side along the sun-baked spaciousness of South Kensington.

He thought she would try to avoid him ; but to his infinite relief she held out her hand, and smiled at him with the friendly look of happier days.

" I am so very glad to see you," she said in a voice that trembled a little.

" Really ? I hardly hoped that."

" Oh, I know, I know how shamefully I behaved. I deserved all you said of me in your cruel letter. But oh, Mr. Wentworth, I think I must have been out of my mind. People had talked and talked till I let myself be persuaded against my own will. And I remembered your agitation at the Briery—and I forgot that having known the unhappy creature"—here she grew crimson and then pale again, and nearly broke down—"it was natural you should be distressed on reading of her dreadful death. I was a blind fool to doubt you—to think—for one instant— that Bee's brother—dear Mrs. Wentworth's son —could—possibly "

Here the fast-flowing tears stopped all speech. Mary felt that she was crying in the face of South Kensington ; and that if by evil chance she were so beheld by any member of Mrs. Smith's visiting circle she would never more be allowed

to walk those streets unaccompanied. So, to Arnold's surprise, she made a rapid rush across the road, and ran into the Natural History Museum, Arnold following her.

Here, seated in one of the rooms, she recovered calmness, and was able to resume the conversation.

" Well, Mary, it is, of course, a great comfort to me to know that you have altered your mind as to the case against me, and that you are at least as indulgent as the Magistrate who let me go; but that doesn't alter my determination to find the real murderer, and to convince you that I had no act or part in Lisa Rayner's death. I am much happier for the thought that I may still possess your friendship."

" And you will forgive me ?" pleaded Mary. " Oh, please tell me that I am forgiven. I have been so miserable ever since I received your letter. When I had read that letter I saw how blind I had been. It seemed as if a thick black curtain was plucked aside, and I saw you in the clear light of truth; and I hated myself for having let other people put ideas into my head. I have not known a peaceful hour since, and I have just drudged at my horrid antique studies—drudged day after day, in the hope of forgetting."

" Well, Mary, there is nothing to forget now, so I hope you will be happy again, and find a pleasanter occupation than soiling your pretty fingers with black lead."

"Will you come home with me and be introduced to Mrs. TreslUian-Smith ? She really is very kind and good and I have been such a wet blanket. She thought I was fretting for my aunt's death ; and I didn't like to undeceive her. Will you come .'"

"As far as your door, Mary, but no further. I am not in the mood for making new friends."

" Then that means that, although you pretend to have forgiven me, I am not to see you again."

" Not till I have cleared my character effectually, Mary; which can only be done when the real criminal is found."

" He will never be found. How can you be so mad as to think it.-' He has left no trace—a lunatic, perhaps, or a burglar, steeped in crime. Who knows \'7d He will never be traced. And is all your life to be sacrificed \'7d Arnold, you do not believe that there is one lingering shadow of doubt in my mind ?"

" I am glad to believe there is not, my dear; but I have my own self-respect to consider. I must be a free man—bound to no one—cherished by no one—till that stain is lifted from my character."

"And how about your poor mother? Is her son to be living so near her, and is she to be made none the happier by his company ? I know how dearly she loves you."

"And you know how dearly my father does not love me. Langton Park is no home for me, Mary. Before this trouble came upon me I had the dream of another home—a home of my own making.

Rough Justice.

But that is all over now ; and if ever I succeed in righting myself it may be too late for that old dream to be realized."

Mary made no reply. Words were so near tears with her to-day, and she did not want to cry any more, or to appear before the Smiths with red eyes.

"We had better say good-bye at the corner of the Gardens," she said, after a silence of some minutes, "if you are not going to be introduced."

And so at the corner of that sunless street which called itself Hexton Gardens, they clasped hands, and said good-bye.

Arnold stood and watched Mary Freeland vanish into the afternoon shadow along the dim perspective of Corinthian porches and projecting windows.

Other Lives,

CHAPTER XI.

OTHER LIVES.

It was a long time before Wilmot Armstrong could persuade his old chum to leave his solitude in those quiet rooms by the river, and share in the various distractions which London ofifers to unencumbered youth theatres, music-halls, suburban race meetings, boating excursions on the upper reaches of the Thames, quiet little dinners at Greenwich, with an after-dinner cigar in the summer gloaming.

Wilmot had come back to his native country with a keen appetite for all these pleasures, and he wanted his old friend to join in them ; but it was only after his interview with Mary Freeland that Arnold shook off his gloomy spirits and consented to do a round of the theatres, and to take a week-end holiday at Maidenhead. There was indeed no reason that two idle men should choose the end of the week, when all the hard workers were crowding the riverside hotels, save to escape from the horror of those London Sundays which had weighed heavily on Arnold's dejected spirits.

Rough Justice.

"I felt so wretched all the week that nobody would suppose Sunday could add a darker shade to my misery," he told Wilmot, "but it did. When I woke in the grey morning and heard the bells ringing for an early service I just turned my face to the wall and groaned aloud, as if I had been Job."

" But you're as right as the mail now, old chap," replied Wilmot. "You've cheered up wonderfully during this last week, just as I was beginning to doubt the agreeable influence of my society."

"Your society has been the saving of me, Will."

"Ah, but there has been something else. The cure was sudden."

Yes, the cure had been wrought by a look from a woman's truthful eyes, the confiding pressure of a woman's hand, a look and touch that told him he was loved, that however hardly Mary Freeland had used him on that bitter day of his release, she was now his to claim when he would. She would wait for him, he thought, wait and go on loving him even if it cost him years to take the stain from his character.

Here was a case in which a girl might fairly be asked to wait for her lover. She was rich, and could live her own life. She was not pining in poverty, dying of the dulness of a rural vicarage, worried by anxious parents, a drudge for younger brothers and sisters. Life had laid itself out very pleasantly for Mary Freeland.

The fragment of essay or speech found in the

Other Lives.

lodging-house had not been traced to its source, in spite of Faunce's efforts. He had enlisted the sub-editor and reporters of a city paper in the search ; but the most careful examination of files of newspapers had been barren of result. Faunce's friend the sub-editor opined that the fragment was part of a lecture the few sentences had the bluntness and strong ring of language intended for oral delivery.

"The man who wrote those lines is a Socialist, but not a member of the working classes," said the Editor. " I'm afraid we must give it up, Faunce. There are hundreds of Socialistic lectures delivered in London that never see print, and any number of meetings that are not reported by so much as a paragraph. I've had all the popular daily papers of November and December gone through for any mention of a lecture likely to include those lines, without result."

Arnold groaned aloud when Faunce repeated these words of the Editor's. He had a copy of the fragment in his pocket-book. He knew the strong, rough-hewn phrases by heart ; and it seemed to him a hard thing that the highly trained criminal investigator could fail to find the man whose hand had written those words. Faunce smiled at his impatience.

"The words may never have been spoken in public," he said. " Who knows \'7d The sentences may have been jotted down at random, while the thought was red-hot. A short-hand writer has a tremendous advantage in that way. He can pin

Rough Justice.

his thought upon paper before it escapes him. The turn of a sentence will slip out of a quick thinker's mind before he can fix it in long-hand. Well, sir, I've done all that is to be done in this direction, and I'm afraid we shall make nothing of the lodger in Dynevor Street."

Arnold thanked him, and again offered to write a cheque.

" No, no, sir ; keep your cheque-book in your pocket, if you please. I'm not a poor man, and I don't want to be paid for my failures," said Faunce.

"But I've caused you to waste your time."

" I've wasted it more to my liking than I should have done in the garden; and the plants and flowers are doing well, which they wouldn't have been if I had had a hand in their management. Wait till I get on to a better line, Mr. Wildover. It will be time enough to think of remuneration when I have succeeded."

Arnold lost all hope of ultimate success, and began to waver in his resolve to keep aloof from the girl he loved.

Why should he be too proud to be happy ." She had sued to him for pardon, had told him that she believed in him, had almost told him she loved him. He had but to seize the golden opportunity, and she would be his loving wife.

Yes, but when the morning of love was spent, in the dull afternoon of life, if her heart grew colder, £is women's hearts do sometimes grow, chilled by the bleak wind of years, what if old

Other Lives.

fears should revive, and she should begin to doubt and wonder, and he should see in her eyes that the mystery of Lisa's death was coming like a shadow between them ? Would not that be hard to bear ?

And while he was longing to jump into the first prowling hansom that crept along the kerb, and drive to Hexton Gardens, he had to endure Wilmot Armstrong's expatiations upon the young lady to whom he was engaged, and finally had to consent to be taken to afternoon tea with the young lady's people.

It was a long time before even friendship and gratitude combined could bring him to this point. The London season was waning, and the planes and sycamores on the embankment were shabby with the dust and grime of a London summer, when he put on a tall hat and carried a pair of light gloves, to walk through the shabby streets between the Strand and Bloomsbury.

"It's rather dreadful for Ida to live in Russell Square," said Wilmot, apologetically, when they were halfway through Endell Street.

" If Russell Square is anything like this it must be dreadful."

"Oh, but it ain't, not a bit. Don't you know Russell Square t"

" I know nothing in this neighbourhood, except Dynevor Street. That got itself imprinted pretty deep on my memory, you see. I remember this street, too, faintly. Lisa and I walked this way after we left the theatre. Yes, it was along here

Rough Justice.

—a mild winter night, soft and grey. I remember what she was saying as we passed that building, and her face as she looked up at me in the moonlight. Do you know what that feeling is, Wilmot, the feeling of not having acted fair and square to some one who is dead—of having done something, or left something undone ? It gnaws like ten thousand rats. Well, don't ever give yourself that pain."

" Dear old chap, I know you wanted to do the best you could for her."

"No, no, I didn't, Will. I wanted to do the best I could for myself. I was sorry for her, and I was grateful to her for the love she bore me; but my love for her was dead."

" What ought you to have done, then Iarry her without caring for her—make a martyr of yourself, for her to find it out afterwards, and be miserable ?"

"God knows! She is gone, and the heart I wounded that night can be healed by no kindness of mine. Perhaps there is a world where she thinks of me and forgives me."

" Arnold, we are close to the square, and I want you to look your brightest."

"Well, I won't be drearier than I can help. I'll sun myself in your Ida's beauty."

"Oh, but she is not beautiful. No, no, that's too big a word. She is only—inexpressibly nice ; and she has a perfect figure."

His tone was apologetic to timidity. Arnold remembered how he had raved about his divinity

Other Lives.

in the summer nights, as they sat in the balcony, smoking meditative pipes, and watching the star-shine on housetops and river.

" Her father is a philanthropist," pursued Wilmot. " That is why they live in Russell Square."

" As how ?"

" The houses are large, you see, and rents much lower than in Mayfair. The rooms do for committee meetings, and deputations, and tea-parties for the working classes, and that kind of thing ; and that is about all Mr. and Mrs. Borrodaile care for."

"Is Borrodaile a Socialist?" Arnold asked eagerly.

"Socialist—no, no, a philanthropist."

" Isn't it pretty much the same thing "i They both affect a monstrous interest in the working man, and both would like to put a knife into their superiors."

"Nothing of that sort about the Borrodailes. Here we are."

Rough Justice.

CHAPTER XII.

NINETEENTH-CENTURY CRUSADERS,

Mr. Borrodaile's house was one of the largest in Russell Square. The doorsteps were spotless, the windows were clean, but there were no flower-boxes no strivings after prettiness.

The butler had a severe countenance ; the hall was business-like, and might have belonged to an insurance office ; the dark red Brussels carpet on the stone stairs had been worn threadbare by the tread of serious middle age; the spacious drawing-rooms were furnished in the early Victorian manner; rosewood tables and chiffoniers, rosewood chairs with red-silk cushions ; red-silk curtains, whereof the deep festoons and heavy fringes seemed carefully planned to exclude light and air. There was a little third room which looked like a concession to modernity and youth, and which was indeed Ida Borrodaile's boudoir ; and in this sanctuary Arnold was introduced to a tall, fair-haired girl, with a long neck and a slim waist, and just pretty enough to appear a goddess to the man who loved her.

Ninetecnth-ccntiiry Cmsaders.

"We are going to have tea here," said Ida, "before the meeting. There will be tea for the world in general afterwards."

"Meeting?" echoed Arnold. "What meeting ?"

" Haven't you been told about it 1 Oh, Wilmot, how shocking of you to trap Mr. Wentworth into one of father's prosy meetings" shaking a reproving finger at her sweetheart. " They are all as good as gold," she went on, explaining the case to Arnold ; " but they make speeches, and speeches are always prosy—aren't they, mother ?" addressing herself to a languid lady, in a pale-grey tea-gown, who crept quietly into the room at this juncture, and was installed in her easy-chair and built round with small satin pillows, which, being of a downy and slippery nature, kept falling out of the chair with every movement of the languid lady, who was a professional invalid, and who acknowledged her daughter's introduction of Mr. Wentworth with the air of a sufferer for whom even that trifling exertion was a painful effort.

Nobody ever remembered hearing Mrs. Borro-daile own to feeling even tolerably well, and no doctor had ever been able to discover the exact nature of Mrs. Borrodaile's malady ; but there were those among her friends of long years who suspected that the lady had resorted to chronic ill-health as the only practicable mode of escape from the weariness of drawing-room meetings and philanthropic labours.

"Your father's speeches are always full of

Interest, upon whatever subject he speaks, my dear," Mrs, Borrodaile said, with dignity.

" It's all very well for you to admire his eloquence, mummy dear. You ain't obliged to hear him," retorted Ida. " I know father speaks well, and to the point; but Lord Hildyard is just a shade prosy sometimes. I think even Lady Violet must feel that."

" I hope Lady Violet knows how to appreciate her father, who is a saint on earth."

" Oh, I know how much he has done—and that he spends almost all his income on the poor ; but even a saint might be boring, you know, mother dearest."

" I take the keenest interest in my husband's noble efforts," said Mrs. Borrodaile, addressing herself to Arnold ; " and it is one of my saddest deprivations that I dare not be present at these delightful meetings."

Gradually, while Ida poured out the tea, and her sweetheart handed cake and bread and butter, and made himself clumsily useful, the nature of the entertainment to which he had been beguiled was explained to Arnold. It was a drawing-room meeting, to be holden in the spacious front room between five and six, the meeting of half a dozen or so of philanthropists, and as many of their friends as could be induced to come and listen to them while they held forth upon the benighted condition of the working man in a certain overcrowded slum of Lisson Grove, and discussed measures for ameliorating the present state of

things, by the introduction of educational, sanitary, and recreative sweetness and light. Subscriptions to this good work would be strenuously entreated i'n the room, and a collection was to be made on the landing as the audience departed.

"It's a shocking trap for people who don't know what a drawing-room meeting means," Wilmot said apologetically.

" People who are not interested in their fellow-creatures are hardly fit to live," said Ida, who had been brought up in an atmosphere of philanthropy.

" We shall have Mr, Greswold, who is a delightful speaker," said Mrs. Borrodaile.

"But a little apt to repeat himself," objected Wilmot. " He is rather too studied for my taste."

"That's because you have no taste, Will," answered Ida, asserting the young lady's right to snub a sweetheart. "Mr. Greswold is simply perfect as a speaker."

"And most earnest and energetic as a man. He is Lord Hildyard's right hand," said her mother.

"And I hope Lord Hildyard will reward his devotion by letting Lady Violet marry him," said Ida.

"Good as Mr. Greswold is, he would hardly be a suitable alliance for an Earl's daughter," Mrs. Borrodaile objected, with a touch of solemnity.

Mr. Borrodaile had made his fortune in commerce, and ^Irs. Borrodaile had never got over

her reverence for the peerage, and her consideration for peers and their belongings as a race apart.

The butler removed the tea-table, and they all went to the large drawing-room, where half a dozen rows of cane chairs were arranged for an audience, and where Arnold was introduced to

Lord Hildyard and Mr. Borrodaile, two large, comfortable-looking gentlemen with bald heads, white beards, and white waistcoats, who were very gracious, and hoped he would be interested in the work in hand, to which end Mr. Borrodaile gave him a descriptive leaflet written by Lord Hildyard, in which the worse than Central African state of life in Millicent Walk, Lisson Grove, was depicted in moving language.

For the remedy of these evils it was proposed to buy the whole block of tenements, with a view to their reconstruction or improvement, and to convert one of them into a mission chapel, and another into a hall of recreation and public laundry.

The room began to fill while Arnold sat in the fourth row reading his leaflet. When he had finished it, his attention wandered to a young lady and gentleman who were standing in the recess of the window nearest him, talking earnestly.

The man was of middle height, thin and wiry, and had lost all the freshness of youth. He was not bald, but his hair was thin, and he had the London pallor, and the London look of late hours

and too much brain-work. A burner of the midnight oil, Arnold thought—a journalist, perhaps. His features were refined, the nose thin and aquiline, the nostrils pinched, the upper lip long and bloodless, the chin square, and too large for perfect proportion. He had fine eyes of a dark hazel, full and large, and the eyelids and eyebrows were good and well-defined. He was a man whom some people might call handsome, and whom nobody could call bad-looking.

His clothes were of that universal and correct metropolitan fashion which invites no attention, and can offend no one.

The girl with whom he was talking was tall and distinguished looking, a brunette, with black hair brushed back from the broad full brow with a severe simplicity which suits one face in a hundred. In an age of hidden foreheads. Lady Violet could afford to leave her brow unshaded. The perfect arch of the strongly marked eyebrows gave character to the face, the small straight nose and firm mouth suggested hauteur; and it was only Lady Violet's rare smile which gave assurance of womanly gentleness and amiability. She was graver than her age and sex warranted ; and it seemed to those who knew her best as if her youth had been overshadowed by the miseries of all those people—from palsied age to starved and neglected infancy—for whom Lord Hildyard had laboured ever since she was born.

To be born in the purple—to have a hereditary right to live in the best society aristocratic England

can afford—had meant nothing for Violet. Of fashionable amusements she knew only the names, A long rural ride with her father in the dewy morning; croquet or tennis with the Vicar's daughters ; or the humdrum house-party of cousins and old friends, or a walk with the Hanoverian governess who had been with her since her mother's death, and from whose sole tuition she had learnt all she knew of the sister arts ;—these were her recreations.

Other girls of her rank in London had Herr Wolff to teach them the fiddle, or were luxuriating in pastels under Mrs, Jopling. Other girls of her rank in the country were following the hounds for a seven-hours' day, wringing the backs of a couple of high-bred hunters. Other girls had their " pals " and their tame cats, and their particular circles, and were Sylphs, or Seraphs, or anything ridiculous they liked to call themselves and revelled in the fantastic and the expensive. But Lord Hildyard's daughter had been brought up to care for none of these things. She saw them only from afar off, and wondered at them ; wondered to see young faces brilliant with painted bloom, and girls of her own age wearing frocks and hats the cost of which would have put new roofs on their father's cottages, or provided good drainage and pure water in villages that steamed and stank under the August sun.

Violet suffered from no sense of loss or deprivation. There had been no parsimony in her father's system; a liberal economy, rather, in which

nothing was stinted and nothing wasted. Her governess's salary was on the highest scale ; her French maid was the best and cleverest, and most conscientious young person, whom careful inquiry among Protestant pastors in Paris could produce. Everything Lady Violet had or wore was of the best that money could buy; and the houses in which she lived, the fine old Stuart Manor House near Beverley, and the spacious house in Hyde Park Gardens, were so bright and gracious in every detail as to dispel the idea that gloom or ugliness had any place in Lord Hildyard's philosophy of life.

" Let us do all we can to make other people's lives happy, and then we can enjoy our own," he said.

And after she had overcome the great sorrow of her mother's death, which happened before she was eleven years old, Lady Violet had enjoyed every hour of her life.She adored her father, with a worshipping love. There was no saint in the calendar whom she would have counted his superior.

" He will live in men's memories as a saint when we are all dead and forgotten," she said to Oliver Greswold one day, when he had been first praising her father, and then complaining of the opposition some of his wisest efforts had to encounter.

Greswold was socially on a much lower plane, but had been admitted to friendly and even familiar relations upon the broad claims of philanthropy. He had gradually dropped—or slid—into

Rough Justice.

the position of his lordship's unpaid private secretary, and was entrusted with matters more delicate than the daily work of the salaried clerk, whose pen was going steadily all day upon the business of charity.Greswold was a Radical, a philanthropist, and a deep thinker, intense in all he did and thought. As a Radical he went far beyond Lord Hildyard ; yet while eager to level downwards he had no enthusiastic appreciation of the upward tendencies, the possibilities of improvement, in the masses whose cause he served. He was a pessimist in politics and though he kept his opinions upon religion scrupulously to himself, Lord Hildyard feared that he was an unbeliever, and that in his creed the narrow limits of this little life bounded the possibilities of human improvement. It was always of the " race " he spoke ; seldom of individual men.The chairs were filling while Arnold sat idly watching these two, interested in both faces, suspecting that they were something more than everyday friends. He was still looking at them when a hand in a pale-grey glove touched him lightly on the sleeve, stretched from the row behind him, and a clear young voice murmured his name. He turned quickly, and discovered Mary Freeland sitting just behind him, charmingly dressed in half-mourning and looking her prettiest.

" How odd that you should be here this afternoon," she said, and then looking at a portly lady

Nineteentk-cenlury Crusader's.

in black satin who sat near her, "Mr. Wentworth, Mrs. Tresillian-Smith."

Mrs. Smith smiled, and held out an affable hand.

"I am so glad to meet you, at last, Mr. Wentworth," she said graciously. " I have met all your people when I have been staying with my sister. Mrs. Wentworth is a charming person. I only hope you are like her. Do you know Lord Hildyard ?"

" Only by his public work. I am here as a guest of Mrs. Borrodaile's. Do you know the Borrodailes ?"

"You never need ask that question," said Mary. "Mrs. Tresillian-Smith knows everybody. She gives the most delightful parties in London."

" I hope you will come to some of my parties, even if you have to scold Miss Freeland for overpraising them."

"I should be delighted only I am too much of a South African savage to trust myself at a fashionable party, I should be doing something dreadful, and you would be sorry you had asked me."

"You are a nasty, disagreeable thing," said Mary, in a shrewish whisper.

" It would take a long residence in South Africa to spoil a son of Mrs. Wentworth's," said Mrs. Smith ; and then a preliminary cough from Lord Hildyard, who was now in his place as chairman, imposed silence.

Arnold, who had not come to hear the sorrows

Rough Justice.

of a Marylebone slum, felt utterly happy in the near neighbourhood of Mary Freeland. How her eyes had sparkled with pleasure at meeting him ! How clear she made it to the meanest comprehension that he had but to ask and claim her ! Paradise—the sweet companionship, the untem-pestuous bliss of united lives, the calm home-haven for which every good man longs, could be his for the asking.

"But then some day she might round upon me and say she always knew I was a murderer," he told himself gloomily, " I should be a weak fool were I to surrender myself to that easy happiness before I have the stain off my name. I should deserve the worst that could happen to me in the future."

He looked about the room—or rather with a wise instinct looked into the corners of the room for Wilmot and his sweetheart, and presently descried them screwed into two chairs near the door, whispering to each other, and demonstratively indifferent to the proceedings.

Lord Hildyard briefly stated the class of wretchedness that he and others were anxious to ameliorate. A medical man followed, speaking at some length upon the health question ; and then a lady in nurse's uniform spoke about nursing; and after her came a speaker who took up the discourse upon the side of morality; and each had specifics for creating a clean and sinless little Eden out of an unsanitary Tophet, if the money were found for nurse and dispensary, mission room

Ninetee7ith-century Crusaders.

and night school, drain-pipes and Bibles, cisterns and infant nursery.

A buzz and whisper ran round the room as the man who had been talking to Lady Violet came to the space in front of Lord Hildyard's table, and prepared to address the audience. He received more attention even before he opened his lips than had been evoked by the highest oratorical flights of the other speakers. This fact alone would have aroused Arnold's attention, had he not been already interested by the appearance of the man.

*' I am so glad Mr. Greswold is going to speak," said Mrs. Tresillian-Smith to her neighbour. " He is a magnificent speaker."

" Too artificial for my taste," replied the gentleman she had addressed, "and he repeats himself odiously. I have heard the same burst of eloquence—the same peroration—half a dozen times."

This Greswold was an accomplished public speaker —a man who had made oratory a fine art. The low quiet voice in which he began penetrated to the furthest corner of the room. Without effort, in the easiest way, he took the audience into his confidence, and told in the plainest language of plain facts which the previous speakers had understated or ignored.

And then—passing from that unadorned statement of cruel sufferings and cruel wrongs, he went on, with a change of voice and manner that thrilled his audience, to the socialist's view of those wrongs, the socialist's scathing denunciation

Rough Justice.

of the rich and happy who know not or will not know the sin and sufferings of the helots that take all the ugliness of life upon their shoulders in ex-chanee for a crust of bread watered with tears.

His views might be exaggerated, romantic, unsound; but his w^ords held his hearers, and among the audience, mostly women, few heard him dry-eyed. There was a thrill in his deep voice which thrilled their nerves, like the silvery boyish treble in a cathedral choir.His words were burning words, Mary Freeland felt like giving up half her income; and even Irs. Tresillian-Smith, who had intended to put half-a-crown in the collecting bag, resolved on the sacrifice of a sovereign.Arnold listened, and owned to himself that speech like this was a great gift and a great power.

"If I were a good speaker I would go into Parliament to-morrow," he thought; and he wondered that this man had not found his way into the House before now.

Suddenly a phrase—a word—struck on his ear as if a gun had been fired close beside him. He leant forward, grasping the top rail of the chair in front of him with both hands, to the derangement of some fluffy decoration upon the neck of the lady seated there, who turned and rebuked his bad manners with a scowl.

He saw not the look. His eyes were fixed upon the speaker. His ears were absorbing the speaker's words.

Niiuteenth-centtiry Crusaders,

Word for word—sentence for sentence he heard the words and phrases copied from the short-hand notes found in the Dynevor Street lodging-house. Every syllable was engraved upon his memory ; he had no need to refer to the paper in his letter-case, against which his agitated heart was thumping.This was the lodger of Dynevor Street the man who had lived his silent, solitary life in a room within view of Lisa Rayner's dwelling, and who had disappeared from Dynevor Street within twenty-four hours after her death.This was the man. He wore no spectacles today ; and from the easy way in which he glanced at his notes during the statistical part of his address he was evidently not short-sighted. The clear, strong outlook of the keen grey eyes was not that of a man who now suffered, or had lately suffered, from any defect of vision. The blue spectacles worn in Dynevor Street were assumed with a motive. The man was in hiding there for some reason or other. The man was there under an assumed name.

Arnold, in his wild eagerness, could imagine, could believe in, only one reason.

The man was there as an intending murderer, lurking, hiding, waiting, and watching for the fatal opportunity.

Such things have been in Italy often enough to be commonplace. The victim has walked the streets of Rome or Florence, the narrow alleys of Venice, the arcades of Bologna, careless, unknowing ;

Rough Justice.

the assassin stalking near, the hired dagger ready to leap from his breast.

But here what motive for stealthy murder? What motive, unless that which Faunce had suggested—" a life to be suppressed."

But the reason for suppressing that obscure life \'7d What could there be in the relations of this man and Lisa Rayner to make her existence a terror or a trouble to him ?

Was he a lover of the past—a lover of whose existence Lisa, in her spontaneous confession, had given no hint ? Did he represent an episode in her life which she, so seemingly candid, had carefully concealed \'7d Some link there must have been between them, if he were indeed the murderer, since his social status precluded the idea of a murder to assist a theft.

The audience rose in a storm of kid-gloved applause, and a murmured chorus of approval, while Arnold sat bewildered.

Greswold had been chosen to wind up the meeting, to make the final strenuous appeal to the hearts and purses of the audience. He was often so chosen ; for the little band of good men with whom he worked fully recognized his power to play upon human heart-strings.

People were moving to the door, gold and silver were dropping into the silken bags which Lady Violet and Ida Borrodaile held, standing on each side of the lofty Georgian doorway, through which fat Joe Sedley may have passed in his hey-day of turtle and nankin.

Nineteenth-century Crusaders.

The room was half empty before Arnold had pulled himself together and was conscious of his surroundings, and of Mary Freeland looking back at him as she followed her portly chaperon.

She lingered long enough to allow of his joining her before she reached the door.

"There is tea downstairs," she said to him. "Would it bore you very much to get some for Mrs. Tresillian-Smith and me \'7d There is sure to be a crush."

" I shall be enchanted."

" How sweet of you! Mr. Greswold's speech gave me cold water down my back. I am going to subscribe at least fifty guineas. I ought to give them a year's income."

"And go without frocks and food for a year .^"

" Why shouldn't I do my share of starving ." It would be better than eating expensive soles in Lent, and calling it religion to go without meat and poultry. Better, at any rate, than to be one of those who don't know, and won't know, how their fellow-creatures suffer. Wasn't Mr. Greswold splendid ? He thrills one with such plain speech, such commonplace words ; and then he spreads his wings like Ruskin or Carlyle."

"You prodigiously admire this Mr. Greswold?"

"As a speaker," she answered quickly.

" Have you ever met him 'I "

"Very often. He comes to Hexton Gardens sometimes—but I have seldom talked to him. He is always in such request."

"Why?"

Rough Justice.

" Oh, because he is really distinguished, I suppose. He speaks, and he writes for the Radical papers, and he is awfully benevolent and philanthropic "

" And religious, no doubt ? A man of exemplary piety."

"No, that is the saddest part of it. Though he is so good, and unselfish, and self-sacrificing, he is not a believer. It is so sad for Lady Violet."

"Why.?"

" Oh, she is so devoted to him ; and I dare say she would be allowed to marry him—though he is of very inferior birth—if he were not a freethinker."

They were in the crowded tea-room by this time, where Arnold had pioneered them into a comfortable corner, and where Wilmot and his Ida presently joined them.

Mr. Fannces Record continued.

CHAPTER XIII.

MR. FAUNCE'S record CONTINUED.

The identity of the spectacled lodger in Dynevor Street with Oliver Greswold, a writer and speaker upon socialistic and philanthropic subjects, of some repute in his own particular circle, having been indicated by a fluke, it became my business to discover his connection, if any, with the murdered woman on the other side of the street. The fact that his residence in an obscure Bloomsbury lodging-house was a secret and stealthy business was proved by the alias and the dark spectacles. I took occasion to see the gentleman several times after Mr, Wildover's discovery, and I never saw him wearing spectacles, or even using an eye-glass ; nor could I hear from anybody that he had ever used one or the other. His grandfather's old man-servant, with whom I became very friendly in my casual way, told me that Mr. Oliver had "the hi of an 'awk."My first business was to find out all I could about Greswold's surroundings and antecedents, before approaching the problem of his association

Rough Justice.

with the murdered woman. To discover the link between those two I must first know what the man was, and what kind of life he had led.

It was easy to know his life and surroundings as the world knew them, since his active share in the good Lord Hildyard's work had made him a public character.

He was known to have very small means in the present, but considerable expectations from his grandfather—a man of advanced age, who led a secluded life in a dreary-looking house on Clapham Common, one of the largest houses in that neighbourhood, and with grounds covering five or six acres, now of considerable value. There can be no interest to anybody in the details of my work. I shall therefore sum them up in a single word, Patience.Patience enabled me to overcome the dogged reserve of the curmudgeon who had been the head of the elder Greswold's house for nearly forty years, and whose memory—unobscured by book-learning— was a storehouse of facts relating to the Greswold family. Patience, and a trifling outlay upon glasses of brandy and water at the Flower Pot tavern in the Clapham Road, placed me upon a friendly and confidential footing with Benjamin Ludgater, butler, valet, and factotum to Mr. Andrew Greswold, of the Belvidere, Clapham, family solicitor, and reputed millionaire. In less than a month from the day when I first dropped into the tavern parlour, where the old man-servant spent his evening leisure—having heard all about

Mr. Fannce's Record

his habits from a loquacious grocer's boy Ludgater and I were familiar friends. He had accepted my own account of myself as a retired tradesman resident at Putney, and strolling over to Clapham two or three times a week in the long evenings for the sake of the walk ; and by slow degrees, beginning with reluctant and churlish assent to my remarks about the weather, or the contents of the evening paper, he had unbent so far as to spend the greater part of the evening prosing at my ear, and to entertain me with interminable stories of the Governor and the family.

From him I heard that old Greswold had begun life in a small way as a solicitor in Hatton Garden, but by the help of certain business associations with the turf had made himself a law and power in all turf questions, and had invested his early savings in the betting Ring to such advantage as to enable him to exchange Hatton Garden for Mayfair within the first decade of his professional career.

In Mayfair he had lived over his offices, and it had been Ludgater's privilege to supervise such little dinners as can only be given by the happy few who live within a stone's throw of Berkeley Square. To such dinners " never less than the Gracers or more than the Musers, as master used to tell his friends" came some of the biggest toffs in London, toffs who looked up to Mr. Greswold as to a father, whose stamped paper filled Mr. Greswold's most sacred despatch boxes, upon whose drags Mr. Greswold was driven to

Epsom, and in whose houses, at Sunningdale or Virginia Water, he stayed during the Ascot week. It was not till Mr. Greswold was past fifty, and beginning to talk of retiring from business—much to the distress of the toffs—that he went to live at Clapham. He might never have gone there had the property not fallen in to him, as part of a bad debt, after the suicide of a young racing man—born of city people—who had been imprudent enough to push his way into the toff-world, and whose plebeian spirit had failed him in a financial crux out of which a toff would have emerged smiling. This low-born tradesman's son must needs cut his throat, rather than face cross-examination in the Bankruptcy Court.

Mr. Greswold married soon after taking possession of the Clapham property, and here he lived for some years in great splendour, Ludgater having a footman and page under him. Here also Mr. Greswold took upon himself a reputation for shining piety. Family prayers morning and evening ; church morning and evening, on Sundays ; liberal subscriptions to charities ; liberal treatment of servants.

He had married a very handsome woman, twenty years his junior, of whose connections and antecedents even his confidential servant Ludgater had discovered nothing.

" She might be dropped from the clouds for all I knew about her—until they took to quarrelling in my hearing, and then he threw things in her

Mr. Faunces Record contimied.

face that showed pretty plain the class she come from," Ludgater told me.

The pair were badly matched, and miserable together, but, whatever her past conduct, the wife behaved like an honest woman in her husband's house. She bore him two children, a boy and a girl. The father adored the girl, and detested the boy.

The mother idolized the boy, and resented her husband's preference for the girl. This was the beginning of domestic warfare. Their first quarrels were about the children. The wife fell into a decline, and died in the south of France, before the children grew up ; and after her death the daughter became practically her own mistress, indulged in every whim, quarrelling with one governess after another, and making slaves of the women servants.

The boy did well at school, and at the University, was called to the Bar, married the daughter of a distinguished Queen's Counsel, for whom he had devilled, and was beginning to be known as a rising junior, when the consumptive taint showed itself, and he followed his mother to her grave in a foreign cemetery.

He left a son of seven years old, and a widow, who was much too pretty to remain long widowed. There had been no marriage-settlement, and the orphan was left wholly unprovided for; so the grandfather took charge of him, and tolerated him. It had never been more than toleration, Ludgater told me.

Rough Justice.

However well his grandson did at school, whatever honours he won at Cambridge, the old man still looked coldly upon him, and always kept him short of money.

Before the grandson came into the house the daughter had gone out of it for ever. She had vanished one summer night, after a violent quarrel with her father, a quarrel that had been more desperate than the worst that Ludgater could remember between husband and wife. The ofirl had gone out of her father's house, angry and defiant, to join her lot with a man whom her father denounced as a swindler—one of Greswold's Mayfair visitors—a man of good birth—"a sprig of nobility," Ludgater called him, but of the worst possible character.

Her father swore never to see her again, and never had pronounced her name in Ludgater's hearing since that night.

" You can chuck all the rubbish out of the south bedroom and boudoir, and lock the doors of both rooms," he told Ludgater.

The old servant opined that the word " rubbish " included all Miss Greswold's personal belongings, so he touched nothing, believing that her father would relent in course of time.

He shut the shutters of all the windows, and locked the two doors, and gave the keys to his master, who asked for them ; and the rooms had never been opened within his knowledge since he closed them.

"You can see those windows, with the old-

Mr. Paunces Record continued.

fashioned Venetian shutters, from the road," Lud-gater said ; " and you may think how thick the dust must lie and how heavy the cobwebs must hang upon everything after over thirty years."

Within a month of Miss Greswold's disappearance all the splendours of the Belvidere, Clapham, had vanished as completely as the fugitive daughter herself Ludgater was now the only man-servant in the great empty house, and the whole indoor establishment was reduced to himself and two women. All the large reception rooms were closed, the furniture covered with brown holland, the Axminster carpets rolled up, and opposing, as it were, an earth-work against the intruder who ventured to pry into those desolate apartments.

Of the seven gardeners who had made the Belvidere flower-beds and hot-houses the admiration of Clapham, one only was left to mow the grass and roll the gravel walks, on which the gloomy owner paced to and fro for hours on end, summer and winter, fair weather or foul. Of all the flowers that had bloomed there, only the hardest perennials remained, to blossom and fade unheeded.

It was at this time that Greswold's piety assumed a gloomier cast. He now took to religion, as some men take to drink. He attached himself to a low-church preacher of the most rigid Calvinistic views, and expected all his household to attend the Sunday services in a hot, ugly church, and to listen to prayers and Scripture readings morning and night.

Rough Justice.

"How does his grandson stand that kind of thing ?" I asked.

" He has to stand it, as long as master lives, if he don't want to be cut off with an angry shilling. Everybody except the master knows that Mr. Oliver don't believe in nothing but earth worms and climbing plants, and such like—I've seen the books on the table by his bed—but he has to go to church, and to eat cold beef and salad on Sundays, or he'd soon get the key of the street, instead of the latch-key that has never been allowed him."

Nothing had ever been heard of the vanished daughter. If the father knew her fate— whether she were living or dead—he kept his own counsel. None of her belongings—clothes, trinkets, girlish possessions—had ever been taken out of the house. They were there after thirty years, mouldering in the sealed rooms.

Ludgater had once heard his master, in a moment of irritation, remind his grandson that he had other heirs—those who might be dearer to him than the offspring of that starched prig, his son. This speech had impressed the old servant; and he inclines to think that the daughter is still living, and that her father may have forgiven her, or that she has left offspring whom he knows and protects.

My progress up to this point was satisfactory, but I found it difficult to get any further, as Ludgater had forgotten the name of the "sprig of nobility," as well as the noble tree on which

Mr. Faunces Record continued.

he grew. That threat of the old man's was an indication that had to be followed—for here was at once the suggestion of motive, could I trace the offspring of the rebellious daughter in the murdered Lisa Rayner. Yet it would be hard to believe that old Greswold could boast of heirs near and dear, and leave one of them to sink so low as that unhappy young woman had fallen, long before her tragical death. If he knew of their existence he would surely have cared for them. If he had no knowledge of them he would hardly have uttered such a threat.

I tried to realize the position of Oliver Greswold —brought up in the house of a wealthy grandfather, ostensibly his sole heir, but threatened with the existence of a hidden rival, or rivals.

Suppose there were one rival only, and the man knew who and what she was—her fallen and friendless condition ; suppose he knew that a will were made in her favour, or were likely to be made in her favour—there was motive enough in the mind of a villain for putting her out of the world. Could I believe a young man of Oliver Greswold's presumed character—a man of blameless life, whose voice was never raised except in a good cause, whose eloquence could draw tears, who had laboured early and late for the help and improvement of his fellow men,— could I believe that under the spotless skin of this philanthropist there beat the heart of a murderer \'7d Well, yes ; after five and twenty years' experience of human nature's dark side I can believe in

Rough Justice,

anybody's wickedness. I set no limit on myself there. My only difficulty is to believe in human goodness.

But somehow I like Wildover, and I like working for him.

My business is now to learn all Wildover can tell me about the unhappy girl's antecedents—he has been very reticent on this point—and to follow up any clue he can give me till I discover her history and parentage. The odds are that, after taking infinite trouble, I shall find her totally unconnected with the Greswold family, and so find myself no nearer the discovery of any link between Oliver Greswold and the murder in Dynevor Street. The mere fact of his being a resident in that street under a false name may have no bearing on the murder ; there are many motives for hiding—debt, politics, love. Yet with a man of Greswold's respectability it is not easy to suppose any such motive; nor was there any hint of a petticoat at the lodging-house.

And there is the curious fact that the man who bought a pistol in Holborn is described as of middle height, slim, studious-looking, and wearing smoke-coloured spectacles.

The work will be slow and may be unsuccessful, but it suits me better than picking caterpillars off the rosebushes, or watering the geraniums, in the long summer evenings.

The 'Boyhood of Oliver Greswold,

CHAPTER XIV.

THE BOYHOOD OF OLIVER GRESWOLD.

After the drawing-room meeting in Russell Square Arnold became on very friendly terms with Wilmot's Ida, and was induced to join the lovers in visits to picture-galleries, and other places of public entertainment, to which the young lady went in custody of a serious aunt, whose piety was tempered by an insatiable thirst for mundane pleasures, and who talked in the same breath of her favourite parsons and her favourite actors. This lady had battened upon her elder sister's bad health, and enjoyed all the privileges of a chaperon, which included every picture-gallery in London, a good many of the best morning concerts, light luncheons at the nicest West End confectioners or cafes, and stalls at the Lyceum and Haymarket for every new play, the expense of which entertainments Wilmot cheerfully defrayed for the delight of being with his Ida.

As he grew more intimate with the young lady Arnold was able to question her freely about Oliver Greswold, and from her he learnt all that the Borrodailes knew of Lord Hildyard's unpaid secretary. He had been allied with his lordship for six or seven years, Ida told Arnold, and his attachment to Lady Violet was an open secret to all the world except that "dear old Mole," Lord Hildyard, who could never see anything outside St. Giles's or Whitechapel.

Did Ida think that he would consent to his daughter's marriage with Greswold ? Ida thought he would sacrifice all caste prejudice if Mr. Greswold were to come into a fortune, and were able to help the great cause with money as well as with his brains. Mr. Greswold had great expectations from a miserly grandfather, who lived in a dismal old house on Clapham Common, surrounded by gardens and paddocks that were supposed to be worth a fortune as building land.

" He keeps that poor young man dreadfully short of money, and wouldn't even let him go to the Bar, because it would cost something. Father says he has just the clothes he wears, and his board and lodging at Clapham ; so it is impossible for him to put himself forward as a suitor for Lady Violet till his grandfather dies. However, as the old wretch is nearly ninety, it's to be hoped he will make up his mind to do that before long."

" But is Greswold sure of being his grandfather's heir?"

" Oh, no doubt such an old wretch might leave everything to a hospital ; but there are no other relations; and Oliver Greswold has been brought

The Boyhood of Oliver Greswold.

up in his grandfather's house, so that ought to mean being his heir."

"And you think Lady Violet would marry him if he asked her ?"

"Like a bird," replied Ida, who had adopted some of her Wilmot's phrases, and prided herself upon them^ as she prided herself upon writing like him, though his penmanship was execrable.

Lady Violet accompanied Ida on one of their picture mornings, and Arnold, who had the honour of escorting her through the galleries, found it very easy to lead her to talk of Oliver Greswold. From her he heard how hard the young man's lot had been, and how the fire of unsatisfied ambitions was consuming his youth.

" He ought to be in the House," she said. " He could help every good cause if he were there—for he is a born leader of men. William Pitt was a power at his age. He would be in the House if my father were rich enough to help him. It is hard to see men who are so inferior to him making great names, while he is known only to a few. You heard him speak ; you know what kind of speaker he is."

" I thought him a very fine speaker ; but eloquence is not everything in the House of Commons, and some distinguished orators have failed there. Greswold may not have the genius of debate."

"You do not know how clever he is, or you would not say that. My father and I have known him for a good many years, and we know what there is in him, and that he only requires a proper

platform. It is so hard that want of money should stop the way—but—

" Every door is barred with gold, and opens but to golden keys,"

concluded Lady Violet, with a sigh.

Her face, which revealed every feeling, glowed with enthusiasm as she talked of the man she loved. She told Arnold how nobly he had assisted every scheme of her father's ; how indefatigable, how clever, and far-seeing he had been. Looking at pictures was a secondary pleasure compared •with talking of Oliver Greswold to a sympathetic listener ; and to Violet's mind Wentworth's eager interest could spring only from genuine admiration for the man she loved.

He asked her if Greswold always lived at Clapham, in the dreary house with the miserly grandfather.

"Always—at least, I only remember one occasion when he lived anywhere else, and that was last winter, when he had lodgings in some street near the British Museum. He is writing a book upon trade unionism, and workmen's societies of all kinds, and he wanted to be near the Museum Library. He had to work there every day."

She knew all about it, then! He had made no secret of his residence in Bloomsbury, This shook Arnold's conviction, and damped his ardour. His spirits sank at the idea that he had lighted on a mare's nest. Yet, if there were no evil intent, why did Greswold disfigure himself with spectacles, and assume an alias ?

"Do you remember the name of the street where he lodged ?" he asked ; and then, as if in answer to her surprised look, " I—I—am thinking of reading up a little mineralogy—in case I ever go back to the goldfields—and I should like to know of decent lodgings near the Museum."

"I don't remember the address—I doubt if I ever heard it. He was with my father every day, and we had no occasion to write to him. But I'll ask him, if you like."

" Please don't; he would think me a troublesome fool. Here comes Miss Borrodaile. She will say I am hindering you from looking at the pictures."

" I am always glad to talk to any one who is interested in my father's work," she said.

Arnold called at Faunce's suburban villa that evening, and related his conversation with Lady Violet, but Faunce received the communication quite coolly.

" The man would have to account for his absence from Clapham," he said, " and, if he is the criminal we want, he would be wise enough to know that the nearer he kept to the actual truth the less risk he would run of detection. There was nothing extraordinary in his wanting to live close to his work, but there's something extraordinary in his hiding his eyes, and changing his name. Lady Violet was told the one fact—which seemed natural enough. Had he pretended to be on the other side of the Channel—or a hundred miles away from London—he would have found it difficult to give a good reason for his absence, and might

have been met in the street any hour in the day.

" But even as it was—how if he had been met, disguised ?"

"Spectacles don't necessarily mean disguise. He would have accounted for them by affecting something amiss with his eyes. No—your Lady Violet has not made any change in my ideas. And now I have something to tell you."

Arnold was all eagerness, and being enjoined to listen quietly, and make no comments, this was the story he heard.

Remembering the murdered woman's custom of wandering about the lonely squares and the Primrose Hill district after midnight, as described by her landlady and her fellow lodger, it had occurred to Faunce that she could hardly have escaped the observation of the constables on duty in those districts, if they were worth sixpence a night as observers of human nature. Alone, or in company, she must have been a noticeable figure in the small hours.

Proceeding upon this hypothesis, Faunce had interrogated the men in the locality, and had finally met with an intelligent Irish Sergeant whose beat lay between Primrose Hill and the Gloucester Road, and who had frequently remarked the lonely woman walking towards the hill after midnight, when the streets and roads were almost empty of human life, or walking towards

London at a still later hour.

He had seen her in the middle of summer

The Boyhood of Oliver Grcsivold.

walking eastward with the light upon her poor pinched face. She always looked pretty much the same, the Sergeant said ; pale and melancholy, decently clad, quiet and respectable. He had never spoken to her, for he was sure that she had seen better days, and that it would vex her to know that she was noticed or watched.

He had never seen her walking with anybody. She was always alone, and her eyes had a faraway look, as if she was always thinking the same kind of thoughts.

One night in the previous November he had observed, to his surprise, that she was being followed —stealthily, and at a distance and he kept his eye upon the follower as long as he could do so without leaving his section. The person following was a youngish man, slim, a little over the middle height, looking like a Londoner, wearing a loose brown overcoat and a brown felt hat. He was puzzled by this fact, as there was nothing attractive about the young woman's appearance or manner; and, while the man was obviously watching her, he made no attempt to stop her or to enter into conversation with her.

He followed for the most part on the opposite side of the road, and far enough in her rear to prevent his footsteps being heard by her.

The Sergeant saw this man shadowing the woman three or four times in the course of as many weeks—in dull, weather, and on fine bright nights ; but though it was obvious to him that the man's purpose was to watch and to follow

Rough Justice.

this one lonely figure, the thing was so done that he felt shy of questioning the man. There was nothing that indicated any sinister purpose up to the night of the 20th of December, when something' serious happened.

The night was dry, but rough. There was a waning moon, which showed occasionally in a sky full of storm clouds.

There was a south-w-est wind, and the night was particularly mild for the season. There had been showers early in the evening, and the earth and the trees about Gloucester Gate and Gloucester Road had a cool freshness which the Sergeant enjoyed. He was hardly surprised to meet the lonely woman walking across the open ground at the top of Park Street, just as the York and Albany was closing. She walked at her usual brisk pace, and she went the way he was going to the Hill.

The moon was hidden now, and had been hidden for the last half hour. He could not see her, though he believed she was in front of him.

Presently, nearer to him than he thought, he heard her light, quick footsteps, still in front, and at the same minute became aware of other footsteps, almost as light as hers, a little way behind him. He stopped, and stood aside, hidden by a group of trees.

The following footsteps passed him, and went on. He waited, and by-and-by the woman passed, retracing her steps, the man following, always at about the same distance. He heard his breathing

The Boyhood of Oliver Greswold.

as he passed, hurried, harder, and more agitated than it need have been, the Sergeant thought, considering the easy pace at which he was walking.

The woman crossed the road at the foot of the Hill, and entered a long suburban street, one of those eminently respectable streets from which every token of human life vanishes soon after eleven o'clock. The man crossed the road as the woman had crossed, less than a minute after her. He was keeping closer to her than usual to-night. The man entered the street she had entered, but kept on the opposite side of the way, as usual, and the Sergeant followed, keeping to the muddy roadway, so that the tramp of his regulation boots should not be heard by the people he was following, silent boots having not yet been adopted by the service.

The sky was clearing, and the moon had looked out from among the clouds several times within the last hour. She leapt suddenly from behind a cloud-bank as the Sergeant entered the empty, silent street, and he saw that the position of the people he was following had changed. They were still upon opposite sides of the way, but the man was now considerably ahead of the woman. He drew aside as she approached, and stood in the shadow of a stuccoed porch. The street was a monotonous avenue of bay windows and pillared porches, the latter raised from the pavement only by a single shallow step.

The man came out of the porch as the woman.

Rough Justice.

approached, and the Sergeant saw him take deliberate aim at her with a pistol. He was just near enough to see the flash of steel in the moon-light.

" Holloa! " shouted the Sergeant, and ran as fast as his boots would let him.

That shout may have saved a life, or only postponed murder.

There was a cross street a few doors from the spot where the man had stood to take aim, and he was away round the corner before the Sergeant came up with the woman, who had stopped at his shout, and had seen the man running away, but may have been unaware of the danger she had escaped.

" Do you know that man ?" gasped the Sergeant, without stopping.

"No."

The Sergeant, still without stopping, called to her to wait for him. He would be back in a few minutes.

The side street was as long as the main avenue, and there were numerous turnings in it; some leading to Camden Town, others towards Regent's Park. He was in an endless labyrinth of middle-class gentility; stuccoed porches, bay windows, larger or smaller, more or less ornate.

He gave up the chase after about twenty minutes, during which he had enlisted the service of a constable on his beat.

Then he went back to the street where he had left the woman, fully expecting to find her waiting

The Boyhood of Oliver Greswold.

for him. Surely a woman's curiosity, even had she no stronger motive, would induce her to wait and hear the end of so strange an adventure.

She was gone. The Sergeant paraded the neighbouring streets for the rest of his time, but could not meet with her ; and he never saw her again. Her nocturnal perambulations in that particular district were never repeated, or the Sergeant must have met her. Whether he reported the occurrence on his sheet, or not, was a question which Faunce had not cared to push too closely.

" Poor soul! She had not long to wander alone under the stars after the twentieth of December," said Arnold, with that dull aching pain which he felt whenever his thoughts reverted to the woman who had loved him.

" You take it for granted, then, that this wanderer was Lisa Rayner."

" Have you any doubt of it ?"

" Not much. If the lodger in ynevor Street was there for the purpose of murder, it is highly improbable that his audacious entrance at No. 13 on Christmas Eve was a first attempt. He would have tried a less hazardous method first; and to shoot his victim in a deserted street was certainly a much safer plan. I have no doubt he had made other attempts before the one the Sergeant saw, and that it was after several failures for, you see, a London street is seldom as deserted as it looks that he grew desperate, and watched for the first opportunity of getting into the house. He was watching you and Mrs Rayner from the

other side of the street, most likely, while you were walking up and down; and he may have crossed the street, and slipped in at the half-open door while you and she were absorbed in that last farewell,"

"Yes that might have been. She was crying, and I took a handkerchief from my breast pocket, and lifted her veil, while I dried her tears. My back was towards the door-step. Any one might have gone in at that moment. I watched her as she went in two minutes afterwards, and heard the door shut firmly behind her. The murderer must have been hiding in the dark passage. I noticed that there was no gas, and wondered whether there were candle and matches ready for her in the hall, or whether she would have to grope her way upstairs in the dark. I was so sorry for her that it was only natural I should think of these details. Her hard life seemed ever so much more pitiable now I was prosperous ; and I feared she was not going to let me help her to an easier life. Well, your Sergeant's story is conclusive—a grand piece of circumstantial evidence."

" Not worth twopence at the Old Bailey. Convincing for you and me, perhaps, but useless for a jury."

" Useless Such evidence as that! "

"An indication only not evidence as against Greswold. You may prove him to be the man who lodged with the Durfins, and called himself Longman: a suspicious circumstance, no more.

The Boyhood of Oliver Greswold,

You have to find whether he, Greswold, had any motive for getting rid of Lisa Rayner. Prove that much ; prove a reason for his wanting her dead and out of the way ; prove, even, by the evidence of the gunsmith, that Greswold bought the pistol; you have still only a weak case against him, a few odd links in a chain, but not an unbroken chain such as a judge and jury would require before they would believe that a man of Oliver Greswold's eminent virtues leading a clean life, of good means, popular and respected—could be a cold-blooded murderer."

" What more is there to be done ?"

" Much, if you want to succeed. But I tell you, again, that if this man is the murderer, I don't believe you will ever see justice done, even though you and I may know that he deserves hanging. A moral certainty is one thing, a case for a jury is another. However, my business now, if I am to go on working for you, is to find out Lisa Rayner's early history, and to do this I must go to Vienna, and try back from the point where her life began when she was tempted away by her seducer: not a very easy task, when you consider that she came to England nearly ten years ago, and that you can give me positively no clue to her name or whereabouts in Vienna. The only scrap of knowledge I have to begin upon is the name in the little Lutheran Testament— Lottchen Noack.

Lisa, von Lottchen Noack."

" My first step will be to advertise for Lottchen

Noack in the Viennese papers. I don't know much of the German language, but I know that an educated German always writes their ridiculous character with a delicate regularity which makes penmanship a fine art. Now, Lottchen's autograph is an abominable scrawl, so I take it she belongs to the lower classes."

" The more likely to be easily found." " No, Mr. Wildover; in cities the lower classes are the nomadic classes."

Having been honoured with Mrs. Tresillian-Smith's card for three Thursday evenings, Arnold was not slow to seize the opportunity.

Two influences drew him to the house in Hexton Gardens. First, the desire to see Mary Freeland, which was irresistible, though he had made up his mind to avoid her ; and, secondly, his ardent wish to meet Oliver Greswold, and to go down a little deeper into the nature of the man whom he had only seen in his public aspect. Face to face, and eye to eye, character might reveal itself, in spite of the severest training in hypocrisy.

Mary welcomed him with her sweetest smile, and to be with Mary was to be in Paradise, even though it meant sitting in a corner of a hot room, made mute by Herr Somebody's fiddle-scraping, for which he cared not a jot, but about which Mary was enthusiastic, and even ferocious.

" Hold your tongue, you Goth," she whispered. «' If you cannot listen to Chopin's nocturne in

The Boyhood of Oliver Greswold.

A Flat, you can have no more ear than an African iage." " I should be sorry to have as much." savage."

He came on the third Thursday, and looked about the room for Oliver Greswold. He had drawn blank upon both previous occasions, and Mary had told him that although Mr. Greswold was expected, he might be unable to be there. He had so much to do for Lord Hildyard in the East End ; and he had his own schemes—workmen's night schools, debating societies endless work.

The third Thursday was an occasion of peculiar brilliancy. Mrs. Smith had secured one of the largest stars who could be wheedled into performing for friendship's sake, and had sent little notes to all her friends, with the promise of fine music. And this time Mary had something more definite to tell in answer to Arnold's inquiry.

" Mr. Greswold can't be here to-night," she said. " His grandfather is dead at last and he has come into an immense fortune."

" Oh ? His grandfather is dead ?"

" He died last week,- after keeping that poor young man in subjection, and almost poverty, all these years. He might have been making a great name in politics instead of wasting his talents upon workmen and night-schools."

"And now I suppose he will cut the workmen ?"

Rough Justice.

*' That's very unlikely. He is steeped in all the Hildyard ideas, and is a Socialist at heart. He will go into Parliament, of course, and will fight for the cause ; and I suppose he will marry Lady Violet, who adores him,"

" Is the fortune very large .""

" Nobody knows anything about it, yet at least, Ida Borrodaile doesn't; and, you see, she is my friend. I am not intimate with Lady Violet, though she and her father came to one of Mrs. Tresillian-Smith's parties."

Mary and her chaperon were going to Suffolk next day to spend a month at the Briery, while Dr. Tresillian-Smith handed over his patients to his partner, and went to Connemara to fish. Of course, all his best patients would be away, and his partner was quite capable of looking after the small fry.

Arnold had spent three evenings in Mary's society, and had been happy indeed, it seemed to him that they had both been happy, and that there was a thrill of joy in Mary's voice when she talked to him ; but no word of love had been spoken. He told himself, even, that he had only accepted Mrs. Smith's invitation on the chance of meeting Greswold in her house; that he would not have been so weak as to go there for Mary's sake, but being there he had "spent the evening in Mary's pocket," as his hostess playfully told him.

He had set a stern watch upon himself, and had breathed no word of love, nor the slightest allusion

The Boyhood of Oliver Greswold.

to a future in which they two might be one. He was much lighter in heart and spirits for the thought that Mary had ceased to think evil of him, but he was resolute in keeping aloof from all questions of love and marriage.

Rough Justice.

CHAPTER XV.

MR. FAUNCE CONTINUES.

My advertisement resulted successfully, and, as I might reasonably have anticipated, the answer to my inquiry in the Viennese papers came to me from London. Germans of that class find their way to London as if by a natural law of gravitation. Fraulein Noack was now engaged as nurse in a family at South Kensington. A friend had sent her my advertisement, and she begged to be informed whether money had been left her, and if so, how much \'7d and would the advertiser send her something on account of such legacy ? In replying to the Fraulein, I begged to inform her that there was no legacy, but that if she would call upon me at my house in Putney, she would be handsomely rewarded for any information she could give me about the person called Lisa, to whom she once gave a Lutheran Testament.

My letter brought Fraulein Noack within twenty-four hours.

"It was my afternoon out," she said, "so if I

Mr. Faunce continues.

hadn't come to-day, I couldn't have come for a week."

She is a plain, practical young woman, and has mastered the English language, which she speaks with an Austrian accent. She is evidently one of those conscientious persons who, being engaged to teach their charges German, direct their principal efforts to making their pupils teach them English ; and it is an open question whether the pupils are not better off without the kind of German Fraulein Noack could impart to them.

Did she remember the girl to whom she gave the book ?

Yes, she remembered her perfectly. They had lived in the same house. What did I want to know, and what reward would I give her if she told me all she could recall about her friend \'7d

I mentioned a sovereign ; but she smiled ironically, and said if she had known I was so generous she would have spent the afternoon with a friend at Earl's Court Exhibition, and would not have wasted her time coming to Putney. Finally I closed with her for a five-pound note, to be paid in advance.

" There is your money, gracious lady " handing her the cash "and now for your information, which in all probability will not be worth five shillings."

"That makes nothing," replied the damsel. "You wouldn't have advertised for me in four newspapers if you were not very anxious to get hold of me."

Rough Justice.

She proceeded to tell him how and when she had made the acquaintance of the girl to whom she had presented the little black book. Lottchen Noack had been a servant in a lodging-house in Vienna when Lisa came to lodge there with her father, whom Lottchen described as a fine-looking man, but a man who had spoilt his health and his appearance by hard drinking. She believed that he was a gambler as well as a drunkard, and that he spent his evenings in low gambling saloons, some of the vilest dens in Vienna. Her master had told her so, and she knew that she herself used to hear his unsteady footsteps stumbling up to his garret in the early morning hours. During the first half-year of his residence he had occupied good rooms on the fourth floor, but towards the last he had moved to three wretched rooms in the roof, and it had been difficult to get even the reduced rent from him.

When he first came to the house Lisa was only sixteen—very pretty, very winning, and very cruelly treated by her father, who left her in solitude day after day, and night after night, and when he was at home would send her on errands all over the city, although she was much too pretty to be trusted alone in such a place as Vienna.

" If I hadn't talked to her sometimes, she would have had no one to speak to," said Lottchen. " I don't think she had ever known what it was to be happy. Her father and mother wandered from place to place till the mother was too ill to move, and in that long last illness her father left her

Mr. Fatmce continues.

alone with the dying mother, in a lodging at Havre, where they had scarcely bread to eat, and where the mother had to be buried at the expense of the State, like a pauper. And her mother told her that she had left a luxurious home and forfeited a large fortune for love of the man who had deserted her."

He came back a week after the funeral, Lisa told her friend, paid the people at the lodgings, and carried Lisa off with him. He seemed to have plenty of money at this time, and he came straight to Vienna, and took the nice apartments on the fourth floor, and lived like a gentleman, but was always equally dissipated, stopping out late at nights, and coming home the worse for liquor.

When Lisa described those sad days by her mother's death-bed Lottchen discovered that she had been brought up like a heathen. No one had ever taken her to church, or taught her to believe in God. Her father and mother had quarrelled dreadfully, she confided to Lottchen, after she had known her some time. She had loved her mother dearly, but she had also feared her, for when she was angry her temper was terrible. She was always complaining of her miserable life, and regretting that she had thrown herself away upon a scoundrel. Many a dinner that they three ate together had been watered with tears.

The man was English, but spoke French and German with perfect facility. His name was Clissold.

Lottchen took Lisa to the Lutheran church

Rough Justice.

occasionally upon a Sunday evening, when she, the household drudge, was allowed to go. She talked to her of religion, and gave her the little book now in my keeping.

As time went on, Lisa altered, and became silent and reserved, and on several occasions Lottchen found her in tears. She was not surprised at this, as the girl's life grew more wretched every day, the father sinking deeper in debauchery, and growing rougher and crueller to his daughter with every downward step.

" I was not surprised when I heard him storming and raging one morning. It was past eleven o'clock, the hour at which his daughter used to take him his coffee, he sprawling in his bed sometimes till two or three in the afternoon. He came down to the kitchen in his shirt and trousers, with bare feet; he had a letter in his hand, a letter of one sentence which he had found in Lisa's garret, where he went to scold her for not waiting upon him. ' I have gone away with some one who will treat me kindly.' That was all the letter. He was furious. If he had been the best of fathers he could not have used more dreadful language. He was deep in debt to the landlord, who lost temper with him, hearing the vile things he said of that poor child, and turned him out of the house on the spot—gleich!"

" Did you ever hear what became of him .-*" I asked.

" Oh, we heard, safe enough; but not for three months afterwards. A body was found in the

Mr. Faunce continues.

canal, and my master thought the description fitted his old lodger, and went and looked at him. It was Mr. Clissold. He had stones in his pockets —heavy stones, and had meant nothing less than to be drowned."

I asked if this was the end of the history—if no inquiries about these people had ever been made of her master. No, there had been no inquiries so long as she lived in the house, which was more than a year after Clissold's death. She had no idea as to the person who took Lisa away — she had never been shown a letter or a present, or any token of a lover in the background—nor had she ever heard from the girl after she left. She had never gone out walking with Lisa except on a Sunday evening. They kept her too hard at work in the lodging-house. When she left it had been to go to Paris with a lady, and in her service she had learnt a great deal, and she was now head nurse at South Kensington, with an under-nurse to wait upon her.

I took down the address of the lodging-house, and I felt that my next inquiries must be made in Vienna. The only thing to be done there would be to identify Clissold as the man who eloped with old Greswold's daughter. But who could tell, even if he were the man, how many aliases he may have assumed, and how difficult it might be to trace the stages of his downhill career \'7d

Clissold .-* There is some association with that name which I cannot for a moment recall. Was

Rough Justice.

it in connection with the great Burford forgery-case—thirty years ago—that the name occurred ? Possibly, for the old butler at Clapham said the lover was a "toff"—and there were several toffs concerned in the Burford forgeries, directly and indirectly,

I must take my evening stroll to Clapham, and have some further talk with my friend Ludgater.

I found Ludgater at his usual post in the parlour of the Flowerpot, and in a state of suppressed excitement.

He had been told nothing about his master's will. The old man's solicitor had arrived upon the scene within a few hours of his death. He had seldom appeared at the Belvidere of late years, but Ludgater remembered his father, Morris Mortimer, senior, coming there three or four times at very short intervals nine or ten years ago, and that on these occasions client and lawyer were closeted together for a considerable time. Ludgater had noticed that Mortimer's visits always occurred during young Greswold's absence. He remembered also that on the last of these visits the lawyer was accompanied by his clerk.

"I suspected the old man of plotting against his grandson," he said, *' and that the clerk might have come to witness a will that would leave Mr. Oliver out in the cold."

The solicitor is one Morris Mortimer, a Jew, whose father was concerned with old Greswold in many of his money-lending schemes—in a word,

Mr. Fmmce continues.

a fellow blood-sucker. I know a good deal about this Morris—the Mortimer is an addition which his father assumed when he moved his offices westwards, and set up his brougham—and I know him to be clever and unscrupulous. The father died three years ago.

Mr. Mortimer spent some time with Oliver Greswold, looking through the old man's papers, and went away without imparting any information to Ludgater, not even to the effect that he would be provided for in his old age, which he considered hard treatment, after so many years of faithful service. I asked if Oliver Greswold looked like a man who had come into a large fortune.

If a large fortune made a man very anxious, perhaps he did ; certainly, in Ludgater's opinion, Mr. Oliver looked eaten up with anxiety. He had condescended so far as to tell Ludgater that he and Mr. Mortimer were sole executors, and that the management of the estate would come upon him. It was a very complicated kind of property, for besides investing in all manner of stocks and shares, English and foreign, Mr. Greswold had put a good deal of money into freehold houses in Lambeth and Southwark, and in East London ; houses that had brought him in twenty per cent, and upwards, but which it was a misery to live in ; and yet tenants were eager to get lodgings in them, and would go on suffering and grumbling, and grumbling and suffering, for a life-time. Ludgater had been round among the Lambeth tenants once when the Collector was ill,

Rough Justice.

and he had seen the kind of den that brought old Greswold a dirty canvas bag of silver every week.

" There was a dozen such bags brought to him of a Monday night," said Ludgater, "and the old man would sit at his dinner-table and count the dirty silver as if it was all he had to depend upon. But I knew he had money in almost every railway in England, and shares in other things that paid better than railways. Once I ventured to drop the hint that he was wasting his life and caring too much for money. He wasn't a bit ofifended, but he looks me full in the face very serious, and says, ' It isn't that I care so much for money as that I don't care for anything else. That's where the harm is,' he says."

After my interview with the old butler I felt more immediately interested in the Greswold succession and in Oliver Greswold's proceedings than in following up the information I had obtained from Lottchen Noack. I might follow up that clue personally later on. In the mean time I knew of a very clever member of the Viennese police to whom I could depute the investigation. He had to find out the man Clissold's antecedents for me, if he could. The man must have had associates in Vienna, and from one of these my friend might obtain some particulars of his past life, and carry the retrospective scent to a point at which I could pick up the line.

I waited a week before going back to the

Mr. Faunce continues.

Flowerpot, and I found Ludgater in much better spirits. Mr. Gresvvold had told him that although there were no legacies or specific provision left for any member of the household, he, Ludgater, should be provided for.

"I take that upon myself," he said, "and will allow you a hundred a year, to be paid quarterly by Mr. Mortimer, as long as you live ; and you can consider yourself your own master, and can live where you please."

Ludgater opined that there was only one place in which life would be possible for him, and that would be within ten minutes' walk of the Flowerpot. He had seen an unfurnished parlour floor in one of the terraces diverging from the Clapham Road which would suit him, in the house of a highly respectable spinster, who had been cook in a good family, and might be relied upon to cater and cook for Mr. Ludgater. He opined also that there were various trifles of disused furniture at the Belvidere which would suffice to furnish these two rooms comfortably. He would be sorry to retire from service in the prime of life—he must have been well over seventy—and feeling himself as fit to conduct a household as he had been when a young man ; but he believed that Mr. Oliver meant to dispose of the Belvidere and to take a house at the West End of London.

Ludgater's good humour enabled me to realize a desire that I had vainly tried to gratify during the old man's life.

I wanted to see the house and grounds in which

Rough Justice.

Oliver Greswold's dreary boyhood and youth had been spent, and on repeating this request, refused hitherto, Ludgater promised to obhge me, if I would call at the Belvidere at noon next day. His young master always left home after an early breakfast, and rarely returned till late in the evening, and we should have the place to ourselves at that hour.

Up to this point I had felt myself to blame for not having hunted up any evidence of the young man's habits and disposition which might be afforded by the rooms he had lived in, and upon which every man leaves some imprint of character and temperament. The clue afforded by such indications might be of the slightest, or there might be no clue; but it would be a fault in me to neglect the opportunity.

With Ludgater at my side, babbling prosily of the days that were no more, I explored the Belvidere from cellar to garret, exhibiting a taste for architecture and old furniture which was, I confess, only an assumption of the moment, and a part of the many-sidedness which is essential in my profession. The prosier the old servant was the more leisure I had for my investigation.

The house told me nothing except that it had once been a stately mansion, built in a day when houses were built to last. Oliver Greswold's rooms were as cold and cheerless as a prison cell—no fancy goods in the way of pipes and cigar boxes, no photographs of pretty actresses, none of the incongruous rubbish to be found in most young

Mr. Faunce continues.

men's rooms, but a rigid order in the arrangement of books and papers which recalled Mr. Durfin's description of the lodger on the second floor in Dynevor Street.

The rooms told me only what I already knew about Oliver Greswold—a man of mathematical precision and of fixed purpose, a character of unwavering force for good or for evil.

Having surveyed the house, Ludgater invited me to see the garden. Now, the garden was not likely to tell me anything about Greswold, who was not at all the kind of man to be fond of a garden, or to devote his leisure to budding roses or training carnations ; but it is a precept in my calling that there is no such thing as a negligible quantity, and I followed Ludgater along the moss-grown gravel walks through grounds which had been neglected for a quarter of a century, and where there remained only the rough indications of what had once been a fine suburban garden, such as the citizens of fifty years ago loved.

It was in a remote part of the grounds, quite out of view of the house, that I found something which at once aroused my curiosity. There is a short avenue of limes inside the high boundary wall, and here, in walking almost ankle deep in dead leaves, I kicked up an old playing-card which, even before I stooped to pick it up, I saw had been used as a target. It was riddled with bullet holes. There is an old Lombardy poplar at the end of the avenue, between the last two

Rough Justice.

limes, and hiding the return wall. I went over to look at this tree, and, as I expected, found the trunk had served as a mark for a shooter. I found a second playing-card and torn scraps of others in the leaves and rubbish at the foot of the tree.

"Mr. Oliver's morning amusement some time ago," said Ludgater. " He ain't had much chance of sport, but he must be uncommon fond of shooting, for he used to be at it of an October morning the year before last almost as soon as it was light, peppering that poor old tree. It was too far from the house for his grandfather to hear him, or he dursent have done it, and there ain't no neighbours on this side of the grounds ; but I comes upon him unawares one morning when I was smoking my after-breakfast pipe.

"He just laughed it off when I expresses my surprise. ' Don't think me a fool, old chap,' says he. ' You see, I've some pals I meet now and then at a West-End shooting-gallery who think no end of themselves ; and I want to show them I'm not quite such a duffer as I look.' 'Well, Mr. Oliver, says I, 'I don't see the fun of shooting if you haven't a hanimal to 'it.' "

My friend Ludgater is irresolute in the use of aspirates, but I don't often trouble to reproduce his vernacular in this record.

I went home to an early dinner at Putney, pleased with my morning's experience. I had found another link in the chain of evidence leading up to a moral certainty, if not to a case for a jury.

Mr. Faunce contiimes.

In the October before last Oliver Gresvvold was shooting at a mark in a quiet corner of his grandfather's garden, and in the following November the Sergeant on the north-western side of Regent's Park saw the skulking figure in the shadow of the porch taking aim at his intended victim. A chance shot in the midnight street would have been a much less audacious crime than the murder in the Bloomsbury lodging-house ; and I take it that in crime Mr. Greswold is the kind of man politicians call an opportunist.

Before parting company with Ludgater I contrived to bring the conversation round to the elopement of old Greswold's daughter, and asked in a casual way if he had recalled the name of her aristocratic suitor—a name which he happened to have forgotten when we last spoke of her.

No, he had forgotten the man's name years and years ago. He was a younger son of a nobleman with whom Greswold had done business—a nobleman who kept racehorses and had gone altogether to the bad, and been sold up, before Greswold came to Clapham. The young man had not been at the Belvidere often. Ludgater believed that Miss Greswold had met him at the house of a widow lady up the river, at Maidenhead or thereabouts, with whom she used to stay for a week at a time. He had heard her father reproaching her for encouraging a worthless fellow, without a sixpence, and with one of the worst names among young men in London. One day when the widow lady, whose name also Ludgater had forgotten,

Rough Justice.

came to the Belvidere, there had been a row between her and Greswold, and his master had told him that she was never to be let into the house again.

This was all that Ludgater could tell me about the young lady and her lover. There was no more to be done but wait patiently for the report from Vienna, and for an inspection of Old Greswold's will, which I meant to see at the earliest opportunity.

The report from Vienna came to hand after a fortnight's delay, during which my friend Wildover favoured me with several visits, and exhibited all the indications of a temperament better adapted to camp life in South Africa than to keeping quiet and playing a waiting game in London. He had seen something of Greswold in the interval, having met him twice at Mr. Borrodaile's in Russell Square, where there were frequent meetings of a little knot of philanthropists, headed by Lord Hildyard. There was a grand scheme in hand for a philanthropic factory, with dormitories and a public eating-room, all under one roof—an adaptation on a smaller and more domestic scale of Louis Blanc's National Workshops, one of those brilliant schemes which usually end in failure.

"The fellow passes for a saint with Lord Hildyard and his set," Wildover said savagely. "They are all deluded by his high head and melodious voice. They don't notice his hard thin lip and stealthy eye—an eye that looks slowly

Mr. Faunce continues.

round the room and inquires, Is there any one here who suspects me ? Is there any one who sees the man behind the mask ? I sit and watch him like a tiger waiting to spring. When shall I be able to take the leap, Faunce ? I long to have my claws in his throat."

" I'm afraid you'll have to crouch a good deal longer," said I.

The news from Vienna brought very little information about Clissold's antecedents ; but my colleague's letter contained one significant fact. He had discovered that he was not the first inquirer upon Clissold's track. A Parisian detective had been in Vienna a year before, making careful inquiries about this very Clissold, whom he had traced from Paris.

Andrew Greswold's will was proved without loss of time, and I took an early opportunity of reading it.

It was neither long nor complicated. He left his entire estate, real and personal, to his granddaughter, Lilian Carford, born in Paris on June 6th, 1865, and christened at the Protestant Church in the Rue St. Honore; chargeable with an annuity of six hundred a year to his grandson Oliver Greswold. In the event of his granddaughter's predeceasing him, the estate was to go to his grandson Oliver.

" I make this disposition of my property with no ill-feeling towards my grandson, who has been obedient and dutiful to me, but as I was a cruel

Rough Justice.

father to a daughter whom I loved better than any other human being, I make this atonement to her daughter, should she survive me.

" I make no bequests to charities, for the simple reason that I have been pestered by the innumerable appeals of charity-mongers until the very look of a subscription list has become hateful to me."

An eccentric will; yet there was nothing in the wording of it to show that the testator was not thoroughly competent to dispose of his property. It was executed ten years before the death of the testator. It was witnessed by James Howell, clerk, and Morris Mortimer, Senior, solicitor, of Albemarle Street; Morris, Junior, being appointed joint executor with Oliver Greswold.

Lilian Carford : Lisa Clissold. The initials were the same ; but that was a trifling coincidence to the mind of a man experienced in meaningless coincidences.

" There is your motive for murder—a great fortune at stake," cried Wildover, when I showed him my copy of the will—" the difference between affluence and a pittance; between wealth that will enable him to marry.the woman he loves, to shine in Parliament, to accomplish every desire of his eager, ambitious nature, and a beggarly six hundred a year. You were right, Faunce. There was a life to be suppressed; an unoffending woman to be cheated out of her inheritance, and by the straightest way—murder. I know the man —I have watched him. He is burnt through and

Mr. Fatmce continues.

through with the fire of ambition. He is all nerve and brain. In Robespierre's place he would have sacrificed as many lives as Robespierre sacrificed, and would have called himself an honest man. Do you suppose such a man would stick at one life? He would murder me to-morrow if he thought I suspected him."

" We are sure of nothing yet."

"Yes, we are—of the motive—the man—everything. Lilian Carford—Lilian My God ! I remember her once asking me if I thought Lilian a prettier name than Lisa. I laughed at her for asking such a childish question. That was in our best days, when I was flush of money, and we were light-hearted enough to talk nonsense. The grand-daughter's age would correspond with hers. She told me that she was four and twenty just before I sailed for the Cape."

I let him rave as long as he liked in his impetuous way; but I reminded him at last that until we could establish the identity of the murdered woman with Andrew Greswold's heiress our chain of evidence wanted the most important link.

An advertisement inquiring for Lilian Carford, or for any information as to the present whereabouts, if living, or the date and place of her death if dead, appeared in the Times daily for a week, and on alternate days for a month. The address given was that of W. Morris Mortimer, solicitor, Albemarle Street, W.

I had some thoughts of calling upon Mr. Morris

Mortimer in relation to this advertisement. It would have been easy to pretend an acquaintance with some young woman called Carford, who might or might not be the person wanted, and of whom I should have conveniently lost sight some years previously; but I doubted if this process would enable me to screw any information out of so artful a card as Morris Mortimer, who might happen to be acquainted with my personal appearance, and would at once be put on his guard. My client's interests demanded the closest secrecy, and any suspicion of an inquiry would make our progress all the more difficult.

I have interviewed the gunsmith's assistant who sold the pistol, and he has promised to assist in the identification of the purchaser if I can bring him where he can see the suspected person, though he cannot at this present hour recall the face of the man we want. The face might come back to him, he thinks, if he were to see the man. My plan is to take him to the next public meeting at which Greswold appears as a speaker. He has accepted a little present in advance for his trouble and loss of time, and I think I have secured silence and secrecy on his part. I have only to wait my opportunity for putting his memory to the test.

Waiiing on Fortune,.

CHAPTER XVL

WAITING ON FORTUNE.

Time wore on, and Arnold saw life full of joys,' emotions, and movement for Wilmot and his Ida, who were to be married early in the coming year ; while for him life was like a stagnant pool in tropical Africa, across which never a ripple breaks, save when the dark bulk of a crocodile stirs below the slimy waters. Arnold longed for movement on the part of that one crocodile that lay like a log at the bottom of his life-pool. He had to stand aside and bide his time, while Oliver Greswold was realizing all the ambitions of his eager temperament. He had sprung at a bound into social importance. Six months ago he had been known only as a clever young man, dependent for his daily bread upon a miserly grandfather, and shining in the reflected light of Lord Hild-yard's patronage, able to help his Lordship's schemes with his brains and his voice, but making no figure in the subscription lists where his patron's name shone conspicuous. He was now known as a man of much larger means than Lord

Hildyard had ever possessed, even before he began to impoverish himself for the benefit of his fellow-creatures. The public voice—or rather the voice of that small public which knew Oliver Greswold—exaggerated the amount of his fortune ; and the young philanthropist and orator was now listened to with a new interest at drawing-room meetings, as a reputed millionaire, while his attachment to Lady Violet was dwelt upon as the most romantic thing in modern history.

He bore his prosperity with a good grace, and for the half-year immediately following his grandfather's death he spoke of himself deprecatingly as only a custodian of the property, and refrained from exercising any of the rights of an owner, even in the way of improvement.

*' Every possible means is being taken to find my cousin, if she is living," he told Lord Hildyard, who had lately been made acquainted with his secretary's hopes, and was warmly interested in his fortunes. " My solicitor and co-executor cabled to America and the Colonies, and advertisements have been appearing all over Australia and the United States, in Canada, South America, and the West Indies, and in a large number of Continental papers. We have spent hundreds upon advertising."

" And without result \'7d "

"With the result of producing twenty or thirty claimants—regular Miss Ortons, not one of whom knew my grandfather's name, or where she, the claimant, was born, or her mother's name, or could

Waiting on Fortune.

oblige us with a certificate of her baptism. In most cases the church where Miss Orton was christened was supposed to have been burnt down, and the registers had perished in the flames. There has been a perennial supply of Lilian Carfords since we began to advertise."

" And you think your cousin must be dead \'7d"

" I won't say I fear so—I should be a hypocrite if I pretended not to want this fortune. I do want it; and I believe I have a higher claim upon it than my cousin, and that only sheer perversity upon my grandfather's part would have left it away from me."

•'Remorse, perhaps, rather than perversity," suggested Lord Hildyard.

"Remorse, yes, if the daughter he had cast off had been living, and he could have atoned for years of neglect—years in which he let her starve and perish. But, she being gone, what had remorse to do with the granddaughter he had never seen the offspring of a man he detested ." I have my own theory about my grandfather. Lord Hildyard. which I would not breathe to anybody but you. I believe that from the day of his daughter's elopement the balance of his mind was gone. He was keen enough in business, perfectly able to look after a very complicated mass of property, and to make sure that no man cheated him of a shilling but I think from that time he was what we call a crank. His whole manner of living was that of a monomaniac, taking into account the extent of his means, and

Rough Justice.

the self-indulgent life he had led previously. He ground the faces of the poor in order to pile up money, which he left reluctantly, first to his granddaughter and then to me. It was the merest hazard that he didn't leave it all to a hospital."

" Did he ever tell you he meant to make a will in your cousin's favour.""

" Never. The will was ten years old. I dare say it pleased him to know the surprise he had in store for me. I don't want to speak of him unkindly he is in his grave, and I am likely to profit by his long life of money-grubbing and deprivation but I cannot forget that in all those years he never gave me a word of praise or a sign of affection. He seemed almost irritated with me for coming out in the honour list at Cambridge. He had never heard of a Senior Wrangler doing much good in the world, he told me; and he supposed there were plenty of seventh wranglers breaking stones in Australia. I was seventh on the list, and I thought he might have flung me a kind word when I went back to Clapham. I had kept rigidly within my allowance, and had been content to keep aloof from all the most popular men of my year, and to rank as a smug the worst possible kind of smug, in some men's opinion—the smug who reads hard and never misses a lecture."

" You have had a hard youth, Greswold; but you will now—if this young woman is dead—have grand opportunities, a magnificent career."

With Lord Hildyard a magnificent career meant

a life devoted to picking the fallen out of the mire, and setting weaklings upon their legs, to looking after the health and morals of the working man, to remodelling the dwellings of those who could not afford to pay sanitary engineers or provide scientific ventilation on their own account. Self-abnegation had become as natural to Lord Hildyard as self-indulgence is to most people. ,

CHAPTER XVII.

FOR THE HAPPINESS OF THE GREATEST NUMBER.

Oliver Greswold's first act of ownership, in the beginning of the new year, was the demolition of some of the most profitable house-property in his grandfather's rent-roll. They had been among the worst houses of the London poor, and had yielded from ten to twenty per cent, to their owner. When rebuilt they were to be among the best and healthiest dwellings open to the working classes ; and they would yield their owner at most two and a half per cent., with a very moderate margin for repairs.

" People can afford to hold land that pays them less," Oliver told Lady Violet. " I have no broad acres to be proud of. I want to be proud of my acres of humanity my great piles of human life rising story above story into the clearer air, in airy rooms and spacious corridors, sweet and clean from basement to garret."

He and Lady Violet had planned the houses with the assistance of an architect who, to Violet's eager mind, seemed very inferior to Oliver in the

constructive arts, but who did occasionally throw in a staircase or a chimney shaft which they would have omitted, and who sometimes showed a glimmer of intelligence in the arrangement of fireplaces and windows. Oliver and his sweetheart were so full of architectural ideas, mostly impracticable, that the professional mind seemed narrow and limited in comparison.

Life and the future smiled upon the philanthropist with a new brightness. He was Violet's acknowledged suitor, and they were to be married soon after Ida and Wilmot. A fine old Georgian house in a park of three hundred acres, within ten miles of Lord Hildyard's Yorkshire seat, had been in the market for the last half-dozen years, had been put up for sale twice during that time at a great auction mart in the city of London, and had drawn down the scathing reprobation of a famous auctioneer, who told the room it didn't know how to bid for a good thing when it was offered. Twice had the estate—some nine hundred acres in all been offered to the British public, and twice withdrawn, and many an attempted private treaty had fallen through ; and now from a despairing owner, banished by chronic asthma and chronic poverty from his native soil, Oliver Greswold bought the property for about half the first reserve price which the proud possessor had set upon it when his courage was high.

Wilverwold Park was a fine old English home. The gardens were spacious, and had been established for the best part of two centuries. The

house had been built and finished while the first George was a stranger in England, and while the English people were still wondering at his strange taste in beauty, as exemplified by his two German mistresses, the fat and the thin. Thick walls, narrow windows, large reception rooms with lofty ceilings, a fine hall paved with black and white marble, a carved oak staircase, and a lantern roof were things for a young wife to be proud of, and Lady Violet was very proud of her future home, having known and admired Wilverwold from her childhood, preferring that sober red-brick mansion to the mock Italian villa which her grandfather had built when Lord Liverpool was Minister, and which had all the faults common to the ugliest period in domestic architecture—a heavy portico darkening hall and dining-room, a low slate roof, impertinent columns and meaningless balustrades, dog-hole bedrooms, and reception rooms whose lofty spaciousness sent away every unacclimatized guest with a cold in the head.

Mr. Greswold had bought Wilverwold House with all its belongings, and amongst the furniture, sold by the dispirited proprietor en bloc, there were pieces of Sheraton and Chippendale cabinet work, treasures of old Chinese black and gold screens which would have fetched high prices if offered at Christie's. In a blind ignorance, having failed to get a good price for the land he overrated, Sir Henry Knowlhurst of Wilverwold let his furniture go upon the valuation of a provincial upholsterer, who told him the things were shabby

For the Happiness of the Greatest Ntmtber.

and out of date " quite out of date, Sir 'Enry, and you're very lucky to get 'em off your 'ands."

There was very little to wait for at Wilverwold. Oliver Greswold sent down three chests of plate that had been lying at the Bank ever since his grandfather turned anchorite. A dozen spoons and forks and a tea-service had been enough for the two men, in a house where a visitor was as rare an event as a thunderstorm. The Morris Mortimers, father and son, and the sour-visaged Nonconformist parson, were almost the only visitors Oliver had ever seen in that gloomy dining-room. But now all the treasures that had been hoarded in the dark were to come out into the sunshine, and were to belong to Violet and her husband. The house at Wilverwold was being got ready for them. They were often in Russell Square, and Arnold, who had been accepted by Ida as her sweetheart's adopted brother, frequently met them there. Oliver was always civil to him —civil and indifferent—worlds away from guessing his identity with the man from Africa who had been arrested as Lisa Rayner's murderer.

"He must have kept aloof from the police-court when the inquiry was going on, or he would have remembered the face of the man in the dock," Arnold thought, and this very fact that Greswold had not once looked in at the Court during the twice-adjourned inquiry might seem evidence in his favour.

Would not anxiety have taken him there, almost in spite of himself, had he been guilty?.
Rough Justice.

No. To have shown himself there ever so briefly would have been an imprudence ; and this man was caution personified.

He was less cautious now, perhaps, having prejudged Arnold as a good-natured oaf, incapable of far-reaching suspicions. He went so far as to betray an interest in the half-forgotten Bloomsbury murder by asking Arnold if he had ever met the man Wildover in Africa.

Yes, Arnold confessed to having known the man.

" What kind of fellow was he ?" Greswold asked carelessly.

" The kind of fellow who would be incapable of cold-blooded murder."

" Oh, then, you think he was innocent ? "

" I am sure he was. Do you suppose he was guilty?"

"Oh, I have never thought about him. I remember thinking the case looked rather black. But I have forgotten all details, except that the man hailed from South Africa. Do you know if he went back there ? "

" If he was wise he would get out of England."

"And I suppose among you gold and diamond diggers he would be thought none the worse of for an escapade of that kind "

" For killing a woman in cold blood, because she stood in his way ?"

" Because she stood in his way " repeated Greswold.

" Yes, I take it that must have been the motive."

For the Happiness of the Greatest Number.

" Only if it was the man from Africa. He might have wanted to get rid of an importunate mistress —the survival of a past that sickened him. If the murder was done by a stranger, gain— the money that had just been given her—must have been the motive."

" I see you do remember the details, after all."

"They come back to my memory as we talk. It was a problem case—and crime-problems are always interesting."

"Naturally. One speculates upon the kind of man, and upon his feelings before and after the deed; how much or how little he may suffer. Experience proves that there is a kind of man who doesn't suffer at all."

" Perhaps. A great General does not count the lives lost in a battle, though a mistake in tactics may have involved the sacrifice of thousands. I don't suppose Marlborough regretted Malplaquet, though there were a good many people who thought that victory was only another name for needless carnage. I don't suppose a surgeon frets because many of his finest operations have resulted in death—one life more or less, in a world where everybody must die "

" Is not a subject for life-long remorse. I like your idea of the philosophic assassin, who can put the memory of his crime away from him as calmly as a resolute man can forget the friend he has cut. And then a man might be good all round, except in that one circumstance of a murder. There are cases even in which he might be of more use to

Rough Justice.

his fellow-men because of that murder. He might have sinned for the happiness of the greatest number."

"That is taking a rather wide view of the criminal question. But men are easier under the burden of crime than you and I, who have not dipped our hands in blood, could imagine. I have seen a good deal of the criminal classes, and I never knew a wife-murderer who did not look upon his victim's death as an unlucky accident a perversity in the Power that governs life, rather than a criminal impulse on-his part."

The two men were standing in the deep embrasure of a window in the Russell Square dining-room, talking together in a friendly way, face to face, while the people who had crowded in to tea after a drawing-room meeting gradually dispersed. Greswold had his cup and saucer in his hand, and sipped his tea in the pauses of his talk. Not a flicker of the eyelid, not the faintest quiver of the resolute lips, indicated that the conversation was in ;any way unpleasant to him. His voice—a little fatigued after speaking long and vigorously had been marked by a calm languor, every syllable uttered deliberately, every word following without break or hesitancy.Never was there less suggestion of suppressed feeling in the manner of a man; yet only by that cruel mouth, Arnold might have known him capable of any act, however desperate, that would help him to realize his ambition, to snatch the happiness for which he longed.

For the Happhiess of the Greatest Ntimber.

His eyes softened as he looked at Lady Violet, when she came to him presently, with some trivial inquiry, obviously for the sake of being near him. The eyes changed and brightened with the light that told of a passionate love ; but the mouth was cruel, even when it smiled.Arnold had no more doubt of his guilt than that the March sunlight was shining upon his face as he stood there. He had made up his mind upon that question, even before the motive had revealed itself.

Could he doubt now, when one lonely woman's death made all the difference between dependence and wealth ? He had seen the power of Gresvvold's new position to-day, and how the influence of the popular speaker, the People's Advocate, had been quadrupled by the knowledge of his fortune. He had been speaking on behalf of a new Rescue Society, a society in which all the workers were those who had themselves been among the fallen who had gone down to the depths, and had been saved from deep waters, and knew the horror of a vicious life as no virtuous woman can know it.

" It is noble heroic in a chaste woman to go amongst her fallen sisters," he said, "but half the time it is heroism wasted, self-sacrifice in the wrong place. These dear saints don't know what to say to the sinners. The fellow-feeling is wanting. Only the bitter experience of sin can teach them the way to their erring sister's hearts,"

And then he had drawn a moving picture of the redeemed sinner—no longer young, no longer

Rough Justice.

fair, pleading with youth and beauty, vain, happy, prosperous, tripping with light foot along the primrose path.

"We don't want to save them only at the last, when the tempters have ceased to tempt, and the trade in sin is over; we want to startle them in the morning of sin, while the sun shines, and their world is full of roses. You ladies can hardly grasp the fact that for these your sisters vice means a life of pleasure, and virtue a life of toil. They were starving in garrets, perhaps, yesterday —and to-day they are feasting in fine rooms, wearing fine clothes, driving in the sunshine, caressed, praised, adored, perhaps. The only woman who can startle and win them is the woman who can tell them what comes afterwards —can show them that hideous future in the fierce light of her own experience a woman who is not afraid to speak such words as you ladies have never heard, and could not utter even if you knew them. Sex to sex, sister to sister, it is the fallen who must rescue the fallen."

There had been tears in his voice, and many of his hearers had been moved to tears ; and the women present had responded liberally to his appeal for the help they could give money, clothes, books, furniture, flowers, for the spacious and comfortable Cld house in a remote north-east suburb which he was about to open as the House of Mary Magdalen. It was among the many small properties in the neighbourhood of London which Andrew Greswold had acquired in the

For the Happiness of tJie Greatest Number.

course of his practice as a money-lending solicitor. Every square foot of the five-acre garden and paddock was now a gold-bearing soil, and would have been promptly taken up by the speculative builder, to blossom into terraces and squares for the lower middle class—a class seemingly infinite. Mr. Greswold's generosity in devoting ground so valuable to the uses of charity had been praised and wondered at, but he had put aside all such praises lightly.

"To be of real use the House of Mary Magdalen must be within half an hour's drive of central London," he said. "When a brand has to be snatched from the burning there must be no question of a journey to some remote village—no long waiting at a railway station, affording time to repent of repentance. Rescue work must be prompt and instant. In the wicked London streets an outcast and a wanderer at midnight; in the Home, sheltered, protected, on the threshold of a new life before morning."This House of Mary Magdalen was only one among many gifts which marked Oliver Greswold's succession to the wealth that had so long been growing with compound interest in the miser's keeping, sometimes lying dormant in some sluggish three per cent, debentures, sometimes speculated with a reckless daring, but with a foreknowledge a " flair" which realized cent, per cent. The game of money had been Andrew Greswold's only recreation in all those long years after his retirement from the law. He had played with his

Rough Justice.

capital with the resolute, far-seeing play with which the proficient plays a fine hand at whist. In all that bold handling of an ever-growing capital there had not been one generous use of wealth; nor had the money-grubber's narrow mind ever conceived the idea of wealth as a means to charitable deeds. No pang of remorse had troubled him in the slow decay of a vigorous old age. If he had left his fortune to a hospital, the motive would have been of the basest—the wish to disappoint an expectant heir.

Arnold Wentworth pondered long and deeply upon the problem of Oliver Greswold's nature. Believing, as he did believe, that this wonderworking philanthropist, whose pleading for sinners could move strong men to tears, was himself a sinner, and the vilest of sinners, he asked himself whether it was possible that such a man could have benevolent instincts, a warm, active humanity, keenly alive to the sorrows and sufferings of others. Could love of the race be compatible with inexorable cruelty to the individual.? Could any sane man persuade himself that the murder of a helpless woman, his kinswoman, who had never injured him, was to be justified by the noble uses he could make of a fortune secured by blood ? Remembering that conversation in the embrasure of the window, when for the first time he had discussed the ethics of crime with this suspected murderer, it seemed to him possible that Oliver Greswold had persuaded himself that such a crime might be justified by its results.

For the Happiness of the Greatest Number.

He recalled that allusion to Malplaqiiet a battle so recklessly hazarded, so disastrous a victory, and he remembered that the great Captain who could risk the slaughter of thousands in order to hold his supremacy as a commander had been the fondest, the most devoted of husbands to a termagant wife. These contradictions and inconsistencies are the stuff of which human nature is Yv^oven—a woof of darkness, a warp of light black and silver threads crossing and recrossing. It came within the limits of possibility that this bold sinner was not the despicable hypocrite he had. seemed to Arnold in the first instance.

And this man was to marry a woman who loved him with the generous confidence of youth that knows not the meaning of falsehood or sin. It was impossible to see Lady Violet and her lover together, or to hear her talk of him in his absence, without discovering that to her he was saint-like, God-like, a being as worthy of worship as of love, and to be very sure that for this woman disillusion would mean death. The blow might not destroy that fine frame, in the perfection of healthy girlhood, but it would take all the joy out of the young life. The heart would break, and perhaps brokenly live on. Arnold Wentworth had not the courage to interpose between Violet and her lover—to try to prevent a marriage that seemed sacrilege, considering the spotless innocence of the bride, the awful guilt of the husband. Faunce had warned him that the chain of circumstantial evidence might snap at any point, and

Rough Justice.

prove Greswold to be the victim of a series of curious coincidences. No; he could not say to Violet, " The man you love is a villain," unless he had stronger proof of Greswold's guilt than that which he had himself accepted as conclusive. Events must take their natural course, and as Oliver's wife Violet would only stand in the place of a woman who has loved a scoundrel, and who, having once loved him, would rather mate herself with the darkest consequences of crime than forsake a repentant sinner.

Violet and Ida had been almost inseparable since the two weddings had been fixed. The useful horse that drew Lady Violet's light victoria knew all the turnings between Hyde Park Gardens and Russell Square, and could with difficulty be persuaded to take any other direction.

There was much less talk about trousseau and wedding pageantry than there usually is between young women at such a time. Lady Violet had been brought up in the ways of self-abnegation, and had been taught to think of what she owed to other people, and never of what was due to herself She was oppressed with no idea of what society expected at the marriage of Lord Hild-yard's daughter. Details all-important, all-absorbing to the average bride, were ignored by her. Her father had given her a cheque for more money than she had ever had before, and had begged her to order all that was needful.

"You have no mother not even a kind aunt to assist you, Vi," he had said, "but you have

For the Happiness of the Greatest Number.

plenty of common sense, and I have no doubt you will manage very well."

" I really want very few new frocks, father. We are to live in the country, except when we are with you, and tailor gowns last so long."

" Oh, but you must be smart, my dear. Our Yorkshire neighbours will be critical about you."

"I think they have known me too long to be critical. They would wonder to see your daughter going in for fashion. Don't be frightened, father! I mean to have nice frocks. I want Oliver to be proud of his wife."

Ida, though reared in a philanthropic atmosphere, had a shade more worldliness, and was altogether business-like in her arrangements, taking upon herself the direction and management of every detail upon the ground of Wilmot's incapacity for any business outside a mine. She had pronounced it essential to her happiness that she should live near Violet; and to gratify this wish Wilmot had explored the country within a twenty-mile radius of Wilverwold Park, and had at last succeeded in finding something secluded and uncivilized enough for his South African taste, a house which nobody else would consent to live in, since it stood on the skirts of a moor, nine miles from a railway station, and five from church, doctor, and butcher. But the spot was pronounced healthy, and some moorland shooting might be had. With the bride of his choice, guns, dogs, and a horse or two, Wilmot felt he could be completely happy at Lingfield Lodge.

Rough Justice,

Ida looked a little doubtful when he described this gem of a dwelling, with a wild garden, and a little wood of Scotch firs between garden and moor; but as she had insisted upon living near her dearest friend, and as Lingfield was within seven miles of Wilverwold, she could hardly withhold her approval.

" I should have preferred being close to a dear little town, with a nice church, and a conscientious old doctor, and a few decent people—parson, and so on—to drop in to tea. I shall have to ride and cycle, and shoot and fish to fill my time; especially as there are no cottagers within a walk for me to look after."

" Not a roof or a barn within eye-range."

"It must be lonelier than Cornwall or Ireland."

" It is. But there are plenty of snipe and plover."

Ida Borrodaile and Mary Freeland had grown fast friends in the familiarity of philanthropic gatherings in Russell Square and evening parties at Hexton Gardens, so Mary was to be the second of two bridesmaids, that modest number being the utmost Wilmot could tolerate. He had told his sweetheart that if she or her people organized a fine wedding, he should inevitably run away before the event.

"You would have fourteen bridesmaids and no bridegroom," he said. "I shouldn't want to do anything so dastardly, but the impulse would be stronger than me—I should bolt."

" Fourteen would be preposterous, but two will be very shabby," Ida answered discontentedly.

Happily for Wilmot, Mrs. Borrodaile's bad health was a powerful factor in the domestic arrangements. As a professional invalid, she insisted upon a subdued ceremonial. Everything was to be in half tones. If she were required at the church, there must be no fuss or bustle. She was not sure that her nerves would stand Mendelssohn's noisy march; but, of course, if Ida insisted upon it, the march must be played. ' A crowded reception after the wedding was out of the question. It would be worse than one of those dreadful drawing-room meetings, which always brought on her neuralgic pains, even though she was never in the room. The noise of people going up and down stairs made her a perfect wreck for a week afterwards.

" I should like to have seen all my friends," Ida murmured. " I shall only be married once, mother,"

" And you can only kill your mother once, Ida. I don't think you would wish to do that."

"Dearest, dearest mother, don't say such dreadful things. The wedding shall be as quiet as you like."

"Thank you, my love. That is a weight off my mind. I have been thinking what a trial your wedding would be for my poor nerves ever since you were born,"

Her wishes being thus complied with, Mrs. Borrodaile acted handsomely in the matter of house linen, and long-hoarded silver was brought out of the strong room in the basement, and Ida felt that, in spite of the quiet wedding, she was

Rough Justice.

being launched upon the matrimonial ocean with all due honours.

Arnold was his friend's best man, and was thus brought again into Mary Freeland's company. He had avoided all chances of meeting her since her return from Eastbourne. He had not even sent her a Christmas card, she told Ida piteously, forgetting, perhaps, what a bitter anniversary Christmas was for him, and how the remembrance of that Christmas tragedy in Dynevor Street might shut out all cheerful and gracious thoughts. It had not been so with Arnold, however; for although his memory had been full of that last Christmas Eve, and the pathetic interview, his own painful sense of being unkind to a woman who loved him, the tears, the sad parting, the unspeakable horror that came afterwards, there had yet been room in his mind for thoughts of Mary, as he passed the smart shops, full of expensive prettiness, where other people were buying gifts for their beloved. He refrained from gift or greeting to his dearest, resolute to stand aloof until he could bring her evidence that would take the stain from his name, the shadow from his life.

On the wedding day it was Mary who held herself aloof, seemingly unconscious of Arnold's existence after the first cold touch of meeting hands. She looked almost as white as her gown and hat, and was not an ideal bridesmaid, her pallid cheeks contrasting strangely with the pink chubbiness of Ida's other friend.

Lady Violet and her betrothed were among the

few guests, and Arnold was touched with that spectacle of happy love, so free from apprehension upon Violet's part, knowing that it was perhaps his mission to change the cup of joy into a cup of bitterness.

"Am I to think of mercy in dealing with a wretch who was merciless—who would have let me suffer on the gallows, and would have gone on his way reaping the harvest of virtue, with a soul steeped in blood ? No, there can be no question of mercy—no relenting or looking back."

Rough Justice.

CHAPTER XVIII.

WHAT HE MEANT TO DO.

Arnold was not an invited guest at Lady Violet's wedding, but he was an attentive spectator of tlie ceremony among the idle young ladies who had got wind of the marriage, and the nurses who had dropped in on seeing the carriages drive to the church door, and the red carpet laid in readiness for satin-shod feet.

The nurses condemned the whole function as a shabby affair, but were agreed that the bride looked as beautiful as a statue, and carried herself like a queen. She was not one of those crying brides whom the nurses spoke of contemptuously, as not knowing their own minds, and spoiling their looks with red eyelids, and upsetting everybody. Nor was she one of those voiceless brides who open tremulous lips and gasp like a fish when called upon to utter the words that mean fate. Low and clear and distinctly audible were her answers to the fateful questions, and even the furthest off among the nursemaids heard and approved that firm utterance.

What he Meant to Do.

Arnold heard her from his place in the shelter of clustered columns, heard her with an aching heart. Truth, love, beauty, purity, all were being given to a man whose guilt-stained soul he knew; and he had done nothing to save her.

"It would have been useless," he told himself. "She would not have believed me. What woman would believe a stranger in opposition to the man she loves ? Love is deaf as well as blind— illogical—wrong-headed. Love is love. No, I should but have made a false move, spoilt my own game, and saved her not one pang. She must dree her weird."

Mary Freeland and Mrs. Tresillian-Smith were among the wedding guests ; a somewhat premature present from Mrs. Smith having reversed the order of the game, and produced the invitation card in response to the gift, instead of the gift in response to the invitation. Mary was wearing her bridesmaid's frock and hat, and was looking prettier to-day in her unconsciousness of Arnold's vicinity than she had looked at the former wedding, when her pale cheeks and air of offended pride clouded her frank English beauty. Mary's was a beauty made for happiness—a delightful Aurora or Hebe, but a very poor model for Electra or Antigone.

They were married, the low-born money-lender's grandson, and Violet, the daughter of a. man whose distinguished lineage was forgotten in the lustre of his benevolence. Philanthropy, public speaking, sympathy with the working man had

Rough Justice.

done this thing for Oliver Greswold; and there were cynics who had watched his career and envied him his talents, and who now went about saying that he had made philanthropy pay.

Bride and bridegroom went to Italy for their honeymoon. They were bound first for Sorrento, travelling by easy stages, and, after seeing Naples, Sicily, and Capri, they were going back to finish their holiday in Rome, only returning to England in time for Oliver to stand for a certain East End constituency in a district where his triumphant return was a foregone conclusion. The present member was a distinguised lawyer expectant of being raised to the Bench, and there was very little doubt that the seat would be vacant before long.

And thus Arnold's enemy vanished out of his ken, while the chain of evidence was still incomplete, and Arnold, sadly missing his friend Wilmot, walked about London idle and discontented, fit neither for work nor play, and heartily wishing himself back at the Rand. If it had not been for Mary's sake he would have gone there, and left the missing links in the chain to Fate or Providence ; but he loved Mary, and he knew that she loved him, and was waiting for him, and loyalty to that unspoken contract kept him at home. Sometimes he had thoughts of running down to Suffolk to see his mother, but his mind was too much troubled for him to find happiness in such a meeting. He knew that she would question him closely about himself, and that he would find it difficult to answer her questions ; so he deferred

What he Meant to Do.

the meeting, and was content to write occasionally under cover to the faithful factotum, and to receive long, fond letters from the loving mother—letters in which she thanked and blessed him for not going back to Africa.

He saw Faunce from time to time, and Faunce was as keen upon discovery as he had been in the beginning of things. He had been in Paris, and he had been in Vienna, but declared that the result was not worth discussing.

"When I have any facts worth putting before you, Mr, Wildover, you shall have them. In the meantime a little moving about does me good. It enables me to shake ofif my Putney sluggishness."

He was firm in his opinion that the question of Lisa Rayner's death could never be reopened in a court of law to any useful end.

"No magistrate in London would accept such evidence as we can produce," he said. "The case would be dismissed as soon as you had made your statement. What witnesses have you ? The Durfins, who might be firm in their recognition of their lodger, but who could prove nothing except that he was living opposite the house where Mrs. Rayner was murdered, and left almost immediately after the murder. The gun-makers' assistant has failed to identify him. I took him to a Mechanics' Institute at the East End, where Greswold was one of the speakers, a week before his marriage, and the man saw him and heard him, and could make nothing of him. The goggles

Rough Justice.

that hid his eyes and the bowler hat that hid his forehead would make a great difference, you see ; not enough to deceive a man like me, with a memory for faces and a habit of registering every feature, but quite enough to baffle the casual observer."

"Well, I suppose, after all our patience and perseverance and lucky hits, the evidence isn't worth much from the legal point of view. But give me the moral certainty. Let me be able to say to the girl I love. That man is the murderer! and to demonstrate his guilt by evidence that I can make as clear to her as it is to me. Help me to do that, and I shall be satisfied—even if I never see him at the Old Bailey, never hear St. Sepulchre's bell toll for him,"

Easter and Whitsuntide were past, and Arnold had heard no more from Faunce, who had taken various other investigations in hand, and had spent a good deal of his time on Continental journeys, since the beginning of the year.

" They will have me at my old work, Mr. Wild-over, whether I like it or not," he told Arnold, who was strongly of opinion that Faunce did like his old work, and liked no other.

The year wore on. Greswold had been returned by his East End constituency, unopposed. His popularity in that particular district was so well known that nobody had cared to waste time and money in fighting him. The fact that he was now a rich man, and that long-needed institutions— baths and wash-houses, and a nursery—were being

What he Meant to Do.

built at his sole expense would have made opposition madness. There was nothing to be done against him in this hey-day of his fame. Every day he lived was an exemplification of the cynical adage—"Nothing succeeds like success." There would come a time, no doubt, when the wheel would turn, and the rabble who were full of gratitude to-day would begin to carp and question, to belittle everything he had done for them, and to talk of all the things he had left undone.

He had been heard in the House very often before the end of the session ; and he had been active upon every question that involved the welfare of the masses. He was among the ultra-Radicals, the men who want to abolish almost everything that makes up old-fashioned people's idea of England, and to create a new England, without an established Church, or a House of Peers, or a great Capitalist, and possibly without a beer-shop along ten miles of dusty high-road—an over-educated and very uncomfortable England, in which Jack was to be not only as good, but a great deal better than his Master.

Arnold heard of Oliver Greswold's popularity in Yorkshire from Wilmot Armstrong, who was pressing in his invitations to his old chum to go and stay at Lingfield, and do a little fishing, or go to all the summer races within a day's journey, by road or rail. Arnold wanted to be at Lingfield later, and he had his own plans with reference to that visit.

It was not till September that he received any

communication of importance from Faunce ; but early in that month a telegram summoned him to Putney. It was the briefest of messages: "News for you—at home all afternoon."

Arnold was in a hansom-cab bowling along the Embankment five minutes after the telegram was handed to him.

"Well," said Faunce, who was sunburnt from foreign travel, and looked as jovial as a man who has been doing nothing but amuse himself, " I think I have taken your business as far as it will go, and that I have been about as much use to you—or as little—as I am likely to be."

"You have been of the greatest use—without you I could have done nothing."

" It's very nice of you to say that. I think I have made that poor young woman's identity as clear as it could be made—having no better evidence of name than that little Lutheran Testament, which helped me to find Fraulein Noack. Without her we might never have discovered the man called Clissold."

" That was not his real name, I suppose ?"

"No, it was not his real name—yet he had a kind of claim to it. I found on looking up Lodge that Carford is the family name of Lord Felixstowe, and that the last Lord Felixstowe married the only daughter and heiress of John Clissold, of the Towers, Wavertree, Liverpool. There is a famous firm of shipbuilders at Liverpool called Clissold, and I dare say this Clissold was a member of that

firm. There, you see, you have the names of Carford and Clissold in close association. Now, the late Lord Felixstowe was well known on the turf, and known as a shady customer, whose stable was suspected of in-and-out running, and whose horses were only backed by the greenhorns. A little cautious stimulation of old Ludgater's memory produced the fact that Lord Felixstowe was one of his late master's most important clients. Tin deed-boxes with his name were still in the loft at the Belvidere when Ludgater left Mr. Greswold's service."

" Oh, Ludgater has left him, then ?" "Yes, he has retired with a liberal pension, and has nothing but good to say of his master's heir, who might have thrown him upon the Union, as there was no provision made for him in the old man's will. There never was such a cruel will, Ludgater said, for if ever a servant had a right to be provided for, he—Ludgater—had that right, and his master of forty years had not left him forty shillings. ' I think he would have liked us all to rot,' said Ludgater. * I believe he felt so savage at not being able to take his money with him that he left it so as to give everybody as much trouble and vexation as possible. Or else he would hardly have given the granddaughter he never saw preference over the grandson who had lived with him and knuckled under to him all his life.' I didn't think it worth while to suggest that this inconsistency was only one of the numerous inconsistencies that make the sum of human

Rough Justice.

nature. If I were describing the average man by figures, Mr. Wildover, the total to be a hundred, I should reckon generosity fifteen, justice five, honesty five, acquisitiveness, envy, and jealousy thirty, inconsistency forty-five. That is my experience of the human race, and that is why no man's conduct can be calculated beforehand. Here you have the least likely will for an offended father to make. Here you have the least likely man to be a murderer. But I am rambling away from our business."

Faunce went on with his story, and did not again diverge into any expression of his own opinions.Ludgater, having been put on the right scent by the mention of Lord Felixstowe, presently, unassisted by any furthur suggestion, recalled the name of Carford. The young man who had come on several occasions to the Belvidere, at first as a client of Andrew Greswold, and later as a surreptitious visitor to the young lady, was the Honourable Ralph Carford, Lord Felixstowe's second son. He lived most of his time near Epsom with his lordship's trainer, and was well known as a gentleman jock, having ridden his father's horses in the crack steeplechases, as well as in a great many smaller races—such as Windsor.Yes, Carford was the man ; a handsome, attractive-looking man, always well-dressed in a sporting style ; age, at the time of the elopement, about thirty. The young lady was under twenty-one.Armed with this knowledge, it had been an

Wkal he Meant to Do.

easy matter for Faunce to trace the marriage of these two before the Clapham Registrar, and, further, to find their whereabouts in Paris, where they occupied a fourth floor in the Faubourg St. Honore, and where the record of Mr. Carford's habits was still existent in the memory of an old woman who had been portress and bonne-d-tout faire in the house, and who now sold newspapers in a kiosk on the Boulevard St. Michel.

From this old woman, hunted down after considerable trouble, Faunce had heard not only the habits of Mr, Carford, his frequent absences across the Channel, his riding in steeplechases at Dieppe and in Brittany, his variable fortunes and variable tempers, his reckless money-spending, late hours, and occasional drunkenness ; but he also heard that all this information had been given two years ago to an Englishman, who spoke French like a native, and who had taken great trouble to discover the ci-devant portress.This had been Faunce's first knowledge of the French-speaking Englishman, whom he heard of after this at every halting-place on Ralph Carford's road to ruin. Wherever he found the trace of Carford under this or that change of name—he also found that the same inquirer had been there before him ; and after hearing this inquiring spirit described by a great many different people—more or less minutely he had not the shadow of doubt as to the man's identity. He must be Stephen Bardhurst, and no other.This Bardhurst was a private detective who had

Rough Justice.

begun life as a gentleman and amateur actor, who had then gone on the stage, and acted at London theatres for three or four seasons, with some success in certain character parts, but with a lack of voice and presence which barred his achieving a permanent position on the boards. He had then taken to the delicate-investigation business, and had done well in it, exacting swinging terms from jealous wives and husbands who wanted to cut the matrimonial knot with the ' " abhorred shears " of the Divorce Court. His experience as a character-actor made him good at disguises; while his education and antecedents had enabled him to hold his own where the average Scotland Yard detective would have shown the cloven foot of the policeman in the gentleman's dress boot. In following up Carford from city to city, from affluent dissipation to penury and ruin, Mr. Bard-hurst had not considered disguise necessary. His own close-cropped scanty head and crooked nose had been good enough for the job, and these, with the freckled complexion, narrow shoulders, and slight stoop, were enough to denote the man. He had traced various stages in the well-born adventurer's career, and Faunce had followed, there being always at each stage some indication that led to the next: although in some cases the scent was so weak as to require much patience and energy on the part of the sleuth hound. Step by step the miserable lives were traced   the daughter's birth in Paris ; the return to London during her infancy; then back to Paris ; then, after three years, to Havre, whence Carford sailed for New York, and where the wife and child hved in decent poverty during his two years' absence, and where the wife died and was buried shortly before his return. Then the departure of the father with his seven-year-old child for Germany; and then, after a dissipated and disreputable career at Frankfort, Hamburg, and Berlin, the final remove to Vienna, where he called himself Clissold, and where he sank to the lowest depth of sordid debauchery, drunkard, gambler, cheat, his miserable death unnoticed save by the police authorities, who recorded it as one of the tragic entries in their calendar of vice and crime.

Faunce had discovered that during all these years Ralph Carford had been drawing an income of a little less than two hundred a year, chargeable upon his father's estate, and paid half-yearly through the family solicitor ; and it was partly by these payments, through local bankers, that Faunce and the sandy-haired Bardhurst before him had been able to follow the reprobate's career.

There was no link missing in the history of Julia Greswold's husband, and no shadow of doubt that the hapless woman known to Charlotte Noack as Lisa Clissold, and to Arnold Wentworth as Lisa Rayner, was Lilian Carford, granddaughter and heiress, had she survived him, of Andrew Greswold. "

"You made no discovery as to the man who took Lisa away from that wretched home in the Vienna lodging-house," Arnold asked, hesitatingly.

Rough Justice.

" No; there are too many men of that class in Vienna. The search would have been endless."

"And it matters so little, after all. The story y^ou heard from the servant proves how bitterly that poor girl suffered before she took the fatal step. What excuses she might have made for herself when she told me the story of her fall! And she made none. She humbled herself in the dust; she thought herself the worst of sinners. Oh, what a life it was, Faunce, and what a death! The sinner who was responsible for the life has gone to his account. The sinner who has to answer for the death shall be my business."

"You don't suppose you can bring him to the gallows to the Old Bailey, even upon such evidence as this ? "

" There is no link wanting. We have the motive. We know that the man was there on the night of the murder within a few yards of his victim."

"Yes, we know he was there or we think we do but that's not the same thing as making a jury know it—or getting a police magistrate to believe that Oliver Greswold, the working man's friend and advocate, is a murderer. The woman was murdered, and he was a gainer by her death ; but we have no evidence that he murdered her. Suppose the Durfins are firm in their recognition of him as their mysterious lodger. What does that prove ? He would give some plausible excuse for his assumed name, some plausible account of his business in that part of the town, and his character would in itself seem a sufficient refutation

of such a charge—unless backed by overwhelming evidence."

"The Sergeant who saw him following his victim ?"

"No evidence that the woman the Sergeant saw was Lisa Rayner, or that the man was Oliver Greswold. We have a strong series of probabilities, a chain of conjectures ; but we have no case for a magistrate, least of all for a jury. In my own mind I have now very little doubt that Greswold killed her. He and Morris Mortimer are close allies, and Mortimer may have told him the contents of his grandfather's will, and so set him upon his plan, first to trace his cousin, and then to get rid of her. Perhaps to a man of that kind it would seem hardly a crime to make an end of such a life as hers. He may have thought her life less innocent than it was, you see and that he, the saint, had a superior right to the fortune."

"Well, he may escape the law of the land," interrupted Arnold, impetuously, "but he shall not escape me. After all, what would it profit her, at rest under the rose trees at Highgate, that this man should die by the hangman's hand ." And what does it matter to me, personally, what the world at large thinks of Lisa Rayner's murderer, when there are only about three people — yourself, Chilbrick, and one other—who know me as the man from South Africa, locked up for a month under suspicion. But I want that one other to know that Oliver Greswold was the murderer—and not I—and she shall know it."

Rough Justice.

"How?"

"From his own confession."

" To whom ? He might confess to the chaplain at Newgate, in the condemned cell; but as you will never get him there "

"His confession to me, Faunce to me, the man who has suffered for his crime, his deliberate statement over his own signature, given in the presence of the woman who is to be my wife, or so given that she cannot doubt it."

" You think you can bring him to that ?"

" Think! I say I mean to do it. I shall live for nothing else. It is only a question of life and time; his life and mine. One of us may die before it is done ; but if we both live, by God's grace it shall be done."

The American Remembers.

CHAPTER XIX.

THE AMERICAN REMEMBERS.

This life has nothing more exquisite than the first year of a love match, a marriage of minds and hearts, a union upon which Heaven and friends and fortune smile. At morning and night, upon her knees, Lady Violet Gresvvold offered up her gratitude to the Creator, who had given her so happy a lot. There was no cloud on her horizon, no fear in her heart that life would ever be less perfect; save that one fear of sickness and of death which lies always at the bottom of all human bliss, the knowledge that in a day, in an hour, the light may change to darkness. Happily, in the glow of youth and health, in a busy life full of duties to be done, the haunting shadow of man's common doom came but seldom across her path. Sickness, old age, and death seemed very far off; especially to one whose parish-visiting had brought her, for the most part, in contact with extreme old age. It seemed to her, indeed, that among those hardy Yorkshire peasants it was more difficult to die than to live. They suffered diseases that would have killed Hercules,

Rough Justice.

and held fast by life for years after any London physician would have condemned a London patient. Seeing such powers of resistance in the lives she knew, it was but natural that she should think of her husband as if he were immortal. Indeed, there were times when she seemed so to think of him, weaving her bright dreams of his future, ambitious only for him, proud only of him.

His success in the House of Commons enchanted her. To her, he was a heaven-born debater. The wrongs of all the ages would be righted now that he was in his proper place, to fight the cause of the lowly born and the oppressed, the hewers of wood and drawers of water, the little children toiling in mills and factories, or in the darkness under ground, as her father had fought for them when he was a young man in the House of Commons. Many wrongs had been righted, much had been gained on the side of enlightenment since Lord Hildyard had come from Oxford to cast in his lot with Reformers and Peace-lovers, but much still remained to be done ; and the people were asking for much more now than they would have thought of claiming when her father was young. The views of the Proletariat as to their own rights had widened considerably since Lord Hildyard began his great fight for the working-man.

Lady Violet and her husband lived at Hyde Park Gardens during Oliver's first session ; and the young wife's fair face and tall, slim figure were often to be seen at tea-time on the House

of Commons terrace, where she loved to sit with her husband, hearing the prospects of the evening's debate, at a httle table apart from those gayer groups assembled for pleasure only. Their talk was serious, and she felt as if the happiness of a people depended on the speech of the husband she loved. To her he was not a unit in the House ; he was the House itself, or all that was worthy to be considered there. Greswold insisted that she should read the whole of a debate in which he took part, and tried to make her see the merits of other speakers on his side, even if she could admit no merits in his opponents ; but to her mind the speeches of other Members were only the quartz out of which the gold of his eloquence was extracted.

And now, when the session was over, and all the smart people were scattering themselves over the continent of Europe, Greswold and his wife were living quietly at Wilverwold House, where he was resting after a really laborious session, in which he had worked with all the unmeasured energy of a man to whom Parliamentary life is still new. The time when he would learn to spare himself, to hold his power in reserve for great occasions, had not yet come ; nor had he spared himself outside the House any more than inside. He had spoken at all the old places, the Mechanics' Halls, and Free Libraries, and Provident Institutes, and Polytechnics, at which he had been accustomed to speak ; he had superintended the beginning of philanthropic schemes which his wealth was to

Rough Justice.

establish. He had worked with unremitting energy; and the result was that he came to Wilverwold looking fagged, and as an American friend who was on a visit to him put it, very-much under the weather.

"A week in our moorland air will cure him," Violet said ; and she made it the business of her life that he should have rest and recreation.

She sent him out upon fishing expeditions with Mr. Somerville, his friend from New York—a man who had been doing in the worst slums of that city very much the same kind of work that Greswold had been doing in East London. She organized picnic-luncheons and long excursions; she contrived a life under the open sky, determined to keep her husband away from those blue books to which so much of his existence had been given. And this out-of-door life she could share with him. Her country habits had made her a good walker, and twelve or fifteen miles seemed no more for her than a walk across Hyde Park for her Bayswater neighbours.

Wilmot and Ida were established at Lingfield, and shared in many of these excursions, every ruin and every waterfall serving as an excuse for a ten-mile drive and an out-of-door meal. Violet quoted " In Memoriam," and compared their talk with the discourse of those bright, incomparable spirits who loved to " banquet in the distant woods," and who

"glanced from theme to theme, Discussed the books to love or hate, Or touch'd the changes of the State, Or threaded some Socratic dream,"

while the wine flask cooled under dusky waters, and the simple meal was spread upon heather-scented sward.

There was talk enough at these rustic meals, albeit the talkers were inferior spirits to Arthur Hallam and Alfred Tennyson. There were youth and energy, ambition, and the love of books worthy to be loved.

Violet thought her husband equal to any man who had lived before him. He was not a poet, but his life was full of aspirations and schemes that he who wrote " Maud " would have honoured, would have woven into immortal verse, perhaps, had he heard the philanthropist expound his far-reaching views, and paint the fairer future of regenerate mankind—poverty that should be no longer sordid or loathly ; toilers who should be no longer dwellers in the dark of ignorance and neglect; a world whose blessings should be shared as fairly as angels and seraphs share the bliss of heaven.The most vehement, and not the least interesting in the little band of talkers, was Laurence Somer-ville, Mr. Greswold's American guest, whose friendship seemed none the less cordial because it was a thing of recent growth.Somerville was Greswold's senior by only a few years, and had been attracted to him by his reputation as Lord Hildyard's lieutenant. The American had inherited a large fortune, and had devoted a considerable portion of his time and wealth to schemes for the public good, and had,

Rough Justice.

therefore, a peculiar interest in such work as Lord Hildyard was doing, together with a settled conviction that nothing done in England could be done as intelligently or as effectually as what he and others were doing in New York.

"I thought I should like to see if there were any strong points in your work," he told Oliver frankly. " Of course, I knew I should find plenty of mistakes. I was keener in getting at your ideas than at his lordship's. He belongs to a played-out generation. Wilberforce and his lot thought they were doing a good deal when they emancipated the coloured man—they haven't seen the last of him yet, by the way—and started a ragged school or two. And even now you think that a night refuge, where your pauper population can be dirty and uncomfortable under cover, is the way to salvation. We've gone you several better on that. We don't think we're doing a heap when we feed one in ten, and leave the other nine to starve. We've got to look after everybody, if we can find the hang of it—and we mean to find it sooner or later."

And then he looked round, smiling at the little circle, as if he had been saying the politest thing possible.He had heard Oliver speak a good many times in London and the suburbs, and had condescended to no word of praise, which reticence would have made Violet dislike him had there not been a pleasantness in the man's voice and face, and a magnetism in the man's manner which compelled

The American Remembers.

every woman's liking. But while she was thinking him a Goth in this matter of non-appreciation, he startled her one day by saying, " I've heard your husband more than once. Well, ma'am, he can speak. He's what we call a speaker. There aren't many of 'em. When I hear a speaker I know it. He was born that way."

Late in September the little circle was increased by the arrival of Mary Freeland at Lingfield, delighted at the prospect of a long holiday from the conventionalities of South Kensington.

"You needn't even wear gloves here, unless you like the sensation," Ida told her. " I never wear mine except for church and visiting. I am always doing something with flowers, or ferns, or dogs, something that makes gloves a nuisance. Of course, I have gardening gloves—but they are generally in my pocket. You have no idea how delicious life is here after a long course of Russell Square. The moorland air makes me feel drunk, and I go dancing along over the heather like a lunatic. If my poor mother would only come here, a dreadful thing would happen to her. She would get well."

"Dreadful, Ida!"

"Dreadful for her, poor dear. She has been ill for years, don't you know. Her illness is her only occupation, the only interest she has in life. What would become of her if she began to feel thoroughly well to have no excuse for listening to herself, as the French call it. It would be too cruel! Mother so enjoys her privileges as a confirmed invalid."

Rough Justice.

Mary was delighted with Lingfield—the solitude, the wide horizon, the heathery wastes, gemmed here and there with a dark tarn that flashed in the sunlight, the marshy hollows above which the peewits screamed and soared, as she and her friends rode by. They had found her a horse that would have carried her all over the three Ridings, Wilmot assured her, "without being sick or sorry," and who was all the better for doing twenty miles a day. So when Wilmot was shooting, and didn't want feminine company, the two girls rode over the moors, or in the grass lanes, at their own sweet will; or went to Wilver-wold, and spent a long afternoon in the garden with Violet, and sometimes with Violet's husband, who would sit and brood over a book, or lie in a hammock seemingly asleep, while the young women dawdled through a game of croquet, or indulged in the mild diversion of garden golf, or sauntered about the gardens. Mary remembered her last holiday with Mrs. Smith, a holiday in which prunes and prism had ever been the first consideration, a holiday which had carried to country lanes and woods the gloves and fichus, and narrow rules, and social shams of Hexton Gardens.

In Yorkshire she had felt more alive than she had ever felt since she left the Saxon. She felt her youth in her veins as she had felt it in South Africa.

" I believe you are Bohemians at heart, both of you," she told Ida and her husband. " I am as

TJie American Remembers.

much at my ease with you as with my dear old uncle and aunt at Johannesburg. I suppose it comes of your haying lived at the Rand, Mr. Armstrong. South Africa is my idea of a liberal education."

" But Ida is a thorough Bohemian. Look at her sunburnt hands! And she has never seen the Orange Free State."

" Ida is like you' as the husband is the wife

"Well, I'm glad you like African rovers, Miss Freeland, for I expect one of them in a day or two; and I hope you and Ida will make him happy here."

Mary blushed crimson, with a sudden overpowering gladness.

" Is it Mr. Wentworth "

"Yes, it is Wentworth. He and I are like brothers, you know. He is not so light-hearted as he used to be ; but I think you can make him forget his troubles."

" I wish I could," said Mary, frankly.

" I don't see why he should have any troubles," said Ida, "or why he should hold himself aloof from some one he dearly loves for I know he does love you, Molly. Don't blush, dear. We have no secrets among us. Why should he trifle with happiness ? He has plenty of money, and you have plenty. Why shouldn't you be married this year, and settle somewhere near us ? There are always nice places coming into the market. He is a fool not to know where his happiness lies."

Rough Justice.

"If you talk like that, Ida, I shall pack my box, and go back toHexton Gardens. Mr. Wentworth has never said a word about marrying me. Nothing is further from his thoughts or from mine."

She had to rise from the garden seat and hurry away to hide her tears after this protest, too keenly remembering that bitter day in Hexton Gardens when he had come to her, strong in the pride of integrity, warm with love ; when she might have made him her own for life ; and when her egregious folly had lost him. To have suspected him, her noblest and dearest, of a cruel murder! She must have been demented. She had allowed her poor weak brain to be made a receptacle for other people's suspicions and opinions. People for whom she cared not a straw had told her that he, her true love, was a murderer, and she had believed them.

There are men not a numerous class who can keep a friend's secret even from a wife. Wilmot was among that faithful band. Ida knew nothing of the dark episode in the life of Wentworth, alias Wildover and knew not the alias ; for there had been no letter-writing between the Orange Free State and Russell Square. Wilmot had gone to the Cape a man on his trial. If he proved Vorthy he might come back some years later and offer himself again as a suitor for Miss Borrodaile. Until he proved himself worthy she must hold no communication with him. His sins had been only the sins of youth, but they had seemed terrible

The American Remembers.

in the sight of Mr. Borrodaile ; and this Draconian sentence had been pronounced against him.

Arnold arrived next day. He knew that his love was at Lingfield ; and, in spite of his recent avoidance of her, he had his reasons for wishing her to be near at hand during his visit. He had even asked Wilmot to get her invited there. But they met as they had always met of late, as if they were on the most distant footing a friendship so cold as to seem little more than a casual acquaintance.He was looking thin and careworn, and more given to intervals of deep thought than a man who had come to shoot and fish and enjoy life at his friend's house ought to have been. He was absent-minded, and had to be spoken to three or four times on occasions, before he could be roused to answer some trivial question about a gun or a dog, whether he would go with the shooters or ride or drive with Ida and Mary. He was curiously indifferent, except when there was a question of joining the Wilverwold party, and then he was always eager.Mary's heart sank with a sickening fear sometimes. Had he fallen in love with Lady Violet.? No, there could not be such a tragedy. She was a jealous fool to imagine such a thing.

"You seem to have taken a great liking to Greswold," Wilmot said; " and yet I shouldn't have thought him the kind of man you would like."

" One may be interested in a man without any ardent liking. This man interests me."

Rough Justice.

" Well, he is a man of strong character, no doubt; but I didn't know you were a student of human nature."

"A new faculty with me, perhaps developed by long idleness. One had no time to study human nature on the Rand; one only wanted to feel sure it hadn't a knife in its hand, or a revolver at one's ear. I am interested in Greswold, and in his American friend."

" His American friend is interested in you. I saw him studying your face at lunch yesterday,"

" Did you > Another student of human nature, I suppose."

Greswold and Somerville were to meet Wilmot and his guest that morning. The Wilverwold shootings included a part of the moor behind Lingfield, and extended over a wide expanse of barren country. There was a keeper's lodge in the midst of this barrenness which had been untenanted for years, no keeper caring to live in a spot remote from civilization, and esteemed unhealthy, while there were cottages to be had nearer Wilverwold village. The deserted hovel was in a picturesque spot, looking over wastes of heather and gorse, and the distant darkness of fir woods. Lady Violet had known the lodge all her life, and was pleased at being able to do what she liked with it. Under her orders it was made wind and weather tight, lined with blue-grey tapestry, furnished with bamboo chairs and tables, and provided with a stove that would cook a luncheon and boil water for tea. This was now

the chosen resort of the shooters when sharp-set after a long morning's tramp, and a favourite rendezvous for afternoon tea, when the home garden was renounced on account of the colder weather. From Wilverwold House to the shooters' lodge was a three-mile walk.

Greswold and his friends had spent the morning on the moors, and had parted company at the lodge, after lunch, Wilmot and Arnold intending to walk back to Lingfield, while Greswold drove his American guest home to Wilverwold in his dog-cart.

Both men were thoughtful, and the rough track between the lodge and the high road made careful driving necessary, and was an excuse for silence on the driver's part. Somerville was the first to speak.

"I don't fancy you've had much of a time today," he said.

" What makes you think so \'7d "

"Well, you looked bored. I don't believe you care a lot for shootinsr."

"I don't. I was not bred up as a sportsman. I shoot because open-air exercise is good for me, and because it pleases my wife to see me tramping about the moor. But I miss a bird as often as I hit one ; and, what's more, I don't care whether I hit or miss. My heart isn't in it."

"No more is that man Wentworth's, though he's no slouch of a shot. I don't think he is here for the shooting."

" What then .? He is here to get rid of his life.

Rough Justice.

perhaps. Half of the people in the world have no stronger motive."

" He ain't here for the girl, eh ?"

"Miss Freeland—a pretty piece of commonplace. The Queen could call out regiments of such girls if they were wanted."

"He ain't here for the girl. I don't like that man's way, Gresvvold. There's something back of it. I don't think he's the kind of man who ought to be admitted into a man's home. Your neighbour Armstrong seems a real good sort, and I don't like to see him making a friend of that man."

" Oh, Armstrong knows all about him; the best and the worst. They were chums in South Africa a kind of adopted brothers digging for diamonds, or gold ; I forget which."

"A gold-digger in South Africa, was he?" exclaimed Somerville, eagerly. " Then my memory for faces didn't play me any tricks—in spite of the whiskers."

" What do you mean ?"

"He is the man I thought. ' I remembered him though when I saw him nearly two years ago he had whiskers that covered up his chin. I was puzzled the first time we were out with him. Where did I see that fellow where when.? Why is his face so familiar to me the forehead and eyes, the way the hair grows at the temples, like the portraits of Henri Ouatre.? I kept asking myself questions all the time we were with him. I am a man who gets worried about that

kind of thing. Where, when did I see him ? Why did his face make such an impression upon me ? He must have interested me more than the common herd, or I shouldn't have such a distinct idea of him. To-day as we were sitting at lunch the place, the atmosphere, the hour of our last meeting, came upon me in a flash, and I was there again, in the foggy London police court— lamps burning in your British daylight, candles on the Magistrate's desk, and that man standing in the dock on suspicion of murder—the man from South Africa."

The hands on the reins made a movement that startled the light-mouthed horse, and he broke from a trot into a tempestuous canter.

" What's the matter ?" cried Somerville.

"A rabbit, perhaps. The beast shies at a feather. Well, I think you are mistaken, Somerville—a chance likeness, and the fact that this man has been at the Cape, have misled you."

" I saw the likeness before you said he had been at the Cape. I tell you, I know the man now, as surely as if I had known him all my life."

" What was the murder ?"

"A poor creature—a woman living alone in a London lodging. A man followed her to her miserable attic and blew out her brains, in a house full of people, at one o'clock on Christmas morning. He hadn't much of your British reverence for Christmas, you see. He had got a way beyond that."

"And you say that Armstrong's friend Went-worth was in the dock at Bow Street ?"
Rough Justice.

"I didn't say Bow Street but I believe it was Bow Street. You remember the murder, I dare say. It made a good deal of talk at the time."

"Yes, I remember something about it and that a man was arrested on suspicion, who had recently returned from the Cape. The evidence broke down, and he was discharged ; but that does not prevent his being guilty. And you say that this Wentworth is that very man ?"

"I would swear to it in any court of law, if his life or mine depended upon my accuracy."

"Curious! How did you happen to be present \'7d "

"I was there for a purpose—to see what an inquiry before the Magistrate upon a serious charge was like. I had been at the Old Bailey, and in most of your great law courts, and I wanted to see how the preliminary inquiry worked. And then, I was interested in the murder as a murder ; and I reckoned I'd like to see the possible murderer."

"Did he impress you as an innocent man.?"

"No! He looked haggard, angry, desperate a wild beast at bay, full of savage impulses yet not without remorse. I made a study of his face, and I could see the agony of his soul when the woman was spoken of—her aspect after the murder all the hideousness and horror of it. He had killed her upon some sudden brutal impulse, I believe, wanting to get rid of a woman who had some strong claim upon him, and who was importunate, and not to be shaken off. He
The American Remembers.

had given her money, you see, and that had not satisfied her. She was hanging upon him, crying, and worrying the very soul of him. Upon my honour, Greswold, if you consider the worrying power of a woman, it's a wonder more of 'em don't get themselves murdered."

" Then you think he was guilty ?"

" Who can doubt it ? The man was there, within five minutes of her death. They were seen together—she was in tears and there was trouble between them. What more probable than that she would admit him to the house, her friend whom she trusted "i What more unlikely that she would admit a stranger, or that any stranger would have been quick enough and daring enough to slip in at the half-open street door, while she and her friend stood talking by the railings t Murderers are not conjurers. The police failed in making a clear case against the man ; and then, no doubt, they fell back upon their usual theory in London, or New York, Paris, or Berlin, they are pretty much the same—the theory of the unknown assassin who is cuter than all the rest of creation."

"You may be mistaken in the man, after all. There are accidental likenesses strong enough to deceive a court of justice."

"Yes, Lesurques and Dubosc, for instance I guess you were going to quote that case. I tell you, Greswold, I am sure of my facts, and I don't like to see a decent fellow like Armstrong, and two nice young women like his wife and

Rough Justice.

Miss Freeland, living on friendly terms with a murderer."

" Come you have no right to condemn a man whom a magistrate refused to commit. Armstrong may know all about the case, and his friend may stand acquitted in his judgment."

"His friend is very artful. A statement he made at Holloway while he was on remand was read in court. He made a plausible story, which sounded like truth, and no doubt was truth as far as it went—leaving out the murder. If Armstrong knows that he was the suspected murderer of that unhappy young woman—I don't recall her name — he has no right to admit him to his house, to bring him into friendly relations with an innocent girl like Miss Freeland."

"I begin to think you have fallen in love with Miss Freeland."

"No, I haven't. I'm past the age when a man falls in love. But I know a nice girl when I meet one—a frank, truthful, whole-souled girl the sort of girl who makes a good wife, not a walking advertisement for a dry-goods store. Yes, I admire Mary Freeland. You've got a pearl beyond all price for your own share, Greswold ; but I hope you don't think you are the only man in the world entitled to a good wife."

" Indeed I do not; and if you can win Mary Freeland you shall have my blessing."

"Thank you. No, I don't see my way to that—I'm too old ; and, what's worse, she is too much taken up with that fellow. I just

The American Remembers,

reckon I shall have to give her a pointer about him."

" What! Tell her your suspicions ?"

"Tell her that he is the man I saw in the dock —not once, but three times. I watched the case all through."

"You had better not. Remember the English law of libel, and that the truth may be libel."

" I'm not afraid of your law."

" If you don't want to win her for your wife you had better leave her affections to take care of themselves. Besides, if she likes this man, nothing you could say would set her against him. She will accept the fact of his not being committed for trial as proof positive of his innocence."

"Guess you're right there. An innocent girl over head and ears in love with a bad man is a difficult kind of beast to herd up. I'd as soon take a rhinoceros by the horn and try to turn him from the way he's made up his mind to go."

" Believe me, you had better not interfere in this case; and, above all, not a word to my wife."

"If you say not, of course I shan't give him away; but I hope you'll let Lady Violet know what sort of angel she has been entertaining unawares."

They had passed the lodge, and were driving up the avenue. Violet appeared in the portico as they approached, and welcomed their return with a smile which changed to an anxious expression at a nearer view of her husband's face. Seldom had she seen that pallid greyish colouring, or that drawn look about his mouth. She made no remark, but he saw her change of countenance and hastencd to reassure her.

"There's nothing amiss, Vio. I'm only fagged after a long morning on the moors. I'll go to my den and rest."

' " I'll bring you some tea, dear, at once, and read you asleep if you'll let me."

It was one of her most valued privileges to read to him in his intervals of rest after exhausting mental work. His acquaintance with light literature—with the poets, novelists, essayists of the past and present—had been gained for the most part since his marriage ; for all his own reading had been of a heavier order, consisting chieily of blue books, and their like, the history of human wrong and suffering, and the work that had been done or attempted by the strong on behalf of the w'eak.

" No, dear. I couldn't stand being read to this afternoon. I want just to lie down and make myself a mindless log for the next two or three hours; and I shall join you and your party before dinner, as fresh as a daisy. I think the Lingfield people are to dine with us to-night, and the Vicar."

" Yes, they are coming, and my father is coming to meet them ; but I can send a messenger and put them all off. They can come any other day. Don't let us have them if you are ill. Don't you think we ought to put them off, Mr. Somerville.-'"

" He was looking pretty bad as we drove home ; but I don't suppose it was anything more than the

effect of a plaguey long walk. You English are never satisfied till you're tired to death."

" I won't have any one put off. I shall be fresh enough for a dinner-party of forty when I have slept off my fatigue," Greswold said decisively.

His den, a large panelled parlour, was at the end of the house furthest from hall and staircase, and from all the movement of servants and visitors. Here, when he shut the door upon himself, he shut out all sounds save the far-away cawing of rooks in the park.

CHAPTER XX.

THE MAN BEHIND THE MASK.

There was an old Vauxhall looking-glass over the chimney-piece, framed in the oak panelling. Oliver Greswold walked across the room and looked at his haggard face, reflected unflatteringly in the tarnished old glass.

"White-livered idiot!" he muttered, "to be so feeble, just when pluck and force were most needed. A man of decent physique wouldn't have turned a hair. But that's where my cockney training comes in—poor blood, and not enough of that. Pluck, force, endurance, what do they mean ." Red corpuscles—perfect physical health. The mind is only the flame, the body is the oil ; and the oil in my lamp has been running low ever since the one bold act of my life."

He had locked the door, was secure of not being disturbed in his solitude ; but he was in no humour for that supreme repose of which he had talked to lie like a log steeped in dreamless sleep. On the contrary, every feature in his clear-cut face was sharpened by intense thought. He walked up

and down the room, where there had been ample space left on purpose for such perambulations, essential to him at all times and seasons in the brief intervals of his work. Everything in this room had been chosen and arranged with a view to his pleasure and comfort:

from the large knee-hole desk in front of the fireplace old Spanish mahogany, beeswaxed into brightness—to the thick Turkey carpet in rich blues and yellows, that covered the floor and made his perambulations noiseless. The only books in this room were the books he wanted for reference, and these filled two substantial revolving bookcases, one on each side of his desk. A large sofa by the fireplace afforded the opportunity for such rest as he had talked of this afternoon. Lady Violet had heaped one end of it with silken pillows, and this was the only feminine note in the room.The three deep-set windows looked into a small enclosed garden, which had once been the " physic garden   of the house-mistress, in the days when every country gentleman's wife v/as learned in herbs and simples, and grew enough rosemary and rue, peppermint and lavender, to make medicine for the whole of her parish. A hedge of clipped yew shut this garden from the outer world, and intensified the quiet of the room by the narrowness of the outlook. Greswold could see nothing above that eight-foot hedge nearer than the tree-tops in his park ; but the little garden was laid out in geometrical beds full of flowers people love best carnations, mignonette, stocks, pansies, heliotrope,

Rough Justice.

and in the middle of every bed a standard rose. A pleasant garden on which to look out with folded arms on the cushioned uundow-ledge, to look out upon in idle mood, with musings attuned to the lazy drone of the bees a pleasant prospect for any man whose mind had room for pleasant thoughts, but not for Oliver Greswold.

" Oh I full of scorpions is my mind, dear wife ! "

Greswold's mind was full of scorpions. To-day for the first time he had discovered that he was not the strong man he thought himself, that the iron nerves of which he had been so proud were not all iron, since at the first hint of peril his courage failed him, or his nerves gave way. It came to the same thing.

" I am not a coward," he thought; " but I could not keep the blood. in my face to-day when I heard Somerville's assertion. If he is right if this Wentworth is Wildover, can I doubt that he has a purpose in being here, in cultivating my acquaintance ? Fool! I thought he was an ignorant admirer a dull, well-meaning fellow, who took an interest in my work ; I looked down at him from the height of a superior intellect; was no more troubled by his existence than if he had been a harmless friendly dog somebody else's dog that fawned upon me."He stopped in his monotonous pacing between the windows and the wall, and laid two fingers on his wrist. The pulse was thin and fluttering the pulse of a man who had let his strength run down,

The Man behiitd the Mask,

and whose nerves had sufifered in consequence. He remembered himself two years ago, a man of iron, indefatigable, alert, prepared for every emergency. Since that time he had been too eager had used and wasted his energies without thought of the future. Sleepless nights had been the only respite from days crowded with engagements. He had risen unrefreshed, and had fought against exhaustion.In those pacings to and fro his mind travelled over all the pages of his life history. If the book could have been begun again, would he have made it different \'7d He hardly knew.His life history as the world knew it was simple enough ; a boyhood passed under the gloomiest conditions, a son left fatherless and dependent on a vain, weak-brained mother, who caught at the first offer of a second husband, married a country vicar, and was very glad to renounce all claim to her son, and to be exonerated from all care and affection for him in the future. He remembered her tearless eyes when she left him in his grandfather's dismal house, her indifference as to the chances of their future meeting. She had harped upon his advantages in the transfer, his grandfather's wealth, which he would no doubt inherit.He never saw her again. She died three years after her second marriage, leaving an infant daughter who did not long survive her. At fourteen years of age Oliver was motherless, and knew that he had no one to look to but the grim old man who sat at meat with him day after day, and

Rough Justice.

hardly ever flung him a civil word. The boy ate his dinner in silence, while his grandfather's spasmodic scraps of conversation were with the confidential servant who waited upon them, and not with the clever nephew, whose observant eyes watched those two withered faces, and wondered if there were many such men in the world, and many fortunes that brought so little pleasure and comfort to their possessor as his grandfather's wealth afforded him.Ill-dressed, ill-fed, ill-housed—for the neglected rooms at the Belvidere were cold and draughty, shabby, cheerless, unbeautiful—Oliver thought with angry contempt of the money piled up at compound interest year after year. Already he had begun to brood upon the problem which the unequal distribution of happiness presents to every ardent mind ; and already he had learnt to pity the poor. He was a day boy at one of the City schools, and his grandfather's generosity went so far as to allow him the bare cost of the omnibus journey between Clapham Common and the Mansion House, with the addition of a shilling per diem for his lunch. He saved on omnibus and on lunch, and bought books, or on occasion gave the money in charity; and in the leisure allowed by lunching on a bun or a sandwich instead of sitting down to a substantial meal, he amused himself by exploring the slums within a mile of his school.Little by little in this manner he made himself familiar with queer neighbourhoods and queer people, and on more than one occasion was

The Man behind the Mask.

shocked at finding that some of the most miserable lodging-houses in East London were owned by his grandfather. He had heard master and servant talking of these houses, and had gone to look at them.

Soon after this he heard Lord Hildyard speak at a meeting in South London ; and dim visions of the good that a wealthy philanthropist might do began to fill his brain. He had read books written by Socialists, and he had already taken sides against the idle rich, the class he had seen in Hyde Park riding or driving in the summer sunset, while the crowd looked on as at the pleasures of a privileged race human butterflies flitting to and fro amidst the roses of life. Having only the London streets for his recreation, he had explored the West End as well as the East, and ever present in his thoughts of rich and poor was the contrast between a lamp-lit dining-room in Park Lane, the women with diamonds in their hair, the table covered with flowers, the powdered heads and solemn faces of the footmen serving wine as if it were a libation to the god of luxury, and a ground-floor room he had seen at the same peaceful evening hour through an open window in Whitechapel, mother and father and children at their wretched supper, an idiot gibbering in his corner, tied into a broken armchair, and in another corner a childish form lying stiff and stark under a ragged coverlet, with a few sprigs of rosemary scattered about it.He thought of his grandfather's hoards and of

Rough Justice.

the good that heaped-up gold might do, by-and-by, when it should be at his disposal. He had no doubt in his mind at this time. His grandfather had adopted him, and meant to make him his heir. Whenever the old man talked to him it was of the wise uses of money, how to make it grow and multiply, how to invest wisely and well, when to be bold, when to be cautious.

" I have never made an unlucky investment," he would say, in conclusion, satisfied that he had fulfilled the whole duty of man.

Morning and evening prayer, the Psalms of David, the splendid imager\'7d' of Isaiah, read by the miser's pinched lips, in a quavering monotone, did not make Oliver in love with religion, any more than the long sittings in an ugly church and the cold Sunday meals. The thing he most loathed in all his unlovely life was the too soon recurrent Sunday. That seventh day to which many people look forward as a day of rest was to him an interval of absolute sufferincf ; and he promised himself that if he ever realized his boyish ambition and won a seat in Parliament, his chief and most ardent efforts would be directed to the abolition of all Sabbatical restraints. Let the fools crowd their churches, and sit in a fusty atmosphere listening to truism and commonplace spread thin over a quire of sermon paper; but let the sensible majority take their pleasure unimpeded by legislation, unfettered by the tyranny of custom. But in the meantime, always mindful of the fact that his grandfather held the golden key to his

future happiness, he was careful not to offend by so much as a hint at his real opinions. He was punctual at every pious observance ; he listened attentively to the weekly morning and evening sermon ; and he was always ready to discuss the last pious discourse either with his grandfather or with the Nonconformist divine who sometimes joined them at the supper table, and for whose entertainment a bottle of the wine of other days was brought up from the dusty limbo below stairs, where the spirits of mirth and good company slumbered in deep stone bins muffled in sawdust, and wreathed with the cobwebs of years.

There were very few visitors at the Belvidere, but those few were always polite and friendly to the solitary boy, and before he was in his teens Oliver had summed up these courtesies as rendered to the future millionaire. Old Morris Mortimer, the solicitor, used to pat him on the head while he was small, and had tipped him with the only half-sovereigns his childish fingers had ever grasped. When he was taller the tips became sovereigns, and the pat on the head changed to a slap on the shoulder.

"You are a good, industrious boy," said old Morris Mortimer, when the lad had brought home a batch of prizes—Milton, Pope, Macaulay in the gaudy prize-binding of crimson and gold ; "and your grandfather will get proud of you by-and-by, if you do as well at the University as you are doing at school."

" Will my grandfather send me to the 'Varsity ? " Oliver asked eagerly.

Rough Justice.

" Yes, if you get a scholarship." " They say I am sure of a scholarship." "Go in and win, then. I suppose you'll be choosing a profession before long ?"

" I should like to go to the Bar, if my grandfather would let me."

"Your grandfather is an old man, Noll, and I dare say you'll be able to do pretty much what you like by the time you're five and twenty."

Later, when Oliver had left Cambridge, after having made his mark there, it seemed to him as if the very fact of his success was unpleasant to the old man, who would harp upon his own lack of education, his squalid childhood, his impecunious youth, and would sneer at those academical distinctions which so often marked the bright beginning of a life that ended in failure. Oliver fancied that in that warped mind there lurked a rancorous dislike of youth that had begun to realize its ambitions, and had a long life before it in which to conquer and enjoy. What was there in front of this miserable old man, when the lean fingers that trembled over piles of dirty silver had lost their sense of touch, and the sunken eyes which brightened only at the idea of gain, were too dim to see the figures in his bank-book ? For him there remained only nothingness and the dark. For the man of twenty, who had lived hitherto only to acquire the knowledge that is power, for him there opened the long vista of prosperous years ; intellectual power used for good ; ambitions realized ; fortune and fame hand in hand.

Oliver Greswold's college career had brought him in contact with various classes of men, and he had made for himself this discovery, that there is no surer or swifter road to distinction than philanthropy. Having discovered this, he determined that the business of his life should be the betterment of his oppressed and unhappy fellow-creatures. He was not a mere calculating machine, with self as the sole motive-power. He had charitable instincts, the gift of pity, or at least a sensitiveness about suffering that moved him to help the sufferer. His joyless boyhood, his stinted youth, had taught him to hate the rich and to sympathize with the poor. He saw undergraduates flinging their money about, wallowing in expensive sports and sensual indulgences ; and he remembered the young men he had seen in the slums— the hollow-eyed students at the Free Library— the lads playing pitch and toss in a dirty alley,' to jump up and scamper off like scared rabbits at sight of a policeman turning the corner. A keen sense of the inequalities of life inspired him with a very real yearning to do some good in his generation—to win happiness for others while he was winning distinction for himself. The poor and the ill-used were to be the ladder by which he scaled ambitious heights; but those who made the ladder should be the better for his ascent.

He had been a hypocrite in his tacit acceptance of a creed that he despised. He had dismissed religion from his thoughts as a bugbear and a dream. But his humanity was real. He believed

Rough Justice.

in man's duty to man. He believed In the capacity for better things latent In the lowest races, from the keen-witted product of poverty and vice cradled In London gutters to the man-eating savage of New Guinea. All of these were capable of regeneration not that regeneration which soothes their misery with visions of a happier world hereafter, but that transformation of creatures that have crawled and suffered In the black night of Ignorance and pauperism to a race of men who dare to stand upright, and face the sun, and claim their portion in the comforts and joys of life. A world In which there should be no hidden misery starving in cellars and garrets. A world where all labour should be performed under the healthiest and happiest conditions which the capitalist's thought and care could provide for the worker; where old age should go cheerily to the refuge the State provided, sure of kindly treatment; and where It would be only the few who would have need of such an asylum, since for the many it would be made easy for youth and middle age to set aside a provision, state-aided, for the years of feebleness and grey hairs.So much had been done since Lord Hlldyard began his life mission! In the mine, in the factory. In the private madhouse, that good man's influence had been a lamp to lighten the darkness. And yet so much remained to be done.The achievements of half a century seemed little to the dreamer of what might be, had he Lord Hildyard's power to inaugurate schemes and draw

The Man behmd tJie Mask.

upon well-filled purses. But for him, Oliver Gres-wold, there would be no achievement while his grandfather lived. He could but bide his time, and make plans for the future, and pace those gardens of St. John's, a solitary figure, choosing the lonelier walks, out of the way of men hurrying to the boats, or playing tennis, aloof from the loud-voiced, empty-headed undergraduate.

It was at Cambridge he first met Lord Hildyard, who had come to see a favourite nephew, and who spoke at a meeting of Johnians bent upon establishing a mission, after the example of their neighbours of Trinity. Lord Hildyard's manner, earnest yet suave, and of an antique courtesy, charmed the young man, who had come in contact with very few gentlemen. The difference between the philanthropist and Morris Mortimer might be more subtly expressed, but was wider than the difference between a Kaffir and an English peasant.Oliver got himself introduced to Lord Hildyard, made a very favourable impression, and was asked to luncheon in the nephew's rooms, where his earnestness and genuine interest in the philanthropist's work was reciprocated by the interest of the older man in the enthusiasm of the younger. Out of that luncheon party, and a conversation which lasted late into the afternoon, arose a friendship which was sustained by devotion and usefulness on Greswold's part. Within a few months after he left Cambridge he had taken a definite rank in Lord Hildyard's house, and he

devoted the greater part of his life to Lord Hild-yard's service ; an employment of his time which the old uncle at Clapham appeared to approve, though he was deaf to any appeal for money in aid of those benevolent schemes which he affected to admire.Lord Hildyard was Low Church, and this fact alone recommended him to Mr. Greswold. Nor was the ci-devant adviser of " toffs " by any means disposed to undervalue the advantages of friendship with a man of the philanthropist's birth and station. He approved, but he did nothing to assist the alliance.In Hyde Park Gardens Oliver Greswold found himself in a new atmosphere. The sweetness of the Christian life among people of education and refinement came upon him as a delightful surprise ; and for the first time since he had begun to think he was sorry he was not a Christian.With regard to his worldly prospects the young man was perfectly frank. He told Lord Hildyard all he could of his grandfather's circumstances and his own rearing.

" I believe my grandfather to be a rich man, and I believe he means to make me his heir. No other relative has ever crossed his threshold since I can remember; and I suppose that when he took mc from my mother and charged himself with my bringing up he may be said to have adopted me."

" Of course he has adopted you—and means you to inherit his fortune," answered Lord Hildyard,

who was of a sanguine temper, and always looked at the bright side of things. "You will have grand opportunities in the future, Greswold. You will be a power for good, when my working day is done."

Lord Hildyard had made inquiries about old Greswold's career, and the sources of his wealth, from one of those men to whom London life for the last half-century is like a book that they know by heart.

" Greswold ? Yes, of course, I remember the fellow. A money-lending lawyer; gave good dinners and ruined half the young men upon town. But he had his redeeming points—never wanted you to take wine or pictures wouldn't look at anything but real property, and was satisfied with thirty per cent, per annum. A long-headed old dog! But you don't mean to say that old Greswold is alive .-' I haven't heard of him for the last five and twenty years."

" He is living, but in retirement. You think he must be rich ?"

"As Croesus! He has eaten up more landed estates than I have worn out boots. He must be a millionaire."

To an enthusiast of Lord Hildyard's temper the idea of Oliver's future means was full of attraction. He had spent as much of his fortune as he could spend without leaving his only child too poorly provided for; and he looked on all sides for funds with which to sustain work that had been begun, but which was too apt to languish, even after the

most prosperous beginning, for want of income. It was easy to kindle the flame of enthusiasm even in the worldly breast; but it was hard work to keep the fire burning. People told him that they were beginning to sicken at charity appeals. There was so many of them. It was impossible to help everybody. The indigent were nowadays the only people provided for.

Everything was found for them: Free Libraries, flannel petticoats, schools^ for their children, hospitals, convalescent homes, days in the country, winters on the Riviera. "We can't get these luxuries, don't you know.? We have to go without," says Flippancy, vexed at having the price of three pairs of evening gloves squeezed out of its lizard-skin purse.Lord Hildyard had been called blind as a bat by those who saw the peril of Oliver's position in Hyde Park Gardens ; but it may be that he was not unaware of the growing attachment between his daughter and his secretary, and that he beheld it with approval. He had infinite faith in the young man's character and capacity ; and he had no doubt as to his future position. He did not commit himself to any promise. Indeed, Oliver, always reticent, had been careful to avoid any revelation to the father, although his hopes were known to the daughter. He told Violet that it was wiser to keep silence until his grandfather's death should place him in a position to ask for her hand ; and Violet had consented to a secret engagement, knowing that her father liked and trusted the man she loved, and having no fear for the result.

The Mail behind the Mask.

This was the state of affairs when Oliver was startled from his dream of bliss by an explosion of temper upon his grandfather's part, a burst of ill humour, the cause of which was insignificant, but the result stupendous ; for in this sudden fury the old man revealed the feeling of long years.

"Do you think I ever hked your Puritanical visage, or relished your damned superior airs ?" he cried. "You were born a prig, like your father

before you. By G , I should have liked you

better if you had been a profligate. And I'll be bound you are counting on making a mighty figure in the world with my money when I am under ground. Your name will top every subscription list with three figures, and you'll be on the committee of every new-fangled scheme for pampering a pack of lazy swine ; and you'll be wanting to pull down my tenement houses, which have paid twenty per cent, for the last fifty years, in order to build palaces that will cost you money out of pocket every year to keep up. That's the kind of use you'll make of my money ; instead of turning your attention to the money-market, and developing into a great financier—as you might have done if you had been of my kidney. Don't be too sure of your chances. You are not the only piece of my flesh and blood. There is living, somewhere, perhaps in dire poverty, while you are wallowing in luxury here, a child of the child I loved best of any mortal upon this earth."

"And who rewarded your love with the basest

Rough Justice.

ingratitude," retorted Oliver, too angry to maintain his usual reserve.

" Oh, you have been told that story, have you ? Yes, my daughter was ungrateful—a viper that I had warmed in my bosom ; but, who knows, if I could have looked forward and seen the long lonely years before me, I might have been weak enough to forgive the viper. I loved her, sir, I am capable of love, though you may not believe it. But I can't love a prig."

This revelation of the feelings of a soured old man was like the lifting of a curtain ; and Oliver did not rest until he had seen Morris Mortimer, and, by dint of diplomatic promises, which amounted to something a little less than direct bribery, had obtained the particulars of his grandfather's latest will.

The will had been made soon after Oliver left Cambridge, and at a time when his thoroughly respectable career under most adverse conditions ought to have won his grandfather's regard. A previous will, made when Oliver first came as a child under his grandfather's roof, left him everything.

"What, in God's name, have I ever done to forfeit my grandfather's good opinion .'"" the young man exclaimed despairingly. " Is it not a hideous injustice in him to prefer the child of a disobedient daughter—a creature he has never seen ?"

" He is a strange being, and his life has been a strange life ever since the girl kicked up her heels and left him. She was a beautiful girl a brilliant,

quick-witted hussey, and she could twist her father round her httle finger. I suppose as he got older he took to brooding upon the past. Old men do, you know; lonely old men like your grandfather live more in the past than they do in the present."

" It is a hideous injustice a hideous injustice," reiterated Oliver, as he walked up and down the office, white with anger. He could find no other phrase to qualify his grandfather's treatment of him. "I have been brought up to rely upon this fortune. I have given all my thoughts and study to the future use of the money that now lies idle —a disgrace in a Christian country. I should use it for the benefit of my fellow man; not for luxury, not for self-indulgence, or for what the world calls pleasure—not for grouse moors, or yachts, or racing-stables. The clothes I wear today, the dinner I eat to-day, would be good enough for me to-morrow if I were three times a millionaire. I have no sensuous longings, Mortimer; no lust for high living or dissipation. The woman I love is the noblest type of womanhood—my superior in character as she is my superior in station. My life lies smooth before me—a good life, a useful life, a noble life ; but it is dependent upon my inheriting that old man's wealth. If he cheats me out of that he will cheat me out of everything."

He flung himself into a chair and sobbed aloud the first tears he had shed since he was told, curtly enough, of his mother's death. He remembered the day as if it were yesterday ; a blazing

Rough Justice.

July afternoon. He had been playing in the neglected garden, longing for a dog, or a rabbit, any living creature to bear him company, when his grandfather came to him with a black-bordered letter in his hand. He remembered also how the housemaid, who looked after him, had tried to comfort him with talk of his future riches, when she found him sobbing in his lonely little bed.

And now the door was shut upon that brilliant future which he had believed in until to-day.

"You mustn't be so downhearted, my good fellow," said the solicitor. " I may tell you in confidence, as I am, and always have been, your true friend, that your grandfather has not been able to find out whether his daughter's only child a girl, whose birth and christening we know all about, and whom we were able to trace up to a certain point is alive or dead. The chain snapped suddenly at Havre, where we found evidence of her mother's death, some years before our inquiry, but beyond which place we could find no indication of the girl or her father. It's as likely as not the girl is dead, or has gone to America, or the Colonies, or has gone to the bad, and that even should she survive your grandfather we may never hear any more of her."

" How long is it since your search ended ? "

" Five years."

" And has my grandfather been content to make no further effort?"

" Well, to tell you the truth, Oliver, I have done all in my power to hinder any further search. You

see. I have known you from a little lad, and up to the day I received instructions about the new will I looked upon you as your grandfathers sole heir; so I was rather lukewarm about the search, and I—well, I confess I employed a highly respectable private detective, who can speak no language but his own, and who is about as intelligent as the average detective."

" But there will have to be a further search made after my grandfather's death, of course," said Oliver.

"Yes, as his executor it will be my duty to make inquiries, to advertise for the heiress. Frankly, Oliver, I hope the girl is dead, and that you will not lose the fortune to which you are fairly entitled."

Oliver thanked him for his good wishes.

" If I do get my chance you won't find me ungrateful," he said.

He did not rest content with this information ; and the search for the girl was begun again under new conditions. It was a secret search, and the man who was employed never knew the real name of his employer. Oliver Greswold had been able to save between forty and fifty pounds from the sums paid for his contributions to some of the better class of magazines. He could write well and vigorously upon subjects that he knew by heart ; and while his pen had served the good cause, the earnings of that pen had been accumulating against some unlooked-for need. The money was just enough to pay the fees and expenses of

Rough Justice.

the inquirer; and within three months after his confidential interview with his grandfather's solicitor, Oliver Greswold knew that the woman who was to deprive him of fortune and status, and to spoil his chance of winning the girl he fondly loved, had drifted to a garret in a dingy lodging-house in one of the shabbier streets of Blooms-bury.

The transaction was completed. The agent who had conducted the inquiry had placed the result before his client in black and white. Every link in the chain was there; and there was no shadow of doubt that the Mrs. Rayner, living wretchedly in a third-floor bedroom in Dynevor Street, walking the dreary streets and squares night after night when all happy people were within four walls, was the only child of Ralph Carford and the very Lilian Carford named in old Greswold's will. The agent had talked with Mrs. Grogan, and had heard all that there was to be told of her history and her habits. Her history a blank, her habits eccentric, but, according to Mrs. Grogan, not vicious.

Oliver Greswold would not believe that story of eccentricity without vice. Of course she had fallen into vicious courses ; or if she had abandoned the ways of vice, it was because vice had abandoned her. He could think nothing but evil of her. The offspring of a disobedient daughter and of a raffish adventurer—one of those sprigs of a noble tree for whose species the hard-headed Radical had ever

The Man behind the Mask.

felt a contemptuous dislike. What good fruit could come of such a tree ? The girl had eloped with the first seducer who offered himself. She had lived the usual life of such facile victims; had dressed fine and eaten and drunk of the best, and when abandoned by her first protector, had found another on a lower grade as to means.

Who could doubt what kind of life she had led when deserted in his turn by this second lover ? The woman at the lodging-house in Dynevor Street would naturally, in her own interests, pretend that all her lodgers were immaculate ; but, considering that the painted lady on the second floor was known to be a disreputable character, it would have been childish credulity to accept Mrs. Grogan's assurance that her third-floor lodger's midnight ramblings indicated only an innocent eccentricity.

No, he had no doubt as to the character of the woman who was to supplant him. This disreputable creature, meagre, hollow-cheeked, and haggard of eye, was to come between him and all those golden opportunities of goodness and greatness to which he had looked forward ever since he had been able to think. He told himself that there was nothing sordid or selfish in his aspirations. Were the fortune his, thousands would share in its benefits. Every sovereign in the yearly income would mean something of comfort for some sufferer —some lightening of the burden under which the weary shoulders and weak knees were daily bending. He thought of the airy and healthful

houses which would rise from the ruins of the Greswold tenements—houses which should offer advantages and comforts slowly planned and developed in the long hours of many a wakeful night, discussed with architects and sanitary ensfineers : houses which were to be the ultimate outcome of modern science in the housing of the poor. He thought of himself in the House of Commons as the people's advocate ; and all that he had of ambition and of vanity thrilled and pulsed in his veins as he pictured the triumphs that might reward so fiery an enthusiasm pleading a cause that so appealed to a universal sympathy. But to plead successfully, to be listened to and respected, he must be known as a rich man who was devoting his fortune to the cause he advocated. Not as the penniless Radical, making capital of the common sorrows and sufferings, would he have his voice heard in the senate-house, where success had ever been his loftiest dream. He had turned his thoughts with contempt from every petty triumph —from the applause of the Mechanics' Institute or the Drawing-room Meeting, to the foreshadowing of that future in which his voice should resound under the roof which had echoed the voices of Ashley, Cobden, and Bright, in the days when philanthropy was a new fashion.

And how would this woman use the wealth that was to be flung into her lap ? Without experience of decent life, without one reputable acquaintance, how could she be expected to deal with a great estate ? She would eat it and drink it, and fling

it to the loose company that would gather about her, swift as vultures sighting carrion. The chances were that her brain would be turned by so sudden a change of fortune, and that a year of wild enjoyment would end in a lunatic asylum. Champagne first, perhaps, and chloral afterwards, would be the epitome of her miserable history. A lover or two, to cheat and bully her ; perhaps a husband to clutch the bulk of her estate and hasten her progress to the grave. Could money mean anything but accelerated ruin for such a human wreck as the cousin whose history he had been told, and whose face he had seen

He had often debated that question which modern thought has discussed as boldly as ever it was argued by antique philosophy. Is life worth living ? And here, he argued, was a case in which the answer was easy and decisive.

Here, in the person of Lisa Rayner, was a life not worth living—a life worthless to its possessor; a life that could only exercise evil influences upon others; a life which for him, Oliver Greswold, meant ruin and despair.

Long days, long nights of harrying thought resulted in a plan of action, which began with daily practice in his grandfather's grounds, and an occasional hour at a shooting-gallery in Soho.

CHAPTER XXI.

A NEW DEVELOPMENT.

At eight o'clock the Wilvervvold drawing-room looked as pleasant a place as the heart of man need desire for the focus or rallying-point of home. It was summer still, though autumnal sport had begun—summer tempered by autumn. There were open windows which admitted the perfume of Dijon roses, while the red glow of a wood fire gave that suggestion of comfort which is wanting where the hearth is cold. Pleasant people were grouped about the pleasant room, and the master of the house, standing by Lord Hildyard's side upon the spacious Persian hearthrug, seemed in no manner out of harmony with the brightness of his surroundings. He was able to answer his wife's pathetic little look of interrogation, as she crept to his side after welcoming her guests, with a reassuring smile.

"Yes, dear, quite myself again. You see how foolish it would have been to put people off."

" I am so glad—I am so happy."

Her hand stole into his for a moment before she turned away.

A New Development.

"Wonderful recuperative power there, Lady Violet," said the American, who had been watching her. " Hard workers like your husband have that power sometimes in an extraordinary degree. But he was just dead beat this afternoon. He oughtn't to walk ; walking over a lumpy country isn't good enough for a man of his mental calibre. It's a waste of nerve force, and a wanton expenditure of blood that ought to be feeding his brain. Do you know how much blood the brain wants to keep it going, Lady Violet? I don't suppose you do. Nobody ever takes the trouble to consider what a glutton the brain is."

Violet listened smilingly, without hearing. She was happy now her husband's face had recovered its habitual repose—a thoughtful face always, but with a look in the eyes when they met hers which brightened the whole countenance.

There was no lack of talk during dinner, though the host himself was silent.

"Our friend is a speaker, and not a talker," Somerville remarked to Mrs. Armstrong ; " oratory, not conversation, is his forte."

"Oh, but I assure you he can talk splendidly upon his own subjects," argued Ida.

" Of course he can! That is oratory. Conversation is the art of talking about everybody's subjects—touch and go pitch and toss catching folly as it flies. That's why your empty-headed man is generally the best dinner-table talker."

The night was unusually warm for the time of year, and when the ladies were gone the men

Rough Justice.

took their politics and their cigarettes out of the dining-room windows and into the coolness of a dewy garden. Somerville hooked his arm through Oliver's, and talked of his last peregrinations among the New York slums, while Armstrong and the vicar sauntered beside them and listened, mildly interested, Arnold found himself alone with Lord Hildyard, who walked slower than the younger men, and who was in the expansive after-dinner mood common to men of his age and circumstances.

"I dare say my son-in-law's work is rather out of your line, Mr. Wentworth," he said, when his cigar was fairly lighted, "but I hope you don't think him a bore, or a faddist. I hope you understand and appreciate his fine qualities and his capacity for work."

"Perhaps I admire him most as your disciple. Lord Hildyard. All the good he has done—or is ever likely to do is the good you began."

"In the dark ages. Well, it was something to help in that beginning of things. In the early forties there were just a few quiet people who cared for the poor; but now humanity has become a universal passion "

"And a fashion."

"And in some cases the Charity Bazaar and amateur play section a fashion. There is a rage for good works, and the sacred cause of humanity is in some peril of falling into discredit by being overdone. There are too many people playing at philanthropy, you see, Wentworth. They block

A New Development.

the way of the workers. But my son-in-law is no dilettante. When I hand on my lamp to him I know that I pass it to a stronger runner than myself."

"And he is in earnest "

" He is terribly in earnest. The work that he is now doing has been the dream of his life. If he had been disappointed at last, as there was some risk that he might be, by his grandfather's perversity in preferring a granddaughter whom he had never seen to the grandson he had adopted and bred up from childhood—if this unknown woman had come forward to claim the estate— I think Oliver's heart would have broken."

"He could scarcely have aspired to your daughter's hand in that case."

" Oh, I don't quite know about that. I am very fond of my daughter, and I am not very fond of rank or of money. I am by no means a flinty-hearted father, Wentworth. But I have very little to give my only child."

"You have had so many orphan children to provide for."

" And if Violet and her husband had depended upon me they must have been very badly off, poor things. He would have been cramped and fettered, and most of his schemes would have come to grief for want of money. However, the cousin has not been heard of, and I think we may make up our minds that the cousin is dead, and the money which she might have spent weakly and foolishly, or wickedly, will be the

Rough Justice.

redemption of hundreds of her down-trodden sex "

"You mean that a great part of this fortune will be devoted to rescue work?" questioned Arnold.

" Yes, that is the work to which my son-in-law has given his greatest efforts within the last year. He is an enthusiast; but he has a cooler and clearer intellect than is often vouchsafed to enthusiasts."

"And this passion for rescue work, I take it, is a new development in your son-in-law's career." "Yes, it is a new phase of usefulness. His earlier efforts were concentrated upon one great work, the proper housing of the poor. All his noblest feelings were appealed to by the miseries of East End London, as he saw them in his school-boy wanderings, a lonely, friendless lad, who had no home pleasures to distract his thoughts from suffering humanity. The subject was brought nearer to him by the fact that his grandfather owned houses as wretched as any of the dens east of his City school. He brooded on the miseries of the poor at an age when the average boy has no heavier care than a Latin imposition or a debt at the tuck shop. Rescue work is a new development, and he has taken it up with an intensity beyond any of his previous enthusiasms. It is no longer the healthy housing of bodies, remember. It is the saving of souls for which he is now working. His House of the Woman of Samaria, his Home of St. Mary Magdalene, will

A New Development.

give shelter and cure, and new life, and useful healthful work to hundreds of women now wandering, painted spectres, embodied miseries, through our midnight streets. I cannot, in this casual talk, describe the magnitude of the scheme to which he has been directing his energies from the hour that he succeeded to his grandfather's fortune; but, if he be spared to complete that work—a task, perhaps, of many years "

" Of many years," Arnold echoed mechanically, as if thinking aloud.

" He will leave behind him a name that should rank with those of John Howard and

William Wilberforce. He will have brought light into the prison-house of sin, he will have emancipated the slaves of vice."

"You think his life a valuable one, then. Lord Hildyard ? "

" A life of infinite value to suffering mankind."

"And you are sure that he is in earnest, that he will not slacken his efforts in the cause of humanity, now that he has won your daughter and made his position in the world .<* Forgive me if I speak too plainly."

"I am not afraid of plain speaking. Greswold is an exceptional man, and the world is apt to doubt the sincerity of philanthropists. 1 have no more doubt of him than I have of myself. He has been my coadjutor for half a dozen years, and I have never known him flag or waver. He has already engaged at least a third of his capital in the work he has at heart, at the hazard of

Rough Justice.

being called upon to re-instate every shilling in the event of his cousin being still alive."

"Oh, you may be sure upon that point. He must know there is no risk of that."

" He has only negative evidence. He knows that all efforts to find her were without result; but he has no evidence of her death."

" Poor waif! " sighed Arnold. " It is in remembrance of her, perhaps, that he is trying to save the wretchedest among her sisters."

" It has occurred to me that such a feeling might influence him," answered Lord Hildyard. " Gres-wold might naturally say to himself, ' Here am I enjoying the fortune which would have belonged to this woman, had she lived to claim it, and not knowing what miseries she may have endured for want of money while she lived, or into what depths of degradation and sin poverty may have sunk her. How can I make amends to the dead better than by saving the living.'" I can fancy him arguing with himself after that fashion, and then flinging hinjself, as he has done, with heart and mind and means and strength into the work."

"Father, are you and Mr. Wentworth going to prowl up and down the grass all night .^" asked Violet's gentle voice from the shadow of the verandah. "Mr. and Mrs. Armstrong are waiting to wish you good night."

"Then I am wanted," said Arnold, as he followed Lord Hildyard into the drawing-room, where he found everybody in the act of departure.

He was silent during the drive home, brooding

A New Developfitent.

over Lord Hildyard's words a life as useful to humanity as Howard's or Wilberforce's— good done to hundreds perhaps to thousands ; for the ball set rolling will always find new hands to push it along.

"A life of useful achievement, a life a thousand times more valuable to humanity than mine can ever be. I have no passion for good works, don't know how to begin them, instinctively pass by on the other side, when my fellow-traveller lies wounded in the dust. My life measured against Oliver Greswold's ? A lucifer match against a star. And yet I know that Oliver Greswold is capable of deliberate murder. I know that with relentless footsteps and unfaltering hand he tracked his kinswoman to her doom, watched and waited for his opportunity, had months in which to waver and repent, and yet held on, inflexible in wickedness, ruthless as Satan."

Could there be two sides to a man's character pity, tenderness of heart, sympathy with sorrow and sin, an ardent desire to snatch brands from the burning, and, co-existent with those feelings, the power to take the life of a fellow-creature who had never wronged him by so much as a word, the life of an unoffending woman, creeping along her melancholy way, bowed down by the weight of her own humility ?

But this woman, humble, unoffending, had been the obstacle between the philanthropist and all he wanted in this world.

He had thought out the question, perhaps ;

Rough Justice,

had weighed the good and evil in his metaphysical scales; and had persuaded himself that one desperate crime kicked the beam when weighed against a life and fortune devoted to good works. What, considered dispassionately, was the value of this woman's life ? To herself very little ; to the v/orld at large, nil. She had neither child nor friend. Fortune flung at her, in her degradation and loneliness, might only spell moral ruin.

Some day she must die. The inevitable end that comes to all must come to her. A little sooner, or a little later. What matter? All that is lovely in woman's life—beauty, chastity, youth, health—she had wasted. The ship was wrecked long ago. What matter how soon the shattered hulk sank under water \'7d

After this fashion mused Arnold, trying to follow another man's argument.

The cruel, cruel murder! A victim so defenceless, so unoffending! But what of his own treatment of that victim, whose moral wreck was known to him, whose tenderness, whose divine instinct of love had saved him from suicide, and who had been his devoted companion through years of trial and poverty \'7d He had left her when it served his purpose to try his fortune elsewhere ; he had come back from his land of Beulah a rich man, intent upon offering her a money compensation for all her sufferings, in order to marry the girl he loved. He had come back to reward her martyrdom of patient waiting by the heartless confession of his inconstancy.

A New Development.

She had turned from him heart-broken, and he had not relented. He had not called her back and cried, " You shall be my wife, and no other. I bound myself to you for life when we parted, and I will keep my word."

To have let her go, crushed and despairing; to have broken that promise made in their poverty and sorrow, sealed with their mutual tears; to have disappointed the hope that had sustained her through years of misery! Was not this as black a crime as murder \'7d Was he a man to drag his fellow-man's misdeeds to the light of the day to bring anguish unspeakable upon the devoted wife, the trusting father-in-law, that benevolent old man whose whole life had been spent in easing the burdens laid on other lives, who had a claim to pity and reverence equal to the saints of old What mattered their virtues or their sufferings to him, Arnold Wentworth ? Had the evidence against him been stronger, would Oliver Greswold have sacrificed himself to save an innocent man's life \'7d No, a thousand times no! The philanthropist would have pursued his beneficent course, the friend and helper of men, leaving a great name behind him in the days to come. Many men, many women, would have been bettered by his existence; but that one man would have gone under, just as that one woman had died, for his and the world's advantage. This is how Arnold thought out the situation, in the darkness and silence of a sleepless night, after the friendly dinner at Wilverwold Park.

Rough Justice.
CHAPTER XXII.
THE ENEMY AND AVENGER.

The Lingfield party were to join Greswold and his American friend the day after the dinner at Wilverwold, the men for a morning over the heather and gorse, the women to meet them at the hut in time for luncheon. The party had been made up in the drawing-room at Wilverwold after dinner. Laurence Somerville had been the chief mover of the plan, and had pleaded that his time in Yorkshire was nearly up, and that this might be his last chance of having a day's pleasure with them.

He had been seated next Miss Freeland at dinner, and had contrived to keep her interested in his conversation. American novelists had taught her a good deal about America, and she was eager to ask questions and compare notes. Was life in the country really as simple and sweet as Miss Wilkins made it. Was Boston quite the Boston of "Silas Lapham " ^ And so on, and so on. Somerville's talk had charmed her into forgetfulness of Arnold's cruelty. He watched her furtively from the other

side of the table, and the pangs of jealousy were added to his burden of care.Perplexed, anxious, at war with himself, yet with a fixed purpose in his mind, he set out for the moor with Armstrong and a keeper, after a seven-o'clock breakfast at which neither Ida nor Mary appeared.Ida's pink cotton frock flashed into the hall just as they were starting, and she walked to the gate with them.

" We shall meet you at lunch. Oh! how pale and fagged you look, Mr. Wentworth, just as if you had been awake all night."

" I haven't done much in the way of sleep but the moorland air will set me up again."

" Be sure you bring us a good luncheon," said the husband, with a kiss for a full stop, before he shut the gate.

Luncheon was over, and the cart was driving off with the game bags, and with plates and dishes, empty champagne bottles, and all the machinery of the feast. The keepers and dogs had lunched in the open, and the cartridges had been removed from the guns. Greswold and his friends meant to shoot no more to-day. There would be just time to walk quietly home to tea, before evening closed over the faded heather, and the autumn mists veiled the track across the moor.

There had been an air of happiness and high spirits during the meal which had harmonized with the popping of champagne corks, and the

rattle of knives and forks ; but all the talk and gaiety, the quips and cranks and ripple of silvery laughter had been provided by four people out of the seven assembled there. Somerville, Armstrong, Ida, and Mary had done all the talking, and all the laughter had been theirs and even of these four the mirth had not been quite genuine, for Mary's thoughts had been divided between a natural girlish sympathy with all things bright and pleasant and an aching anxiety about the man she loved.He was sitting next her to-day, had indeed taken care to seize that position, and in the midst of the laughter that followed one of Somerville's stories, he startled her by an unexpected address.

" Mary, when you and the others are walking homewards, I want you to give them the slip, and come back here. Can you ? Will you do it, dear."" he said, in a voice too low to be heard across the table.

" But why ?"

" I want you here half an hour after the rest have left—except Greswold. He will stay here with me. We have something to talk about—and there will be something for you to hear. Will you do it, Mary ?"

"You know I would do anything to please you."

" It isn't a question of pleasing me; it is a question of our future lives—my fate and yours. You'll come, won't you ?"

" Yes."

"I don't believe Miss Freeland heard a word

The Enemy and Avenger.

of my story," said Somerville, who had been watching these two. "Mr. Wentworth might reserve his confidences for a more convenient time. I don't suppose all the secrets he could tell are calculated for a picnic party."

Mary blushed, and Arnold looked angry.

" If we have lost a particularly choice example of American wit, I dare say we shall stumble upon it some day in Bret Harte or Mark Twain," he said.

The party broke up after this. They had been sitting at lunch nearly an hour and a half, the liberal temper of the new wife having permitted cigarettes with the coffee. The men pulled themselves together, explored their tobacco-pouches to be sure of a provision for the journey home, while the women put on jackets and gloves, and all were in marching order.

Lady Violet headed the column with Armstrong ; Mary, Ida, and the American following. When these had left the hut Greswold paused at the door, waiting for Arnold to precede him.His keepers and servants had gone; his wife and his guests were walking briskly away in the westering sunlight. He was alone with Arnold Wentvvorth the man against whom he had been warned. His wife and his friends were distant by hardly a hundred yards ; yet he felt as if he were abandoned and defenceless, face to face with all the horror of his life.Suddenly, while he waited, looking at his guest interrogatively, Arnold clapped the door to, locked

Rough Justice.

it and put the key in his pocket, and then stood with his back against the door, facing Gresvvold.

" At last! " he cried. " I have waited for this chance, and it has come. Murderer! "

*' What are you raving about, Wentworth ? Open the door, and don't play the fool!"

He tried to treat things lightly, and bore the shock well. His spare frame was drawn to its full height, rigid as if made of iron. His thin lips were tightened into a straight line. All that was hard and daring in his character expressed itself in his face; but the ashen pallor of that face, the drops that stood like dew upon his forehead, the wild despair in his eye, were so many confessions of guilt. No innocent man, surprised by an inexplicable accusation, ever hung out that white flag of surrender.

"You don't know who I am, or why I am here. You know me as Wentworth—a good-for-nothing chap who has made a little money in South Africa, and is loafing about in a harmless, good-natured way, and has been brought by chance to your door. That's what you thought of me, perhaps, Oliver Greswold, when you gave me your casual hospitality. You were wrong. It was no chance that brought me to your door. I come as an enemy and avenger. I am the man—Wentworth, alias Wildover—who stood in the dock at Bow Street to answer for your crime—to answer for the life you took."

"You are the stronger man. and I can't stop your raving."

The Enemy and Avenger.

Still the cold dew oozed from the pallid forehead, and the eyes were still widened with agony. Carry himself as he might, with a careless shrug of his shoulders, a contemptuous motion of his head, the inward agony of the man showed itself in outward signs that were unmistakable.One thought and one name were in his mind. "Wife! Violet!" What would she not suffer if the evil he had done were brought home to him \'7d He had won her, as it were, with a cast of the devil's dice ; and if she were to know that he had bartered his soul to win her she who believed in souls, and heaven, everlasting reward and everlasting punishment her heart would break.

" Violet! Violet! "

The dear name repeated itself in the confusion of his brain. He scarcely knew what Arnold was saying to him, though his eyes were fixed upon the speaker's face, and though he seemed to be listening.

"You gained fortune wife, fame, and station by a cruel murder. I stood in your place in the dock, and left the court with a stain upon my life. Had not poverty compelled me to sink my real name, this stigma might have broken my mother's heart. It was dark enough to part me from the woman I loved. I would offer myself to no pure-minded woman while there was doubt as to my guilt I waited for you, the guilty man, to remove that stain. The time has come for you to do it."

He took a folded sheet of foolscap paper from

Rough Justice.

his breast pocket, a little ink-bottle such as a collecting clerk might carry, and a pen. He laid the paper on the table, and placed the ink-bottle and pen beside it. All this was done rapidly. The instant it was done he resumed his post of vantage against the door.

" I came prepared for business, you see. I didn't expect to find a shooting-lodge provided with stationery. Sit down, and write as I dictate."

"Stand away from that door. I am not the kind of man to be trifled with, or to humour a madman."

I "Mad or sane, you have to reckon with me. One of us will have to knock under. If you want to leave this house alive you'll have to write a confession of your guilt. Make it as short as you like ; but it must be plain enough for the woman I love to understand."

Greswold looked round the hut. The guns were gone. There was no weapon within reach^ not even a poker on the hearth, for there had been no fires burnt yet, and nothing had been provided against winter weather. He looked at Arnold. He was armed, perhaps ; carried a revolver or a bowie knife in his pocket. The man of civilization, who had never lived out of London till now, was prepared for any act of violence from this South African adventurer—gold-digger, ruffian— who for years had held his life at a moment's purchase.

" You came here prepared for violence," he said. " You are armed, no doubt ? "

The Enemy and Avengef.

"No. I came to meet you on equal terms man against man ; clean hands against hands dyed in blood. You needn't look at the window noticing Greswold's swift, sudden glance that way. " I shan't let you out of this hut till you have written that paper."

" Then it comes to a question of brute force broad shoulders against narrow, six foot two against five foot ten, fourteen stone "

"Or thereabouts."

"Against nine."

" Call it so. I mean you to write your confession !"

" And you mean to hang me with it.-'"

" No. I have no hunger for that kind of vengeance. I don't care a jot what becomes of your miserable carcase, for I know there is something inside it mind, memory, conscience, blue funk call it what you like that must prevent your ever knowing a happy day. I want one woman in the world the woman I love to know that you are the man who murdered Lisa Rayner. When you have made that clear to her she will be here presently, to witness your deposition I care no more what becomes of you than I care what becomes of the bats that are skimming past that window as we stand here talking."

" Then it is not for the dead woman's sake you have hunted me down not a vendetta for love of her, not for your old mistress ?"

" No . The wrong I did her is a wrong that no penalty you can pay could lessen or atone. She

lies in her grave. I might have kept faith with her, and I broke it. I might have made her happy, and I didn't. I know my sin. No punishment inflicted upon you can lessen that. Come, sit down and write: ' I, Oliver Greswold, declare myself the murderer of Lisa Rayner.' "

"You are a fool or a madman to suppose that even brute force would extort such a confession from an innocent man."

" Oh, you still deny your guilt. That is a detail. You have to exculpate me by that acknowledgment. You have to reckon with a desperate man, whose life's happiness is at stake, and who won't stick at trifles. If you refuse to do what I want, only one of us shall leave this place alive. You can guess which that one will be. Will you write.?"

He sprang forward, laid his hand on Greswold's shoulder, forcing him into a sitting position. The hand of the man whose thews and sinews had been braced by years of rough open-air life weighed like iron upon the town-bred student's slender frame. The man who had cultivated brain at the expense of body bent like a reed under that firm grip-Greswold dipped the pen in the ink, and sat for a minute or so, deliberating calculating his chances. Should he try his strength against this man fight for his life, and lose it; let himself be found brutally murdered skull battered, limbs broken, in a fight with a savage foe, or strangled by that iron hand which was now pressing on his

The Enemy and Avenger.

shoulder ? If he had the fortitude to accept such a doom his wife need never know him for the wretch he was, and the man who killed him might swing for that brutal murder.

This were the nobler course, the only manly course ; but this meant surrender and death ; and that long vista of a fair and honoured life, the love that was his, the wealth and power that he had bought with that one crime, ail must go; and instead of these would come that dreary end which he had never dared contemplate annihilation. His quick imagination fancied himself lying at his adversary's feet, breath ebbing, sight fading, and in his brain but one thought Life, life, life ; the worst, the most degraded life is better than death.

" If, to avoid a struggle in which I must be worsted, I write the confession you ask, will you swear that it shall not be used against me most of all, that my wife shall never see it, or be told ?"

"I want it for the sake of one woman. When she has seen it, I shall be satisfied."

" Mary Freeland ?"

 Mary Freeland."

" How do I know that she will keep the secret ?"

" You must trust her as you trust me. I cannot promise for her. I know that she is generous, kind, compassionate. If it comes within the limit of her charity to pity a cold-blooded murderer, she may pity you. For your wife's sake I think she will deal mercifully with you, as I shall And

now let there be no more talk. The confession has to be written,"

" So be it. You are master of the situation."

He began to write—slowly—with a hand that moved steadily along the paper, and he spoke the words in clear unfaltering tones as he wrote them.

"I confess that, with a deliberate purpose, and under the belief that I was justified in suppressing a useless life, which blocked my way to a career of benevolence and usefulness, and in the interests of the many as against the few, I shot my cousin, Lilian Carford, alias Lisa Rayner, on the morning of Christmas Day, 189 ."

A light knock at the door startled him as he wrote the date,

"Stay," cried Arnold, unlocking the door. " Here is my witness. You shall sign in her presence."

Greswold's whole manner had changed after he had taken up the pen. The livid countenance, the ghastly horror of the man who unexpectedly faces death, had changed to a pale resolve which was not without dignity. The man who had made his own law of life, and who feared neither God nor devil, reasserted himself. He looked up at Mary Freeland with a cynical smile upon his lips.

"This paper has been written for your satisfaction. Miss Freeland. I don't know whether Mr. Wentworth has prepared you for its contents. It is not an everyday document."

Mary looked at him in blank astonishment, and then looked from him to Arnold. Her hair had

The Enemy and Avenger.

been blown about by the evening wind upon the moor, and her face was pale with anxiety.

"I don't understand," she said.

"You will understand when you have read that paper which Mr. Greswold is going to sign in your presence. You will read it while the ink is wet. You will have no doubt that his hand wrote it."

And then, without looking at the writer, Arnold pointed to the blank space below the written lines.

"Sign," he said.

Greswold, that cynical smile still upon his bloodless lips, signed his name in full, with an untrembling hand. He was thinking what weight such a document might carry in a criminal court, whether if he declared that it was written to appease a homicidal maniac, there might not be people to believe him. For the rest, it was written because he could not help himself; and again his thoughts went back to that one image which filled his heart, the only being he had ever loved.

"Violet, my wife!"

"Read," said Arnold, handing the paper to Mary.

She took it from him mechanically, with a bewildered air, and again her gaze wandered from one face to the other; her eyes questioned each in turn.

"Read, read," Arnold repeated impatiently.

She read, and the new horror grew into her face. She looked at Greswold—a look of loathing— dropped the paper as if it had been an adder, and then flung herself upon Arnold's breast, clinging

Rough Justice.

to him as in a wild terror of some monstrous creature never seen before.

" Do you understand, Mary ? "

"Yes, yes, I understand. I knew you were innocent. I have known it ever since that one miserable day when I let you leave me in my misery. But I never suspected, how could I have ever thought "

"That such respectability as Oliver Greswold's could stain its fair record by murder. No, you never thought—the world would be slow to believe " —he stopped to pick up the paper which Mary had dropped at his feet. " I am going to give this man's confession into your keeping, Mary. It holds the hazard of his life, or almost the certainty of an ignominious death. Will you promise to keep the secret ? It is meant for your knowledge only. No good can come of the world's knowing. One life cannot buy back another. And I, too, have been a sinner. I, too, have to suffer remorse. And there are others who would have to suffer for his crime if it were known. It is better, as I think, that he should escape than that those innocent ones should suffer. For these reasons, Mary, I have pledged my word to him that his secret shall rest between you and me."

" I promise," she said.

" As you hope to be saved ?" urged Greswold.

"As I hope for mercy, and as I believe in a merciful God."

She kept her eyes averted from his face, even while she addressed him, as if she wanted never

to look upon that face again. And then she took the paper to the window and read the Hnes again by the waning hght, slowly and thoughtfully this time.

" Have you any matches, Arnold ?"

" Plenty."

" Light one, please."

He obeyed her, guessing her purpose, and held the match while she lighted the paper.

" For your wife's sake," she said, addressing Greswold, but not looking at him.

A guttural sound that might have been a stifled sob came from the man who sat at the table, and who had not stirred since he signed the paper.

Mary held the paper till two-thirds of the sheet were burnt, and then let it flutter blazing to the ground. No vestige of the writing remained after Arnold had set his foot upon the blackened ashes.

"You have got off very cheap, Mr. Greswold," he said, "for your wife's sake. I leave you to your conscience, and your God. Come, Mary,"

He drew her trembling hand through his arm and led her out of the hut. Neither of them turned on the threshold for one last look at the stricken wretch who sat there, cowed and broken, his head bent, his face hidden, his dry lips dumbly shaping one of those cries of self-abasement so familiar to him in the years of his probation, when his grandfather's harsh voice in biting winter mornings, or the oppressive heat of a London

summer, made the language of the Psalmist a weariness and a disgust.

" The terrors of death are fallen upon me. Fear-fulness and trembling are come upon me, and horror hath overwhelmed me. Bloody and deceitful men shall not live out half their days. I sink in deep mire, where there is no standing ; I am come into deep waters, where the floods overflow me."

" But I am a worm, and no man ; a reproach of men, and despised of the people."

The words came back to him in a wave of agony, words his unheeding ear had heard so often that they had sunk into his memory unawares.

The mists of evening were rising from tarn and bog when Arnold and his sweetheart left the hut to walk to Lingfield. They had walked about a mile when they met a dog-cart, driven by one of the Wilverwold grooms, who stopped to inquire about his master. Lady Violet was alarmed by Mr. Greswold not having overtaken her, the man told them, and had sent the cart for him.

" I hope there's nothing amiss, sir ?" added the groom, who was an old servant of Lord Hildyard's, and had broken Lady Violet's first pony.

" No, there's nothing wrong. You'll find your master at the hut."

The dog-cart passed them half an hour later on their homeward way, the groom still driving, his master sitting beside him. Arnold and Mary

stood and watched that drooping head and bowed figure, as the cart vanished in the thickening mist.

" Will he tell his wife ?" she asked.

"Not he. The shock was a rough one, and he may be some time getting over it; but he will take his secret to the grave v/ith him. If we are silent Lady Violet will never know. I don't suppose she'll have a happy life with him. He's made of hard stuff, but even he won't escape the worm that dieth not, and the fire that is not quenched ; and she will discover sooner or later that in the midst of prosperity and domestic love, and the world's respect, he is about as miserable a wretch as ever walked the earth. His malady will be called nerves, spinal disease, tumour anything the most distinguished medical guessers choose to call it. But his malady will be the deathless worm and the unquenchable fire ; and his victim will be amply avenged."

He told her briefly the story of the murder. She had no thought to-night for anything else— not even for happiness, and the knowledge that the man she loved belonged to her henceforward, and that all she had ever hoped for in life was to be hers. In England or in Africa, in poverty or in wealth, it mattered to Mary Freeland nothing how her days were to be spent, so long as they were spent with him.

No word of love was spoken between them that night. It would have seemed horrible to expatiate upon their own happiness after that scene in the

Rough Justice.

hut; but the next day and the next, and for all the days Arnold spent at Lingfield, love was their only theme—love and love's fruition, the happy days that were coming for them with the coming year. They were to be married at Lingfield Church on the first anniversary of Wilmot and Ida's wedding.

"We shall run the show," said Ida, who had adopted all her husband's slang phrases. " We are quite old married people now, yon see."

In order that nobody's sensibilities should be outraged, Mary was to return almost immediately to the sheltering wing of Mrs. Tresillian-Smith, and the Worth and the Doucet of South Kensington and West Brompton were to be set to work on the young lady's trousseau ; a modest little trousseau, in which provision was to be made for a long honeymoon in South Africa, where Arnold was to take his wife over that Tom Tidler's ground on which, while other men. were laying the foundations of gigantic fortunes, he had esteemed himself lucky in securing a competence.

Before Mary left Lingfield she had to undergo an unexpected ordeal in an interview with Laurence Somerville, who solemnly warned her against the man to whom she had engaged herself—a man who had stood in the dock at Bow Street as a suspected murderer,

" I know all about that," Mary answered quietly ; " but, you see, I knew Arnold Wentworth years and

years before he stood in the dock as Alfred Wild-over ; and I knew—or I ought to have known "— she hesitated at this point, remembering those dreadful hours of doubt—" that he was no more capable of murder than I am."

Somerville sighed.

"I think you might do better for yourself, Miss Freeland—a young lady of your remarkable attractions—than to marry a man who had ever occupied that—dubious position."

And then he told her that he had never admired any woman as he admired her—never had known what love meant till he knew her.

She stopped him as quickly as she could.

" Don't; pray don't! " she exclaimed. " You are so kind, and clever, and altogether nice—and I can't bear to pain you—but I have been in love with Arnold ever since I was twelve years old, I was wearing pinafores when I began to adore him."

"That will do, Miss Freeland. You're as straight as a die. The man you love is a man the President of the United States may envy; but Fm out of the running. I shall go back to New York on the next boat. Life hasn-'t been very lively at Wilverwold since you dined there that night."

" Is there anything wrong ?"

" Greswold is too full of his rescue work to be good company beside the domestic hearth. He's a remarkable man, Miss Freeland. His ideas are in advance even of ours, and he's sure to do a great work if he lives; but he's not a lively

Rough Justice.

companion, and his wife is over-anxious about him —watches every shadow that crosses his face; watches his plate to see if he eats, his glass to see if he drinks; looks miserable when he is out of the room for half an hour; wants to keep him in sight when she is talking with her visitors ;—a perfect wife, but a shocking bad hostess. So I shall cross on the next boat. Good-bye, Miss Free-land."

The wedding at Lingfield Church was all that is rustic and pretty in a country wedding, even though there was no glory of summer roses to brighten the grey walls and outshine the old glass in the chancel window. It was not by any means a smart wedding, and it passed unrecorded in the Society papers ; but what can any bride desire more than to be completely happy ? And Mary's happiness was too deep for words.

" I have always loved him," she whispered, when Mrs. Wentworth, who had come all the way from Suffolk to assist at the ceremony, hugged her in the vestry, while the fateful book was being signed.

" And I have always loved you, dear ; and always wished for this day. And I hope you will soon be tired of Africa, and come and settle down in your pretty house at Mervynhall."

" I will go wherever Arnold likes, and live wherever he can be happiest," said the bride, being of the worshipping and upward-looking order of brides long since voted old-fashioned.

The Enemy and Avenger.

Lady Violet and her husband were in Egypt when Mary Freeland was married. They had left Wilverwold for London early in November, and had left London in a P. and O. steamer for Alexandria at the advice of a famous specialist whom Violet persuaded her husband to see. The specialist pronounced Greswold a sufferer from mental strain, no doubt the result of prolonged over-work.

" Take him to the land of the Pharaohs, my dear lady, and let him bask in Egyptian sunshine, and not write so much as a single letter, or read one, if you can help it, till you bring him back in the spring. So valuable a life as Mr. Greswold's must not be jeopardized. He has a frame of iron— slight as he looks; a will of iron, too, I fancy. Heart and lungs are undamaged. All he wants is rest, and the capacity to enjoy life—a capacity which a good many hard workers lose ; and they don't know till they have lost it what a valuable quality it is."

Lady Violet and her husband are at Cairo; but all his plans for the help and comfort of his fellow-creatures are going on apace during his absence. The Home of St. Mary Magdalene, the House of the Woman of Samaria, are full of human brands snatched from the burning. The workmen's dwellings which he planned, exercising in many details an intelligence and an inventive power that have gone beyond the trained abilities of architects and sanitary engineers, are rising

Rough Justice.

skyward, solid, commodious, and not unbeautiful, eagerly competed for by the most respectable of the working classes. And everywhere, among the people who try to leave the world better than they found it, the name of Oliver Greswold commands admiration and respect.

THE END

Miss Braddon's Novels.

Printed in Great Britain
by Amazon

61057201R00092